DARKNE

REALM
OF
HOPE

E. L. LI

Paperback: ISBN 979-8-9855401-0-9
Hardback: ISBN 979-8-9855401-2-3
Ebook: ISBN 979-8-9855401-1-6
Library of Congress Control Number: TXu002299042

First edition January 2022.

Edited by Kereah Keller
Cover art by Miblart

Starlight Publishing

❀ Created with Vellum

For anyone who has supported me.

TRIGGER WARNING

This book contains sensitive material relating to:

trauma,
death,
PTSD,
suicide,
violence,
& more.

CAST OF CHARACTERS

Star Strike: Astro Strike
Zephyr Lumière—Leader
A tactician who utilizes his clan's glyph abilities in battle. Wields Gale-force, his trusty katana.
Skye Hikari—Powerhouse
A member of the Farien who harnesses the energies of the stars and boosts her powers with limits. Wields Excalibur, a sword with two forms.
Shadow Hikari—Defender & Healer
A member of the Gwymond who possesses dark powers. Wields Diablos, an axe that can also transform into a bo staff.
Aurora Candor—Mage & Healer
A descendant of one of the greatest mages of all time with immense aura control. Wields Helios, a tome that channels her aura.
Leif Underwood-Moreno—Ranger
A skilled user of the earth element. Wields chakrams.
Spark Knight—Secondary Powerhouse & Defender
An aspiring Lightning Master. Wields lances.

Star Strike: Nova Strike
Luna Zedler—Leader
A jack-of-all-trades unit with some Lumière clan abilities and strong aura sensing skills. Wields Executioner, a powerful whip.
Blaze Stryker—Defender
A tracking and sensing unit. Is a Beast Morpher.
Stream Calderón—Tech Expert
A unit with aura point disabling abilities skilled in breaching and building advanced devices. Wields retractable claws.
Glacieus Thorn—Recon Expert
A marksman who gathers intel during reconnaissance missions. Wields tonfas.

Twilight Treader
Adriel Ronan—Leader
A member of the Sylfira capable of producing black flames. Wields an axe.
Saylor Devaux—Powerhouse
Skilled with manipulating ice. Wields fist cuffs.
Evelyn Devaux—Recon Expert
Skilled with manipulating metal. Wields needles.
Senna Clark—Defender
Skilled with manipulating earth. Is a Beast Morpher.

Raven Mist
Tristan Avniel—Leader
Non-aura user. Wields a spiked ball.
Laken Harper—Powerhouse
Non-aura user. Wields fist cuffs.
Amber Mendoza—Recon Expert
Earth Master. Wields an iron fan.

Trinity Trio
Ava Carello—Leader
General within the Combat Agents. Bird Morpher.
Tiamat Carello—Defender
Ava's brother. Dragon Morpher.
Fang Westwood—Powerhouse & Healer
Blaze's mentor. Beast Morpher.

Wings of Order
Aqua Lumière—Leader & Powerhouse
Lieutenant General of Lumière Inc and Zephyr's eldest sister. Wields a lance.
Clay Thorn—Healer
Glacieus' eldest brother. Wields a staff.
Blossom Lang—Ranger
Head of the Lumière Tech Department. Wields a bow.
Zetta Petrov—Mage & Recon Expert
Top Recon and Intel unit. Wields magical orbs.

Triple Strike
Sunny Reyes—Leader & Mage
Fire Master. Wields magical orbs.
Sully Reyes—Healer & Mage
Water Master. Wields a wand.
Swifty Reyes—Powerhouse & Mage
Spark and Aurora's mentor. Lightning Master. Wields a staff.

Dawn Brigade

Elena Cohen—Leader

General within the Combat Agents. Manipulates sound waves. Wields a halberd.

Iyar Cohen—Ranger

Elena's younger brother. Wields explosives.

Ambrose Vincent—Recon Expert

Master of metal manipulation. Wields knives.

Lucia Rayne—Healer & Recon Expert

Member of the Farien. Wields a staff.

Oscar Rockwell—Powerhouse

Skilled user of light. Wields a scythe.

Calypso Andino—Mage

Water Master. Manipulates aura only with her hands.

Typhon Strike

Mercury Levisay—Leader & Powerhouse

Darkness Master. Weapon unknown.

Electro Stallard—Tech and Recon Expert

Lightning Master. Wields fist cuffs.

Ariadne Driscoll—Mage & Healer

Special abilities unknown. Weapon unknown.

Ursula Sharpe—Ranger & Powerhouse

Bara clan member. Weapon unknown.

Researchers

Jacques Caraway
Member of Ice Tetra.

Valeria Fern
Member of Ice Tetra.

Raphael Willis
Member of Ice Tetra.

Sarai Schnee
Member of the Sirens.

Alix Chen
Member of the Sirens.

Medics

Trent Thorn
Head of the Lumière Medical Department.

Ellen Thorn
Higher-up within the Lumière Medical Department.

Celia Thorn
Higher-up within the Lumière Medical Department.

Eila Lumière
Second-in-command within the Lumière Medical Department.

Catria Wexler
Eila's assistant.

Cerberus

Wren Navar
Heracles Serum test subject.

Mabel Whitethorn
Heracles Serum test subject.

Remi Skinner
Heracles Serum test subject.

Hosts

Dove Hart
Skilled Wind Specialist. Wields a spatha.

Storm Ashford
Skilled Lightning Specialist. Wields a staff.

Teddy Whitlock
Prodigy with all elements. Wields a gunblade.

Eloise Hale
Distant Thet Royalty. Wields blades.

Astrid
Descendant of Celeste. Wields swords.

Deities

Celeste
Goddess of Balance and Peace. Many heroes in history are descended from her.

Celestria
Adoptive mother of Celeste. Goddess of Light.

Gemini
Goddess of Wind. Created the worlds of Eta Geminorum and Tau Geminorum.

Pisces
Goddess of Water. Created the worlds of Eta Piscium and Tau Piscium.

Misc

Seren Hikari
Skye and Shadow's mother. Member of the Farien and Gwymond. Grand-daughter of Lumina Rayne. Teammate of President Ziel.

Lukas Hikari
Skye and Shadow's father. Member of the Hikari clan. Teammate of President Ziel.

Cynthia Hikari
Younger sister of Skye and Shadow. Studying to become a Specialist at Garnet Academy.

Rolf Candor

Aurora's father. Teammate of President Ziel.

Anaïs Candor

Aurora's mother. Teammate of President Ziel.

Ari Candor

Aurora's elder sister. Ice Master and mage on Team Phoenix Force.

Ziel Lumière

Zephyr's father and grandson of Capala Lumière. President of Lumière Inc.

Rosalie Lumière

President Ziel's former teammate and wife. Higher-up within Lumière Inc.

Tandy Lumière

Ziel's third youngest daughter. Agent Trainee.

Suzie Lumière

Ziel's youngest daughter. Agent Trainee on the same team as Cynthia.

Capala Lumière

Founded Lumière Inc.

Elara Zedler

President Ziel's eldest sister and Luna's mother.

Starla de Cordelia

Late Queen of Cordelia. Descendant of Celeste.

Astra Lumis

From the kingdom of Orwyn. Descendant of Celeste.

Solace Aegis

From Piscium. Fastest known descendant of Celeste.

Lumina Rayne

Also known as "Lumina Blackburn". Descendant of Celeste.

Panda

A mysterious merchant.

Eta Geminorum

GRAFFIAS

ANTARES

STELLAE

SCORPION

AQUARIUS ISLANDS

WAVES

GWYNERVA

Brian Ligae

PIAN

Desert

ES

SNOWHOLT

Polaris

FAIRHILL

Lastalia

Millmead

CASTOR

pollux castum Inn

pollux

pondley

VERTBARROW

ASTURIAS

Emerald Forest

THE WANDERING DEEP

ORWYN

Assassins keep

BSC Tower

Chaim 2021

PROLOGUE

SKYE HAD TWO WISHES SHE WANTED TO BE GRANTED BY NIGHTFALL: the stars would shine for once, and that she'd end up on the same team as her friends. Fulfillment of the latter was more likely, however. With the hustle and bustle of Garnet City and the influx of airships blocking the view after dark, it was often difficult to see the celestial bodies, even with the magnificent view behind her home.

During daybreak, Skye had no trouble admiring the sight of the sun blooming onto the horizon from her bedroom window. Petals of gold scattered, weaving their way into the blue hues. Skye cherished the stars and the sun, since most of her notorious ancestors were named after them. She felt it was only fair to have a proper way to gaze at both, even though only the starlight would've enhanced her power.

Skye decided to awaken her brother—she'd been up for two hours and couldn't fall back asleep. They had an hour before last-minute training, but Skye wanted to squeeze in extra time.

It always gave Skye a thrill to see her aura techniques continue to grow as she learned more about each element. Light aura was her specialty. Watching it manifest in her hands made her feel alive.

Her twin's room stood across the hall from hers. Grabbing the doorknob, she burst through the door. Shadow's body laid face-down on his bed, cocooned in blankets. For a six-year-old, he snored loud.

Skye grabbed Shadow's side and shook him. "Shadow! Get up!"

After more aggressive attempts at shaking him, throwing pillows at him, pulling his hair, *and* yelling at him, she left the room with a huff and returned with a bucket of ice-cold water.

Shadow yelped as soon as the clear liquid flattened his jet-black hair. The cotton t-shirt he had on clung to his tanned skin.

"Morning, Shadie!"

Shadow's eyes darted between the bucket in his sister's hands and his drenched state of being. "What the heck!"

"C'mon! Get dressed! We gotta train!"

As soon as breakfast was over (and Skye's mother, Seren, reminded her twice to not wolf down everything), they were in their backyard, where they first learned how to fight. Dummies, weapon racks, and practice targets served as a significant contrast to the flower field further behind their property.

"Let's go for some sparring first," said Seren as she led the twins toward the dirt training ground that stood between the weapon racks. Her light brown locks and hazel eyes shone in the sunlight. "And, Skye, go easy on your brother."

Skye smiled sheepishly, grabbing her training axe. "Okay!" She strived to be like Seren one day, along with their ancestors. Her mother was of the Farien, descendants of the Heavenly Goddess. Seren raised the twins to follow their people's principles the best they could.

Shadow retrieved his axe from the racks and faced his twin. They had the same golden-amber eyes, except Skye's had a lighter tint.

A cool breeze swept strands of Skye's black hair with caramel-brown highlights into her face, and she brushed them aside. Physically, Skye only possessed the same heart-shaped face, tawny complexion, and almond eyes as her mother. The rest was a unique blend of physical features from her father and other relatives.

"Begin!"

Weapons clashed several times. With a single blow, Skye knocked Shadow across the training yard. Skye dashed toward him, glowing white and gold, releasing a miniature blast of light.

A red shroud surrounded Shadow's body, protecting him from her attacks, and jumped back up, slamming his axe onto the ground. A thread of darkness emerged from the axe, and Skye dodged every attack.

The twins' father emerged from the backdoor and joined his wife in spectating.

"Skye's getting more powerful by the day. Shadow's aura control is looking better too," noted Lukas. "Skye has nothing to worry about. They're going to end up on the same team as Zephyr and Aurora. Their synergies are very high."

Seren remembered the discouragement on her daughter's face when she heard the differing media speculations about Skye and Shadow in terms of future abilities and team compositions.

"Hopefully tonight's exam results and predictions will simmer down *some* of the obnoxious buzz regarding the kids."

"Exactly. No matter what abilities they inherit from past heroes, their legacies as Agents will prevail, like ours in our prime. People should know that."

Target practice followed. Seren instructed the twins to focus their aura onto different parts of their body and their weapons, releasing them as all nine elements, one-by-one, onto the bullseye.

After meditation exercises, the twins ran laps back and forth to the flower field. A dirt trail separated their backyard from the field and part of it led to the woods that the twins and their friends liked to play around.

Every time, Skye arrived at the vibrant display of flowers first. They flooded the ground, spanning multiple kilometers. The faint sound of buzzing bees flew, gathering pollen. Delicate aromas of fuchsia and magenta petunias paired well with the white daisies.

Shadow ran over, bending and panting.

"Gotta keep up, Squirt!"

"Just cuz you're taller doesn't mean you can call your older brother 'Squirt!'"

"We're the SAME AGE!"

"Nine-and-a-half minutes doesn't mean 'the same!'"

Skye puffed her cheeks, and Shadow grinned.

This was their last lap before returning to the training yard. Their aura and energy needed to replenish enough for the exams, despite Skye wanting to train more.

For as long as Skye could remember, she wanted to be a hero, like in the stories their mother read to them at bedtime. Her parents described their mission days in extensive detail with their extended family and friends. She and her brother started at the hip, and she prayed it wouldn't end soon.

The time she'd been waiting for came, and excitement rushed through Skye's veins. Her destiny was to become an Agent of Lumière and she couldn't wait to see which collection of heroes she inherited the most from. Regardless, she wanted power like her mother. Her mother always fondly told the twins about all the times she saved the day with her Farien abilities.

"Let's go," said Seren.

Hikari Residence to the Lumière Base was hardly a commute. Their suburban neighborhood, Daybreak, heaped with nuclear families, seemed straight out of a commercial. All it took was three blocks to see towers belonging to business moguls and skyline apartments with terraces to die for in the distance. Horizons of metals, fleets of aircraft, and hordes of trains that spun and went upside down in the Financial, Industrial, and Interplanetary Districts made Garnet City the way it was—a civilization of future unity and innovation. It set an example for the rest of the world of Eta Geminorum, and few cities could compare. Electronic signs floated near its entrances, displaying the text: *Welcome to Garnet: Our World's Pride and Joy.*

Skye loved the Explorer's Square, situated at the southwestern portion of the city—bordering the leftmost harbors. While the twins' closest friend, Zephyr, could spend days at the historical monuments and museums, what caught Skye's eyes was the Garnet Commercial Hub. She and Seren preferred it over the Market District.

The high-walled, outdoor complex divided itself into several rings in which several restaurants and boutiques could be seen. It housed numerous levels, with some shops being two-tiered. Skye and Shadow were fond of the citrus aromas wafting from the perfumeries and all-you-can-eat dumpling huts.

If the rest of Eta Geminorum was similar to Garnet City in terms of protection and ultra-modernism, the world would've been a utopia. More than half the world, however, was far less technologically advanced and stuck in its more ancient ways, either by lack of resources or for the sake of preserving history.

The Base was the largest building in Garnet City, southwest of Daybreak, past Aurum District and Garnet Hills. It was dark blue and comprised three domes connected by bridges. Although it looked made of glass, most of its material was made of almost indestructible Azoth—a material native to Tau Geminorum's Aot Nation. Standing at the top of the main dome was the iconic Lumière symbol.

Agents stood within the main gates.

"The time has come, Lukas, Seren," said a female Agent. "Any guesses on what the Fates have planned for the twins for the future?"

"I suspect they'll resemble their ancestors further along the family tree than us for aura abilities," replied Seren.

"Yeah, the most they inherited from me, from what I can tell, are my hair and eye color," joked Lukas. "They don't seem to have much from the Hikari clan at all."

"Regardless, this must be a nostalgic time for you. Since Anaïs, Rolf, Rosalie, and President Lumière have their kids taking the examination this year, too," said another Agent.

"Indeed. To think it was so long ago when we took this exam at their ages." Lukas smiled at one of the male Agents. "You were there, too, Dr. Lycaste."

Dr. Lycaste nodded. "So much has changed throughout the years. Each generation's becoming stronger, and this year's cohort will be no exception."

Seren sighed. "Which works out. Their missions will be harder than ours back when our powers were at their peak." She and her husband retired from field missions as soon as their power faded out—conveniently, right before the twins were born. "Sometimes, I wish I could've done more."

"You needn't dwell on that. Both of you have done so much in your youth. Leave everything else to the other descendants of Celeste," said the female Agent.

"We'll always do what we can to make our ancestors proud," Lukas replied. "But, anyway, I'm sure we've taken a bit too much of your time!"

Seren faced her kids. "We'll come get you right after the exams."

The parents smiled at the twins and left while Dr. Lycaste escorted them toward the waiting area, making friendly conversation with the children as they passed the metallic blue walls and windows that faded to opaque.

Portraits of the best Agents of all time and their accolades lined the walls along with maps of all six of the worlds in the Mortal Realm: the two Geminorum worlds, the two Piscium worlds, Eta Taurium, and Eta Sagittarium.

A boy with spiky chocolate brown hair and turquoise eyes lingered around the hallway. He towered over both twins and his defined jawline made him look slightly older than others his age.

Skye's eyes brightened more than usual whenever she saw him.

"It's about time you guys got here!" exclaimed the boy.

The twins walked up to him, smiling when he looked at Skye. He gave one of her pigtails a playful, gentle tug.

Her face pinked when their eyes met once again. For as long as Skye could remember, the twins followed Zephyr's lead. Zephyr was the mastermind, the one with the ideas. The one with the plan.

"Hello, Zephyr! Ready for the exams?" asked Dr. Lycaste.

"Of course, sir!" Zephyr flashed the researcher a charming smile.

"Great! Many of us are excited about seeing what you're capable of and what sort of massive power you'll possess as a Lumière clan member."

Children of Agents were usually indoctrinated with the belief that they were granted the privilege to serve with the abilities they possessed. It was honorable to use what you were given from the Fates and other immortals. These values were taught since the little ones could crawl.

"I know he'll do really good!" chimed in Skye.

"Yeah! I'm excited!" replied Zephyr.

"Are you going to join us in the waiting room?" asked Dr. Lycaste.

Zephyr shook his head. "No, I'm waiting for Mother. There are some things we have to take care of."

Dr. Lycaste nodded. "Very well."

Zephyr turned to the twins. "Wanna meet here after the exam?"

"Sure!" replied Skye.

Zephyr smiled, giving her pigtails another tug.

A woman with silky blonde hair and green eyes exited a room. Her plump lips and beauty mark underneath her left eye set trends within Garnet City. Socialites and the like sought artificial procedures to look like the President's wife. "Zephyr! We have to get going!" She smiled as soon as she noticed the twins' presence. "Oh! Hello, there!"

"Hi, Mrs. Lumière!"

"Lady Rosalie," greeted Dr. Lycaste.

"Any early predictions, Professor?" asked Rosalie.

"I can tell these three will do very well, as expected. Of course, anything can happen."

"Indeed. I'm afraid Zephyr and I will have to finish up our business soon, so I'll leave you to it. Good luck, you two!"

Zephyr followed her out of the hallway, waving at the twins.

The twins made it to the waiting room, where many other five-to-six-year-olds were already present.

A girl with wavy, red hair, fair skin, freckles that dotted her cheeks, and minty-green eyes entered the room, stumbling and tripping.

"Aurora!" Skye helped her up and grabbed her friend's left arm, pulling her toward the empty seat beside the twins. She and Aurora were inseparable, practically sisters.

"I'm nervous," said Aurora. "What if I fail?" Her face fell, staring at the floor.

"There's no way!" replied Skye. She rocked on her chair, legs kicking back and forth. "We'll be on the same team! All four of us!"

After more chatting, proctors called the children to stand in a single-file line to leave the room and into the examination area. It took ten minutes for some of the little ones to comply. Skye wondered which of them had parents who worked for the organization. Testing your child for eligibility to become an Agent was voluntary, but an honor if successful.

"But I don't wanna go in there!"

"Can I go home? I'm hungry!"

Skye puffed out her cheeks, annoyed, as she waited with Aurora and Shadow in line. "I wanna show the grownups what I can do already!"

After another five minutes, they finally took a step out of the waiting room.

Examiners split the examination room into several sections to test different capabilities, with each area having a number. The first open area comprised targets, training dummies, and small robots, appearing color-coded, dividing into red, blue, and green. Sensors and surveillance cameras surrounded the room.

"We'll start with combat trials," began a proctor. "For the targets and training dummies, a different color marks each one. Blue ones are to be hit by aura users only while red is for physical attacks. Green is for either."

"We're testing your overall strength, speed, aura control, any magical abilities, things like that. And don't worry about the robots —they can't hurt you," said another proctor.

"Once done, we can move onto the Medical, Aura Control, and the other trials!"

Skye wondered how the proctors could get some kids to do any of this, but stopped paying attention as soon as a blonde girl released lightning bolts, decimating a dummy. She could only hope to be as powerful as that kid.

Skye did her best to show the proctors who she was—a descendant of Celeste. This was *her* portion of the exams to shine in. Once she finished showing what she'd done in training, she watched in awe at a boy who created black flames while another turned his hand into ice.

Medical trials had a smaller section—with patients set up with basic cuts and scrapes. Meanwhile, the Aura Control trials had tables with matchsticks, cards, and crystal orbs for the children to pour their aura into.

"If you can't transform your aura, don't worry! You can take a break until the next set of trials!" The proctor pointed at an empty section of the room.

The Intel trials were last, along with additional tests related to it. Stations for headsets, monitors displaying various shapes and symbols, and simulations of mazes and forests filled the two sections.

"We'll test your memorization skills along with how well you can strategize and gather information," said a proctor.

The aforementioned were popular departments to get into for those who couldn't manipulate their aura. Retired field Agents transferred to those departments or became researchers since most Agents never stopped serving the organization until their deaths or retirement.

"ANAÏS, you're right. Those are Circe's abilities," said Rosalie, staring at replays of the footage. She tapped her chin with a manicured finger. "Best aura control seen in generations."

Zephyr, Aurora, and the twins' parents were in one of the security rooms. Monitors featured Aurora, where a white glow emitted from her hands, allowing her to illuminate a matchstick. Such a feat was difficult, even for adults.

Another monitor displayed graphs for potential growth rates in aura control and other magical abilities. Circe was one of the greatest magic user of her time. The differences between her and Aurora's datasets were slim when compared side-by-side.

"Aurora'll be at her most powerful from her late teens to mid-twenties," said Rosalie. Those with stronger abilities often lost their power at an earlier age. Strength of aura peaked within the same timeframe as muscle mass. Aura potency and reserves declined exponentially faster after a mortal's prime.

"I'm proud!" A petite woman resembling Aurora, with short red hair, freckles, and brown eyes, smiled. Her white teeth shined as if they were pearls. "She'll be like her sister!"

"You should be," said a lean man who possessed the same hair color as Zephyr. His turquoise eyes pegged him as a member of the Lumière clan. Around his former teammates, he looked like a giant, making him appear powerful with a substantial presence. "I've seen no one else at six with that kind of control."

"Man, I thought she was taking after me for aura control!" A lanky man with Aurora's eyes and brown hair sighed. His fuzzy beard was a subject of envy amongst other men in their mid-to-late thirties.

Lukas laughed. "Rolf, you owe me ten Gold."

Zephyr's footage was next. His weapon of choice was a wooden sword, and he glowed green, transferring aura from body to sword, releasing two glyphs. Each was a flat, green circle of aura. In its center rested the Lumière family symbol, marking its territory as a technique exclusive to his clan. He twirled his weapon, side-stepped, and struck the dummy in front of him.

Graphs outlined the predictions of his combat skills throughout the years. Categories included speed, strength, how powerful his aura was at each age. Like Aurora, his prime would end around his mid-twenties, where the graphs sloped downward.

"He seems to have a high affinity for aura-based attacks, Ziel," commented Seren. "Everything else seems balanced all around."

One clip stood out where Zephyr directed small robots to retrieve an item around a simulated maze. He saw the maze's layout provided for him, memorized it, and came up with a plan within minutes.

President Lumière scrutinized the footage and related data. "He's more of a tactician than a fighter."

The twins were up. Skye had her tremendous speed again, able to seemingly disappear and reappear behind the training dummies and knock them across the room with a swing of her wooden axe. She landed another strike while glowing white light, causing the dummy to explode into nothing.

"Just like Solace Aegis," observed Seren with pride. "She may not be as fast, but she'll come close."

"Powers from three Daughters of Light, hm?" asked Ziel. "But none from the one she's directly related to."

"She seems to have the most physical power out of them all," said Rolf. "The Fates sure had fun granting her all this."

Shadow stood out in a clip where he glowed green, mending a cut on a swimming fish in a bowl of water. His combat clips were notorious as well, with him being able to glow a red color and protect himself from hits from a training bot. He manifested a black aura around his body and landed a strike, causing a dummy to explode.

"Defenses from Astra Lumis and Gwymond abilities from Lumina Rayne." Out of anyone, it would make sense for Seren to understand her ancestors' abilities the best, especially with Lumina being her late maternal grandmother.

"That's the most out of Celeste's descendants with this year's cohort," said Lukas.

The twins possessed abilities from some of the most powerful figures in history, all descended from Celeste, the Goddess of Balance and Peace. Seren knew all eyes would continue to be on her children now that they had proper confirmation of who their abilities came from.

"This is it... This is a Dream Team." Everyone turned toward the President.

There weren't many Dream Teams, but each one included those with objectively the best combinations of abilities, both combat and non-combat. They were the ones the world paid the most attention to with access to the best resources for preparing them for their time as fully licensed Agents. The best instructors provided Trainees endless opportunities to improve, all intending to retaliate against the impending threats upon the Mortal Realm.

Not a single person in the room questioned what President Ziel had to say. The previous President selected him as most eligible to lead the organization out of his siblings. Ziel would one day do the same between Zephyr and his sisters if he decided to not default to picking the eldest.

"These four?" asked Seren.

"No, this'll be a bigger team. Other outstanding candidates will pair with them."

Although it sounded promising, Dream Teams were no guarantee to end the interplanetary threat within the next twenty years. Intel divisions predicted worsening states of the world soon, and anything was possible.

"If we're not able to make any more breakthroughs for a while, this will be the best we can do. We can only hope the other worlds are doing the best they can. . ." Ziel looked at his comrades, who had been by his side for thirty years.

"I hope we'll be able to travel between worlds once again," said Lukas. "I don't know how much longer Tau Geminorum can last if all we can do is contact them for the time being."

The room dulled to a silence.

SKYE AND SHADOW left the examination area, waiting for Aurora to join them, and they all walked out together.

"See! Told ya it was easy!" said Skye, tossing a pigtail over her shoulder.

Skye imagined themselves as young adults, slaying monsters and saving the world side-by-side with Zephyr on the front lines, Aurora and her brother in the back. They would be unstoppable, like the heroes in the books.

"We can save every world!" chimed in Shadow. The twins exchanged identical, optimistic grins. They only hoped it would be contagious enough to lift Aurora's spirits.

"I hope I did okay…" said Aurora.

Shadow patted her on the shoulder. "Zeph said you did good!"

Realization hit Skye's face. "Oh yeah! We were gonna meet with him!"

Dr. Lycaste came up to them. "Skye Hikari." She looked up at him, eyes round with innocence. He smiled at her. "We found something special about you and we want to test it again. Could you come with me?"

Skye looked at Aurora and Shadow, and back at the Agent. "I'll be back!"

She followed him, wondering what this additional test would be like. Skye wondered if it involved other weapons or more things she could do with her aura. Whatever it was, she felt ready to give it her all. Her rambunctiousness and zealous nature may have gotten her into trouble, but her fiery spirit in battle was unrivaled.

The halls in front of her were blurry for a split second, and for the first time in the central dome, Skye couldn't recognize where they were. Her eyes narrowed, glancing from left to right. They never played together in this area of the Base…

"Come in." He led her to the door.

Not a single soul was present.

The room went dark as the doors shut and locked.

Skye's eyes widened, and her heart lurched.

Zephyr walked further down the halls, having sensed Skye's aura nearby.

"Skye? Are you here?"

Unfortunately, one of Skye's wishes didn't come true.

PART I

GENESIS

1

ON OUR OWN
ZEPHYR

AFTER TWELVE YEARS OF TRAINING, SHADOWING AGENTS AND instructors on missions, and days spent in the classrooms at the Lumière Base... Today was the day. Hardly a single person on the face of the earth didn't know who Star Strike and their subgroups, Astro Strike and Nova Strike were. For any large-scale missions that required both, the public referred to them as Star Strike.

When the news broadcast that Zephyr, Aurora, and Shadow would take the Specialist Examination, the public went wild, especially since Zephyr was the Dream Team's leader. Star Strike spent years living in an era of hype and excessive publicity.

Zephyr exited his chambers, closing the double-doors. He barely slept a wink the night before, but had more energy than usual.

"Good morning, Master Zephyr," greeted Antoinette from the floor below. The woman practically raised him and his younger sisters, Tandy and Suzie.

Antoinette made it up Lumière Manor's grand, spiral staircase, armed with a pile of gift baskets, careful to not let any slip. Those baskets arrived at his doorstep every day for the past week, and there was already a mountain of them in his room. Zephyr never thought he'd see the day when he'd tire of chocolate, pralines, and nougats. His sofa smelled like caramel.

"Give some of them to Tandy and Suzie!" Those two wouldn't have minded seeing the contents of a mini-gift shop in the comfort of their own home.

Zephyr descended, heading toward the main floor, greeting staff members passing through the grand hallway, which served as the primary avenue of traffic. Most disappeared into adjacent rooms, equipped with paint cans. His mother wanted Lumière Manor to resemble classic styles originating from the clan's home world, Eta Taurium, in contrast to their former, modern-day Silvatican themes. He wondered how long it'd take to repaint their high ceilings, replace mantels of birch wood, and remove all ornamental keystones. They'd been like that for three generations, ever since the clan erected Lumière Manor.

He twisted the brass knobs of the varnished wooden doors with colored glass panes. Lumière Manor had three dining areas, two of which were for parties depending on the size. The final one had a walk-in pantry, supply room, and windowed doors leading toward gardens. Silvatican Cardinals rested on the perches of the birdhouses outside.

A sweet scent flowed through the air, making his stomach rumble. A hearty breakfast was exactly what he needed to start his day and first mission as a Specialist.

His sisters sat at the wooden table on the left. Five empty chairs surrounded them. Plates piled high with pancakes and their pillowy, buttery goodness. Syrup bottles, butter dishes, and a bowl of whipped cream rounded out the spread.

"Did Aqua leave?" asked Zephyr.

"Yep. And Eila didn't come home," noted Tandy.

It was only a matter of time before Tandy would follow in his footsteps as an Agent since she only had two years of training left. Suzie was likely to do the same since she looked up to Star Strike. Especially Skye.

"What kinda mission are ya going on?" asked Suzie, swaying in her chair, and looking as if she was about to jump out of it. Zephyr thought their chefs replaced the usual maple syrup with a less sugary alternative, but he guessed not. Tips of her curly, brunette hair glistened with stickiness. "Are you rescuing people? Or destroying things? Or escorting people? Or-"

Tandy shook her head in dismay. "Let him breathe!" Her own curly, blonde hair was sticky-free.

Zephyr served himself a blueberry pancake in opposition to his preferred double-chocolate ones. "Whatever they assign us!"

"Will you be back by lunchtime?" asked Suzie. "They're making galettes today."

"Don't you have classes?" asked Zephyr, reaching for his fork.

Tandy grabbed a butter knife and cut a miniature square. "Today's our off day for training. You forgot, didn't you?"

Zephyr stuck a fork in his stack. "My mind's been on our first mission. I haven't had time to think of anything else, but I'd imagine we'd be back by noon." Maybe even sooner.

"You better tell us ALL about it! Star Strike is all they ever talk about at school!" exclaimed Suzie.

Zephyr grinned. "Will do." His parents, Aqua, and Eila often recounted the details of their own first missions, always eliciting excitement from Zephyr and his younger siblings.

Tandy and Suzie hugged him before he left and exited the double-doors. His boots hit the cobblestones, passing through the hedges and fountain and out the gates which shut behind him.

Zephyr waited for the streets to clear off any traffic before stepping forward. Garnet's Base was further east, within more urbanized districts—a short walk from Aurum District.

"Good luck, Zephyr!" cheered Garnet citizens. His friends liked to dub them as "Garnetites," though Zephyr believed it sounded outlandish.

Aurora and Shadow waited at the entrance. Zephyr assumed Aurora must've dragged their best friend to the Base almost right after Cynthia stirred him awake.

As soon as Zephyr informed Star Strike of his certification plans,

Shadow and Aurora worked their tail ends off to prepare for the examinations. They didn't want Zephyr to enter his first mission alone. Nova Strike was completely certified. Once Spark and Leif got their license, Astro Strike would be as well. Zephyr felt his duty as a leader was to check in on everyone regularly. Luna found it amusing but encouraged him to continue.

"Are ya ready?" asked Shadow.

"I know YOU are, considering how you're not late for once," teased Zephyr. If Shadow was early AND not clueless, it'd be a sign of the apocalypse.

Shadow side-eyed him. "Yeah, yeah! Whatever!"

Zephyr glanced at Aurora, who bit her lip. He knew that exact expression on her face too well—Aurora was filled with doubt and uncertainty in herself. "You'll be fine."

"Uh-huh! Nothin' to worry about!" Shadow chimed in. "Especially with ME around!"

Civilians clamored their cheers in the distance.

"Goooo, Dream Team!" exclaimed a passerby.

Aurora sighed. "This makes it *even* more nerve-wracking. All eyes are going to be on us when I mess up on a mission."

Lumières learned how to deal with the pressures of being in the public eye from an early age. Not all notorious bloodlines and families had such successful methods, however.

"Come on." Zephyr put a comforting hand on her shoulder. "You're the best magic user in our class *and* one of the best healers."

Aurora took a step forward, tripping onto the concrete pavement. "Ouch!"

The boys hurried to her side, extending their hands to help her up.

Security Agents guarded each sector of the Base's exterior. They possessed the same enthusiastic grins and wished them good luck as they entered the automatic doors that scanned entrants before opening. Anyone new to the Base would've believed it was a maze with all its hidden corridors, entrances, and ways to get to other domes. Surveillance and security were top-notch. Garnet

City's Base prided itself on being the safest building in Eta Geminorum.

They passed the portraits on the walls—dedicated to late Agents. Their ancestors were on display. Beside them, the Typhons' images hung proudly. The leader, Mercury, stood out with his wispy silver hair and red eyes, poised in a manner that commanded respect. Typhon Strike had been the blueprint for modernized Agent teams with record-breaking awards, inspiring Star Strike and its subgroups' names. Zephyr aspired to be Mercury and sought to accomplish his level of feats.

Past the paintings and on their right was a large common area with holographic screens displaying mission information and geographical locations on a map. Agents stood, perusing it for their next tasks. A circular desk sat at the center of the room. Surrounded by the sea of monitors was the diminutive receptionist.

The receptionist looked up from her screen. "Mister Zephyr!"

"Hello! We would like to start our first mission."

"Lumière blood or not, I would like to see verification."

The trio fished out their Communicators from their pockets and handed them to the receptionist. Communicators were almost indestructible and functioned as a foldable holographic tablet. The backside of the Communicators had a white seal attached to the center. Such a seal only belonged to a licensed Specialist.

"Congratulations! Since you're likely going to be on your own for most missions, your Communicators will need upgrades." She pulled out a device bigger than the Communicators' and put each inside, emitting a white glow. "It now displays mission objectives and details. There are also more sensory features, and you can store more objects and combat gear inside."

Shadow beamed. "Sweet!"

The boys enjoyed these additions for more than missions. Upgrades would allow for a better experience overall for gaming and their other "nerdy" shenanigans. Their antics exasperated Aurora.

"Now, your first mission should be easier. Perhaps an E-rank."

The receptionist typed away at her computer and a holographic list of missions followed by their descriptions took shape.

An E-ranked mission was standard for rookie Specialists. Risen may have been far more horrifying than regular monsters, but even preteen Agents-in-training had no trouble with the Level 1 creatures of darkness. E-ranked missions had Level 1 and Level 2s.

For Dream Teams, a beginner level mission was child's play. In their case, Zephyr thought a Level 4 Risen wouldn't have hindered them either.

We can take on Level three Risen fine. So, the second-to-last level shouldn't be too far off.

"How 'bout the one at Wellsprings Cave?" suggested Shadow.

"Sure!" said Zephyr. This mission was going to be over within record time.

The receptionist nodded. "Log in the information and you're set."

Three additional holographs appeared, prompting them for their credentials. Green check marks displayed onto the screens, signaling their validity.

"By the way, what kind of mission is Skye Hikari on right now?" asked Shadow.

The woman pressed some keys on her keyboard and glanced at the screens. "An A-ranked at an underwater fortress. She's done and heading back now."

Zephyr couldn't remember the last time he'd seen Skye for over a day at Garnet City.

"We can finally spend time with her again," said Shadow with a hint of sadness in the undertones of his voice.

"Oh, yeah!" Aurora's face brightened. Years back, they dreamed of going on their first mission as licensed Agents together.

"Can you imagine being on par with her and Luna?" asked Shadow.

After selecting their mission, the trio stepped to the side to suit up. Donning their combat gear showed their state of duty. Agents had the liberty of designing their own clothing. Attire for missions was notoriously durable and they weren't ordinary garb. They seldom got dirty, being sweat-proof as well. With a press of a button on their Communicators, a flash of light replaced their current outfits with one of their choosing. Star Strike thought it'd be cool for the guys to select outfits comprising collared or hooded jackets to coordinate. The girls had more variety in their outfits due to differing fashion sense.

Zephyr had on his signature costume, the one he was the most recognized in: a black jacket reaching a little past his thighs with the Lumière symbol on the back, a dark blue v-neck, black trousers, matching fingerless gloves, and high-top boots. People joked about how out of Star Strike, he, Shadow, and Glacieus dressed the best out of the guys on the team. It wasn't like Zephyr minded, because it was a coverup for how he "secretly" wanted to dress as cool as his favorite comic book characters. Otherwise, he didn't care, but he had to maintain an image for the public as instructed.

Shadow had a black t-shirt, khaki pants, a dark gray hooded jacket with an X pattern and emerald hems, black fingerless gloves, and dark green and white sneakers. Almost all of his outfits had a hood and sneakers. According to the media, all Hikari's had head-turning looks; any descendants of Celeste had her god-like beauty.

Aurora wore her favorite lavender dress with a sweetheart neckline and straps which hung diagonally on her shoulders, a white undershirt, and gold hemming that matched the gold sash around her waist. Her tight, red waves had two gold clips on either side of her hair, which also matched her gold and brown, knee-length boots. Like always, she slipped on white and gold bracelets.

"New outfit?" Zephyr asked Shadow, who nodded. "It reminds me of Draco the Slayer's costume in Edition thirty-nine! And in his vintage action figures!"

"Are you talking about those dolls in your room again?" asked Aurora.

"They're ACTION FIGURES! With real, LIGHTNING-PUNCHING ACTION!" replied Zephyr in an almost too quick and defensive manner.

Aurora facepalmed. "If you say so."

"Action figures! I repeat! THEY ARE ACTION FIGURES!" said Zephyr, fist-bumping Shadow.

The trio could find the closest and most used teleportation panels in the Lumière Base at the Hangar, a few sections away from the common room.

"Do you think we can go on missions with Skye soon?" asked Aurora, following Zephyr and Shadow toward their destination.

"It's possible," replied Zephyr. "Even when Aqua got certified before the rest of her team, she helped guide them on beginner missions."

This wasn't an uncommon occurrence with veteran licensed Agents, especially with Dream Teams. Zephyr cherished every memory with Skye—they stamped themselves into his mind. His heart palpitated at the mere thought of her and her soft voice.

"But Aqua never disappeared as much," Shadow pointed out. "Skye always disappears, one mission after another, with no breaks! Like a workaholic!"

"I never realized how odd that was until the others got licensed," said Aurora. "They might've had longer missions or bigger projects, but at least they took breaks, and we could spend time with them."

Last time they teamed up with Skye was six years ago, before joining a customized training program within the Combat Squad. Although the four of them planned on becoming Specialists together as kids, Skye's plans changed, and the President believed it was the best choice for the team. In her view, Skye wanted to compensate for being "helpless" since the night of the exams.

Zephyr tended to think about that chilling course of events.

Dr. Lycaste was a renowned scientist, a higher-up who planned most of the exam. He came up with a new test to see how Skye's power fared against a captured Risen. It spun out of control, and it pained him to think of that innocent girl witnessing the slaughter, paralyzed out of sheer terror. If Zephyr hadn't found her lying in a pool of blood, almost lifeless, she would've ended up dead like the rest.

"Hope it happens soon!" said Shadow. He wished the four could be as close as they all were six years ago. It might've taken some time, but it wasn't impossible.

The Hangar split into two—an outside portion holding Lumière aircraft, battleships, and an indoor counterpart containing encapsulated warp panels. They were the only ones visible—others were only seen through Communicators for security. Agents memorized most panel locations, which helped in a pinch. As a precaution, Communicators tracked how close Agents were to each panel.

"Let's go!" Zephyr patted his friends on the back as they stepped on the panel together after selecting their destination.

The party disappeared into the gold beam.

Within seconds, they arrived in the middle of sections of thickets, beside the area's warp panel. Various luscious springs connected to waterfalls nearby. Herbs and flowers clung dense and sweet over this portion of the forest. On the surface, it seemed like a peaceful spot for an evening stroll.

A cave, hollowed between hillsides stood before them. Its entrance appeared as a natural void with outsides overgrown with moss.

"Such a pretty area. Hard to believe it's overrun by Risen," commented Aurora.

"I'm assuming the fresh Risen nest took over the cave and killed the wildlife inside," said Zephyr.

Shadow scratched his head. "Level one Risen like Wolf Risen can't take down bears and wolves. Right?"

Zephyr nodded, remembering lessons taught in their academy days. "Wolf Risen probably took down the bats. Whatever's scaring anything bigger than a deer was probably a Level two."

The nest might not have been a large one, but a wave would expand soon. The Agents' best option was to eliminate it swiftly before the Risen attracted higher levels.

Anything Level 2 and onward was a threat to civilians, as determined by the organization. Each type of discovered Risen was divided into one of the five tier levels, with each tier based on what critters, civilians, and Agents of varying rankings could take on and how easy they were to kill, depending on the type of monster.

"Welp, you better get on with the leading stuff, Zeph! Put all your training and whatnot to good use!" exclaimed Shadow.

Zephyr grinned. Their team had the most formidable Agents Eta Geminorum had ever seen. They were going to put an end to the misery that overstayed its welcome in this era. All the enhancements, extra resources, extra training—all of it was for this purpose.

Wolf-shaped creatures resembling shadows flooded the cave. They stood on all fours, with red eyes and claws. Wolf Risen might've looked menacing, but their claws were as dull as a butter knife.

They pressed a button on their Communicators, and golden beams in the shape of their respective weapons appeared in their hands. Diablos in Shadow's, Helios in Aurora's, and Galeforce in Zephyr's. Galeforce was a gift from his parents to celebrate his promotion to Specialist. The katana had layered tamahagane steels with a range of carbon concentrations. Sword wielders either wielded katanas originating from Kadelatha or from Thet. Zephyr's fighting style was better suited for shorter, lighter swords with sharper cutting edges.

"Get in formation!" said Zephyr.

That's what Mercury would say! Those words made Zephyr feel powerful, like he could do anything as a team leader and beyond. Was Capala watching from above?

Aurora stayed behind Zephyr and Shadow.

Shadow pressed a button on Diablos, transforming it into axe form. Galeforce shined in the dark cave, and he pointed his blade at the Level 2 Risen. It turned light blue, and he landed a blow on one foe.

The Risen became an icicle and shattered upon contact with the sword, which absorbed the icicle particles and sliced the air, unleashing a vacuum wave shooting ice shards toward other enemies within range.

Zephyr side-stepped to stab another Risen in a sequence, before charging and shooting lightning bolts out of his sword.

Shadow shielded Aurora from attacks that might interrupt her spells. He swung Diablos and allowed the head of the axe to fly around the battlefield while the staff shot bullets made of water aura. The head made it back to the top of his staff like a boomerang and he struck the ground with it, creating a slight tremor and allowing stones to pelt the Risen.

Opening her tome, Aurora drew the aura from her body into a magic circle. This required concentration and took more seconds than a standard, aura-based attack. The circle was a reddish-orange color, and the tome allowed her to draw additional power for her spell. Once her aura channeled, her circle vanished, and balls of fire rained upon the remaining Risen as Helios lit up.

"Heh! Piece of cake!" said Shadow. They set out to explore the cave for any more waves. "Actual difference is we don't got instructors tellin' us what to do!"

"I've never seen you pull those kinds of attacks, Zeph," observed Aurora.

"Heh, I saved it for the first mission!" Shadow mentioned that Zephyr could've been a Unity Squad Trainee.

Zephyr wondered what it would have been like to go through those regimens, rather than his custom Lumière one.

"Guys, how did I do?" asked Aurora. She was the only one on Star Strike born with the ability to use her aura as magical spells. Everyone on Star Strike had innate, enhanced ways of manipulating their aura. All strongest teams had aura users.

"Your fire magic is stronger," commented Zephyr, wiping Galeforce's edge. "I'd imagine we'd have to face stronger Risen, the further we get into this cave so that'll come in handy."

"What about meeee?" asked Shadow.

"You did well, too. As always," said Zephyr.

Shadow beamed. "I know! Wanted to hear ya say it!"

Their Communicators beeped—it might have been important. Alas... It was an anomalous frog picture with morose eyes sent from

Leif to their group chat. Usually, something of the sort had a response of laughter images from Glacieus.

"Where does he get those?" asked Aurora.

Zephyr laughed. "I thought it was a news alert."

Shadow shook his head. "There ya go again with the news! Checkin' it ALL the time!"

"Maybe because it changes every day or something," said Zephyr sarcastically.

"Whatta nerd!" joked Shadow.

Aurora rolled her eyes. "Shadow, you can be such a child!"

"You know, with all of this extra storage space, I wonder how many emulators we can put on here!" A twinkle appeared in Zephyr's eyes as the boys did another fist-bump.

Aurora sighed. "*Both* of you can be such children."

More Level 1 Risen scattered throughout the cave, and it didn't take long to eliminate them. This mission was going almost too well, if that was possible. Wellsprings Cave was an area for beginners, and it showed.

"Noticed ya didn't miss any spells yet!" said Shadow to Aurora after another successful battle. "Actually, ya haven't missed since-"

"DON'T BRING IT UP!"

Zephyr remembered when Aurora accidentally lit Leif's pants on fire. And instead of dousing the flames with water magic, she unintentionally used lightning.

"It's not funny!"

Shadow burst out laughing. "Still got the video, Zeph?"

"You HAVE A VIDEO?"

"He recorded it!"

"Really, Zeph? Really?" Aurora's face filled with judgment. "You REALLY enjoyed that, didn't you? Gods, you're spiteful!"

Zephyr smirked. "I think panicking and trapping him in a water bubble was the best part."

"I think I'd rather get trapped in a water bubble and drown right now," muttered Aurora.

The last stretch of the cave was expansive. Risen emerged,

more anthropomorphic than the wolves and resembling Level 2s that Zephyr had seen before in textbooks. Agents-in-training and newbie Specialists sometimes had trouble with Level 2s. With the success rate the trio had so far, they were nothing of consternation.

"The aura around here is a lot stronger," noted Zephyr. "All Risen come from this area… Probably spawning from a bigger one."

"Like the one up there?" asked Shadow, pointing above his head.

A Beowulf remained attached to the cave ceiling. None of them encountered one before, but Zephyr recalled they were one of few types capable of spawning Wolf Risen offspring. They were also classified as Level 2s.

As soon as the Beowulf spotted the party, it shrieked and landed onto the ground, activating a tremor. The Beowulf struck, but Zephyr dodged and jumped up into the air, landing a slash onto its side. Wind glyphs shot out from his blade as he slashed the air, creating small tornadoes that swept it up above as he spun around. A blast launched from the Risen's mouth and missed.

Zephyr countered, vertically slicing its body with Galeforce, covered in a white glow.

The Beowulf could self-regenerate, so they had to relentlessly attack.

Shadow swung Diablos, allowing the head to detach and fly off, striking the Beowulf. Once the axe returned, Shadow gathered more momentum, leaping up and slamming the bit against its body, charged with his signature, Gwymond Darkness.

A yellow magic circle surrounded Aurora. She levitated above the ground and a ball of electricity generated around her. A bolt of lightning appeared, landing on the head of the Risen, causing it to disintegrate into nothing.

Shadow punched the air. "We did it!"

"Wait! What's that?" Aurora pointed at the ceiling, where pools of darkness and more Risen emerged from them.

Shadow gave Zephyr a thumbs up. "Your orders, Zeph?"

Zephyr grinned. "I got a plan!" Their first mission was one battle away from being over. How much harder could reinforcements be to take care of, anyway?

Everything coming from this last part of the nest seemed miniscule. All except one. A void made of darkness appeared in front of them as soon as they annihilated the fodder. A large humanoid, Risen, revealed itself; half-dead, dark, and beaten up. Zephyr created more glyphs to latch on and hold it back.

"I've never seen that type of Risen before." Zephyr pressed the "Scan" button on his Communicator and holographic blue light emerged.

He glanced at the most relevant data. *Name: Eraser. Level: 4. Known Weaknesses: Light & Lumière aura. Known Behaviors: Sometimes erratic. Sometimes targets units with highest strength first, whittling them down until one last blast to eliminate all of its enemies simultaneously. Known Abilities and Characteristics: Darkness blasts, needle-based attacks, powerful blows from its spiked club.*

"Can we take on a Level four?" asked Aurora. "Why's it here?"

"It's weakened!" said Shadow. "We can take it! Especially me!"

Aurora and Shadow's aura levels were plentiful. No damage yet, as well. Given its weakened state and how Zephyr's abilities could counter it, this fight should've had a desirable outcome.

Weird how a Risen like this would warp here, thought Zephyr. *There's not as much information recorded about this one.*

Their options were to stop the Risen or call for reinforcements. The latter was unnecessary. Especially for them.

"We'll be fine!" said Zephyr.

The glyphs enlarged once Zephyr waved his hand. Cyclones shot out of them and trapped the Eraser inside. No damage taken, as displayed by the holograms. A spiked club surfaced in the Eraser's hands, and everyone avoided the blows from it.

Zephyr struck, dealing no damage. He conjured glyphs with another movement of his hands, landing green slashes on the enemy. Still nothing.

Shadow's axe-work and Aurora's magic both did nothing. Before Shadow jumped and attacked, the Eraser landed a direct hit, throwing Shadow to the ground. Parts of the cave floor crumbled. Chunks of earth shot up and repeatedly crushed against Shadow's body, and the passive, transparent shield always covering him dematerialized.

Floating chunks of earth blocked Aurora and Zephyr, giving them no choice but to break through with their attacks.

Blood gushed out of Shadow's sides.

How'd it break through Shadow's natural defences? thought Zephyr. Shadow was one of the most defensive units on Star Strike, thanks to his passive ability to withstand more hits than most. It didn't cost any aura to activate, unlike all durability techniques.

It threw Shadow against the cave wall, leaving him almost unconscious.

"Shadow!" screamed Aurora. She unfurled her palm, releasing bursts of wind at the chunks and put on a spurt of speed toward Shadow.

The Risen outran her, slamming her to the ground as well and crackling the ground. It grabbed her by the neck, about to land a fatal blow.

Five wind glyphs seized the Risen. It dropped Aurora, and a glyph cushioned her fall.

"Zephyr... Get out of here..." Zephyr barely heard her as she struggled to move.

"Guys... No!"

Every muscle in Zephyr's body tensed.

His heart rate sped up and his head spun. He was almost out of aura, but he needed to use up the last of it as much as he could. If to save his friends, he would take it, no matter the odds. Zephyr charged Galeforce with as much blue electricity as he could muster, standing his ground in front of his friends. The Eraser's club filled with intense light at a rate faster than the eye could see, turning the entire cave's interior white.

Before the beam landed, a figure appeared before him.

"What the. . .?"

2

NEVER BE THE SAME

ZEPHYR

M<small>IRACULOUSLY, THE BLAST DIDN'T HIT</small> Z<small>EPHYR</small>.

As soon as the figure appeared, the light vanished. For a split second, Zephyr thought either he was hallucinating or illusions had made a return to the Mortal Realm.

She was there.

Skye's iconic long sword, Excalibur, blocked everything in its path in its golden form. She grabbed a knife from her belt and slashed the Eraser, releasing a shock wave throughout its body. Such a technique would paralyze it for a short time.

Skye faced him. "Hey."

"How did…?" Zephyr stared at her in disbelief.

"Now isn't the time to explain." The Communicator in one of the brown pouches strapped around the side of her thighs lit up and three Elixirs appeared in her hands. She tossed them to him. "I need you to take care of them."

"What about you?"

"Help them." Skye gestured to Aurora and Shadow. "They need you."

The Eraser would recover from its paralysis any second now.

Skye twirled her sword, drawing aura from her body to the blade.

"How'd... she know?" asked Shadow.

Zephyr crouched by Shadow's side and Aurora's, untwisting the cap off one glass bottle, pouring the green liquid down Shadow's throat. Once empty, Zephyr took the second one and gave it to Aurora. The Elixir was sweet, almost like agave nectar. It was tastier than Potions and Ethers. Both had an aftertaste akin to illness medicine.

Skye's status displayed on the hologram when Zephyr scanned. Her aura levels were three-fourths depleted. Bandages wrapped around her legs—a regular occurrence. Zephyr could tell how worn down she was by her bowed shoulders she attempted to hide by straightening her tall and muscular frame.

Under these conditions, Skye and the Eraser fought toe-to-toe. She narrowly avoided a hit from the spiked club. Skye ran up the cave walls and jumped off it, aiming another knife at the Eraser.

Zephyr wanted to help but needed to recover. He made enough mistakes in one day. If he tried to do anything, he would just get in her way. Their earlier loss was already enough of an indicator that they bit off more than they could chew. Dream Team or not, they weren't limitless.

Skye disappeared in front of the Eraser and reappeared right behind it, dodging a blow, and moving so quickly it looked like she was teleporting. She landed a direct hit on its back. The Eraser bent over, exposing its weak spot, giving Skye an opening for throwing a third knife.

The Eraser launched another massive beam at Zephyr.

Skye grabbed Zephyr with her left arm, pulling him out of the way. Her blade was in her right hand, blocking another ray.

"Skye...!" His face flushed, seeing how close they stood together. Her cheeks also pinked.

Parts of the ray hit her, and she winced. In rapid-fire succession, more rays launched, and Skye leaped back and forth, blocking them. Some hit as she shielded him, however, turning into mini-explosions upon contact. Skye closed her eyes and a golden glow manifested in her eyes, boosting herself. She remained unscathed and a clear aura surrounded her, activating her durability shield.

Skye's aura gauge depleted. She twirled her blade once more, and it lit up, cutting through the air, emitting a white flash toward the Eraser, and slammed her fist onto the ground, causing a tremor and knocking the Eraser against the wall.

Skye was the only one capable of boosting her strength, speed, durability, or elemental abilities with limited usage. The drawback was how much stamina it took, depending on how much she enhanced it.

Zephyr recalled the times he heard of Skye collapsing after missions or tough battles. He wished she used the power more wisely.

Skye did a front handspring and struck, inflicting a scratch. Before she could dodge, the Eraser slammed her to the ground, and it cracked once more. She took minor damage, despite getting thrown against a stalagmite with an impact so hard it shattered. Uppercutting the Risen, she sent it flying to the cave ceiling. Her knives glowed and multiplied, encircling her. They flew at the Eraser, lodging themselves into its body like a pincushion. Thousands of needles jutted out of its body and Skye flipped back and forth, evading every one.

Skye turned into a ball of sparks, knocking the Eraser back and forth at a pace faster than the speed of light. Although her natural speed and physical strength surpassed most, seeing them enhanced was a miracle to watch.

She probably has one boost in her left before she collapses, thought Zephyr. He remembered the times he carried her on his back after she fainted during training as kids.

Color returned to Aurora's face, and she sat up. "So, this… is the power of a Marauder."

Skye's power changed in ways nobody predicted. It spiked earlier than expected and to this day, as far as Zephyr knew, it was an unsolved mystery. The data predicted for her to have a handful of abilities that ended up not existing and vice versa, including the enhancement techniques. Others believed she mutated. Zephyr and Shadow thought her power was related to Dr. Lycaste's rumored experiments, though it was strange, considering the organization refused to experiment on children.

Star Strike was designed to beat the odds. It comprised prodigies in technology, recon, magic, sensory, marksmanship, and super soldiers. Skye was the latter. Built as a super soldier and only that.

Skye glared at the Eraser and boosted herself again. A blue shockwave emerged from Excalibur and the Farien symbol on the hilt glowed, as it always did whenever she unleashed significant amounts of aura. Red sparks followed, and they filled the entire cave. The rest of the party found themselves knocked against the opposite side of the area's walls from the impact. A yellow ray came after, along with pools of water, bursts of fire, stones, sheets of ice and metal. Lumière Inc. predicted her specialty to be light, but it required the same amount of aura as any other element.

Skye leaped up into the air, raising her sword and slicing it down onto the Eraser. All the forms of aura she created exploded onto it and the sword multiplied into five copies, spinning around her.

The cave's interior illuminated.

When the light disappeared, the Eraser disintegrated.

Skye bent over, clutching herself.

"Are you okay?" asked Zephyr, running over with Shadow and Aurora in tow.

Green sparkles came out of Helios. Skye jumped to her feet, withdrawing Excalibur. "I'm fine, thanks."

"When d'ya get back?" asked Shadow.

"Not long before I came here. They said you took longer than expected."

"Right after your mission, too... You're exhausted, especially after your previous mission," said Aurora, looking down with guilt.

A heavy, suffocating feeling stirred in Zephyr's chest. "I should've called for help. I should've known we weren't ready to take on a wounded Level four. We shouldn't have had any exceptions." They were doing so well on their first mission. All the buildup, hype, cheering, the gifts, and initial successes caused more harm.

What kind of leader was he? Zephyr had to lead a fully formed Star Strike one day, but he failed to lead a mission for less than half of his team. He made a decision no leader of a Dream Team should have carried out.

"It's not your fault, Zeph!" said Shadow.

"As soon as they detected it on the radar, they sent me. I'm glad none of you are in critical condition," said Skye.

"So, we had a successful mission!" said Shadow, grinning. "Last part was unexpected and didn't count! We did great!"

"We can head back," said Skye, diverting her gaze from Zephyr when their eyes met—just like when they were kids. Her pupils dilated and face flushed. The sight of it made him beam every time.

Zephyr thought back to the warm feeling of relief when he saw her standing before him. He recognized those loose waves reaching halfway down her back and her outfit better than anyone… As soon as anyone saw a teenage girl in those clothes; they knew they were in excellent hands. She had on her iconic, sleeveless jacket and remained a little unzipped, revealing a white undershirt. Combining it with white shorts, brown combat boots, black finger-less gloves, and gray and turquoise bracelets completed the look. As a Hikari and descendant of Celeste, she had to look the part for the public.

"So! Are ya coming on missions with us sometimes?" Shadow smiled at his sister, and she nodded. "You'll see how crazy good I've gotten in battle!"

"It'll be so nice having you around like old times!" exclaimed Aurora.

"Thanks for saving us back there, Skye." The familiar sweet feeling pooled in his body once his turquoise eyes met her golden-amber ones once more.

"No problem." Her voice was particularly softer around him. With her around, Zephyr felt safe. She had always been his best source of comfort. Despite the adversity at hand, she continued to push forward to become the hero she dreamed of.

"It's nostalgic, ya know? Repeating the same scenario with us!"

"A while ago, yes," agreed Skye, readjusting her gloves.

Zephyr chuckled. "I remember Aurora tried to follow you multiple times."

Aurora's face turned a shade of her hair. "Hey! Let's not bring that up!"

Zephyr could've sworn there would be an exclamation mark appearing above Shadow's head if they were in a video game. "And then ya tried to-"

"I SAID DON'T BRING IT UP, YOU DUNCE BUCKET!" Aurora smacked Shadow upside the head, making Skye giggle.

Zephyr thought they were adorable together, like an old married couple.

They arrived at the teleportation spot, back where they began.

With another key press, they disappeared and reappeared in the Lumière Base hangar.

"Just report everything to the receptionist," said Skye, sneaking another peek at Zephyr.

"Where are you going?" asked Zephyr.

"Have some errands to take care of. I'll see you around." They waved and went their separate ways.

"We finished our first mission!" Shadow high-fived his best friends.

There was no point in appearing anxious in front of Shadow and Aurora—it would've worried them more. Zephyr figured he'd set his concerns aside and talk to either Aqua or Skye about his mistakes later when he had the chance.

"Very well. Thank you for your work," said the receptionist, after they reported their findings to her. She said nothing about the Eraser and Zephyr assumed the veteran Agents were the ones to discuss it.

"We'll pick another one tomorrow then," said Aurora.

"Let's hang at my place," suggested Shadow.

It was too late for lunch at the manor anyway... Zephyr messaged his sisters, explaining the delay, but they didn't mind. He braced himself for questions they'd ask later that night.

"Guess daily missions are the new norm," said Shadow. "No more sittin' around in classrooms five days a week."

"I'm going to miss turning and seeing you asleep in class," teased Zephyr. Shadow would not-so-subtly face plant the desk, leaving Zephyr to sit at an angle so their instructors wouldn't notice. Either that, or Shadow spent his time doodling in textbooks or laughing at their teammate, Glacieus's pranks. Or partaking in said pranks.

"That was ONE time! We had those annoying exams in History, Magic, Recon, AND Tech! That's pure torture for kids below the age of ten! For one day!" exclaimed Shadow.

"Hmmm... It wasn't just once. Remember all those times Leif drew on your face in Combat lecture?" Retrieving his Communicator, Zephyr pulled up the exact photo and smirked.

"Oh, COME ON! HOW do you have these pics? From SO LONG ago? Do ya got pics of EVERYTHING? For AMMUNITION? What's WRONG with you?"

They passed by the flower field and the brown, red, and white brick house came into view. Zephyr wasn't sure what was more of a second home to him: Hikari Residence or the Base. His family and the Candors were there often in their cozy, lively house.

The front door sprung open as they approached the front steps.

"How'd it go? How'd it go?" The other enormous ball of energy of the Hikari Household was there, taking turns hugging everyone.

"We made it!"

Cynthia resembled preteen Skye. Her black hair with caramel-brown highlights was shorter than Skye's and tied into their usual high pigtails. She and Suzie were best friends and teammates, and Zephyr found it sweet how they had their own personal cheerleaders.

Zephyr ruffled her hair. "How'd your Weapons Exam from last week go?"

Cynthia grinned. "Passed with flying colors, thanks to you, Zeph!"

"You didn't need me, Cindy. You always sleep through class and manage fine."

"Just like her brother," said Aurora.

"I'm no ditz!" replied Shadow.

"Who are you calling a ditz? Are you talking about me? Tell me more about your mission! And where's Sissy? I thought she was coming home tonight!"

Shadow waved his hand. "We'll tell ya if ya let us get inside already! Skye had to take care of a few things first!"

"What few things? She's hardly ever home! She worries me, Shadie!"

"Same here…"

"I hope she's not pushing herself too far," said Aurora.

Zephyr could've sworn he saw a lightbulb appear above Cynthia's head.

Shadow's youngest sister had a twinkle in her eye. "Maybe YOU should check up on her, Zeph! She's probably still at the Base! I know you like being alone with her! Especially with the way you look at her!"

Zephyr scratched his head. *Yep, this is where the family resemblance ended.*

"Run along now! Rest of us'll be here!" She and Aurora looked at each other knowingly. Zephyr supposed he deserved it after his earlier teasing.

"Wait… What's goin' on?" Shadow's head tilted to the side.

Zephyr sighed. "If you insist."

Cynthia pushed him away. "Shoo! Run along now!"

"Have fun!" Aurora winked at him.

"Someone explain what's goin' on!" Shadow looked between the girls, seeking answers.

Zephyr speed-walked from Daybreak toward the Base. Maybe this alone time he could have with Skye could be meaningful. For years, Zephyr tried to get proper reads on everyone. Skye was the only one he couldn't completely assess and analyze. He knew she kept a lot from him. From everyone.

"Zephyr! What are you doing here?" asked an Agent upon reaching the central dome.

"Oh, I was looking for Skye. Have you seen her?"

"Last I heard, she was at the Medical Wing."

Medical Wing was on the left side of the central dome, ran by Glacieus's parents. It looked like any regular hospital with cots, curtains, and carts full of medical supplies and healing concoctions. The aromas of medicinal herbs wafted the room. Some smelled fruity and others were overwhelming, but felt therapeutic, almost soothing.

Skye was the only one in the sectioned off area and something glowed in her hands. She turned a bit as soon as she saw him to hide it. "I was going to come home in a few."

"Are you hurt?"

"I need to rest."

He hung his head. "It's my fault. You wouldn't be like this if I called for help as soon as we ran into the Eraser. They almost got killed because of me…"

"Don't blame yourself."

"I got way too caught up in the moment to analyze and see how dangerous it was. I got overconfident and failed as a leader on my first mission as a full-fledged Agent!" The raw wound of guilt overcame Zephyr once more. It bled a trail that would never wash away. Zephyr was forced to cradle it.

Skye winced. "Zephyr-"

"I know I worried you and you had to go through extra trouble for us. I'm sorry, I thought I was-"

"Don't worry about it so much," she said in a firm tone. "You can't expect to know what to do all the time while you're learning."

"You're right…"

"Being a Specialist is only the beginning. You're fine, just be more careful next time and let this be a learning experience."

Zephyr smiled. "Thanks. Want me to keep you company?" He

could get a better view of her up close. Skye had always been cute. But now? She was seriously breathtaking with her sweet face, elongated legs, and curves. His Communicator background pictures always included team pictures, and his eyes had a habit of fixating on her.

She looked like she was about to nod but hesitated. "That's okay."

Zephyr's smile faded. "See you later, then?"

Skye nodded.

Zephyr could've sworn he saw her wince again when he left the room. He sensed the same aura glow in her hands once again.

3

SIDING WITH WINNERS

ZEPHYR

Zephyr stayed up late. Ever since his first mission, he did this, but not out of excitement. He repeated the words Skye said in his head for three weeks now. If he didn't learn from his mistake, he couldn't be what everyone expected him to be. There had to be a zero percent chance he would ever make the same mistake again.

He sat at his desk in the study section of his bedroom. His displays showed profiles for his teammates, and he jotted down unique plans of action.

Zephyr extracted the data from every mission to determine the best positions, angles, and techniques to use against different opponents and situations. He believed this would suffice for their next mission. That's what he believed the first time, however…

Scenarios of what could go wrong with each strategy distracted Zephyr, and it didn't help with his pounding heartbeats and creeping migraines.

Subsequent missions were similar. The only difference between their E-ranked missions and their later years at the academy was that they involved no instructor. They had more nest extermination jobs, and Skye accompanied them on a few. For higher-ranked missions, she was to stick with Star Strike, ensuring their safety. With all the resources pooled into making the Dream Team the way they were, someone needed to make sure they stayed alive. Otherwise, it'd be for naught. Ramp-up processes existed for every team, even ones projected to be elite. Everyone had the same E-ranked missions early on. Zephyr was okay with taking time before adjusting to something more difficult—he was only getting comfortable with E-rank, as pathetic as it seemed.

⠂⠄❨⠄⠂

THE TEAM STOOD before the job listings in the common room the following day. Zephyr's eyes made a beeline for the easier missions near the bottom of the lists before Skye made a suggestion.

"Bandit tribes? Oh snap! Those exist?" asked Shadow, peering at the mission description.

"I've heard nothing about them," said Aurora. There was a lot the media didn't want to show, and the news reported less on matters appearing only in a nation or two.

"Hmm, well Sevinnon law enforcement must have a lot of trouble if they need our help," said Zephyr. Affairs to be disputed within nations and kingdoms didn't involve Agents focused on protecting worlds from interplanetary threats militaries couldn't handle.

As superhuman as Specialists were, they had limits. Zephyr tried his best to hide any hint of anxiousness regarding their potentially hardest mission yet.

"It's mostly beginner teams who deal with it, if nations request our help," said Skye. The warmth in her eyes soothed him whenever he intently glanced at her. Up close, he could smell her sweet vanilla scent.

"Why they gotta make more trouble for the world?" asked Shadow.

The organization classified a fair amount of information amongst higher-ups. Newer Specialists gradually became more desensitized with increasing exposure. Zephyr wondered what they would reveal as Star Strike ranked up.

"Some help Risen to avoid getting killed by them," said Skye.

"It's cowardly, for sure," said Zephyr. "Crazy to think how some Risen could become that intelligent." Agents eliminated most of them.

"If they can't beat 'em... They join 'em for immunity?" Shadow stared at Skye in disbelief. "But... why?"

"People have different ways of looking at things. Times are drastic and some gave up on Agents," said Skye.

"A mission dealing with people would be good for us, right?" asked Aurora.

"Right. You need to get accustomed to dealing with different missions, since until now, you've only destroyed nests and swarms as Specialists these past weeks. First six months of your time as Specialists revolve around this. Your focus is experiencing different types, before making bigger contributions to the organization."

Missions in their training days sheltered them. Their missions involved eliminating swarms, escorting people, protecting people, or rescuing them... Not fighting against them.

"We'll be saving lives! Either way! Which is our job as heroes!" said Shadow. "Though, I wanna know how somebody could think that way!"

If these tribes were smart enough, they would've stayed out of Silvatica. No mortals would dare to stand a chance of being so close to the primary Lumière Base in Eta Geminorum. Zephyr hoped to never see Garnet City get invaded in his lifetime or ever hear of it.

Once arriving at the Hangar, Star Strike teleported to the outskirts of a plains area within Sevinnon's borders, outside a forest with trails leading toward several mountain ranges. A sign with multiple arrows marked its warp point, showing different exits and entrances.

Further west was a plateau of semiarid grassland, followed by farmland renowned for the growth of rootsnips. Similarly, to carrots and parsnips, the burgundy crop had an earthy taste. Kilometers away, they'd be able to spot orchards filled with fig trees, some possessing the rare silver color that was said to bring good fortune. Supposedly, when the Wind Goddess, Gemini created Eta Geminorum, she placed certain geographical landforms in "weird locations," according to those who weren't from the wind worlds.

This portion of the mountains had travelers and Risen tended to not spawn here. The shift in the laws of nature hardly affected the forest, so it only had regular monsters that were a nuisance.

Zephyr wanted to rip the bandage off and find the hideout. Delays in their search built up more of the clawing, nagging feeling inside of him caused his heart to thud.

"So, these tribes would migrate and conceal themselves with magic," said Aurora. "That's why it took Sevinnon law enforcement so long to find them?"

Sevinnon was far less technologically advanced than Silvatica. Farms and villages were plentiful, with few major cities bordering up north by The Glassy Sea.

"Hmm, I'd assume so," replied Zephyr. "Which led them to ask Lumière Inc. for help."

"Wish we did earlier!" said Shadow. "We can't leave people in need! No matter how big the problem is!"

"We'll do what we can," said Skye. "It's impossible to help everyone." The way she said it reminded Zephyr of the times his father repeated those exact words.

Shadow had a look of determination on his face. "We'll make it happen! If not, *I* will!"

The Skye I knew would've had the same response as Shadow. What happened?

On missions, Skye was focused and stoic. Stone-faced. Alert for any threats. Like a hardened veteran.

It didn't take long to reach the timeless, ancient trees that seemed to disappear into the sky. The distinct aroma of soil mixed with leaves and rustling sounds of critters scurried around scattered branches. Rays of sunshine filtered through, illuminating patches of moss.

Star Strike crept their way in, trying not to draw unnecessary attention from bee and hawk monsters (Zephyr had to remind Shadow several times to not go after them).

Before long, Zephyr sensed concealing magic ahead.

Zephyr pointed north at a clearing. "It's there."

They approached, following Skye, concealing themselves behind a cluster of trees.

Skye pressed a button on her Communicator, revealing the campsite to the party. They made quick work of the scene. Scattered tents and piles of stolen loot from raids engulfed the area. Bandits went about their day; unaware they were visible.

"Let's go!"

Zephyr stopped Shadow from charging in. "We can't yet."

Shadow and Aurora glanced at him, surprised by the more serious tone in his voice.

"We need to sneak in and take them out from behind." Zephyr looked at Skye for approval. They could've taken them all on right away, but there were too many unknown factors.

"Right. There are plenty of objects spread around the campsite we can use for hiding."

"And if we get seen by too many at once, they'll try to surround us. We'll need to take them down quickly." He waited for Skye to approve once again.

No risks this time.

If Skye took more than a backseat on their mission, it'd defeat the purpose of her being there. She was around to guide them and let them hone their skills, only stepping in when necessary.

Skye and Aurora were to enter first from one side of the campsite, Shadow and Zephyr for the opposite. This was a good matchup since Skye ensured Aurora wouldn't take any blows from enemies while remaining hidden. Zephyr could keep Shadow from doing anything impulsive—he made Zephyr the most nervous as much as he loved the guy.

When the opportunity came and no bandits were within the line of sight, Shadow and Zephyr separately went into the site, each hiding behind crates. A bandit came close to Zephyr, and he struck him with the pommel of Galeforce, knocking him out and hiding his unconscious body behind the crates.

Shadow jabbed two individuals with Diablos' handle.

Zephyr peered to see if there was anyone else within range. Wind glyphs appeared below their feet and spun, sending them flying to the ground. With enough precision, more glyphs muffled any sounds coming from the bandits and cushioned their falls to avoid drawing attention. Shadow pressed Diablos onto the ground. A small whip made of darkness surfaced, traveling underground. The whip reappeared from underneath a group, wrapping around them, muffling sound, and draining enough aura to render them torpid.

It was only a matter of time before more bandits would discover their fainted colleagues.

A message from Aurora arrived—their side had enough taken out to where risking getting spotted was okay, according to Skye. Zephyr did a quick look through their side and forwarded the details to the girls.

The party reunited, and they proceeded toward the central section of the campsite, fighting their way through the remaining bandits attempting to stop them. One came out with two henchmen on either side of him. He wielded an electric hammer, and the henchmen appeared well-equipped, too. This had to be their leader.

Zephyr's hands became extra clammy.

That hammer could paralyze all of us. I could use my glyphs to disarm him, but what if I'm too slow and the henchmen get to me first? Vice versa could happen, too. Skye would take care of those... But what if she's too busy helping the others? And I can't rely on her either. How is that going to help me? But what if...?

Hundreds of strategies filled his head, and he tried to think of the best one. Every detail, everything that could go wrong, hindered his focus.

"Stop what you're doing, right now!" said Shadow.

Skye put a protective arm in front of him, preventing him from taking any further steps.

"Did you have to be so rough with my men?" asked the leader, looking more irritated than concerned.

"I thought we weren't important enough to bother with," said a henchman.

The Bandit Boss glimpsed at Shadow. Then he looked at Aurora and Zephyr.

Aurora took a step closer to Skye, looking intimidated, leading Skye to stand in front of her as well.

"How cute," remarked the Bandit Boss. "You three are new." He stole a glance at Skye. "That grim look in your eyes tells me everything. You've seen it all, haven't you?"

Shadow glared. "Whattaya mean by that?"

"The naïve and clueless air around most of you tells me everything I need to know."

Shadow's face turned red. Darkness flowed out of him, leaving Skye to grab his wrist, restraining him further. "People in the world are already suffering! Why make it worse?"

"You can take us down however many times, but you're not changing anything," said the Bandit Boss. He slammed his hammer onto the ground, unleashing an electric wave capable of paralyzing anyone who got hit by it. With a snap of Zephyr's fingers, glyphs appeared below each party member, lifting them above the ground. The henchmen retaliated, shooting their venomous crossbows in rapid-fire.

This was nerve-wracking, but Skye spent her time deflecting each arrow, giving the others opportunities to focus on landing hits.

Shadow threw Diablos' head at the two henchmen, and Aurora's spell finished casting in time. Bubbles appeared behind the henchmen and the poll of the axe knocked them into the bubbles, trapping them.

"Nice, Aurora!" exclaimed Shadow.

A barrier appeared around the Bandit Boss in the form of electricity. He raised his hammer into the air and summoned lightning bolts, raining them down on the party.

Skye boosted her speed, blocking each bolt with Excalibur. Zephyr dodged each one and Shadow tanked the hits, taking no damage.

One almost hit Aurora, but Skye pushed her out of the way.

Shadow launched more blasts of darkness at the enemy, partially breaking through the barrier and narrowly hitting the enemy leader, leaving him no choice but to dodge more of Shadow's attacks and focus his aura on keeping the barrier up.

A brown magic circle appeared around Aurora and earth walls shot up in a circle around the Bandit Boss, negating the barrier. Glyphs shot out of Zephyr's katana and latched onto the Bandit Boss, and a green thread shot out of the glyphs, rendering him unable to move.

◖

It didn't take long for the Sevinnon law enforcers to arrest them. Returning what they stole back to their rightful owners was up to them, leaving the party to stick around in case they had questions.

Patrolmen donned the olive collared uniform top, trousers, and cap with the red Sevinnon crest on their front pockets. Government officials, including the Prime Minister wore those colors, with slight variations in their attire. Each crest bore the nation's official symbol—a crossed pickaxe and a diamond, representing two of Sevinnon's primary sources of income.

Each individual Zephyr had encountered from this nation possessed that "Sevinnon niceness" he had heard so much about. The officers were far more talkative than the average citizen, however.

An officer nodded at the team. "Thanks for the help."

"Do you know why they wanna do somethin' like this?" asked Shadow.

Zephyr spent the grace period trying to analyze the sequence of events that occurred with the bandits. Their tells, demeanor, and the tone in their voices told him they were frustrated. Exhausted with the state of the world.

The officer sighed. "Most of 'em need a scapegoat to justify their selfishness. From what we've heard about past tribes, they believe Agents can't win against the rising darkness long-term. Or they think you're running out of time."

I see. That makes sense, thought Zephyr.

"What?" asked Shadow. "We got plenty of time!"

The officer shook his head. "I'm afraid others think we have a year left. Sorry, kid. But those who don't worship you, including parts of Sevinnon, are impatient and have been ever since we could no longer travel between worlds."

Zephyr assumed by their accents and style of clothing that the bandits were from Eta Taurium. He found it fascinating how everyone spoke the common tongue passed from the Gods when they once roamed the Mortal Realm. Each world had their own dialect.

Zephyr sighed. "Not to mention losing the opportunity to contact other worlds. Rising casualties and damage inflicted on civilization are nails in the coffin. There are people out there who think we give false hope and failed them."

"Some tribes are from other worlds and not being able to return fifteen years ago caused a downward spiral. I can't say I blame 'em entirely for their rationale. Darkness has plagued the realm for nearly a century now and has gotten worse over the past two decades."

As little faith Zephyr had in himself, he clung onto hope for the organization. They HAD to have more than a year left—that was a detail they couldn't conceal so easily if it were true. Capala Lumière and Zephyr's other ancestors knew the Mortal Realm was going to be in danger for an entire era and beyond. There was a reason there was a push for the organization to stay for the long game.

They may not have been able to stop the inevitable, but without the Agents, darkness would've razed the entire realm long ago.

After all, the shift in laws of nature made the darkness element so powerful, which caused the Risen to become so erratic. This was out of their control.

"It's complicated. Been that way the last twenty years," replied Skye.

Zephyr placed his hand on his chin, thinking. "People like that have always existed. Either way, remember what we're here to do. We're doing what we can to stop the Risen and reunite the worlds."

"We got family in other worlds! We don't know if they're alive! So, we gotta work together to end this!" said Shadow. "Be the heroes like our parents! We've made progress and we're gonna make a comeback! Our generation *will* change everything!"

"We should set aside all our differences, like what the Solarian Continent and the Asturias Continent have done," said Aurora. "And the Piscium and Geminorum worlds way back when."

The bandit tribes weren't the only ones who conspired against them. There were even rogue Agents. Not everyone was noble, like the Marauders or other higher-ups. Agents have left the organization before, thinking it was a waste of their time and effort for what they believed was a lost cause.

Others only stayed for fame, pay, and other benefits, such as guaranteed protection for their families in danger. It shocked Zephyr when he heard these things from Luna. Of course, this sort of thing was one thing to hear about, an uncommon thing to experience for oneself

Another officer approached them, holding the Bandit Boss's hammer. "I wonder how many of these tribesmen are ex-Thanatos members. They would've had a weapon like this."

Shadow pulled his eyebrows together, glancing at Zephyr for answers.

"Thanatos formed years ago to put an end to Lumière Inc, composed of people who didn't qualify to become Agents or the children of older members who became Agents to learn how to kill them," explained Zephyr. "They thought of Lumière Inc. as a corrupt, tyrannical company trying to take over the realm by making all world leaders submit to them as the first phase of their plan."

"That's nuts!" exclaimed Shadow. "Our families have been with the organization ever since it started! They would NEVER do that! I can tell ya that much!"

"It's dissolved ever since, but ex-members still run about, looting destroyed cities like they used to as an organization." Zephyr turned to Skye. "You and Luna helped take them down back then, right?"

Skye nodded. "Mhm. If the bandits are former Thanatos members, they're ones who surrendered and were let off with smaller punishments by whichever nation they were from."

Shadow faced his twin. "Oh, snap! I didn't know you did all that."

"Yeah. We thought they could've been purposely causing the Risen to become a lot worse over the last twenty years since they tried to put an end to Lumière Inc. Shift in laws of nature made them bad enough and we didn't think it was natural for it to continue getting worse. Pretty much why I wasn't around a lot."

"But you're always gone…" Shadow's voice was a near whisper.

"We'll look into it some more," said the officer. "In the meantime, you can take off since we have no more questions."

⁙

AFTER DINNER, Zephyr went straight to his room. He sat at his desk until the heavy yellow moon dominated the scattered stars in the night sky at its highest point. Zephyr spent a majority of the night revising and reviewing the different Risen seen on E-rank missions and their weaknesses. The most time-consuming part was figuring out more strategies that didn't put his teammates in harm's way.

He heard a light knock on the door.

"Come in!"

Tandy approached him, carrying a lacquer tray. A steaming mug and two plates piled with baked goods rested on it. The macarons caught Zephyr's eye. Tandy and Antoinette must have taken a trip over to the twins' aunt's bakery after class.

"Why are you still up? Don't you have a field mission with Professor Juniper tomorrow?"

"Well, SOMEONE wasn't taking my advice about staying up late! Since none of us could stop you, I figured you'd like a snack or two." She set the tray down at his desk.

He smiled and took a sip of the coffee imported from the Aquarius Islands. Its caramelized and nutty scent soothed him. "Thanks."

She knew how much he loved anything from Magnolia Bakery. Zephyr remembered going as a kid regularly, before training got hectic. Sometimes the Hikari kids helped behind the counter when they weren't too busy trying to eat the merchandise.

"I've never seen you stressed before and for so long." She and Eila always complained with envy about how he required little time to study to do well in school.

"Yeah, the licensed Agent stuff is a lot harder. It's nothing like your training days."

Tandy pondered for a minute. "Huh... I guess the pressure is even higher on you now. Everyone's paying even more attention to you as you rank up." She mentioned earlier at dinner how she heard about their mission today from the news.

As far as he knew, the media swept the blunders made on his first mission under the rug. When he confessed to his parents what went wrong, they said little. They knew it was going to be a learning experience and seeing the guilt and fear on their only son's face was enough punishment.

It didn't seem like they lost any faith in his future, as far as he could tell. His father was the only one he had trouble reading out of his family.

"I can't afford to make any mistakes. Especially with how quick people were to give up nowadays."

4

PHOTOGRAPHIC
SHADOW

THE NEWBIES' NEXT MISSIONS WENT WELL. SHADOW KNEW THEY WERE on the track to being the heroes they always wanted to be. He couldn't wait to boast to his relatives about Star Strike's cool adventures. And his own feats. Mostly his.

Their days would've been more fun if Zephyr didn't train or study after every mission. After bribing and attempts at "puppy-dog eyes," Shadow FINALLY convinced Zephyr to relax for once with him and Aurora at his place.

They sprawled out in the living room. Shadow and Aurora looked through old albums, and Zephyr focused on petting their family dog, Mochi. The electronic display showcased the evening news. The white fur ball always followed them around. Particularly Zephyr.

"The Thet-based organization, Cerberus, recently announced their most recent update in efforts to bring back lost bloodline abilities," said the news reporter. "Higher-ups, Wren and Mabel are here with us today for an exclusive interview to tell us more."

Zephyr's eyes darted to the screen. "Been a while since I've heard about them."

A lanky man with auburn hair, sepia skin, and gray eyes appeared next to the reporter.

Some woman stood beside him. Her bright orange locks tied into a bun stood out and Shadow couldn't tell if her matching irises were natural or the result of colored contacts. Freckles splattered across her cheeks and her face showed little sign of friendliness.

Both wore the standard Cerberus uniform—white, sleeveless jacket, black, long sleeves with matching pants, electric-blue boots, and gloves. Obnoxiously displayed on their chests was the Cerberus symbol—an electric-blue wolf.

So boring, having their employees wear the same thing. Blech.

"Welcome, Wren, Mabel!" The reporter pointed her microphone toward the duo. "Tell us more about Cerberus's progress in their pursuit!"

Wren nodded. "Cerberus confirmed through their experiments that as long as the user possesses the DNA of a former wielder of such power, the potential lies dormant in the recesses of their aura reserves."

"Impressive! And what are you planning on doing with this information?"

"Oh, come on! Lumière Inc. already discovered that," grumbled Shadow. "Guess they're trynna take credit."

"We're in the earliest stages of development, but we have a serum called Heracles. It's designed to draw out that dormant power," said Mabel. "We have permission from other nations to use their resources to supply our most ambitious project yet. We'll be combining ingredients that can react to one's DNA and ultimately restore much of what has been lost."

"Our best will take the serum. Powers unlocked will quell the raging darkness in the world. Perhaps the entire Realm, eventually," said Wren. "I'm afraid that is all we can disclose for the time being, but please, stay tuned in our journey!"

Mabel smiled like a crocodile. "We appreciate every form of support in Cerberus's goals."

"Thanks for your time! And now, we'll continue onto the next feature revolving around Kadelatha's Restoration Plans!"

"They went from making medicines and Strength Boosters and defence supplements the past decades to straight up trynna copy us for two years," said Shadow, side-eyeing.

"They're more ambitious and persistent than past organizations attempting to do the same thing," said Zephyr. "I'm curious about this serum, though, and if it has any side effects."

Other failed companies either lost money or had most of their members killed by Risen. Last Shadow heard, Cerberus members could only take down Level 2s. Nobody could be a "better Lumière Inc." Cerberus might've hated Agents, but they could never be them.

"At least their other business ventures have been successful," said Aurora.

"D'you think they'd succeed?" asked Shadow. "In bringing 'em back?"

"Maybe," said Zephyr. "It could take years before that happens. I mean the Typhons tried to do the same thing in the past. They might bring a whole new set of issues to deal with, though... But if they could bring back portaling abilities, that's another story. If they're able to help the overall cause, then maybe we could work with them."

Aurora tucked a stand of hair behind her ear. "It won't be easy, considering how much they hate us."

"It's stupid. Can see them coming to their senses eventually," said Shadow. "And realize how wrong they are about us!"

The news shifted over to some weird, boring soap opera that would've put Shadow to sleep. Since it was even less interesting than listening to Zephyr's history rambles, his attention returned to the albums.

Cynthia trotted into the room with a plate of cookies. "Where's Skye?"

The scent of browned sugar and butter perked Shadow up. He practically tasted the melted chocolate. Cynthia's cookies were always soft and chewy.

"She left on another mission after we got back," said Shadow, taking a cookie and sinking his teeth into it, tasting warm, gooey, and sugary goodness.

"Without you? And two in one day?"

Zephyr reached for a cookie. "It was urgent."

Shadow wished his twin could spend more time with them. Just like the good old days. Back then, he envied her fast growth rates. People praised *her* more than him. He figured he'd catch up to her and was a late bloomer. Mystery behind her power was still unexplained, but maybe the same could happen to him.

I dunno if I'd wanna miss out on living life as a kid. If I joined Unity or Combat.

Cynthia tilted her head. "Whatcha looking at?"

"Class pictures!" replied Aurora.

"I wanna see!" Cynthia set the plate on the coffee table and leaned over to look.

Star Strike was about ten or eleven in one of their team's photos. If Shadow remembered correctly, this was before they chose their specializations. That was also the last time they had all classes together. At least Spark and Leif had most classes with them.

"Hey! That's right before everyone goes their ways!" said Cynthia, hands to her hips. "We took ours not too long ago and I'm missing the rest of my team."

Zephyr took another cookie. "Everyone had to do their own thing first. In our case, eight of us had at least two or three classes together, while Stream and Glacieus were busy with Tech and Recon."

"They were a lot happier there!" said Aurora. "Blaze, too! And Luna belonged with the Unity Squad."

"Yup! We have something like that, too—an Intel specializer in Recon and one in Tech. And Suzie's starting her Lumière training soon," said Cynthia. Her smile faded. "I don't even remember the last time I've been apart from her."

Zephyr patted her on the head. "You'll be together again before you know it."

Cynthia would've had a few classes with her best friend. In three years, they'd have weekly missions together.

Shadow remembered the last time the team was all together in school, all seven hours. Suddenly, he was a ten-year-old, a kid with little responsibilities aside from sleep-inducing homework.

It was picture day.

He and Skye'd walk together with Zephyr and Aurora to Garnet Academy. The leftmost dome of the Lumière Base had another entrance. Lumière Inc. dedicated it to Agents-in-training and only opened during school times.

Spark and Leif came together, Luna would get dropped off by her butler, Blaze came with his older siblings, and Stream often dragged Glacieus over.

They'd meet in the courtyard, hanging out under their usual spot by an enormous Celestial Blossom tree. Leif, Shadow, and Zephyr had game devices with them. The girls talked about something girls liked that Shadow didn't understand. Blaze and Glacieus did their own thing Shadow couldn't remember. If Skye wasn't at therapy before or after school, she'd be with the girls.

The school bell rang.

They'd go into the building together and go up the first flight of stairs on their right. Fifth-years had their classes on the second floor, sharing it with sixth and seventh. Classes further than that were on the fourth.

Glacieus giggled uncontrollably when they made it upstairs.

"What is it THIS time?" asked Stream, facepalming and sighing.

Shadow beamed. "I wanna know! Is it another banana peel? Or marshmallow gun?"

The prankster grinned. "Replacing Saylor's cola with soy sauce!"

Shadow, Leif, and Spark burst out laughing.

Aurora rolled her eyes.

Skye seemed confused.

Blaze and Luna shook their heads.

Stream facepalmed again.

Zephyr looked conflicted.

"Yikes," said Luna. "It's always poor Saylor." As close as she was to Adriel and Saylor's team, she remained neutral.

Everyone made it to the classroom.

The teachers aligned desks in rows and columns of five each. Instructor Elm's desk was at the front of the room, behind the holographic board. Holograms of the six worlds floated around the rightmost wall. Left side had flat maps of the nations and kingdoms of Eta Geminorum.

Shadow sat behind Zephyr in his usual spot—the back, leftmost seat in the room.

Skye, Aurora, and Spark were on the opposite side, also near the back.

The rest were in the middle.

Glacieus swiped Saylor's lunch bag from his desk and grabbed the cola bottle.

Shadow covered his mouth with his hand to avoid laughing too hard. Sometimes, he helped with planning the pranks.

Saylor was their favorite punching bag, since he was a good sport about it.

Glacieus's partner-in-crime, Adriel, kept his teammate, Saylor, distracted with random chatter. With swift movements, Glacieus retrieved the soy sauce bottle, a funnel, and another empty bottle from his Communicator inventory.

Instructor Elm sat at his desk and Zephyr'd talk to him excitedly, like the history dork he was. Conveniently, it worked as a diversion.

Class would begin and Shadow spent the time asleep. They were learning about the First Solarian War for the fourth time. Despite his ancestor, Queen Starla's role in it, sleeping was more interesting.

Once the bell rang and Zephyr woke him up, they'd go to Intel class across the hall. Instructor Castro never tolerated tardiness and was especially strict, known to throw remotes at sleeping students if caught. She filled her classroom with diagrams of Risen, other monsters, status effects, and theories of aura.

Shadow sat behind Zephyr. Almost as if nobody could separate them.

Instructor Castro uploaded a diagram of an orange liquid onto the electronic board. "Today, we'll be covering petrification. If you get petrified, you get turned into stone. This is a panacea, a medicine that can undo the effect. For missions with monsters who can petrify, it's highly recommended to come prepared."

An image of a human with skin the color of slate-gray stone, resembling a sculpted statue, appeared on the screen, replacing the panacea.

"If an Agent is petrified, teammates must come to their aid as soon as possible. Smarter monsters will continue to attack those who are frozen and cannot defend themselves. The worst-case scenario is if your entire team gets petrified."

Shadow didn't know when he drifted off, but the sound of the intercom blaring somehow woke him up. He assumed Zephyr covered his sleeping state so he wouldn't fall victim to a flying remote.

"All fifth-year Trainees are to report to Auditorium A," said a robotic voice.

Everyone from their class went down the stairs and toward one of the first doors on the main floor, led by Castro. The double-doors propped open, and Shadow descended more steps, following Zephyr and the others.

Each team had to stand together by the stairs leading to the auditorium stage. Some camera guy and his assistant were there, readjusting lenses. Shadow assumed they set up the lights, light stands, reflectors, and a camera on stage in front of interconnecting platforms.

"All right, we'll have Team Willow Strike go first," said the camera guy.

Four of their classmates stepped onto the platforms, posing. A few flashes of light occurred, and the camera guy motioned for the next group.

"Dream Team, you're next!"

Stream, Glacieus, Blaze, Zephyr, and Leif stood in the back while the "shorter ones" were in front. By that point, Skye was "a tad" taller than Shadow and Spark was "more than a tad" taller, much to his annoyance.

"That's it! Three... Two... One..." The camera snapped a few times, and the camera guy gave them a thumbs up. "Good to go!"

Star Strike returned to where they stood earlier.

"Whew! Glad that's over with," said Leif. "Is it lunchtime yet?"

"Still got twenty minutes," replied Blaze.

"Booooo!" said Glacieus, putting his thumbs down.

"You should've stood up straighter!" said Stream, making Luna grin.

When Stream, Luna, Blaze, and Glacieus announced they were specializing, Shadow felt happy for them. They were picking fields they were most interested in or suited for, like the exams predicted. Those four were whizzes at what they did, like how Skye was with combat.

Shadow knew the day would come. What he didn't know was how much he missed being with them all the time until it was gone.

"Shadow?"

Aurora's voice snapped him back to the present. "Huh?"

Zephyr took a bite out of a cookie, wiping his mouth with his sleeve. "I was telling Cynthia about all the great things everyone's doing right now."

"Oh, right! Yeah! When we're all ready, we'll be together as Star Strike! Since Leif's certified, we're all Specialists now!"

Astro Strike would finally work together soon!

News of Underwood getting his license inspired Shadow and Aurora to dig through memorabilia. He was going to join them, and they'd have half their team!

Shadow couldn't wait for Spark to finish perfecting her skills— even though he hoped she wouldn't surpass him in terms of power, Luna to complete her bigger projects, and Blaze to finish getting the other two more accustomed to combat-oriented missions. The day Star Strike reunited as an official team was something Shadow felt most excited about.

Zephyr let the others continue to do their thing until they were ready. In the meantime, the newbies needed more experience. Especially before coming together with the veterans. He felt it was the best decision to make.

Shadow supported it like any order from his leader.

"Yay! I better be seeing everyone else come over soon!" said Cynthia. "And I better keep hearing your feats as a leader, Zephie!" She hugged him, squeezing the life out of him. "So proud!"

"Ouch!" Zephyr looked at the clock on the wall. "Oh, it looks like I need to get going."

"Where ya goin'?" asked Shadow.

"I have to go home and train some more," replied the overworked leader.

Shadow wondered if the "puppy-dog eyes" he not-so-secretly copied from his dog would work a second time.

"Ya need to relax more!"

Zephyr shook his head. "It's okay. I already relaxed enough for today."

5

TRAINING DAZE
SKYE

Skye returned to the tree outside of her bedroom at dusk. She assumed her siblings would be asleep and jumped onto her balcony, opening the window as quietly as possible. It'd been a long night of no new discoveries, and she was ready to crash.

At night, when the stars were out, Skye's power grew. Her enhancements increased, but it took the same amount of stamina, and one misstep could cost her. It was one of few Farien abilities that remained. She cherished what hadn't been stripped away from her when she became a Host and lost her humanity.

Mochi laid on her bed. He wagged his tail with excitement, earning a soft smile from Skye. She put a finger to her lips so he wouldn't make any more noise as she sat down and hugged him. The dog alternated between whose room to sleep in to not pick favorites. Mochi broke the pattern to make up for lost time whenever she returned. When she'd leave halfway through the night, he'd wait for her.

Once Skye finished getting ready for bed, she buried herself beneath the covers.

"We found no leads for so long now." Skye turned to Mochi, who rested his head on her lap as she stroked his fur. "Even now, it's always been Aqua and the others piecing things together. If I could do something other than being a Combat Agent, we'd come closer to figuring it out."

Being a Host was the only reason Skye qualified for Combat Squad. Twelve years and they didn't know why her power and the other Hosts were the way they were. Or how to break the curse. It had to be kept secret, so there wouldn't be a panic... and... to protect her friends and brother.

The sun was barely visible by the time Skye arose.

Although there hadn't been night terrors in ages, Skye had a lingering paranoia about their reappearance. In years past, Skye felt comfort in having the family pet with her throughout the nights where she'd awaken with cold sweat on her skin.

Their first pet was a therapy dog who kept her paws on her shoulders whenever she had a panic attack. Her family no longer needed to worry. Darkness from her Host power continued to affect her mind and amplify her feelings of dread as she aged, but Skye learned how to hide them better.

Wincing as she attempted to repress her further thoughts, Skye headed to the bathroom she shared with Cynthia. Nobody except her parents were out of bed yet—they went to work early in the mornings most days.

After her simple morning routine and avoiding her reflection in the mirror, Skye donned a navy blue, sleeveless vest with a sweetheart neckline. It had white trim, remaining unzipped, revealing a gray, mesh tube top underneath. She paired it with white shorts, knee-length, black boots, black pouches and belts, and a gray pauldron on her left shoulder with a navy pattern. Her usual bracelets and bandages remained, assisting with covering the noticeable scars throughout her body. Stream designed her outfits and coined this one as "The Dragon Slayer," which made Skye feel powerful. As much as Skye loved her multiple black vests, Stream insisted she change it up. Skye appreciated how many pockets she had. There were never enough of those.

Skye retrieved a few bottles of blue and red liquid from her

Communicator storage and placed them in her pouches before she forgot. She restocked on Ethers and Potions the night before. If she had any healing abilities like her siblings, this wouldn't have been as necessary.

Random civilians assumed she had them for aesthetics, and rumors popped up in the tabloids. In reality, it was because she was faster at grabbing them in a pinch. It took more than enough button presses to access the storage feature, and she didn't want to risk it, since she often pressed the wrong ones.

Thinking about it reminded her of the time she couldn't get her Communicator to update recent software patches and tapped a ton of keys, only for her to open her inventory, causing all the potion bottles to smash onto the ground.

Skye cringed, remembering Zetta and Clay red in the face from laughter. That mission made Skye feel woozy; they needed to get from place to place urgently. She moved at the speed of light one too many times and it took her days to recover from exhaustion.

Unless anyone likes the feeling of their face peeling off, the freezing cold, and disturbing noises, I don't recommend doing that ever again.

Her Communicator beeped, leading Mochi to jump awake. "Sorry."

Skye accepted the call request, and a holograph of Aqua appeared. "How's my brother doing?" Her hair color resembled Zephyr's, except it reached past her shoulders and was straight. Even in the image, the Lieutenant General appeared tall with eyes that looked piercing, yet as gentle as sea foam.

"He has a lot of potential."

Her mentor grinned. "I figured. But he has a lot to work on, right? Same with the others?"

Skye nodded.

"It's time you showed them what makes them special and taught them skills that'll help them advance. Like how I taught you."

It took time to figure out what to teach her teammates. The Agency encouraged training days for honing skills. Skye's fighting style wasn't the same as the others, so they'd have to seek guidance from other elites for advanced training. She knew this day would come, ever since Ziel assigned her to protect her teammates. The organization expected her to guide them by daylight and disappear by nightfall.

Spending time with her team spread genuine joy within Skye. Aurora was as kind-hearted as ever, Shadow had always been fun to be around, and Zephyr... Well, Zephyr was as perfect as ever. Zephyr was the spot of sunshine in the clouds of gray. Skye's heart sank whenever she turned down their after-work invitations. It was for the best—she had no choice.

⸺☾⸺

"AND THEN I shot these water bullets from my dual blades!" exclaimed Cynthia, seating herself beside Skye at the kitchen table.

"That's awesome," replied Skye, reaching for the butter dish. Whenever she was at home, Cynthia would ramble for eons. Skye beamed upon hearing about Cynthia's progress. Her sister was content and secure, and that's what mattered.

"Morning!" Shadow sauntered into the kitchen, grabbing a plate from the cupboard, and helped himself to Dad's famous waffles.

"Would you want to train today instead of going on a mission?" asked Skye, watching Cynthia douse her breakfast with blasphemous amounts of syrup to the point where the waffles practically drowned.

"I'm game! You'll getta see what I can do firsthand!" Shadow sat across from his sisters and grabbed the bottle of sweet brown liquid, drizzling it on his stack.

Skye stifled a giggle. *You can't call yourself a "Hikari" without consuming a year's supply of sugar a day.*

The twins left as soon as Shadow finished scarfing four waffles and half a bottle of syrup.

Daybreak thrived as people went about their business, leaving their homes with glass-paneled doors and windowsills laden with potted ivy. Joggers maintained their pace on the trails and through the parks near the lake. Its veneer-empty surface and cosmic luster enhanced the calm atmosphere as damp grass reminded Skye of the picnics the twins had with their family. Skye waved at and greeted every dog the twins passed by.

Up the street was Garnet Hills—one of the wealthiest residential areas aside from Aurum District. Musicians strummed their instruments at coffeehouse entrances to rehearse for night shows. Melodies floated out of the bars and taverns with styles from every world after sundown. Whenever Skye returned late at night, she'd hear excited bellowing in the distance.

Near the entrance, a teenager exited his house, with wavy, blond hair, burnt silver eyes, a face splattered with freckles, and slight stubble along his jawline. He was muscular for his age and a lot bigger than when Skye had last seen him—before she joined Combat Squad.

"Hey, Saylor!" called Shadow.

Saylor never looked unhappy, always bright-eyed and goofy, like a bubbly puppy. "How's it goin'? Haven't seen ya since graduation!" He turned to Skye. "And haven't seen YOU in forever!"

"Uh, good." Saylor often fell victim to Glacieus's pranks that Shadow helped with. Part of the reason he was such an easy target was that he found the practical jokes funny.

"We're about to go training!" said Shadow.

"Oh, yeah? That's tight!" said Saylor, walking beside them. "I got a mission today, but Twilight Treader can train with Star Strike sometime! Someday, we'll become a Marauder team, too! Just you wait! We'll keep moving forward!" Last Skye heard, Saylor was becoming a powerhouse as expected—he was a late bloomer as a kid.

"Sure, sure! By the way, I forgot to thank ya for the gift basket! Your baking could rival our aunt's bakery, ya know!"

Skye fondly remembered the chocolate chip muffins—moistened, buttery, and almost as good as cookies. She had little appetite for anything other than sweets, which concerned Mom especially and why their family had sugary treats at their house—better than starvation. Apparently, Saylor sent baskets to every family from their graduating class to commemorate their careers.

In a Realm filled with gore and destruction, we need more people like Saylor. Of course, they won't see a lot of that yet.

Saylor scratched his head. "Aw, don't mention it! It's not THAT great!"

Northward was Aurum District and rows of manors and mansions became more visible. Part of her hoped to see Zephyr appear from that direction and her heartbeat danced, thinking about the times their eyes met. His pools of turquoise sparkled in sunlight, reminding her of days she spent getting lost in them whilst laying in grass, watching clouds as kids.

"How's your team? We've been taking out bandit tribes left and right!" said Shadow. "All the towns we've helped LOVE us! As expected!"

"Well, Senna's gotten so much stronger; she could be a power-house if need be! She's unlocked this cool barrier thing, too!" Saylor's face brightened as he gushed about his teammate, grinning from ear to ear.

He brightens up the room. That's what I wanted to be when I was little.

"And Adriel?" He and Shadow were rivals, particularly in axe-work and darkness. Whenever Shadow won, he'd broadcast it to the universe.

"His Sylfira techniques are really comin' together. Better watch out, Shadie!"

"Heh, we'll see about that! Let's spar sometime!"

As they arrived at the Base's entrance, drones buzzed, sprinkling disinfectant and other cleaning liquids along the exterior walls. The three side-stepped around their paths to avoid getting sprayed.

"Welp! This is my stop!" Saylor waved at the twins and disappeared into the Base.

The twins passed the central dome, heading toward the training courtyard. The familiar sight of weapon racks, paved battlegrounds, and stadium-seatings came to view. Aurora and Zephyr were already present.

"Hmm, this feels nostalgic," said Zephyr. He smiled at Skye, who looked away before he could catch her gazing at him.

Last time they were here together was during their academy days. Daily sparring and target practice took place, followed by training in weapons and aura techniques. Skye's grades in combat-related classes were the highest, which offset her otherwise average marks and almost failing grade in Tech that Zephyr tried to help her with.

Fighting and training... Only things I'm good at. How hard would teaching it be?

Skye followed what her instructors, mother, and Aqua did, remembering their lessons. She had them practice on a training bot. Aurora's casting time decreased and Shadow's aura techniques did more damage. It didn't surprise her that this was the subject where those two shined the most, and Aurora had the best aura control out of the entire team.

It was Zephyr's turn, and there was something Skye cursed herself for noticing. Today, he had on a short-sleeved jacket and his golden skin glowed in the sunlight. Skye wondered when he attained such a toned physique.

As if on cue, Skye's heart started to hammer. Skye grew irritated by the fluttering in her stomach. Zephyr was a friend. A family friend. He was ZEPHYR LUMIÈRE, and she was "only Skye." Regardless, Skye had trouble burying the intense warmth in her body and her increased heart rate around Zephyr these past months. It was the most human she felt in years and happy. . .

"Whoaaa!" said Shadow, as Zephyr enlarged his cyclones and combined them with glyphs. "Looks like training paid off."

"I still have a lot to improve, though."

"You're fine! We all are!" Shadow turned to Skye. "Especially me, right?"

Skye didn't want to see Aurora's face fall. "Y-yeah. . ."

Zephyr shot Skye a glance. "You can tell us the truth. Not telling us would only hurt in the long run."

Her face heated up—he was right.

Skye took a deep breath. "You all have some areas to improve upon."

Shadow cocked his head. "What do *I* need to work on?"

"Mobility and attack speed... And Axe techniques."

That didn't seem too harsh, right? I don't wanna offend them.

If Luna didn't have her hands tied with what was going on in the Eastern Hemisphere and guided them instead, this would've been a lot different. Skye selected her words carefully, as she hated seeing her brother anything other than happy. He deserved it after all the times she worried and disappointed him as kids...

Shadow tipped his head. "What about my Gwymond Darkness? And other stuff?"

"Pretty good."

Her twin grinned. "I'll show ya how much better I can get! With other stuff!"

Zephyr opened his mouth before Skye could say anything else. "I know what I have to work on—pretty much building up as many aura reserves as I can so I can unlock the Mark of Lumière. And more swordplay, building up endurance, that sort of thing."

Skye knew how hard Zephyr trained to unlock the Mark. The number of aura reserves the user has could delay it and how long it took to manifest had the possibility of depending on the Mark's power itself.

He never had as many aura reserves as the other Lumière blood-line members, which was why Zephyr limited the amount of aura he used in battle, in case. In battle, his fighting style was more graceful with strategic usage of the glyphs and only using aura when necessary. Zephyr always analyzed the situation at hand and planned out his moves. It never bothered him as much as before, but this was a process. His other cousins took half a year after becoming Specialists to activate the Mark for the first time.

Zephyr had been using aura-draining gloves, a training method the clan conducted. Wielders had their aura sapped out of them, allowing them to build up resistance and create more reserves. Like building muscle, the gloves reacted to blood of a clan member and wearers depleted their aura at faster rates. Such a device forced users to allocate less aura for stronger attacks and training with them was especially exhausting and painful to use.

"I know what I have to do, too," began Aurora. "I always rely on not getting hit and being protected by people. And a lot of other things."

They're too hard on themselves.

"You're doing better than you think." Skye hoped her words would reassure Aurora.

Aurora's eyes darted to the ground, and she sighed. "My magic takes too long to cast, and I need protection all the time! And if I'm out of aura, I'm useless! You saw back there! Compared to you guys, I feel like a liability."

"That's not true!" sputtered Zephyr.

Aurora was the great-granddaughter of Circe Fowler, the greatest magic user of her time. Her bloodline was renowned, and she worked alongside the famous Lumina Rayne. All her descendants had at least fragments of her magical power. The constant pride, comparisons, competition, followed by how Aurora simply was as a person ever since they were little... It was a lot to handle. And it worried Skye to see how it affected her like this.

Aurora refused to look them in the eye. "I should be at the peak of my abilities by now, but I'm not where I should be."

Skye blinked, studying Aurora's face. "We all have things to work on, but you, being a liability, is untrue. We'd all be in trouble without aura, and I've seen how you've improved."

"You got plenty of time, Rory!" said Shadow.

"You're a powerful magic user who isn't at the full extent of her abilities and you can't see your full potential yet," added Zephyr.

"Maybe, but my weaknesses outshine everyone else's."

Every Agent had weaknesses. Even Gods and Goddesses had weaknesses because of Balance.

"That's what teams are for," said Skye. "What you don't have, another may have."

They need positive reassurance. I'll make sure that happens often.

Algorithms matched teams according to strengths, weaknesses, compatibility, stuff like that. Skye didn't have the extent of aura techniques or as potentially powerful aura like some others, but made up for it in physical strength, speed, and evasion. Her boosting ability served as a double-edged sword. She could perform unheard of feats if she wasn't too busy fainting and fighting off exhaustion.

"As for protection, that was one thing I was going to cover today."

Shadow perked up. "We're learning how to create durability shields! Right? Wow! One step closer to being elite!"

Instructors never taught durability to Agents-in-training. It was too dangerous due to how one would have to shape their aura to get it to work. They reserved this type of protection for veteran Agents to instruct when the rookies were ready. Anyone A-ranked and up could use it with ease, and it was stronger than any passive forms of defensive barriers, even more than Shadow's or Blaze's. Agents without abilities a Defender possessed, used durability more frequently. It served as a good, extra form of protection for anyone, especially against a Level 4 or higher... Or even worse.

"This'll be a big help to us," said Zephyr. "I remember seeing the data on those explosions you tanked back when you saved us. They were only a fraction of what you could withstand, which makes sense for the elite."

"How much can Marauders take?" asked Shadow.

There was a dorky look on Zephyr's face, the same adorable look that appeared whenever he raved about history or his games. "Highest recorded amount Skye could withstand is several billion kilograms of explosions when boosted. Elite are similar in numbers." Zephyr talked about her feats in a way enough to make her body temperature rise.

"Oh, snap!" Shadow's eyes widened. "Ugh, I need to catch up!"

"Try combining it with how fast she moves," said Zephyr. "Definitely one thing fans mention the most about her. Interesting how they call her 'Queen of the Blades' online."

"Aw, cute! They have a nickname for her, like the other S-ranked Agents!" exclaimed Aurora.

Now that Skye was to work with Star Strike, she was in the public eye far more often. Beforehand, it was easier for Skye since she was constantly out of town. Those who liked her only did for her looks and feats in battle. There wasn't much she could do after everything she'd done. She was supposed to be a hero with the power of the Farien by her side, but that was blown to bits… Skye was raised to be of service. As an Agent.

Skye scratched her head. "I'm… surprised you caught onto all of that."

Zephyr's face flushed, and Aurora smiled.

"It's hard to believe," said Shadow.

"Goes to show how strong Risen can be these days," said Zephyr. The organization modeled the power of the most formidable bots after the Risen, after all. "Especially anything Level four or higher."

One day, Shadow, Blaze, Glacieus, and Spark's durability shields should've been stronger than Skye's. For now, it was up to her to protect them until that time came, maybe even after.

"So! Where do we begin? So, I can catch up! To you!" said Shadow.

"Focus your aura on your whole body."

Zephyr turned to Skye. "Where are we focusing on?"

"Oh, the chest area. From the chest to your hands."

"Like this?" Shadow's chest shrouded in darkness like Aurora's did with light. Skye shook her head, demonstrating it again. "What do you think of? To get it to not turn into any element?"

"I clear my mind."

"I don't think that'll work for us, since it'll naturally default to our specialized elements," said Zephyr patiently.

Skye wanted to facepalm. "Sorry. I should've planned this out better." She then paused, attempting to remember Aqua's words during training sessions. "You'll have to think of where it's being drawn from and where it's supposed to protect. Those without high aura control levels have to be extra calm for it to work, too."

Zephyr struggled the most, while Aurora covered her left hand with the clear shield. Even with Aurora's control, that was going to be the most it could get unless she used it repeatedly. It was going to take some time before it could even manifest thoroughly and power up enough to take hits.

Weird... Zephyr's aura control should've been enough to at least manifest a glow.

Skye had them repeat the exercise, just like Aqua did.

Once they took a break, Zephyr sat down, looking the most exhausted. "Fates have a way of trying to balance things out, huh? We've only adapted to grow stronger than our ancestors because of the way the Risen are."

All Agents could tank, act faster, and fight far better than a regular mortal. When one combined inherited abilities with rigorous training, every Agent became superhuman. Despite how durable they were, how fast they were, or how much damage they could deal, they continued to struggle against Level 4 Risen and beyond.

"It's time you guys found instructors who can teach you more advanced attacks and spells. Someone closer to your fighting style and field," said Skye.

"Like Spark and her lightning mastery training with Swifty!" said Aurora.

"Right. I'm no licensed instructor, so there's not a ton else I can teach you guys with techniques."

"I see. Fine by me," said Zephyr.

There was only so much Skye could prepare them for, and she was glad the Agency selected her to guide them now more than ever. She hoped she could continue protecting them before it was too late.

"We'll be unstoppable!" said Shadow. "Ya know, Skye, it's almost like you're... not human."

That's the thing, thought Skye. *I'm not.*

6

OUT EAST

LUNA

WEEKLY REPORTS CAME IN FOR THE ROOKIE SPECIALISTS WITHIN STAR Strike's subgroup, Astro Strike. As soon as Luna had downtime, once she and Blaze returned to the inn for the night, she took a look. Astro Strike's performance for weeks now was above amateur. Calling themselves the "Dream Team" would've been empty words with these consistent results, and Luna hoped this was an odd phase. Luna's job at the moment wasn't to inform them to step it up to be outstanding, so Skye should've spoken up. It wasn't Skye's job to monitor them all the time, but she had to do better.

Astro Strike joined up, primarily taking down more bandit tribes and swarms over the past months. This would change soon, however. The organization assigned Leif and Spark to fill in for teams at the Lumière Base in Gwynerva, since they weren't ready to go on the more advanced missions with Zephyr and the others yet.

"Developments for Project ASTEROID have begun," said the news reporter on the electronic screen sitting in the middle of the rightmost wall. An image of Stream, Blossom, and a few other recognizable faces from Lumière tech popped up.

"First time I've seen Stream on-screen with the Tech Department," said Blaze. He exited the bathroom with damp hair and a towel over his shoulders.

"Same here," replied Luna, smiling at how gorgeous Stream looked on camera. The story went into more detail, covering how powerful the mech suit would be once complete.

Images of Aurora, Shadow, and Zephyr came next. "Speaking of Star Strike, the President's son, Shadow Hikari, and Aurora Candor have advanced to C-rank Agents!" They were in their most recognizable Agent gear, and there were clips of them in action on their latest mission.

Blaze sat on his bed. "Didn't take long at all. Wonder if they'll take the same time as Nova Strike to hit B-rank." Everyone within Nova Strike except for Luna became certified four months before Aurora, Shadow, and Zephyr.

"Hopefully, they take less than half the time of a Unity Squad member," said Luna. The news ended and everything left was some drama reruns, so she shut off the electronic display.

"Chances are, you'll all be in the same rank for some time." B-rank and A-rank felt like an eternity, even for Dream Teams.

"Part of me wishes they restructured the criteria for each ranking," said Blaze. "Having it based on combat prowess makes sense to some extent, but it doesn't work as well for high-level missions that require little fighting."

"I see your point." Those qualified for Unity Squad weren't designed to fight all the time, since they were a jack-of-all trades for skills necessary to become a Specialist, which was why Luna felt stuck at A-rank much longer than her Combat Squad counterparts. "Would take a while to make a change like that."

Through Unity Squad, Luna had permission to earn her certification two years before the rest of Star Strike, albeit with restrictions for more dangerous missions. Skye went through something similar, though the timelines blurred on her end. As the more experienced Specialists, it was their duty to guide their teammates.

Being a jack-of-all-trades was the best for her team, organization, and Zephyr. Luna was Zephyr's second-in-command for Star

Strike, and out of all the Lumière candidates to select as his future assistant and VP, everyone knew he'd pick her if chosen as heir.

Her exam results all those years ago predicted how balanced her non-combat strengths were. It was the most out of any Lumière ever seen and why she advocated for a specialized Unity Squad training program, instead of the Lumière regimen. It took some convincing, but her uncle was a fair person.

｡･:ℂ:･

WHEN LUNA WOKE up the next morning, Blaze's bed was empty. He'd always been an early riser, and she appreciated how silent he was when getting ready for the day. Trinity Trio might have already been awake, so she made haste.

Luna brushed through the layers of her shoulder-length, sandy brown hair. Sometimes she wondered what she'd look like with long hair, however, like the other women on her team. She didn't have the patience to get those glossy, luscious locks Stream and Aurora had and maintain it.

Fortunately, Agent attire adapted to any temperature. As ridiculous as it seemed to wear sleeveless clothing in snowy areas, frigid climates didn't affect Specialists too much with the automatic heating and cooling system sewn into the fabrics. As soon as Leif found this out, he rejoiced. Luna could only name a handful of times where Leif wore something longer than a pair of shorts.

It took a few seconds for Luna to decide to wear her collared, camel dress-coat whose hemline reached down to her calves, black belts that crossed when they wrapped around her waist, black leggings, camel boots reaching up to her thighs, and black gloves. Engraved in white on her left chest was the Lumière symbol, as with all her outfits. In addition, her whip remained attached to her belt, along with a few knives for instant access.

Blaze was sitting down at the breakfast bar on the first floor. Placed in front of him was a plate of muffins as he read off his Communicator.

He wore a black shirt, brown belts wrapping diagonally across his waist, a loose, white-collared jacket, brown boots, and black, distressed jeans with the flame symbol on the pockets. As usual, a brown chain hung around his neck with his red Morphic crystal.

His outfits make him seem like he's trying too hard to be "edgy," thought Luna. *Well, at least they're better than most other guys.*

"Morning," said Blaze. Nobody was around at the mini buffet-like area.

For an inn as small as this, it had a decent spread—a juice bar, waffle-maker, and tins of pastries. Most of the time, Agents didn't have to pay for staying at the inns. No global law existed, but people liked to provide free services for the protectors of the world.

Had there ever been one, there would likely be more of an uproar for those who believed Lumière Inc. was corrupt and in over their heads. Even now, it irritated Luna to hear how some thought that way about her clan.

Luna picked up a tart with tongs. "Have you seen Trinity Trio yet?"

"They were here for a bit when I came down."

It didn't take super long for her to wolf everything down. Today was going to be a tiring mission, so she took energy capsules as well. Luna wasn't sure if they were effective or just a placebo.

Fang and Tiamat were outside the door when they left the inn. Ava's green feathers were in the skies, soaring.

"Sleep well?" asked Fang.

Blaze smiled and nodded at his mentor.

"Good. It would suck to be out there in this cold, running on little sleep," said Tiamat.

Ava flew down to the party, glowing green. Her hawk silhouette turned into the shape of a human and the surrounding light disappeared, shifting her out of her avian form. Within seconds, she appeared as a human, towering over Luna.

Ava and Tiamat had the same mousy brown hair, but had a single streak of their respective Morphic color, being brother and sister. Ava's cropped, layered hair enhanced her face. Underneath her pale-gray eyes was a scar on her left cheek. She always had bandages wrapped around her wrists, like Blaze.

Tiamat's hair was close to the same length, but his eyes were a darker gray, reminding Luna of storm clouds. His cheekbones were so sharp, they could practically perform surgery.

Fang's black hair also had a red streak. He had a burly build and showed no sign of distress, even in the heat of battle. Despite his physique, his soft features gave him a gentle demeanor.

Attractive, strong, and smart. A triple threat.

Ava grabbed her Communicator to jot down everything she had seen and sent the update to the Bases. "There aren't many Risen around here. Just Golems made of ice and yeti monsters. Whatever you sensed must be out in the mountains, Luna."

They were in the middle of nowhere and it would continue to be that way until they got closer to the capital city of Polaris, further north. Pine trees stood scattered on the sheets of snow and ice.

Luna sensed something amiss in the province of Snowholt when she was in Vertbarrow. If it were a swarm of Risen or one extremely powerful, they would've detected it on the Risen radars by now. Whatever she sensed, it had to be something else. She couldn't pinpoint the exact location, so it was better to do a deep search when necessary to not miss any details as a precaution. Nobody questioned her sensory abilities. Morphers may not have been able to sense auras, but they could detect any changes in nature, so Luna sent in a request for help.

For a team that underwent huge reformation years prior because of teammates getting killed by Level 5 Risen, it amazed Luna how Trinity Trio became S-ranked. Ava and Fang once belonged to Beacon Brigade. Tiamat was a year below, on a different team.

"All right, let's head toward the mountains and see if what you're detecting gets even stronger than a signal," said Ava.

Blaze clutched the stone on his chain and closed his eyes, focusing on his aura. He flashed red all over and he disappeared into a silhouette of the same color. His human shape turned into the form of a beast and the glow evaporated, revealing a mix of a tiger and a wolf. His red fur significantly contrasted the snow.

Fang followed suit with the same transformation sequence. His Beast form was larger than his mentee's and was a dark red. It was interesting to see how skin tone correlated with how dark Morphic fur, feathers, or scales were. Sizes also depended on age to some extent.

Ava reverted to a bird, while a light blue silhouette covered Tiamat. His size doubled as his human body disappeared, replacing it with the form of a dragon. Wings protruded from his back on either side and a thick, scaly tail, followed by claws and fangs, completed the transformation.

The Beasts remained on either side of Luna, and Tiamat stayed behind. Their leader remained in the air. Since it wasn't a stealth mission and the four Morphers had more stamina and endurance than the average shapeshifter, they could remain in their shifted forms for almost the entire day.

"Ride on my back so we can travel more efficiently," said Tiamat.

The snowy terrain would've been a pain on foot. Glaciers amalgamated, forming ice sheets. Kilometers ahead, one could reach fjords and glacial deposits with eroded surfaces. Mountains past Polaris could be treacherous beyond measure. Howling blizzards could freeze travelers to the ground until their joints could snap off.

Areas of crystalline rocks would've been nice to admire if Luna didn't hate the cold, despite not feeling much of its harshness. Clearly, if one could see their own breath as a fleeting, misty cloud, there was something wrong.

Can't wait to get out of here.

It didn't take long to run into a horde of Ice Golems. Even regular monsters here were more challenging for any average Agent.

A Golem cast a blizzard spell at Blaze, who shook the attack off him, almost as if he had been drenched with water.

Luna struck the air with her whip as she landed on the ground, leaving Tiamat to focus on other foes. Spikes from her whip came out and stabbed through Golems while the whip wrapped around another.

Another icy wind blasted out of a Golem, this time in Luna's direction.

Blaze blocked the hit, shaking it off his fur as if someone had sprayed it with water.

Luna activated the Mark of Lumière and focused her aura onto her weapon, allowing her to absorb aura from the Golem. She charged it up for a few seconds and dished out enhanced lava pools.

Ava turned her wings into metal, diving into the battlefield and cutting straight through foes. Any retaliating hits didn't affect her. She created a maelstrom with her wings, taking more down with a single strike.

Having routed the enemy, Luna returned to her spot on the dragon's back. Tiamat flapped his wings, rendering them both airborne.

"Excellent job, you two," said Fang, readjusting the bracelets around his wrists. "I know for sure Blaze'll surpass us. It's in your blood."

Luna's lips curled as Tiamat lifted them higher into the air. "Top Morpher in our class for a reason." She expected this of Blaze, who had potential to be the deadliest Morpher of all time.

As they soared higher, Luna could see Polaris. They'd return to the skyscrapers and pointed towers later that night to rest. The city was otherwise gorgeous and snow-filled with stringed lights and mini areas for ice-fishing. If Zephyr was around, he would go on a tangent about random historical tidbits that would've bored her to death.

Blaze looked up. "Any updates, Luna?"

"We can continue forward toward the icy mountains. I think whatever I detected is there. I can sense it more clearly now."

If there was anyone out of Star Strike, Luna enjoyed going on missions with the most, it was Blaze or Stream. Though with the former, it was because of their friendship. Growing up, they usually paired together or swapped between Stream and Glacieus. The opportunity came up about them going into more specialized, non-combat areas at age ten and they took it. Nova Strike and Astro Strike conceptualized. Astro Strike focused almost entirely on the combat side, while Nova Strike dabbled in more of the rest, with Stream and Glacieus being notoriously prodigious in Tech and Recon, respectively.

Scattered Risen greeted them at the foothills of the mountains containing portions of evergreen. This was naturally an area concentrated with aura, and Risen swarms often appeared here and tried to invade Polaris. There wasn't quite a swarm yet, but something was off about these Risen...

Luna felt something powering them. But what was it? It was best to take them down while they could before they grew to the size of a swarm.

Tiamat unleashed an icy breath, freezing the Risen in his path, and disintegrated one with a swift swipe of his claws. He stomped his foot, creating an earthquake splitting apart the ground in front of him, causing the Risen to fall into the crevasse. With a flap of his wings, it returned to normal.

Fang turned himself into a ball of fire, zipping back and forth, soon creating pillars of magma from underground. He was moving faster than the Risen reacted, and he destroyed them with a single hit, just like the rest of his team. His fighting style focused on devastating physical power and allowing his claws to be sharper than most blades.

Blaze somersaulted into the air, slamming his body against one of the Risen, knocking it into a tree and causing it to split into pieces. Flames appeared in his claws, and he slashed his way into the knocked over Risen. He then spun in a circle, generating enough fire aura to spread out into a heatwave.

Luna made a vertical slice into the air and a light blue pair of fangs shot out of it. The fangs grew and followed an enemy, chomping down on it. Shards of ice scattered from the icy fang. Silver aura appeared in Luna's hands, and she snapped her fingers, causing metal pillars to shoot out in front of her, sending Risen flying into the air.

Using her whip to latch onto one of them, Luna powered her aura to grant her the strength to lift one pillar and repeatedly smash it against the victims. With another snap of her fingers, the forms of metal exploded into bullets.

Blaze smiled. "Impressive. I didn't know you could use the Mark of Lumière to boost your strength like that."

She deactivated the Marking so it wouldn't drain her aura. "Recent discovery. Think it boosts up to fifty percent." After her great-grandmother's time, not having the glyph abilities became less rare. She had to make up for it somehow.

Zephyr lost patience with not unlocking the Mark of Lumière yet. Predicting the activation of such an ability as accurately as possible was one of those things their tech could not yet accomplish. Luna theorized the Fates might've had a role in his development.

She wondered what abilities the Marking would grant him. Either way, Zephyr resembled their great-grandmother in various aspects.

Hopefully, he doesn't end up being an insufferable nag like her, too, thought Luna. She heard stories of Capala's youth, before she founded the organization and stopped micromanaging. The idea of anyone nagging her for eons made Luna want to bash her head against the wall. Repeatedly.

"I'm pretty sure whatever is powering up these Risen near the top." Luna jumped onto Tiamat's back, situating herself as he and Ava flew to the top of the mountains.

The area became more desolate and spectral. Down below, Blaze and Fang leaped from place to place, digging their claws into the solid rock. From a distance, the mountains appeared majestic and blindingly white, but not in this area.

"What the…?" Luna paused when she spotted it.

At the snow-capped peak and hidden behind the taller cliffs was a sphere made of pure darkness. It was extremely dense, and the aura matched up to what was covering the Risen.

"I've never seen such a thing before," said Tiamat.

"How did it get here?" asked Fang.

Luna scanned it. There was little to no data picked up other than how high the aura levels were for it.

"I'll destroy it," said Tiamat.

As soon as he flew up to it, a creature made of darkness appeared. It had a white skull with blood dripping all over it, horrifying fangs, legs that looked like a mix of darkness and human bones, and a mouth on its belly.

"Luna!" yelled Blaze. The entire area became shrouded in darkness.

It let out a blood-curdling scream and claws shot out of its legs, grabbing Luna. Every ounce of metal aura she mustered out of her body struck the Risen. It shook off the attacks, however, and thrashed Luna in the air.

Luna focused, activating her durability shield.

Gusts of wind from Ava attempted to sweep the Risen away, but it didn't budge.

Blaze's flames exploded onto the Risen's face.

The Risen screeched again, seeming more irritated than anything.

Blaze attempted to leap onto the fiend, but a sound wave emitted from it, blasting him away, leaving Ava to catch him with her talons.

Tiamat released a blizzard, stirring the storm into a frenzy.

The Risen blocked it with a shield of darkness from its mouth and claws.

Blasts of darkness landed on Luna, but the clear shroud around her protected her.

More of its legs wrapped around her body and limbs, stretching them further.

Luna winced in pain as almost all of her aura transferred from her to the Risen, shattering her shield. She struggled to keep her eyes open, trying to repair her shield with little success, while sound waves sliced off one of the enemy's legs.

"Luna! Hang on!" shouted Ava.

Ice shards lodged into the Risen's legs, causing a few to retract.

All Luna saw was pure darkness and she could hardly make a sound as the metallic taste of blood tainted her lips and tongue.

Explosions occurred along with the sound of other blasts of metal, and her weakened body fell through the skies, only for Ava to swoop down and catch her with her talons.

"T-thanks," she gasped. A green, magic circle appeared around Tiamat, and he flapped his wings rapidly, creating an aura link between him and herself. Her aura replenished as he transferred some of his to her.

Ava flew over to Tiamat, dropping her onto his back. Their leader went in a circle around the Risen, gathering a hurricane.

Tiamat cast a spell onto the conjured wind, electrocuting the fiend.

Fang leaped up into the air and a ball of light shot from his claws, negating the darkness in the area, returning it to its usual state.

With one last jump into the air, Fang turned himself into a sword made of pure flames and sliced himself onto the Risen, causing a chain reaction of explosions.

It disintegrated and Tiamat unleashed an icy breath at the Dark Sphere, creating a barrier around Luna before it exploded. Darkness burst out at the two, but they remained unscathed.

To think I feared this thing... And the Marauders handled it so easily, thought Luna. *This is probably a Level four.*

Blaze's reddish-brown eyes filled with worry. "Are you okay?"

"Yeah, thanks to you guys." What happened back there wasn't anything new. Years ago, she would've been petrified by those claws.

The nearest warp point wasn't too far away, about a kilometer. Once arriving, they teleported to Polaris's entrance for the night.

Luna's Communicator stood in the middle of the Trinity Trio's room at the nearest inn. The device projected a virtual, three-dimensional image with a blue light that shrouded a live recording of President Ziel, making him appear nearly transparent.

"Dark spheres? This is the first time I've heard anything about this."

"I hope we'll be able to get more information out of that Risen," replied Luna. "We were going to re-investigate the area for any leads tomorrow."

President Ziel nodded. "Very well. Keep up the excellent work and get some rest, everyone."

They got ready for bed as soon as their call was over, and Luna looked over Zephyr's strategies for his group's next mission. At some point, he needed to stop asking her and Skye for feedback all the time, but she was fine with it for now. She figured Skye would never tell her future lover this, so it was up to her.

"Are you awake?" Lights were out, and they both lay still in their beds.

Luna blinked. "What's up?"

"It's going to get worse from here on out. Dark Spheres, no sign of communication coming back, and another city destroyed just now. At this rate, we won't end all this misery with our generation, and we're supposed to be one of the strongest the public's ever seen."

"Obviously, power's not enough. If we had the same level of skill as the Typhons with technological advancements and discoveries, could've been different."

"Agreed. I wonder if things would've gotten this bad if they were alive. Would they have reconnected the Mortal Realm by now?"

Typhon Strike was the original Dream Team, eventually combining into a subgroup of the Agency, referred to as the "Typhons." Responsible for most of the organization's earliest tech and research. Every Dream Team and Marauder aspired to be them.

Pangs of dread formed in the pit of her stomach. "No guarantees. Could've happened regardless."

7

NO PLACE LIKE HOME
SHADOW

BEING ON THEIR OWN FOR MISSIONS WAS A CINCH! THREE MONTHS flew by. Shadow felt happy about his progress. Catching ex-Thanatos members, slaying Risen—all went according to plan. The path to becoming a Marauder was well within Shadow's horizon.

It was Aurora's idea to go through the Market District. She wanted a hot beverage from their favorite bistro that served the most mouth-watering hariberry tarts Shadow had ever sunk his teeth into. The golden fruit was native to Silvatica, tasting like a cross between a mango and a strawberry.

Rich cocoa beans and cinnamon bark rode the air.

Shadow brushed his hand along hoops of barrels containing powdered spices and herbs while the other held a disposable cup of hot chocolate. He couldn't stand the bitterness that "contaminated" his tongue when it touched coffee.

Shadow didn't know how Aurora or Zephyr liked that stuff and sipped it without looking disgusted. Skye ordered a cookie after accidentally budging in front of a civilian. He supposed some things never changed.

Garnet's Marketplace was the number one spot for shopping, split between exterior and interior sectors, stuffed with street vendors. The outside squished together with its stalls, forcing people into single-file lines. Wagons with mountains of fresh produce parked off the side of the street in one sector, neatly lined up shops and restaurants in others. Teenagers rode their Leviboards meters above the pavement, conducting numerous flips and tricks as they cheered for one another.

Stream and Aurora usually looked for succulents and other snazzy plants, making everyone follow. There'd be deals at kiosks or fairs with cuisines from all over the world.

"Oh my Gods, it's ZEPHYR!" squealed some feminine voices from the succulent stand. "He looks gooood."

One came up to Zephyr, grabbing his arm. "Can we get a pic with you?"

Skye's nostrils flared. "It'll have to be quick. We have business to attend." She was less than friendly.

"What's *her* problem?" muttered one girl, watching her friend lean in for a picture and lift her mobile device. "Talk about possessive!"

"It's not like they're together," whispered another with disgust.

"Hey!" interjected Shadow. "We have a meeting soon!"

"Huh... Okay."

Once the girls finished, they shot his sister another dirty look before leaving.

Seeing it made Shadow want to smack them. Hard. *Farien Principle Number Three: Have forgiveness and mercy.* As much as Shadow liked how fans preferred his personality over Skye's, he couldn't stand having people talk badly about his twin.

Two blocks past the district was the open area with the Base. People liked to pass by and stare. Especially at Shadow, much to his delight. Reporters and camera crews lingered often.

"Star Strike!" The reporter lady with the chin-length, dark green hair and brown eyes was the most recognized one on the news. A red microphone was always in her hands, and usually some dude with a red sports cap followed her around with a camera. "Do you have time for a quick interview?"

Zephyr nodded. "Sure."

Reporter Lady pointed her mic toward him. "Awesome! How do you feel after taking care of all the bandits?"

"Accomplished," replied Zephyr in his public voice, filled with charm. "They've allowed us to learn a lot more about the state of every world and travel to areas we've never been to. It's rewarding to see towns succeed without them around."

"Yes, you've been the talk of the towns!" She eyed Skye, looking between her and Zephyr. "How do you feel about working along-side a Marauder for a longer time?"

"It's been great having her around. She's helped us newer Specialists with transitioning and getting accustomed to being on our own."

"What do you have to say, Queen of Blades?"

Skye scratched her head, avoiding eye-contact with the camera. "Um... They've done well. . . Yeah."

The reporter nodded. "You four grew up together and stuck together until six years ago! Now that you're all reunited, what do you like to do for fun? To make up for lost time?"

Skye looked at Zephyr, who motioned for her to continue. "Training..."

"But what about for fun?"

"Oh... Uh... Nothing."

Reporter Lady's smile faded, and she moved the mic toward Shadow.

Skye wasn't the best at talking to certain types of people. There were two types who disliked her. Either they thought she was awkward, or they didn't like her relationship with Zephyr. Though the same couldn't be said for Zephyr and Aurora, and Shadow couldn't figure out why. Shadow didn't know what was going on. As usual.

"Shadow! What do you think about being a foursome again?"

"Reminds me of old times! Skye's sometimes busy with other missions! But I love spending extra time with her!" He had to look as good as possible for the cameras.

Reporter Lady beamed. "Awesome!"

Once they finished asking Shadow, Zephyr, and Aurora questions (and didn't ask Skye anymore), the four entered the Base and toward the left dome's auditorium. Last time he came here was for the Specialist Graduation Ceremony. They donned weird caps and gowns and got a piece of laminated paper. All that blood, sweat, and tears for a stupid piece of paper hung on a wall felt silly.

Shadow had never seen so many Agents in one area and wondered if they called everyone who was in the city at the moment to meet up. As soon as he saw the Wings of Order enter the room, he pointed them out.

"Must be a pretty important meeting," said Aurora.

More legendary teams entered the room, and several others Shadow recognized.

They sat in the middle row of the auditorium. Wings of Order came over to them. Shadow liked Aqua—she was the big sister he never had. Aqua trained both Skye and Zephyr. If Shadow was her mentee, perhaps he could've been stronger in battle.

"Seems like you guys are holding up fine," said Aqua. "Glad to see you're taking care of your powerhouse." She winked at Zephyr.

"R-right!"

Shadow wondered why Zephyr's face looked sunburnt.

"Once my brother joins up with you guys, be sure to take care of him. He's a handful!" said Clay.

Clay had the same eye color as Glacieus, and Shadow would've almost mistaken him for his friend, but he had darker hair. They had the same tanned skin, dimples, and lanky build.

"He sure is," joked Zephyr.

"I wonder when all ten of you will start working together officially," said Zetta, casually leaning toward Star Strike as he remained seated. "It's hard to predict what will happen as of now with the most ambitious initiative out of all the Dream Teams."

Zetta's sandy hair was extra light in summers. Shadow thought his pure-gold eyes looked cool. He had a faint scar above his upper lip, rumored to be from a sparring match with Aqua.

"I'm sure they'll be fine," said Clay.

The Wings of Order were the best of the best. Star Strike admired them the most out of the Marauders. They and the Dawn Brigade were the most successful present-day Dream Teams.

"You may have countless resources at your disposal to ensure your success, but don't let it get to your head. Always keep moving forward," said Zetta.

Shadow saw the look on Aurora's face. He had to say something. "We'll be fine!"

"That's the spirit, Shadow!" said Blossom. Her eyes were a bright green, glistening like emeralds, and her inky-black hair curled. She wore outfits that matched her eyes and it stood out against her sepia skin tone. The woman gave off a graceful presence, even in battle.

Blossom was in magazines for her tech skills, while Aqua and Clay appeared on-screen for their battling and medical prowess. Zetta was the "Brains" of the team, seen more in scholarly articles.

The meeting began as soon as President Ziel walked onto the stage. Luna's parents were there as well, and the room fell silent. Cameras were on. More interviews were coming their way.

"Good morning, everyone," said Ziel. "First off, I would like to thank you for all you've done for Lumière Inc., and for maintaining Capala's vision. These times caused some to give up on hope, but we must press forward and remind ourselves of what those in history have worked tirelessly for. The least we can do is continue their legacies."

Shadow looked around the room—everyone hung onto Ziel's every word.

"So far, we've reached several milestones in this past year alone. Prototypes for Battle Suits made significant progress and Marauders eliminated a record-breaking number of Risen. Funding from our biggest donors has also increased, further contributing to our research and technological innovations. Soon, we may make progress with airships and artificial portals that can break through the rifts of light separating our worlds possible."

Everyone clapped.

Portaling capabilities were exclusive to a few: Lumière's and Light Mages. Over time, Lumière's lost the ability and Light Mages became extinct, making interplanetary transportation impossible. At that point, Mortal Realm could keep in touch via Communicators. During Ziel's presidency, networks disconnected from other worlds, making it impossible.

"Our ancestors foresaw the rise of the Risen and their increasingly devastating power. However, these past twenty years have been unexpected, and our theories remain standing with causes being unnatural. We believe someone caused this, created the recently discovered Dark Spheres, and disabled communication between worlds, thanks to new leads and a reported sighting of a cloaked individual disappearing into a void by Wings of Order."

It saddened Shadow to say he got used to people giving up. And do bad things. As a descendant of Celeste, the idea was impossible to wrap his head around. His whole life, they had taught him to be a hero, every principle of the Farien, and about doing the right thing.

"From this day forward, we will dispatch all field Agents worldwide to unravel who is behind this. We need to band together or else the Mortal Realm will be in more trouble within the next few years. We need to push uncovering this mystery by conducting a deep search within Eta Geminorum. Agents can return to any city with a Base and rest up, ideally returning weekly for reports. That will be all, thank you."

Ziel took a bow and left the stage.

"We have even higher expectations as the Dream Team, now," said Zephyr, face pale as they exited the room.

"Right…" Aurora was more or less the same, and Skye's facial muscles looked stiff. She was a lot like Cynthia for that sort of thing —something Shadow didn't notice until recently.

"You became Specialists at an interesting time. Don't worry. We're all in this together," said Aqua.

"Skye and Luna'll show you the ropes, guide you, and keep you safe as you pick up on these new types of missions," said Blossom. "They're your closest resources for guidance."

Zetta grinned. "Anything to keep the Dream Teams around and as strong as can be."

"It's still pressure to contribute a lot," said Aurora.

"We're not expecting you to contribute much now. Focus on gaining experience and mastering skills—those are your major responsibilities," said Clay.

"Zephyr, use the Mark of Lumière as needed in the future. It'll come in handy." Aqua nodded and left with her team.

"If only I could even activate it," said Zephyr, clenching his fists

"There's a lot to catch up on," began Aurora. "We're thrown in with every Agent."

Their parents were in the hallway, waiting for them. For a second, Shadow felt like they were at another family dinner. All that was missing were everyone's siblings and countless dishes served.

"Seeing you in the room together reminded me of our mission days," said Mom.

"I can't believe they're sending all of us out there," said Aurora, shaking her head. "We've only been Specialists for three months!"

"They'll be easier on you, dear. You may come back more frequently if needed, and they'll have you search through less dangerous areas," said Rolf, waving his hand.

Shadow knew Rolf was being sincere and trying his best to comfort Aurora, but he and Anaïs were the least competent in reassuring their youngest daughter. If they were better at it, maybe Aurora's self-worth would be higher.

"Right, and you're more ready than you think. Your sister was ready for these harder missions by the three-month mark, so you should be fine," said Anaïs. That had to sting, even if Aurora's parents didn't mean it to be hurtful.

"I know you're all smart enough to know your limits! Don't take on more than you can handle," said Dad, patting each twin on the shoulder.

Shadow appreciated how his parents never made his siblings compete. Both the Hikari clan and the Farien bloodline valued seeing the good in what each person's kid could do with their power. Everything was for the greater good.

"Agreed. Follow what Skye has to say and you'll be fine," said Rosalie, nodding at Star Strike.

"I'll do everything I can to make sure of it," replied Skye.

"I'm proud of you," said Mom. "Take your time with preparations before you leave."

"And we'll be rooting for you!" said Anaïs.

⁙⁙⁘⁙

"Take as much as you need." Dad handed him small plastic bags of onigiri and sandwiches as soon as they got home. He always overfed the Hikari kids and basically anyone else who came over to their house. It was a Kadelathan thing and, of course, nobody minded.

"Whoa! Dad, when did you make onigiri?" Shadow closed the double-doors of their aluminum fridge. Salmon onigiri with furikake seasoning and bonito flakes always made his day.

Dad chuckled. "I knew you guys were going to be gone for a bit and since none of you can cook, this should help."

"Aw, thanks, Dad! Did ya make Skye's favorite, too?"

Cynthia came into the kitchen and removed bags of chocolate chip cookies from the walk-in pantry. "I did!"

"Of course." Shadow scanned the foodstuffs.

They disappeared in a flash of golden light. Shadow didn't understand how the Communicator kept food fresh *and* at any temperature needed. He figured Stream had an explanation with fancy scientific jargon thrown in.

"Remember to not be too hard on your sister," said Dad.

Skye had days where she disappeared on other missions. All they mentioned was how she was "destroying stronger Risen." Shadow knew there was something his parents weren't telling them. They held in extra breaths, according to Zephyr.

Shadow was grateful he could spend more time with his twin, but they didn't hang out outside of missions. He barely knew her.

Skye was helpful in training or on missions but kept to herself otherwise.

Zephyr and Aurora came through the front door.

Mochi bolted over to Zephyr from his spot on the green doggy-bed in the living room, wagging his tail and bouncing all over him. He wagged his tail so much that Shadow thought it was going to fall off and onto the cream-colored carpet.

"I brought tons of bakery snacks," said Zephyr, scratching his head. "Well, and other things, too, but Tandy went all out again."

Magnolia was the best. Shadow tried to help out at his aunt's bakery, years back. He kept eating the cakes and cookies from the display cases and it was glorious. Sadly, he got "fired."

It's not MY fault they were THAT tasty!

"We could never replicate those macarons," said Dad. "The day I retire as an Agent is the day I'd start working at the bakery."

"You're goofy," said Mom. She came downstairs with Skye behind her.

Their parents were awfully cute together—a real power couple. Shadow thought of him and Aurora. It was weird to him, and he couldn't figure out why he was thinking about it.

"Anyway, word of advice: if you see any Dark Spheres, let Skye destroy them. Remember that she's there to protect you," said Dad. "We don't have enough info on them, since we haven't been able to even detect them on the radars yet." Shadow wondered if Stream was working on the tech getting the feature implemented.

"Got it!" said Shadow.

"Here, I know it's not much, but it'll help!" Cynthia handed him a pile of Potions, Ethers, Elixirs, and Antidotes from her Communicator storage.

She must've insisted on paying for them. Shadow beamed at the idea of how she convinced their parents not to help her. Elixirs especially were expensive, and Cynthia must've saved up a ton.

"Aw, thanks, Cindy!" Zephyr's face softened, and so did Skye's.

"I don't know how dangerous it'll be out there... So, I did what I could!"

"Don't worry! We'll survive this week! Promise!" said Shadow.

The rest of his family wished them the best of luck before they left the house and toward the warp points.

"Coming back once a week, huh? We'll do what we can," said Zephyr.

"Oh, come on! We'll be fine!" said Shadow.

"But what if something happens?" asked Zephyr

"Don't think about that! Anyway, where ARE we going?" asked Shadow.

"Asturias Continent. Right, Skye?"

Skye nodded, looking grim. Shadow assumed Zephyr talked it over with his parents. There'd be Agents already searching there. They'd most likely go to areas with weaker Risen.

"This time won't be the same as our escort missions," said Aurora. "This mission is essentially a long quest."

Skye paused. "Follow my lead and stay close."

"There's something on your mind. What is it?" asked Zephyr.

She sighed. "These new missions aren't like what you've dealt with before."

"I'm ready!" replied Shadow. "We could do so much more than stopping bandits! And we'll show the world what we can do!"

Risen could destroy cities at insane rates. Shadow had never seen it happen up close. It didn't matter; Star Strike could protect every city they came across. That's why the Dream Teams existed. The experiments let them make the impossible possible. *He'd make the impossible possible.*

"You're about to see a taste of what the state of the world is like. We're not going to be super involved with solving the mystery, while we work mostly on ranking up for now, but our investigations and times where we'd help people out will not be like our previous missions."

"Is it going to be worse than bandits?" asked Aurora.

The only missions they had so far were around caves, forests, and finding hidden camps. Shadow heard people talk about the state of the actual world, but there wasn't much detail. He thought they were talking about corruption or governments acting weird because of outbreaks.

"Much worse than bandits," said Skye. "I didn't want you exposed to this so early on, but we have no choice. Just... brace yourselves for anything to happen."

It took years for Shadow to understand how trauma worked. He remembered asking his parents about why his sister was acting so differently. Since the night of the exams. All the therapy sessions, nights where he woke up to her screaming in her sleep, times where she kept surrounding herself with friends to feel safe. It was part of what led Shadow to grow out of his envy toward his sister.

8

FIRST TASTE

ZEPHYR

Lastalia was one of their first stops in their quest, a city once full of brightness, almost always sunny. It had a joyous, colorful atmosphere and was the last city erected before the shift in the laws of nature occurred. The city was a symbol of progress, serving as a popular vacation destination for the Lumières, Hikaris, and Candors.

In a world with a dichotomy between high-tech and ancient areas, this part of Eta Geminorum would've been one of the last spots Zephyr imagined would get attacked and destroyed. The superstructures of Lastalia once gleamed, connected by precarious hanging walkways and colonnades of arches. Its primary form of public transportation involved stepping on floating, steel panels to get to and from stations at each district. Those who could afford it opted for their own solar-powered hoverboards.

Lastalia's most bustling hotspots were within its floating districts—Sector 1 through 3, containing solar circles on each wing, supplying the districts' aerodynamics. Restaurants known for their grilling and barbecuing mostly remained there. Zephyr fondly remembered the scent of flames, smoke from the grills, and lotions preventing him from getting sunburnt.

Zephyr's gut hardened upon arrival.

Dead bodies littered the streets, including Agents. No winds blew, and time seemed to stop in this state of ruin. Not a single hoverboard, floating panel, or floating district. Aura here was darker than anything Zephyr had ever detected. Skies were gray and a dark hole sat above, causing pieces of dark matter to scatter everywhere. Risen patrolled the blocks. Scents from corpses overwhelmed.

In the distance, a hollow shell of the Lastalia Commercial Centre stood. Zephyr could only recognize what the building once was by its dome roofs that were now cracked. Iconic crimson flags with golden wyverns turned into confetti. Macabre piles of bricks, steel, and concrete slabs dirtied the streets around the center. Bent store signs laid scattered between the ground and bloodstained walls.

Zephyr remembered its five vibrant floors overflowed with shops, stalls, and stuffed wyvern souvenir stands. Neon lights scorched out at visitors, drawing them toward the biggest international gadgets from Silvatica and Kadelatha. Every cuisine imaginable was available at the food courts, ranging from Snowholt's battered fish fillets to fried cactus flavored with savory spices from Taonia. Lastalia Commercial Centre was one of the top tourist spots, a place for leisure and further brightness.

This can't be happening... There's no way.

"What's this?" Shadow's voice edged with fear.

Aurora's expression grew dark. "This was the happiest city in the world..."

"Where are the Agents?" yelled Shadow. "There were tons here! Protecting Lastalia!" Skye put a hand on Shadow's shoulder.

They had to have been dead or retreated from a fight they knew they couldn't win. Zephyr assumed Agents stayed behind to buy time for others to escape.

They heard of the attack in the middle of their search for information regarding the surging darkness and arrived as soon as they found a warp point closest to the city's entrance. There were no panels within the city that remained intact. City entrances had the most stable warp panels compared to the rest scattered throughout the area, so this was a surprise.

Zephyr did his best to stay composed, seeing how Aurora and Shadow were.

Skye had her arms crossed, glancing at the scene. Once she saw her brother and Aurora's demeanor, she bit her lip. She did that or clutched Excalibur whenever in a state of unease.

Zephyr imagined how hard this would be for her, as someone who knew about this for so long. Seeing how Shadow reacted to the bandits was one thing, but she had never seen her childhood friends and family like this before. This was a sample of what she wanted to protect them from. Whenever she looked down, he felt an urge to make her happy and take care of her.

Zephyr understood what Skye was talking about. There was a glaring contrast between hearing about casualties and the damage in the news and in history versus witnessing it. He assumed so, and this confirmed everything.

Children ran around, laughing and playing while their parents stood around chatting maybe hours prior. None of them had any idea they'd be dying today, along with their loved ones. All was as good as gone as soon as the dark void appeared in the skies and transported the Risen.

Enormous piles of rubble stood below where Sector 1 would've been. A third of a broken wing laid in one pile. Next to it were more corpses in pools of blood. Each body had gashes all over them.

"They're fresh," said Aurora. "I'm guessing they died an hour ago."

Their eyes remained open, revealing their dilated pupils. Jaws and hips seemed more pronounced. Unlike the dead bodies seen earlier, they didn't have reddish-purple discoloration and not all their muscles stiffened.

"The Risen must've gotten to those who were in the floating districts last," said Zephyr. "The others were stationed further from here and are even more recent."

"Do ya think... whoever's behind the rise of darkness is directly behind this attack?" asked Shadow. "Could they've done something with the districts?"

"I don't know," said Aurora.

"Maybe there's people out there we can still save. Right, Skye?" asked Zephyr.

"We can proceed with caution as long as we stick together," said Skye.

Shadow quickened his pace. "How can you be so calm about this?"

It was nothing new, but Zephyr wasn't expecting to see complete destruction of a city so soon. Exposure became more gradual over the past months, yes, but now seemed like an exponential jump. They were expecting to play at least a minor role in helping to protect people... Not... this.

Skye hesitated. "I've seen it happen before."

"People go through so much," said Aurora, sticking close to Shadow. "Can you imagine losing Garnet City and seeing everyone you know dying?"

"Okay! That's enough! We gotta keep going," said Shadow. "There's gotta be someone out here... Someone I can save!"

They eliminated any Level 3 Risen in their way in record time.

Sector 2 had none. Discolored bodies showed at least two hours passed since their deaths. Most bodies at Sector 3 were young children.

Shadow remained shaken as he searched through the corpses. "These are harder to tell. Could be one hour... Or multiple."

Skye held a bloodied blade. It had the symbol of the Farien and next to her was a child wearing the same symbol on his bracelet. Attached to his body was a sheath for the sword, and multiple bodies had stab wounds in the blade's shape's pointed end.

Zephyr swallowed a lump in his throat, flinching at the sight of the severed limbs belonging to the children. "Did. . . he kill them on his own accord?"

Skye shook her head. "I hope not. Risen could've forced him... Somehow. Or maybe someone killed them with the sword."

"Nobody's breathing. . ." said Shadow.

Zephyr turned to Skye. "Hmm... Our job's close to being done here, right? We only have a couple other areas to check."

Skye surveyed the excess bodies and the dark skies. "Source isn't here, and there aren't any leads I can see. Recon and Intel teams will cover this area at some point more thoroughly."

Aurora bit her lip. "Looks like we're-"

Skye's eyes widened. "Aurora! Watch OUT!"

"Huh?" Behind Aurora was a Risen wielding a giant blade. It was about to strike her.

Skye boosted her speed and pushed Aurora out of the way, blocking the blow with Excalibur. Excalibur shrouded with electricity, and Skye and the Risen exchanged hits concurrently. This happened so fast she couldn't activate her durability shield to cover herself as her body intercepted the blade.

A massive gash appeared at Skye's side while the Risen remained temporarily paralyzed.

Skye stabbed the Risen in its static state, killing it upon contact.

"Are you all right?" Zephyr hated seeing her wince and clutch her side. He didn't get the chance to press "Scan" on the Communicator to get more information on the Risen within that time-span, but he assumed it was less powerful than a Level 5 Risen, judging by how Skye could paralyze it.

Zephyr wondered how Skye was unable to activate her durability shield in time with that speed boost. The aura flowing through her felt weaker this time around...

"It's my fault for not being careful..." said Aurora.

"Don't worry about it. It's just a scratch." The hand at her side was slick with wetness and red.

Shadow took out his staff and moved her hand to see the wound. A big gash emerged on her left side, cutting through her top. Blood seeped, forming a puddle.

His staff glowed green and sparkles flooded the cut, halting the bleeding. "Can't believe they got blades sharp enough to tear through," said Shadow.

"You lost so much blood because I wasn't being careful," said Aurora. "Thank you. I'm in your debt."

Seeing a Marauder get scathed like this, after hearing how fast, strong, defensive, and durable they were from his classmates, was enough to wrack Zephyr's nerves. He'd never seen a member of the elite shed blood before his very eyes.

Skye pressed the "Clean" button and scanned her glove and body to disinfect herself. "Thanks, Shadow. Anyway, what matters is that you're safe, Aurora."

We need a change of plan, thought Zephyr. *Skye and Aurora need repositioning.*

A mental image appeared in his head as he thought of different angles and coordinates that would allow Skye to not get hurt like that again.

No, if Skye was there... we'd end up in the same scenario. But what if another Risen even stronger comes along and drains her aura? It could happen, even if I'd never seen it happen. Maybe Shadow could defend her? But that puts him at risk as well.

"Zephyr! Behind you!"

Zephyr used his glyphs to back away hastily from the Dragon Risen behind him.

This was the last time he'd get caught off guard again. The horrors and everything else distracting him would've cost him, just like their first mission.

"What's the plan?" asked Shadow.

Zephyr pressed the "Scan" button.

The Risen's information appeared in a holograph. The Dragon Risen was a Level 3. This monster was a glass cannon, and Zephyr would need Skye's evasion and durability and Shadow's defences.

The dragon's strength laid in its tail, and a single whip from it created tremors spanning throughout the entire city. It was best to avoid the attacks or let Shadow tank the hits. The former would've been more desirable.

Skye looked at him, wondering why he hadn't given an order yet. She blocked its tail before Zephyr was ready to give the plan.

"Aurora, trap it with your whirlpool! Shadow, keep guarding at that spot. Zephyr, use your glyphs to send it flying!"

After Aurora created a whirlpool, trapping the Risen in place, Zephyr stabbed the ground with his katana, producing a giant glyph from underneath the dragon, sending it flying into the air. He used another glyph to launch himself into the air, powering his sword with metal, allowing it to triple its size, and sliced straight through it. All of it went by before Zephyr had any extra time to think.

He waited too long, overthinking everything, and it could've cost him if Skye hadn't blocked its tail. He messed up... again. This time by trying to be over-prepared... Zephyr wanted to say something to Skye, but she was already on the move.

Now isn't the time. . .

Fallen streetlights and power cables blocked their path. Zephyr pushed them away with glyphs. Seeing shattered statues of past warriors made his heart sink, but it made him realize they were almost at the final unexplored part of Lastalia.

A group of Risen leaped on top of a weakened man, causing him to fall over. He struggled to move—his aura could only protect him for so long.

"I gotta help him!" Shadow was about to charge in, but Skye stopped him before Zephyr could. He vowed to not overthink it this time.

"Not so fast."

"But-"

Skye gripped Shadow's arm tighter. "If we jump in like this, it'll take us longer. Multipliers reproduce quickly and expand their power as soon as they see a group of humans. We need to take down most of them before they can spot us."

"We can hide behind some destroyed buildings and strike from afar," said Zephyr.

They were at the edge of the city, and a landslide was nearby.

"Aurora, aim for the landslide," said Skye. She probably thought Zephyr was going to repeat his mistake from earlier...

A brown magic circle appeared around their mage, and a stone ball appeared. The ball spun around, generating more stones toward the landslide. When the landslide crumbled, Zephyr's glyphs bounced the pieces toward the Risen. He was also within range to create more to protect the man from falling debris. This was the most amount of glyphs he had ever conjured up at once.

When enough Risen cleared, the four dashed into the area. Shadow went toward the man. There was enough Risen to allow Zephyr to generate enough glyphs to deter them from attacking Shadow.

Skye vertically sliced through a few before they could multiply. Her sword glowed blue and made a horizontal slash, causing some to dissolve into drops of water.

Zephyr threw his sword into the air, catching it, and landing a finishing blow on another. Small air thrusts of wind appeared in Aurora's direction.

After annihilating the enemy, they rushed over to Shadow.

"Shadow?" called Aurora.

He bowed his head. "He's… gone. I f-failed to save him." Shadow couldn't avert his gaze from the man's lifeless body.

Shadow never had to save someone's life before with his healing arts. Zephyr could feel how crushing the situation was for him. He remembered seeing how excited his best friend was whenever he volunteered to let him practice first aid on him.

Zephyr hugged him, voice gentle. "It's not your fault. Everyone was at the wrong place at the wrong time."

Shadow didn't budge.

"Come on. This is out of our control, and we're all exhausted. Your aura is running low, and you need to get some rest."

"All right…"

Just like with Potions and other medicines, healing arts had their limits, no matter how strong they were. There was a threshold for how much a human body could take into their systems, whether it was magic or medicine when weakened enough. If spamming Elixirs was a tenable solution, there would've been far fewer casualties.

Star Strike exited the city in silence. Waves of fatigue hit Zephyr. Unsurprisingly, considering the number of glyphs he produced.

Once they made it to an open field, Skye turned on the camping feature with her Communicator, and it set up two electronic tents and a campfire.

"I can't get those images outta my head," said Shadow after a while. They sat on logs around the fire and Skye grabbed a blanket, putting it around her brother. "Like, is any of this for real?"

Aurora fidgeted. "Shadow…"

"All I ever wanted as an Agent was to do the right thing and save lives. I already failed once! We're supposed to be heroes! I'm supposed to save lives as both a healer *and* a fighter!"

"Don't blame yourself," said Zephyr. "We can't save everyone. All those successes you heard about past teams? Media highlighted those, not the failures. Almost got us killed on our first Specialist mission, and nobody heard about it. We have a lot to learn. We have to learn as Agents and expect losses at some point, whether it's a battle or trying to save people."

"I guess. . ." said Shadow, unconvinced.

"We've prepared for this our entire lives. But now, we have to prepare ourselves for what it means to be an Agent. Just know I'll be right by your side, growing and learning with you."

Shadow went to bed early, and Zephyr couldn't blame him. In the meantime, Skye checked inventory, and Aurora practiced her casting on training bots.

"Looks good to me," said Zephyr, checking on Aurora's progress.

"Casting helps me focus and not think about today. Plus, practice makes me more useful."

This was going to challenge Aurora in more ways than ever. She always wanted to make herself useful and live up to her title and lineage. Despite her uncertainty in herself, she never stopped trying, and Zephyr admired her. They always inspired each other, and that was the beauty of Star Strike's friendship with one another.

"You are useful, though. Having a healer on our team helps minimize our odds of dying. You and Shadow are both vital to Star Strike."

Nobody in Star Strike lost patience with Aurora's sense of self-worth. Otherwise, he would've fought them on it, as much as he disliked confronting his friends.

Aurora turned in for the night not long after, and Skye remained, checking inventory.

Skye's supposed to help guide us in what could be the hardest time of our careers, thought Zephyr. *She's here to help. She can help me.*

"Hey, can I talk to you about something?" She nodded. "I'm having trouble spending too much time worrying and coming up with a proper plan on the spot. I know we can't guarantee anything about anyone, but it's far easier said than done."

"That's something you'll get accustomed to. Leave most of the paying attention to people's states in battle to me and focus more on the aim for now. Learn to think fast, and not too hard in the meantime. You'll learn to achieve that balance with time and experience. It'll become second nature."

Is that what leaders like Aqua and Mercury did?

Zephyr scratched his head. "I see. I always wonder if I'm overlooking something. That's why I keep asking if what I'm planning is right, in case you've ever wondered these past months."

"It's good to be cautious, but not to where it can harm you and make you more stressed. You'll need to find the balance there, too. Besides, your battling tactics are fine and you're on the right track by acknowledging the hard facts."

Skye had that familiar, reassuring tone in her voice, the same one used when comforting Aurora. It felt like she held back from whatever she had to say. Less positive feedback occasionally popped up if it hindered anyone's growth, but even those were as sugar-coated as possible.

Strands of her side-swept bangs fell into her eyes and Zephyr resisted the urge to brush them away. Heat rose to Zephyr's cheeks and that fuzzy, warm feeling spread throughout his body. He tried to not look deeply into those amber pools framed by long lashes, to avoid getting mesmerized. Up close, he could tell her heart-shaped face matured over the years, and she became a woman with the figure to prove it.

She noticed him gazing and diverted her attention back to the inventory, cheeks flushing as well. "You've taken the steps. The rest is going to get better with time. I mean, none of us started like this. Not even Aqua."

Skye mentioned years prior how she admired his ability to strategize on the spot after gauging stats of the party and their opponents. This was one of the fundamental things making him stand out amongst his clan… With his recent blunder, was he even capable of performing those feats that impressed anymore?

His training program for the past thirteen years was something else. All the training, however, wasn't enough. Clearly, he had to have more experience and practical application and improve or else he'd have to relinquish his position as leader. If he wasn't up to the task, it didn't matter for him to no longer possess it. What mattered was the future of the organization, not his own desires.

"You've seen so much in your life with Combat Squad. You went on missions like this much earlier and look at where it's gotten you."

Learning strategy, leadership principles, history, and all that other stuff wouldn't have prepared me enough for this, thought Zephyr.

His clan, even in ancient times, focused a lot on these subjects. Combat lessons covered their basic fighting styles and using what made Lumières the people they were.

"That's true. They taught us how to deal with every fighting style out there. We had a lot more exposure to the real world with the missions we shadowed."

"You guys also accompanied older teams for periods of time, right? Not just you, but everyone in Combat Squad?"

She nodded. They became protective powerhouses, and all elite and dream teams had at least one from either squad. Their sole purposes were to protect, sometimes help train newly licensed Agents, and be the biggest threats in battle.

"Yeah, Lumière Trainees would've benefited from more than

going on the same missions as all the other Agents. A mix would've been nice."

It helped with getting me used to leading teams, but at least I had instructors supervising and correcting my mistakes back then.

Perhaps, in the future, Zephyr would have newer generations of Lumières get more of a mix of missions Combat and Unity Squad Trainees would receive. Maybe... Skye would be by his side, helping him. Much like how his mother helped the President and his missing second-in-command.

"I thought we would be like the heroes in history—the ones to save everyone. People place the Agents on a pedestal, seeing them as a 'Beacon of Hope.' Except in history, they make it sound so simple; there's a lot of stuff textbooks neglect to mention." Zephyr rubbed his neck, chuckling a little. "Sorry if I'm rambling."

"It's okay."

He smiled. "Thanks for listening."

She nodded, and there was a moment of silence.

"Are you turning in soon?"

Skye shook her head. "I'll take the first watch."

"You've had a long day, too. Are you sure you don't want me to take watch instead?" Zephyr also wanted her to get more sleep.

"That's all right."

She was still as stubborn as ever. "All right, but you better get some sleep eventually, tonight."

"We'll see."

9

TURNING OVER A NEW LEIF

SKYE

SHARING A TENT WITH AURORA REMINDED SKYE OF THE SLEEPOVERS they had as kids. Sometimes, they "camped" outside in their backyards until the mosquitos feasted during warm months. The boys had their own tent, and Zephyr tried to tell ghost stories by the campfire Dad built for them.

Skye enjoyed sharing a blanket with Zephyr when they sat together on the logs as she watched him roast a marshmallow for her. The night before triggered that exact memory. Conversing with him late at night almost made her feel ten again, loving the color of turquoise, and holding onto everything Zephyr had ever given her. Although she still loved the color turquoise and held onto every gift from him, it'd never be the same as years ago.

Skye didn't wake up in the tent covered in bug bites—there weren't any itch-inducing bugs around the northeastern part of the Asturias Continent. The night before, Aurora asked her why she donned her belts, bands, and bandages at all times, even when they slept. Skye mumbled her excuse about how she wanted to prepare in case of an invasion to hide the fact that she wanted to cover her scars.

Skye wondered what her friends' social activities were like once she joined Combat Squad. The past six years comprised Skye going back and forth between missions and training... And solely that... She became too focused on her objectives to know what it was like to be a kid anymore.

"I woke up in the middle of the night and you disappeared," said Aurora, checking her flawless hair with her hand mirror. She awoke not long after Skye and usually was a heavy sleeper. "Where'd you go?"

"Went for a walk."

"Are you sure you didn't go on a romantic stroll SOMEWHERE with SOMEONE?"

Skye stared at her. "Wait... What?"

"You're not denying it! You and Zephyr were alone out there for quite some time." Skye internally prayed to Celeste the conversation was going to end soon.

After having her prayers unheard and more back and forth about whether anything happened with Zephyr, the girls made it out of their tent. The boys were already outside.

Sunbeams cast in every direction, illuminating the skies. Skye noticed how the Asturias Continent had more radiant sunrises this time of year. She enjoyed seeing it and watching the stars shine, though not as much as when she was little.

"Where are we going next?" asked Aurora.

"Leif messaged me," said Zephyr. "We'll meet him at Pollux before our investigation for leads today."

Pollux was on the opposite end of the Pondley Nation and one of the safest cities to be in. It had an underground Lumière Base and it wouldn't hurt to check it out.

If Leif finished helping the teams in Gwynerva, where was Spark? Those two were never apart. They made their team dynamics even more lively, much to Skye's enjoyment and entertainment. It surprised Skye when she found out they didn't become Specialists, but it made sense for Spark to prioritize her lightning training.

Shadow grinned with anticipation. "Awesome!"

"Oh, boy." Aurora lived next door to the rivals and dealt with their shenanigans. When they were younger, she preferred hanging at the Hikari Residence, since it was far less noisy than Spark and Leif's houses.

They found a warp panel on a historical landmark a few miles away—a statue of Astra Lumis. Pondley had an odd habit of erecting these statues of the twins' ancestors at random spots within their borders.

The sunlight grew harsher as they made it further toward Pondley. If Skye wasn't wearing her Agent gear, she would've been covered in a sheen of sweat.

Zephyr rambled about the historical significance behind the statue-like the dork he was. Skye found Zephyr's spiels to be endearing, even though they reminded her of history classes that didn't interest her, unless it involved feats of heroes. She caught herself staring at him for the billionth time.

Aurora rolled her eyes, Shadow pretended to listen, and Skye listened, since she enjoyed seeing Zephyr happy.

Skye hoped what she said to Zephyr the night before wouldn't cause more worry. He was skilled with hiding his emotions, but him always asking her for reassurance about his plans and decisions made her realize how he felt. She paid close attention to each teammate to get to know them better, after six years of being away. Remembering even the minor details helped in that regard. It was Skye's duty to maintain the wellbeing of those she cared about. Even if it was from a distance.

Skye had to be strong. Ready for anything. Ready to take care of them.

"And that's how Astra convinced the Asturias Continent's governments and militaries to-"

"Ooh, that's pretty!" said Aurora, pointing at Pollux's entrance. It consisted primarily of a garden and marble fountain with a statue of Starla de Cordelia. Park benches adorned with floral designs were plentiful, and the elderly strolled.

"Why are so many wearin' the same hairstyle?" asked Shadow,

pointing at the various women with their hair pulled back with a claw clip. "This some trend I don't know about?"

"Native Pondley civilians usually wear their hair in ponytails of some sort, especially in villages and small towns," explained Zephyr. "Having your hair loose means you've either lost your honor or you're not from around here." Skye assumed an enormous city like Pollux would've had fewer follow that tradition, thanks to the plethora of immigrants. Having a Base here also contributed to the diversity.

Acrobatic troupes practiced their routines in the spacious portions as witnesses cheered. Most wore uniforms coated with crimson—the national color. Their flips and twirls reminded Skye of her fighting style. She was nowhere near as graceful as them, however. The way they maneuvered reminded Skye of a spider.

Wyverns soared through the skies, roaring their greetings to passersby.

"Wouldn't it be cool to ride one?" asked Zephyr. Wyverns were only around Cordelia and Leriann, and since Pollux had close ties to the Solarian Continent as a whole, it made sense for them to congregate around here. Licensed tamers provided transportation services for those willing to pay a fee. Some Agents used them in place of airships, but they were pricier to maintain.

"We're early," said Shadow, checking the clock on his Communicator. "Leif won't be for a while. Wanna sightsee?"

"I'm down!" said Aurora. "We both haven't been here before."

"Sure," said Zephyr. "Hmm, we can check out the Magistrate's office!"

"No!" yelled Aurora and Shadow.

"But there's historical significance behind why it's placed where it is! It's not the same with the other provinces and Magistrates within the nation of Pondley!"

"But it's not interesting!" whined Shadow.

Zephyr snorted. "Yeah, for *you!*"

Most buildings were of gray brick or clay, while the Base stood in the center of the city, divided into two domes, and made of

Azoth. Pollux was more condensed than Garnet and cities alike, so most houses and commercial buildings had more stories. Like Garnet, Pollux was a diverse melting pot of different cultures, thanks to the Base.

Immigrants from other worlds congregated here since it'd be cheaper to live in than Garnet and it was always warm. Their principal forms of economy came from Lumière Inc., along with tourism, history, and arts.

"We can check out the shops," suggested Aurora.

Zephyr side-eyed her, making Skye giggle. "Fine."

Shops were in the southeastern portion, and wooden stalls stuffed with food that reminded Skye of home. The key differences she could see were more vendors selling jewelry, paintings, pottery, and clothing made of the same fabrics found in Cordelia and Silvatica. For a nation that claimed to value taking pride in one's identity—they sure enjoyed worshipping the Solarian Continent.

"Think Stream would like these?" Aurora pointed at hair scrunchies hung on a rack.

"I think so."

Skye didn't know what was in style these days. Stream didn't trust Skye with assembling her own outfits, because of her affinity for "panda-themed" clothing and other prints Stream said were "gaudy," so she gave her a set to choose from.

Some female Agents shamed others for more feminine attire or for primping themselves. She wondered why they were so proud of being "not like other girls" and what it meant. What made them so unique that they condescended others for it? Did they have magical tails? Of course, if she had a life outside of being an Agent, she'd take the time to get into fashion and cosmetics.

"Hey, it's Star Strike!" said Polluxians.

"You're even prettier in person," said a guy, extending his hand. "With beauty like yours, you could be a starring actress."

Skye looked at it, flinching. *Yeah, with these scars... maybe in horror movies.*

She was aware of her beauty… outside of the "badges of honor" covering sections of her.

The man retracted his hand with a blank expression.

"Uh… Thanks," she replied. "You, too." Was she supposed to reciprocate the compliment? Or was she supposed to thank him? Skye did either, though the former led to funny looks of confusion. There wasn't a point in rectifying her awkwardness.

"Wow, Skye! You're reeling in the compliments! You, too, Rory!" said Shadow. "Not as much as ME, though, heh!"

Skye wondered why Aurora frowned. Maybe Aurora was as protective as she was over her brother because of their close friendship. Like Shadow, she rarely knew what was going on.

At the end of the marketplace was the Panda Emporium. The famous anthropomorphic merchant was there, wearing his recognizable, green yukata. Even though he looked like a baby panda that stood on hind legs, he was believed to be immortal and existed since even before Celeste's time. He was the only of his kind that didn't stay hidden.

A watermelon stand stood next to the panda's shop.

The panda waved at them.

Aww, he's so cute! Skye wanted to give him a hug. And squeeze him. He reminded her of Mochi. She sure missed that sweet dog.

"Last time I saw him, he was at Lumière Manor," said Aurora.

The adorable bear liked to visit them and hung around the Bases. He was a traveling merchant who sold weapons and other equipment such as medicine and tools. The panda's prices were fair, and his weapons never ceased to amaze anyone. He remained an enigma, however. He teleported everywhere and could make weapons appear out of thin air.

They perused the assortment of weapons: swords, lances, axes, bows, arrows, guns, electric claws, and anything else one could think of. Skye recognized the Phoenix Forge logo on some and wondered which one of Spark and Leif's family members made them at their shop back at Garnet City.

"Good stuff! I dunno what half these things are!" said Shadow.

He picked up a remote with a giant, red button in the middle of it and an arrow marked at the top. On the arrow was a wind symbol. "What does this do?"

"I think it shoots out air at a high pressure in the arrow's direction," replied Zephyr. "Maybe it's making things float without wind aura?"

"I wanna try!" Shadow grabbed it, pointing the remote at a stun gun. A small gust appeared, surrounding the gun, and levitating it. "Cool!"

Panda clapped as he jumped up and down. Skye giggled at how adorable the little creature was.

Seems simple to use, even for me, thought Skye.

Aurora peered at the tomes, and Shadow checked out other gadgets.

Skye stared at the remote, wondering how it worked, until a girl walked up to Zephyr, catching her attention.

"Can I get a picture with you?" asked the girl, fluttering her eyelashes.

"Sure."

The girl squealed.

Skye suppressed the urge to roll her eyes. *It's just a picture. No big deal.*

The girl moved *uncomfortably* close to Zephyr, wrapping her left arm around him, letting out a giggle that made Skye's skin crawl. She raised her right arm, angling her mobile device and pressing the "Camera" button. With each click, she moved *even closer* to him.

Celeste, Skye wanted to hit something. Maybe a training log. Maybe the girl.

Zephyr shifted slightly away from her, tensing up. "Sorry, I'm not comfortable being this close to fans."

The girl clutched him tighter. "Wow, you're buff! How often do you work out?" Her hand trailed toward his abs.

Skye boosted her speed, grabbing the remote, pointing it at the girl, and pressing the button. A gust of wind blasted the girl out of the way before she could continue harassing Zephyr.

The girl fell onto the nearby cart of watermelons. Rinds and watermelon flesh exploded into pieces, splattering and staining objects and other civilians in the crossfire. Skye's target became covered with red and seeds.

"MY WATERMELONS!"

"WHAT IN THE NAME OF TARTARUS?"

Zephyr, Shadow, and the panda looked at Skye.

Aurora pressed a hand to her forehead. Witnesses held their mobile devices, recording.

The watermelon vendor shook his fist at Skye, yelling strings of choice words she'd rather not reiterate.

Gods, thought Skye. *What have I done now?*

Skye's initial feelings became replaced with pangs of guilt. "I... I'm sorry."

"This was my favorite dress!" Watermelon Girl wailed and glared at Skye, storming toward her. "You DID THAT ON PURPOSE! Gods, what is WRONG WITH YOU?"

"Hey!" yelled Shadow, stepping between Watermelon Girl and Skye. "She apologized!"

Skye reached for her wallet. "Here... I'll cover the damages. For the watermelons. And the dress. I'm really sorry."

Farien Principle Number Four: Never use aggression unless for the greater good.

After more series of apologizing profusely and severely depleting Skye's cookie funds, they received a message from Leif, who finally arrived. Apparently, hordes of Risen delayed his arrival.

It would've been hard to miss Leif in a crowd. His shaggy, two-toned silver hair with black roots and spikes sticking out from all angles and the tendency to wear orange sleeveless shirts and brown shorts made him stand out. Skye thought of him as a colorful, comical character who served as the mood maker of the team.

Leif was in the city square. His hair looked lighter than normal, which Skye assumed was from more frequent exposure to the sunlight. His white teeth contrasted his darker skin.

"I'm back!" Leif grinned. "Hope ya didn't miss me for too long!"

Shadow looked smug. "Ya DID miss eight fans fawn all over me! Asking for my autograph and everything!"

Leif smirked at her twin. "Bet I could get more of 'em! All the ladies love the Leif Meister!" He ran his fingers through his hair. "Especially when I do that!"

"Sureee they do," said Zephyr, raising an eyebrow. "At least you're not scaring them away like last time!"

"Don't worry about it!" exclaimed Leif.

Zephyr chuckled and smacked Leif on the back. "Either way, glad to have you back with the team."

"Course ya missed me! Who wouldn't!" Leif's grin widened when Aurora rolled her eyes. "Admit it, Rory! You missed your old pal!"

"Maybe."

"Don't worry, Leif!" said Shadow. "*I missed playing Monster Quest* together!"

"Again, with the obvious! Now, if Zeph quit being lame and over-preparing, the three of us can play together again like old times!"

"Sometime," said Zephyr.

"You always say that, Pretty Boy!" said Leif. "And hasn't happened in like forever!" His brown eyes shifted and gave him the side-eye.

"Anyway," Zephyr began. "We better start investigating for today."

"What's the plan?" asked Leif. "For the next part in our quest thingies!"

"We'll be going northwest of Pollux, at what used to be an Assassin's Keep. Assassins used to spread out around Asturias, and I figured we could check the one closest to us out."

"Think a Dark Sphere could be there?" asked Aurora, twirling a piece of her hair with her finger.

"Well, they seem to congregate around bigger landmarks. Either that, or it could've been an area housing suspects behind the increase in darkness."

Skye doubted the latter, but it was worth checking out.

"Do ya think ex-Thanatos goons could be behind this stuff?" asked Leif once they headed toward the exit.

"I don't think so," said Aurora. "Ones we took down didn't seem like they could've had some type of power to increase the darkness like that. Or smart enough."

"True. Lots of possibilities," said Zephyr. "For all we know, there could be more competent members running around. People we ran into could've been random, lower-ranked lackeys."

It wasn't *impossible*. Thanatos disbanded, and members' home nations dealt with their punishments. It wasn't Lumière Inc's duty to determine what would become of the international coalition and their members based on the severity of their actions—the organization protected the worlds; they didn't run them.

When Skye and co. suspected them years back AND believed they could've been behind turning her into a monster, they could disprove both theories. As far as they knew… Maybe Agents overlooked something. Maybe Thanatos had them under a ruse this whole time.

Since they didn't have enough evidence, Skye wasn't concerned.

Leif gave them a thumbs up. "Welp, whatever's goin' on, Leify wants in on the action!"

Having Leif around again was nice. His choice of weapon was unique… just like him. Both he and Stream could someday move at supersonic speeds. Although he didn't deal as much damage in a single hit as the others, his attacks doubled since he wielded two chakrams in either hand. He could also fight well at long distances.

There was hardly anything unordinary on their way from Pollux to the Keep. Bear-like monsters and harpies existed, but they wouldn't attack unless provoked first.

Skye had to stop Shadow from taking them on and wasting his aura. That boy was a handful—especially with showing off his skills and asking Skye for recognition. It made him happy whenever she gave him affirmation. She wanted to keep his mind off what happened in Lastalia.

"We made it!" said Leif once they arrived at the Keep. "Okay! What are we doin'?"

"Search and scan through the area," replied their leader.

Skye couldn't detect any signs of worry from him, but that wasn't an accurate indicator. Now that they were on their mission, she had to set aside her unease around Zephyr, after the embarrassing watermelon episode; she'd worry about that afterward.

The Keep resembled a fortress—nobody bothered touching the place for centuries for some historical reason Zephyr knew about. It seemed moldy, with rusted chandeliers hanging on the ceilings. Place was rundown with crates and barrels lying about. It was also littered with cobwebs and dust.

There was a blend of regular monsters and Risen wandering about, but Zephyr showed no sign of sensing any Dark Spheres or anything unordinary. It was probable there would be little to nothing to report about this location, but too soon to make the call.

Star Strike had been out of harm's way. Skye didn't know how she'd be able to handle it when the time came for them to tackle much more difficult missions. Ex-Thanatos members were as strong as a Level 2 Risen. She dealt with far more powerful ones in the past, which Skye assumed should've been dead or kept captive. Once Lumière Inc. completed their job and took care of threats, they cared little for the aftermath. Their focus was on whatever was the next biggest menace. Nations often kept their affairs secret from the organization and vice versa.

Whatever happened, Skye braced herself for the unexpected, especially with Star Strike thrown into the mix. Anyone who *looked* at Star Strike the wrong way would find themselves on the other end of Excalibur.

"A hidden cellar?" Aurora pointed at a door on the ground floor.

"Looks like it's stuck," said Leif, trying to yank it open.

"Lemme try!" said Shadow. "Bet *I* could get it open first!"

"Oh yeah? Wanna bet?" asked Leif.

"Children," sighed Aurora, rolling her eyes.

Skye snickered out of amusement—the door was rusted shut and it would've been a waste of time to keep pulling at it. She walked toward the door and the boys moved out of her way.

"Go, Skye! Use your monstrous strength!" Aurora smacked Leif. "Ouch!"

Monstrous, huh?

Skye punched the door, decimating it, revealing a staircase underneath.

They continued their exploration, using the flashlight feature on their Communicators to light the pitch-black pathways. The cellar was massive, spanning underground.

Aurora got startled whenever a Level 1 or 2 Risen jumped out of nowhere, clutching Skye's left arm. If it were Stream, she would've squeezed the life out of her arm AND screamed at a pitch unknown to humankind. At least, that's what she did when they were kids— Skye didn't know what Stream was like nowadays and looked forward to seeing her again.

"Bet I can take down more of these Risen than you, Shadow!" said Leif, clutching chakrams in either hand.

"Oh, yeah? How 'bout five Gold?"

Another group of Risen emerged from the shadows. Leif threw the chakrams at the enemy, and they enlarged, illuminating the area. A light force of aura shot out of the chakrams, spinning around, generating many sparks and other rays.

"All right! Five of 'em down! Better catch up, Shadie!"

Last time Leif was with them, Skye told him to not rely on the earth element. It took time before Skye spoke up to Leif about the issue, but the guy didn't seem to mind. He was at his most powerful when he used earth-based attacks, yes, but it was best to not use solely the element one specialized in—if they specialized in anything. Doing so would make their attack patterns far too predictable.

"Whoa, Leif! When'd you learn to do that?" asked Shadow.

Leif took out half a larger group attempting to surround them. He threw both chakrams into the air, combining and forming a cyclone. He rode on it around the room, hitting everything in his path. Meanwhile, Shadow created several dark chains, holding the Risen in place, allowing him to flip around his staff and thrust at them with ease.

"Well, I saw Zeph do something like his glyphs earlier! And thought it looked dope!"

"Wait, you winged it?" asked an impressed Zephyr.

"Uh-huh! As expected from the Leif Meister!" Leif grinned whenever he used his self-proclaimed title.

"Nice work," said Skye.

"What about me? How'd I do?" asked Shadow.

"You did well, too."

Exploring the hideout ended within the next five minutes once the team reached a dead end. They had found nothing noteworthy, leading Skye to tell her friends to head back.

"At least we've got some battle experience here," said Zephyr. "Hmm, this might bring up more questions than answers regarding Dark Spheres and their locations."

"Yeah... Wish we could've done somethin' more useful today," said Shadow. "Or found something about who's causing this terrible stuff to happen!"

"Mhm. We might have found nothing related to the cause, but at least we've cleared the area. And everyone knows this place is free from threats," said Skye.

10

CLASH

ZEPHYR

SOUTH OF ASSASSIN'S KEEP WAS POLLUX-CASTOR INN—THE HALFWAY point between sister cities. The plan was to search around the area. Last time anyone reported searches for and between those cities was months ago and a lot could change in a month.

Even though they found no actual evidence regarding the cause of the rise in darkness, they'd keep searching, like the Wings of Order told them earlier. In the meantime, they'd focus on ranking up so they could play a bigger role, eventually.

The inn was a giant rest area. Travelers between Castor and Pollux gathered, along with tourists. Conveniently, the Panda set up shop when they arrived. Other merchants selling the same products avoided areas he appeared in, knowing they couldn't compete with the cuddly bear.

"Welcome to Pollux-Castor Inn!"

The inside of the inn reminded Zephyr of a wooden cabin with a fireplace, log couches with tree-patterned cushions, magazine racks, and a large flat-screen display showcasing highlights for the most recent StrikeBall Tournament.

"I'm sure you're exhausted with all the work you've done," said the receptionist, handing them the keys before they had the chance to pay.

Shadow and Leif's eyes remained glued to the screen as the receptionist gushed about the amenities.

"Let's check out our room!" said Aurora, dragging Skye with her up the stairs.

Skye had a long day. Zephyr had seen her act somewhat hostile around female fans before, but never to *that* extent. Her heart, however, was in the right place and Zephyr was glad she owned up to it, showing remorse as well. He had never been physically harassed like that. So, Skye made a slip up; that didn't change how he felt for her.

The media always made Agents look as good as possible, but people would talk. Regardless, he'd expect to see *some* townspeople treat her differently.

The boys got a triple, and the beds in their room looked fluffy. There were a generous amount of feather pillows, and they had an extra-enormous bathroom the size of a mini swimming pool. Two nightstands stood in between with wireless charging stations.

Hopefully, this time Shadow doesn't break a charger and try to blame it on "a raccoon that broke into the room."

"Sweet! Look's way comfier than a sleeping bag!" said Leif. He set up one of his game systems by the giant display screen and plopped on the couch.

Between practicing to not take as long to plan and training, Zephyr was swamped. He had to practice. As much as he yearned to play with his friends, it had to wait. He wished he could pick up things as easily as Leif.

After they got settled, Zephyr checked on the girls. He knocked before coming in, in case anyone was indecent. From outside of the room, he could hear Aurora's voice, albeit muffled.

"We're in the middle of a conversation here!"

Aurora sat on her bed while Skye leaned against the wall, desisting from looking at him. She reminded Zephyr of a puppy who chewed up a shoe and got caught.

"Sorry. What are you even ranting about?"

"About men!"

Zephyr assumed their conversation was about the incident earlier… Or about Shadow's obliviousness. He was curious why she didn't rant to him, but Aurora had her reasons and Zephyr wasn't a relationship expert.

Skye was oblivious to nearly all romantic implications, including how Aurora felt about her twin. Zephyr conducted several bouts of mental gymnastics to deduce how every sibling could be dense in their own way. According to Suzie, Cynthia at least knew about the romantic interests of the twins but was unaware of her own. He could've sworn the siblings were denser than most rocks.

"All right, I'll leave you two to it. See ya."

Zephyr returned to the guys' empty room. He sat at the desk to come up with a plan for the next part of their quest. Today's mission was far more tame and served as a breather. He pulled up the map on his Communicator and added markers for different battle positions, accounting for multiple scenarios that could occur.

Zephyr's mind wandered to their mission for the day, keeping track of everyone's improvements. Skye's training regimes put them to work, especially Zephyr.

Aurora's spells are stronger, Shadow's darkness uses less aura than before, and Leif is faster. I gotta catch up to them.

Once Zephyr's head spun, he decided to venture outside for fresh air. And to squeeze in training. It'd been some time since Zephyr worked with the aura-draining gauntlets his clan utilized. Zephyr placed his Communicator back into his pocket, getting up to his feet. Pushing the chair into the desk, he exited his room and traversed down the staircase. He wondered what the others were up to.

Zephyr heard whacking noises as he exited the inn.

Shadow gripped Diablos as he sliced a log on a stump to the left of the inn. Piles of chopped and unchopped wood laid to rest beside Shadow as he placed the fresh pieces into the chopped pile.

Shadow wiped sweat from his forehead with the sleeve of his

jacket and grinned at Zephyr when he approached. "Inn lady asked me to help her out!"

Near the inn's entrance, Aurora and Leif stood together. Aurora had Leif's training chakrams in her hands and threw one. It looped and bonked Leif on the head as Skye reached the outside and made a face. Luckily, those were wooden and didn't have blades like the ones he used in battle. Otherwise, Leif's head would've sliced open by Stumbles' clumsiness.

"Ouch!"

"That's rough, buddy," muttered Zephyr, sifting through his inventory for his aura-draining gauntlets.

"What happened?" asked Shadow, looking up from his chopping.

"It was an accident!" sputtered Aurora.

Shadow grinned. "This is just like the fire on the pants accident! And the lightning instead of water! And the-"

Aurora shot him a venomous look. "Don't make me 'accidentally' hit you, too!"

⋅ ⋅ ❲ ⋅ ⋅

ONCE TRAINING WRAPPED UP, the team helped themselves to a decadent spread of cuisines found in the Eastern Hemisphere in the inn's dining hall. Zephyr assumed most of the hearty ingredients came from the inn gardens. The stews smelled rich, with a balanced blend of savory and spicy. Herbs, such as thyme and rosemary, complimented the taste.

"Bet I can eat more chicken nuggets than you!" said Leif, setting down his enormous plate piled high with breaded cutlets, disrupting the once peaceful meal.

That's a CUTLET! Not a CHICKEN NUGGET, you uncultured swine!

"We'll see about that!"

"You're going to be way too loud!" said Aurora, groaning while Shadow sat down with a mountain of crispy goodness, failing to sub in for Stream as the "mom" of the team.

"I got twenty!"

"I've got... twenty-one!"

Zephyr wondered if Aurora's eyes were going to get stuck with the amount of times she rolled them.

Skye watched everyone with a twinkle in her eye. Aurora was too busy getting exasperated by Shadow and Leif to lecture her for munching her way through an entire plate of cookies.

After dinner, the guys returned to their room. Leif and Shadow played *Monster Quest* while Zephyr returned to his desk, double-checking his initial plans for the next day.

Thoughts of the worst cases flashed in his head, but he did his best to shove them away. Migraines crept in, and he had to take an abrupt break and painkillers before continuing.

Remember the aim at hand and how you can't save and account for everyone every time. Including your teammates.

⋯⋅◀⋅⋅

BY SUNRISE, Zephyr had gotten only three hours of rest. He put on a black vest with a red Lumière symbol on his left chest, white collars, and matching white material reaching from hip to hip around the waist. Zephyr completed the look with dark gray trousers and matching gloves.

An alert beeped on everyone's Communicators: *Attack on Castor.* A flutter of unease passed through Zephyr as his ribcage tightened.

"Great..." said Leif.

Their quest had to be on hold, and Zephyr reminded himself of what he coached himself to do the night before, ignoring the creeping migraines before they consumed him.

Everyone met outside of the inn. A fleet of Lumière airliners headed toward Castor, soaring through the skies.

Lumicarriers had sustainable repulsor engines with seaborne capabilities, armed heavily with ventral guns and cannons. Their flattened, dome-like shapes had two saucer platforms on either side could detach and hover.

Everyone disappeared into a flash of golden light as soon as they reached the inn's teleportation panel.

"No…" said Shadow once they arrived at the entrance.

The air reeked of smoke and became more suffocating deeper into Castor. Flames burned deep red and orange, lividly licking up the air. Zephyr didn't know what was louder—the sound of buildings falling, or the harrowing bellows of agony from the unfortunate.

We can't save everyone.

His heart rate didn't slow down, and he swallowed the bile rising in his throat. Thoughts raced and he once again tried to shove them away, looking at Skye to calm down.

Medics ran rampant. Agents evacuated the civilians to the saucer platforms—at least ten here. For a city with a land area of fifteen kilometers, fifty to sixty Specialists should suffice… Anyone available to help had to notify the organization that they were on their way.

A trio forming a bird, beast, and dragon attacked the terrorizing Risen. Bracelets around their legs, worn in honor of their fallen comrades, revealed exactly who they were: Trinity Trio—one of the Marauder teams.

Zephyr focused his aura onto his katana, turning it into three copies. They followed his hand movements and flew toward the Risen. Without turning, he used his glyphs to create gusts of wind to sweep the Risen that were about to lunge at him from behind. With a snap of his fingers, the swords spun around, shooting a fire blast.

Leif struck the ground with both chakrams. Water with high pressures spouted from underground rapidly, shooting from a multitude of angles. He zipped, slicing and dicing through the enemies.

"Glad to see you again, Trinity Trio!" said Shadow. With Trinity Trio and half of Star Strike side-by-side, clearing the area of any Risen would be a cinch. Most of Zephyr's worries washed away with such a competent team by their side.

Tiamat chuckled. "Your moves are flashy."

"That's Star Strike for ya!" said Leif, winking at Ava. "We fight with style!"

"They ordered us to sweep through this half of the city," said Ava. "Other offensive teams are taking care of the other half, while everyone else with us was told to evacuate, heal, and protect civilians."

"I was going to help the Medics," said Fang. "And could use back-up." He nodded at Aurora and Shadow.

The two healers looked at Zephyr. "Go ahead."

Skye eyed them. "Stay alert, okay?"

"Don't worry 'bout us!" said Shadow.

Pride washed through Zephyr as he watched them leave. When Zephyr heard about Blaze working with Trinity Trio and Luna, he had a similar feeling. Skye trusted them with Fang's guidance, as anyone would've, which made Zephyr rest easier.

Tiamat smiled. "And the rest of you can help with fending off the remaining Risen."

"Let's see what half of Star Strike can do," said Ava.

Zephyr smiled. "It'd be beneficial to see how you lead your team, Ava."

Ava nodded. "Watch closely."

They made it to what was Castor's most bustling district. An army of Risen spawned, and edifices burned and crumbled down.

"Stay back," said Tiamat.

Tiamat flew to the heated buildings, prioritizing the ones with people still trapped inside. He released an icy breath, and his ice withstood the flames, holding the burning buildings in place.

Ava created a single gust of wind strong enough to sweep away half of the army. She and Tiamat expanded their bodies. With a flutter of her wings, Ava manipulated the wind to grab onto the civilians and transfer them to her and her brother's backside.

Wow...

"We'll be back." Ava nodded at them and took flight, soaring into the air with Tiamat closely following.

"Our turn," said Zephyr, trying to replicate Ava's calm and collected disposition.

Skye shot silver beams at the Risen army. Pillars of metal appeared around a section of the army, caging them inside of it. She disappeared and reappeared by the pillars, slashing through them with a single swipe, causing all the pillars to explode in a chain reaction. Shards of metal lodged into Risen. Leif put both disks together and a light blue aura formed. A swirl of ice shards shot out of it, freezing a few Risen.

Tiamat and Ava returned, seeing the district devoid of Risen.

"Good work," said Ava. "Let's check the others."

"So far, it looks like we have mostly gotten Level threes and a few fours," said Tiamat. He looked at Zephyr, most likely hearing his quickening pulse. "Do not worry. Us Marauders will take care of those. Take care of the Level three Risen in the meantime."

Star Strike dashed across the streets with Ava and Tiamat flying above.

Wounded, unconscious Agents laid strewn about—one pile on the left and another on the right. Civilians were nearby, panicking as more Agents meant to protect them got slammed to the ground.

Airborne Wyvern Risen came into view. Morphers shot out blasts of their specialized elements, creating numerous explosions. While reinforcements appeared through the skies, dark voids also appeared on the ground, close to the civilians.

Skye's knives whirled around her as she sped rightward. "Take the left!"

Zephyr stabbed the pavement with Galeforce. Three glyphs sprang forward, latching onto Risen on their left, preventing them from taking any further steps toward the townspeople.

Leif flung his chakrams at the trapped Risen.

Dark shields popped before them. Chakrams bounced off and sliced straight through the civilians. The sheer sound of the clash between blade and flesh pierced the air as joints scattered. Thin red lines grew wider at their sides and shoulders.

"No!" yelled Leif. A gasp erupted from his lips.

They screeched, crumbling to the ground with a thud. Their eyes were open, shining with wetness as red fluid pooled into puddles. The coppery, rusty stench of blood spread throughout.

Leif's knees buckled as he quivered.

The imploding pain of a migraine struck Zephyr as despair loomed inside, consuming him. He created a tornado, attempting to sweep up the Risen, but they didn't budge.

Dark shields turned into armor, coating their bodies. They launched blasts of darkness at Zephyr. He created a ball of wind, shielding and buying him time. It felt as if someone had pressed a hot rod against the side of his head—a pulsating pain mixed with every heartbeat and bit of nausea and dizziness.

Further ahead, Skye had an abundance of cuts over her body as more dark voids encompassed her. She guarded the surviving Agents and civilians, panting and shaking as she clutched Excalibur.

How is she already out of boosts?

More dead bodies were off to the side than before, dismembered or with half their bodies ripped open. Bones jutted out of the dismembered limbs, along with guts and innards spilled.

Even Marauders can't save them all.

"Leif! I need your help!"

His blood-covered chakrams lodged inside a corpse. Leif stood, paralyzed with horror. "What have I *done?*"

Mild fatigue hit as Zephyr powered up the ball of wind, tanking stronger blasts.

The enemy's next hits were directed at Leif, knocking him toward piles of debris.

"LEIF!" Zephyr moved the ball of wind, sending the chakrams flying toward Leif's direction before more Risen could dive after his friend.

One Risen grabbed Zephyr by the neck, but he powered Gale-force with metal aura, stabbing it in the back. The surrounding armor exploded, and Zephyr severed its head.

Leif caught the chakrams. Blood dripped from them, staining his shirt.

"Aim for the middle of its back! That's its weak point!"

Before another could strike at Zephyr, Leif threw a chakram at its back. Leif did a flip, catching it as it whirled around, knocking more to the side. His other chakram spun out spikes of metal, lodging themselves into the vulnerable spots of the Risen.

Using a glyph, Zephyr had its wind take him toward the Risen with shattered armor. He charged, swung, and created a vacuum wave, sweeping one away from Leif. A glyph appeared, latching onto it, twisting its body. One last spike struck its backside.

Zephyr hunched over as sweat dripped down his forehead.

Leif rushed toward the corpses, checking for signs of life, and grit his teeth. "Dammit!"

Tiamat and Ava remained in the air, tanking explosions from what Zephyr guessed could've been Level 4 Risen—he hadn't seen them before.

Zephyr ran over to the unconscious Agents. Their aura levels were low. "We need to get those still breathing to safety. Fast."

"How'd we fail?" exclaimed Leif, shaking his head. "We're the Dream Team!"

"You didn't fail. You're alive," said Skye, walking toward them. The sight of her on her feet put Zephyr more at ease.

"Some of 'em died cuz of me!" said Leif.

Skye shook her head. "We can't always succeed. I failed, too. At least we're okay."

Before Leif could further object, Tiamat and Ava landed by them.

"We'll take them to safety," said Ava.

"Do you think you can manage without us?" asked Tiamat. "I am sensing more getting incapacitated as we speak."

"Hmm... We don't have a choice," said Zephyr. "We'll do what we can."

"Right," said Skye, gauging Zephyr and Leif's states. "I'll keep them safe."

"Hopefully, the rest of the civilians, too," said Leif.

Ava nodded, and Tiamat gave them a look of sympathy.

"West wing's next," said Zephyr.

As they made haste, Skye remained close to the guys, clutching Excalibur.

Most of the areas passed were clear. All that remained were more dead bodies and debris. At least they had a silver lining—no Risen around those parts gave them time to rest somewhat.

Although he tried not to show it, Leif ran out of aura, which was astounding, given how many reserves he had. His movements also slowed. Zephyr felt dizzier than before. He hadn't released this much aura in rapid succession before and internally kicked himself for not being wiser about his usage.

Upon entering the west wing, three women in white Lumière Medic uniforms stood afar. One had dirty-blonde hair, another had her red hair tied up into a high ponytail, and the third had brown hair cropped at chin-length.

A team of armed Risen further away cornered them. The brown-haired woman bellowed.

"Eila!" yelled Zephyr, dashing over.

Act like Ava.

Leif threw his chakrams, drawing attention from the Medics.

Zephyr was finally within range to create his glyphs and send them to create wind walls to separate the Medics from the Risen.

The Risen wielded swords, while one was a mage, and another held a staff. *A healer.* This would make the battle tedious and were more rare types of Risen.

"Leif, take out the healer first with your chakrams," said Zephyr. "It looks like the mage is their leader, so we should take down that one next."

Your battling tactics are fine.

Zephyr blocked a hit from the swordsmen with his sword.

Skye stabbed one and tossed her knives at both the mage and the healer, knocking their weapons out of their hands.

Leif slammed his chakrams into the healer, taking it out with a few slashes. Tossing his right one at the mage and using his left to block any magical attacks, Leif distracted the mage.

Taking advantage of the opening, Zephyr stabbed the mage, disintegrating it. He did a backflip, raising his sword above him, and beheaded another swordsman.

Skye landed the final blow, thrusting her blade through the remaining two. Her movements slowed as her aura depleted. Subtle, shallow breaths released from her. Zephyr felt ready to catch her if she collapsed at any moment. He would do anything to carry her to safety, no matter how weakened he became.

Medics ran to the party. "Thanks, little bro!"

"Everyone okay?" asked Zephyr.

"We took down a bunch beforehand, and a lot of our magic got drained after we healed all of those Agents. Otherwise, we're fine," said Celia.

Zephyr thought she looked like an older, female version of Glacieus, though the complete opposite, personality-wise. He stood out compared to his full-siblings, step-siblings, and half-siblings.

"Have you seen anything further west yet?" asked Skye.

"No, we haven't gotten there," replied Eila.

"Let's keep moving," said Skye.

Explosions occurred west, prompting everyone to speed toward the commotion. Upon arrival, hordes of Dragon Risen were present, breathing gigantic fire blasts at every standing building and piece of rubble. Heaps comprising statues, pillars, and roofs fell on townspeople.

Few Agents spread out, taking out mini armies of Risen in blocks further ahead.

"ZEPHYR!" Skye pushed him out of the way as the skyscraper above cracked.

Twirling Galeforce, Zephyr used the last of his aura to create glyphs to blast the trio and the Medics horizontally, away from the timbering edifice.

Across the street, flaming pillars arranged in a circle, entrapping Castorites. Smoke erupted from the pointed ends of the pillars. Shrieks emitted, contaminated with agony, echoing through Zephyr as his head throbbed.

The dragons breathed more fire, this time toward the trio and the Medics.

Skye stabbed the ground, creating an earth wall. Her knives floated up into the air and she moved her hands, slicing the dragons' wings off and Leif threw his chakrams, piercing through their hearts.

Leif sped over to the pillars, trying to put out the flames, shooting out water aura, almost collapsing from exhaustion. Fortunately, the flames doused, and water pressure knocked the pillars out of the way. Unfortunately, they were too late.

"Gods..." said Eila, hand covering her mouth.

In front of them were now singed bodies, nearly unrecognizable. Their eye tissues melted along with pieces of clothing blended into their charred skin. The sickeningly sweet smell of hair and burned corpse seared into Zephyr's memory, rendering him bilious and a shade of chartreuse.

"We could've saved them!" said Leif, face fallen. "We failed. Again!"

"It would've been too risky to try," said Skye. "We had bad timing."

"But our job is to take risks! And succeed! How can you be so okay with us failing?"

Skye bit her lip. "You would've died trying. We're going to have casualties—it's inevitable. It's our duty to save who we can so long as it's feasible and not too risky for you."

"We at least had a better chance of surviving! They had nothin'!" said Leif. "We're supposed to try to save all lives!"

"If you're dead, we'll be saving a lot fewer people in the long run. I swore to protect you at all costs as long as I'm around and I'm keeping that promise. I'm here to prevent you from making a risky decision like that. We need the Dream Team alive to save even more in the long-term by stopping this rise of darkness."

Would Aqua and Luna have said the same thing?

"Man... Thought you and Shadow were the same-"

"Guys, that's enough," said Zephyr, as Skye looked down with remorse. "Discuss this another time."

"Right," said Eila. "This isn't good for any of us right now." She hated fighting. Verbally or otherwise—why she was a Medic.

"I can't agree with Skye, but we can debate over ideologies elsewhere," said Celia.

"But-"

Dark voids manifested, surrounding them. Level 3s inundated.

Gods, what do we do now? Anymore aura depleted, and Zephyr would've succumbed to unconsciousness.

Galeforce felt heavier in Zephyr's hands as he gripped its tsuka.

Skye moved closer to him and Leif raised his chakrams. Both looked as if they were about to pass out from exhaustion. It hurt to even brainstorm, let alone come up with the best strategies in seconds.

Right as several were about to rush at them, a revolving hailstorm burst out, zooming back and forth throughout the battlefield, separating the enemies from Star Strike and the Medics. Ice bullets froze some in their place and exploded with a clicking button press from what appeared to be pale blue shot gauntlets.

Leif gaped. "Saylor?"

Zephyr sighed in relief.

The powerhouse of Twilight Treader stood before them. "We'll take it from here!"

A sheet of ice covered the battlefield with one snap, and Saylor jumped, slamming his fist onto the ground, shrouding the area in mist. Icicles obtruded from below, impaling Risen. He uppercut one, spin-kicked another, using recoil from his blasts to augment the force of his punches and launch him further into the air. Saylor picked up a Risen and threw it over his shoulder, releasing an explosion from his gauntlets at it.

Needles shot from further ahead, jabbing at aura points as his teammate, Evelyn, arrived. A hatchet covered in black flames twirled around, striking the last of the foes and circled back to its owner, Adriel.

"Tides have turned, eh? Figured you'd be saving *us*!" said Adriel. His violet eyes shined beneath his mop of unruly, raven hair. Twilight Treader's leader had the type of lanky build and jawline fangirls drooled over.

"No need to rub it in!" said Evelyn.

"Either way, glad we came in time!" said Saylor.

Anyone who knew the two were siblings could deduce they weren't biologically related. Evelyn had dark skin, cinnamon curls, gold eyes, and a petite build. Saylor's family adopted her after her parents got killed by a Risen invasion.

"Yeah, thanks for saving us," said Zephyr. "We're exhausted."

Twilight Treader was strong, but no Dream Team. Saylor was the reason they were above average in terms of capabilities in their graduating class. Saylor would've been a member of Star Strike if he had ancestry related to a past hero or powerful bloodline.

"Where's Senna?" asked Leif.

"Helping your other teammates," said Saylor. "Ran into 'em earlier!"

Adriel nodded. "We got here late and wanted to help."

"Convenient," said Eila. "Well, the more the merrier. You have our gratitude."

"No prob!" said Saylor with a thumbs up. "Should be wrapped up soon! Everyone's convening at the entrance."

"If everywhere else is clear, we can go back," said Celia.

Agents swept away most fallen pieces and extinguished most fires. The scent of ashes lingered.

Zephyr grimaced upon seeing parts of the city gone as opposed to how it was burning down earlier. Lastalia might've gotten decimated by the time they got to it, but it wasn't the same as watching a city burn down in stages. He also had never seen people get killed like that, and dead bodies of Agents thrown around as additional casualties.

Castor might not have been destroyed, but that doesn't mean much. Half the cities are gone. Plenty of lives were still lost. Having short-term successes won't do much for us long-term.

"You okay?" asked Saylor, walking close to Leif.

Leif grinned. "Why wouldn't the Leif Meister be?"

His facade would've fooled everyone else. *He's going to act like his and Skye's disagreement didn't happen as well.*

It was habitual of him to not get closure for conflict, opting to push it aside and hoping any tension would resolve itself, eventually.

It'll only be a matter of time before it blows up again.

"How's everything?" asked Leif once they arrived at the entrance.

Trinity Trio, Senna, Shadow, and Aurora were there with some airships stationed close by.

"I'm beat!" said Shadow. "Being a Medic is hard work. But! I did great, saving everyone I tried!"

"Hey! Senna helped you out a lot, so don't take all the credit!" said Aurora.

Shadow shrugged. "Yeah, Senna was great, too."

"Course she was," said Saylor.

He stared at Senna the way Zephyr did toward Skye. The way she beamed at him back made it obvious the feeling was mutual.

Zephyr understood why. Senna's eyes reminded him of rubies, and they complemented her sepia skin, luscious, silver hair, and long lashes. She seemed graceful, with long limbs, and didn't have the build of a Beast Morpher. Her voice was soothing, reflecting her gentle nature.

"Uh-huh! How'd it go on your guys' end?" asked Shadow. His face brightened, as if glad it wasn't like what happened at Lastalia.

At least they and Twilight Treader were luckier with what they witnessed.

"Was all right," said Leif. "Don't worry about it!"

Skye looked at him. "Yeah. Did what we could and made it back in one piece." She might not've seen eye-to-eye with Leif, unlike how the old Skye would've been, but at least they could agree here: it was best to not worry them further.

"It's too bad we couldn't have prevented more destruction," said Saylor. "Could be worse!"

"Yeah, I've never seen things happen like this before," said Adriel.

"Unfortunately, it's something you get accustomed to," said Ava.

"Any luck with clues?" asked Zephyr, facing Trinity Trio's leader.

Ava shook her head. "Seemed like any other Risen attack."

"Seein' places destroyed like this is sad, but it's why we gotta keep moving forward! So, we can save more!" said Saylor.

Ava chuckled. "That's the spirit."

"Someday, Twilight Treader will be just like Star Strike! And maybe... just like Trinity Trio, too!"

I envy his optimism. But how'd they react if they saw what we saw exactly? Or if they came across another Lastalia?

It was a long day, and an even longer week. Zephyr wanted to sleep for days to recuperate, but knew it wasn't workable. He physically couldn't bring himself to do so, however; he hadn't had a proper night's sleep the past three months.

11

RECUPERATION
SHADOW

SHADOW GREW TIRED OF SEEING PLANT LIFE WITHIN EMERALD FOREST. They made little progress in their quest. No leads. He and Leif assumed ex-Thanatos members could've been the culprits, but there had been no encounters with them. After weeks of no progress, Ziel assigned them to work with Recon Specialists in the kingdom of Orwyn.

Twigs snapped beneath Shadow's boots as the scent of soil remained fresh. Rabbits scampered away further ahead when the party came close. Jays screeched from the canopy of the trees. Shadow would've rather seen dingles—Orwyn overflowed with the creatures that seemed like a mix between a raccoon and a rabbit. Some kept them as pets, training them for sensory processing.

Get me outta here, already!

They already cleared most of the forest from Risen—the place didn't have as much as expected to begin with. Shadow hoped they could stop by a nearby town for a powderberry milkshake. Somehow, the fruit turned into a powdery consistency when squeezed enough.

Zephyr stopped. "Picking up aura signatures. There's five people here… surrounded by Risen. Let's move quickly."

"Gotcha!" said Leif.

Star Strike and the Recon Specialists followed Zephyr's path, passing through shrubs and mossy rocks.

Wren and Mabel stood within the clearing, beside others, donned in matching uniforms. Threads of darkness connected Cerberus members to the Level 2 Risen.

Almost like they were… powering them.

A twig crunched once Shadow stepped on it.

Cerberus members turned.

Mabel snapped her fingers. Bursts of light emerged beneath the Risen, eliminating them upon contact.

"What are you doing here?" asked Wren, glaring at Star Strike. He sounded the opposite of how he appeared in the news. "Oh, that's right. You're all on that giant mission they obnoxiously announced."

Zephyr frowned. "What were you doing with the Risen?"

"I'm sure the President's son of all people would know about Heracles," sneered Mabel. "And I'm sure even you could deduce that we're testing it out."

"Testing out what?" asked Leif.

A girl with dark blue hair rolled her eyes. "The serum, of course."

Shadow stared at them. "You've completed it already?"

"What's with the surprise?" asked Mabel.

"You're not the only ones who can make progress," said Wren.

"What? Can't handle competition?" taunted the blue-haired girl. Her smirk made Shadow's blood boil, and he wanted to hit something. "Looks like I've hit a sore spot."

"Don't waste your breath, Remi," said Wren. "They're not worth it." He waved his hand, gesturing for his group to leave.

"Guess we'll be runnin' into them more often these days," groaned Mabel, shaking her head as they left the opposite direction.

As soon as they were out of earshot, Shadow spoke up. "That was weird! I wasn't the only one who thought their darkness was powerin' the Risen, right?"

Zephyr shook his head. "No aura was transferred from either side, so I couldn't tell."

Leif turned toward the Recon Specialists. "What d'ya think?"

"It looked like regular darkness from first glance," said one of them. "Not as potent as Dark Spheres."

"Hmm... For all we know, what we saw couldn't have been everything," said Zephyr. "Had we arrived seconds later, maybe the darkness would have appeared different."

"Seemed like they were destroying anything suspicious as soon as they noticed us," said Aurora. "I couldn't tell if they were angrier because they hated us, or that they had to hide something."

"Mhm. Whatever the case, that IS something to note when we report back," said Skye. "Jot down everything you noticed."

"It's suspicious!" said Shadow. "Isn't it weird how they announce Heracles 'round the time Dark Spheres were discovered?"

"Yeah!" agreed Leif. "What if they're purposely doin' this with the darkness? To increase demand for Heracles. And get a ton of profit!"

Zephyr scratched his head. "That's not... an improbable theory. I'll mention that, too."

"It's important to consider," said a Recon Specialist. "I'm sure this will not be the only encounter with Cerberus soon."

Cerberus took care of the remaining Risen in the area—whatever they were doing with them beforehand. The rest of the trek through Emerald Forest went smoothly, with no other glaring concerns. Since Cerberus disappeared, there was nothing else they could do about them now.

"Thanks again, Star Strike!" said Recon Specialists once they made it out.

The grassy hills beyond the forest's exit were more pleasant to look at. Sun was brighter on this side of Orwyn, too.

"Hopefully, you'll reunite with Mister Thorn soon!" said another Specialist.

Glacieus worked with their group before Star Strike came. He was going to travel all over the globe at this rate. Shadow wondered what it'd be like to visit the humid Gemini Desert for recon. It didn't sound fun.

After the Recon Specialists left, Zephyr went on about the BSC Tower, royal castle, and current king while they set up camp. The BSC Tower changed names so many times that it was hard for Shadow to keep track. Shadow listened because Orwyn was Astra Lumis' home kingdom. Mom emphasized the importance of understanding what the Daughters of Light had to go through. People liked to compare him to Astra thanks to their defensive abilities. Shadow loved hearing about that.

"So, that was when both Hemispheres first interacted a lot with each other, thanks to the arising technology! With that, also came the violent clash between those who could manipulate their aura and those who couldn't. Good thing we don't have to worry about the disconnect between types of mortals these days, thanks to Capala! People had their skepticism, but her party got Piscium and Geminorum to coexist!"

Zephyr continued rambling while everyone set up camp and got foodstuffs out.

Only Skye listened as she munched on her noodles and cookies. Last time she had only cookies for dinner, Aurora scolded her. Skye Hikari, slayer of Risen and stoic warrior who destroyed robots the size of a skyscraper with a single punch... eating a plate of only cookies was a sight to see.

Is THAT how she got unbelievably strong? A cookie diet?

Shadow chuckled at the crumbled cookie crumbs edging at Skye's lips. "Skye! Wipe your face!" If only the fans saw how silly this looked.

Skye's eyes darted toward Zephyr and flushed.

Aurora grabbed a napkin and reached for her face, wiping it off. It reminded Shadow of when they were kids, when Skye's clothes and hands usually had chocolate stains.

After dinner, Zephyr and Skye left to practice training on nearby Risen.

Meanwhile, Shadow watched Aurora practice her spells, taking a seat beside Leif on a log. Both were grateful Aurora wasn't using *them* as target practice.

"Y'all are tryhards," said Leif, peeking from his gaming device.

"We can't all be naturally gifted," said Aurora.

Leif put his arms behind his head. "Livin' up to the title!"

"Nobody uses that 'title,'" said Aurora.

"They will! When we hit S-rank! And they'd call YOU, 'Stumbles'!"

"At least Rory didn't pick her own title!" said Shadow.

"We couldn't find many Risen," said Zephyr, returning with Skye closely following behind. "What'd we miss?"

Leif smirked. "Shadow siding with his lover. Like always!"

"So, nothing new," said Zephyr, setting up training bots with his Communicator.

"You'd do the same for Skye!" said Aurora.

"Why'd he do that?" asked the twins, earning facepalms from the others.

Shadow tapped his forehead, trying to comprehend what was happening. Zephyr stabbing the ground brought Shadow back to the present. Their leader's glyphs surrounded the bots and moved beneath them, pushing them into the air.

Zephyr conjured another, using it as a launchpad. He struck, creating vacuum waves sending them crashing to the ground.

How'd he do THAT?

"Maybe… try with smaller hand waves so you do the same thing, but with less aura," said Skye. "It's looking great."

Aurora created twice the usual amount of icicles, pinning a bot like a porcupine. With a flick of her wrists, an ice cube encased her target.

"Excellent. You're both close to B-rank level."

What about me? I gotta be pretty close, too! If they don't talk about me combat-wise as much as those two, it'll be real sad!

Shadow jumped up. "I wanna try!" He had to master his durability shields and increase his mobility, but figured he was fine.

There was plenty of time before his peak ended and Skye never pushed him.

Earlier in the forest, Shadow's power manifested in a way unseen before on a Risen. Unfortunately, there weren't any witnesses... Now, it was the perfect debut. Everyone would get reminded of how great he was, too!

Grabbing Diablos, his signature, Gwymond bloodline-powered darkness appeared. It was darker than three months ago, and Skye hadn't pointed it out as much as he liked her to. "Zeph, use your darkness on me!" A dark aura covered Zephyr. As Shadow spun Diablos, the darkness vanished.

"Whoa... When d'ya learn that?" asked Leif. "One of 'em Gwymond gimmicks?"

"Yup! Happened in the forest!"

Skye grinned. "Nice."

Nice? That's it?

"Am I close to B-tier, too?" Skye nodded. "Heh! Let's see what else I can do!"

"Yeah, that combined with your near-immunity to negative effects of darkness will come in handy," said Zephyr. "We haven't run into any Risen with darkness mind techniques yet, luckily, but we've got you." Even his great-grandmother, half-Gwymond, didn't have Shadow's rare ability! Only pureblood Gwymond were completely immune, but "close enough" was sufficient.

Shadow continued training, hoping for more compliments. Once satisfied, he called it good for the day. He was well on track and didn't need to train much for a while! He'd earn as much praise as his sister one day—he was well on track.

∴ ☾ ∵

LEIF POINTED at the others the next morning. "You bros better come over sometime!"

"Wouldn't miss it," said Zephyr, putting away camping gear.

Shadow was ecstatic about coming home. Star Strike went back and forth a few times now, and Shadow missed his bed. They were all able to play games with each other again on their time off.

"Yeah, cuz you're finally resting! For once!" said Shadow. "With all that analyzing and whatnot, your brain needs it! So does your aura! Remember what Instructor Cross said? About using as little as possible! To recover fully? Yeah! We gotta do that!"

"Agreed!" said Leif. "I gotta rest up, especially. Now that Sparky's rejoining us, gotta stay energized! Can't lose no competitions!"

Spark either helped research teams, filled in for other teams, or took time off to train with Master Swifty. Zephyr always praised her for being a versatile unit on the battlefield.

This was the second longest time Spark and Leif had ever been apart. Spark returning gave Shadow a break from Leif's competitiveness. Nobody else was better suited to be Leif's eternal rival other than Spark. Shadow hated losing competitions he knew he couldn't win.

With Spark back, Astro Strike would be complete again!

As soon as they wrapped up, Star Strike headed toward the closest warp panel—a twenty-minute walk from their general area at a road sign.

After they gave their reports to the receptionist in the common room, a girl with sunflower blonde hair tied up into its usual ponytail came in.

Leif waved at her. "Spark!"

"Heyo!" Spark speed-walked to them, giving Aurora a hug. She did it to Skye afterward, and Shadow laughed when she stood there awkwardly, patting the blonde on the back.

"Nice shield. Did you design it?" asked Zephyr.

A new one strapped around her upper left arm. It was circular and made of silver. She always had a piece of armor and a shield attached to her body. Her light blue eyes twinkled. "Sure did! I'll tell you more about it after I report my latest mission to the lady!"

"Receptionist," coughed Aurora. She shot the receptionist an apologetic look.

Once done, Spark went into detail about the design process and her role in building the shield. Zephyr probably didn't know all the fancy words related to weapon-making, but he listened to all of it while Shadow paid little attention.

Leif yawned. He was used to weapon talk all the time at home.

Spark grinned, as they exited the Base. "So! What's everyone up to for their day off?"

"Home first, then figure it out," replied Zephyr. "We could meet up later to hang out, though."

Everyone nodded and dispersed.

He and Skye made it home. Mom and Dad wouldn't have been around since it was morning and Cynthia was probably at class.

Shadow went up to his room across the hall from Skye's. He liked how he and his siblings had a room with the same size and shape. Their furniture and the placement were the same, just in different colors. He thought the dark green walls paired well with his black furniture.

Aside from the axe-polishing station, the rest of his room looked like a typical teenage boy's. The walls had three StrikeBall posters and a flat, electronic screen. There was a display case under it with his consoles and games. Off to the side were shelves containing his action figures and comics.

After putting his recently gained souvenirs on a shelf, he went downstairs to the kitchen. Thanks to Cynthia's constant baking, there was normally something tasty to eat. He was grateful how aura usage burned calories super fast.

"I'll be back," said Skye, coming downstairs and heading toward the front door while Shadow grabbed a cupcake from the fridge.

He licked off frosting before peeling off the wrapper. "Where ya goin'?"

"I'm going on a walk."

"You're not hangin' out?" Whenever he asked, she had something else to do. Whether it was maintaining her weapons, getting supplies, training, meditating, or having business back at the Base, Combat Squad seemed to have busier lives.

"Sorry. I need to clear my head."

Shadow sighed. "You should be with us!"

"I'm sorry." She apologized too often. "These weeks have been... rough."

"Rough? How?"

"We, as an organization, made little progress in figuring out who's destroying every world, aside from a few speculations, when we have a few years left before the Realm's time is up. And there's all those places getting destroyed, not only Lastalia and Castor. Sometimes, I need to clear my head now and then to digest it."

Sure, they weren't always successful, but they bounced back every time. From every close call. Shadow clung to the idea that Star Strike was invincible and could accomplish beyond everyone else, given time. Like the other Dream Teams. Shadow forced himself to think of happier thoughts whenever the disasters came to mind. Witnessing so many dead bodies and people he failed to save were already hard enough to deal with. It bruised him and his ego.

Skye never said much about how she felt. About anything.

"See ya later, then?"

Skye nodded. "Later."

His Communicator beeped, not long after she left. There was a message from Leif about meeting up at his house. Perfect, just what he needed to keep himself occupied.

The Underwood-Moreno Residence was a ten-minute walk from his place.

Five of his teenage neighbors were outside, playing bounce ball in their driveways a few doors down, when Shadow exited the Hikari Residence. They were probably skipping school. Shadow was thankful he didn't have to deal with regular school like most kids. Seemed much worse than Garnet Academy.

"Is Skye on her way to attack another fan?" asked Luther.

"Or destroy more watermelons?" asked Boyce. "Man, we knew she was weird. Didn't think she was a jealous psychopath either." Shadow didn't care for them enough to tell them apart—they had similar pug noses, stringy, brown hair, muddy brown eyes, and nasty sneers.

Shadow glared at them. "Shut up! She apologized!" They never liked the twins. They were just jealous they had nothing to contribute to the organization.

"Guess all that power and looks went to her head. There's a reason she didn't hang around towns for all these years. She HAD to look good fighting monsters and didn't wanna expose her ugly side to the public but slipped out inevitably."

"The media LOVES to kiss your asses, but at least the online forums are honest. We KNEW the 'Queen of Blades' could never be 'The Next Seren Adnet.'"

"I SAID, SHUT UP!" The Gwymond Darkness surrounded him, turning into chains, pinning them to the ground.

Some shuddered.

Luther and Boyce smirked.

"Really wanna expose your ugly side too, huh? Oh, that's right, you don't THINK you have one, because you're a buncha self-righteous Farien with chronic hero syndrome that always wanna look good."

"Careful, Hikari. Do you wanna end up with a bad rep like your sister?" Luther purposely pronounced it like "HIH-CARRY," just to rag him off.

He had a point. Shadow took a deep breath, making darkness disappear.

"You know nothing! You wouldn't have the same smirks on your faces! WHEN one of us has to save you!"

Shadow shot them a dirty look one last time and stormed off before he could make himself look even worse.

Leif, Spark, and Aurora lived in Capala Hills—east of Daybreak. Directly south of them was Startown, where Stream, Glacieus, and Blaze lived. Capala Hills was more casual with its parks, StrikeBall fields, and stadiums—perfect for the "Rival Duo." It differed greatly from Startown's murals, trendy boutiques, theatres, and random sculptures lying around.

"Shadow, hey!" Saylor and Senna waved at him. "Something happen?"

He sighed and told them everything.

"Aw, that's too bad," said Senna.

"No kidding! What jerks!" This was the closest Shadow had ever seen Saylor get to being "angry." He never got upset, reminding Shadow of a teddy bear.

"You ever run into people like that?"

"Relatives get like that," said Senna. "You know, since I'm the first person with Morpher DNA in the family in eighty years. Always accusing me of showing off or trying to be the hero."

"Oh, forgot about that," said Shadow. He vaguely remembered Saylor being the one to listen and help her with issues growing up.

"Pay 'em no attention!" said Saylor. "It's different now since you're in the public eye more than before as Specialists. They're projecting and trying to feel better about themselves."

"That's pathetic," said Shadow. "We're heroes! We're HELPING them! Being envious of us is a given, but they don't gotta be so rude about it!"

"Keep doing great things. Once you become Marauders, most'll forget about slip ups. Dawn Brigade had stuff like that happen here and there, and nobody remembers. They'll thank you one day." Saylor gave him a thumbs up. "Keep moving forward! You got this! Ya know, I always looked up to you. Even more than Adriel!"

Shadow's eyes widened, and a grin crept over his face. "Oh, snap!"

"Shhh, don't tell him I said that."

Shadow pretended to zip his lips. "Heard nothin'!"

"When you become a Marauder, I'll get your autograph. And I'll catch up!"

"Don't forget about our sparring match!"

"I won't. Promise."

"Okay! Wanna come over to Leif's?"

Saylor's face reddened. "Actually... Senna and I have... plans."

Shadow tipped his head. "Oh? What are ya doin'?"

"It's an outing," said Senna. "A romantic one."

"WHOA!" Shadow heard the rumors for years about their speculated romance. They said the same thing about Star Strike members, too, the most interesting "pairing" being Luna and Stream. He didn't think any of it was real. "Well, congrats! Have funnnn!"

"We will!" They smiled at Shadow and left in the opposite direction.

It took a few minutes to make it to the Underwood-Moreno Residence. Leif's house was between the Candor and the Knight Residences. It was a spacious and almost entirely made of brown wood, reminding Shadow of a cabin.

Shadow entered the house through the main entrance. The Underwood-Moreno's always had visitors. Most of the time, it was someone from Spark's family.

"Hi, Shadie!" greeted Leif's three-year-old sister, Flora. She might've been cute and innocent but was fiercely protective of her brothers. Leif claimed she could crush an apple with one hand. This wasn't hard for Shadow to believe because his own younger sisters had capabilities like that at her age.

Shadow stepped down to the basement. The last time he was here was before they got certified. After classes, this would be a hangout spot big enough to fit everyone.

Zephyr and Leif were on the couch, playing *Street Brawler*.

"You're late!" said Leif. "You missed me destroying Zeph earlier!"

Zephyr handed Shadow a controller. "I'm rusty!"

"Where's the other one?" asked Spark. She and Aurora sat in the sports bar. They often used it for StrikeBall game watch parties and movie nights, making full use of the soda fountain and other drinks on tap.

"Out for a walk."

"What took ya so long? Yer usually late to everything except hanging out!" said Spark.

Shadow filled them in. They didn't seem the least bit surprised about the blossoming romance between Saylor and Senna. For some reason.

"What in the name of Tartarus?" asked Leif, setting down his controller.

"Those guys were always infuriating to deal with," said Zephyr. "I'm glad they weren't able to get more on video. You shouldn't have used your power, but it's a good thing you stopped in time."

"Yeah... That was irrational," agreed Aurora. "And stupid. But at least you stopped."

"What did they mean by 'self-righteous?'" asked Spark. "We're Agents! You're Farien! It's in your blood! Ugh, I wanna pound 'em one!"

"I'm sure the media will try to make her look as good as possible in the next articles and reports," said Aurora. "That'll appease some of them."

"Happens to all of us," said Leif. "Won't please 'em all, but it's somethin'."

Zephyr sighed. "It's sad that this has to happen. We need all the public support and morale boosts that we can get."

12

MONSTER I'VE BECOME

SKYE

SKYE WENT TO THE FLOWER FIELD BEHIND HER HOME. THE SCENT OF endless daisies and petunias soothed her as she strolled along the nostalgic path. Shadow chased her, Zephyr, and Aurora around this field as kids.

There were important matters for Skye to attend to, matters that her friends and brother couldn't know about yet.

Skye was to work with Triple Strike later that night to continue their search. Years spent seeking leads with little progress for the latter made Skye want to give up and think it was a lost cause. Being around Emerald Forest brought back painful memories that she couldn't stop thinking about and the darkness didn't help either. Unfortunately, sorrows that came with the night of the exams over-powered her brief, pleasant, and warm recollections of being in the flower field.

I was here... Right before we went to the Base for the exams.

Her power grew at an unexpected rate at age eight. She was no longer afraid of Risen after repeated exposure in therapy and taught to channel her fears into fighting spirit. Despite issues, she domi-nated Combat classes. The invigorating high she felt from winning and gaining strength pushed her to train until collapsing.

At age eleven, she arrived at the Orwyn Mountains' main warp point—a sign showing to "proceed with caution." Mountain ranges stood on either side of Emerald Forest at the northern portion of the kingdom. Peaks of brown rock jutted into the skies, laced with powdered snow, and concealed in gray mist.

Dove, Storm, and Teddy were with her. She would've been on a Combat Squad mission, but those three had to help her control her power after recent spikes that were far more difficult for her to handle than before.

Skye had trouble manipulating the smallest grains of the elements. She couldn't move pebbles with her aura—she split the earth instead.

Skye spent endless nights on training bots, bound with training bracelets suppressing her power. One was on each wrist, connecting to each half of her body and the aura points on either side. Dove said it was time for the next step—less restrictive settings on the bracelets and fighting Risen.

The dirt path was moist, and Skye smelled an earthy scent as she trudged along it, eyes peeled for any Risen lurking behind endless rows of pine trees.

"First Risen we see'll be the one you try your earth and wind aura on," said Dove as they passed through.

Dove was everything Skye wanted to be, aside from Astrid. She might've been cursed like the others but Dove always kept a smile on her face. Skye admired that, knowing she could never match up to her.

Dove was gorgeous with platinum blonde hair, coffee-colored eyes, and golden-bronze skin. She had perfectly arched brown eyebrows, red lips, and notoriously thick eyelashes.

It was Dove who told Skye what she truly was: a Host. Astrid was there but was too choked up with tears to say anything. Astrid was her role model and hero, and Skye had never seen her so vulnerable in her entire life. Until then, Astrid put up a facade for Skye's sake and waited to tell her the truth.

Astrid was with the Wings of Order. Dove, Storm, and Teddy's teams had all been killed during their endeavors to destroy all the Undead Hosts. So far, Wings of Order was the only team with mostly humans that could avoid getting killed by them, as long as Astrid was around.

"There's one," said Storm, pointing at a Golem Risen behind the trees, ten meters away.

"Boost yourself and shoot the earth out of your axe first. Blast wind next," said Teddy.

Storm was short, with porcelain skin, raven hair, and violet eyes. His jawline and nose were sharp, which made him seem intimidating, especially with his raspy voice. He looked older than Teddy and Dove, even though they were all close in age.

Teddy was large and muscular, with cropped, brown hair, ebony skin, and gray eyes. Despite his size, his round face made him appear friendly. He reminded Skye of a cuddly koala bear.

Skye grabbed her axe and focused, coating it with earth aura. Boosting herself, she slammed her axe onto the ground as the glow grew brighter in her eyes. An earthquake emerged and dozens of stalagmites sprang, trapping the Golem. Pointing her axe at the Golem, she spun the axe and created a twister. It ripped apart the stalagmites and spread out in all directions, disintegrating the Golem, as well as nearly hitting everyone in the crossfire. Hundreds of trees were decimated, and Skye blew herself backward, leaving Dove to catch her.

"Sorry..."

"Don't worry! Let's try again. We'll up restrictions some more," said Dove. She pulled out her Communicator, pressing some buttons. Bronze bracelets around Skye's wrists tightened and glowed.

Beowulves, more Golems, Wyvern Risen, and Gargoyle Risen were next. Even with less aura at her disposal, Skye's power went haywire.

"We should call it for today," said Storm, sounding disappointed. "You're going to destroy the entire forest and mountain range at this rate."

Dove saw Skye's face fall, shooting Storm a look, and slung her arm around Skye's shoulder. "You'll get it right, I promise."

Dove's words penetrated Skye's ears, but not the rest of her. The other Hosts didn't have this degree of trouble with their boosting ability. Skye's power was even more uncontrollable at night.

Skye shook her head, avoiding Dove's wise eyes. "How? I'm a descendant of Celeste and one of the Farien! I'm supposed to protect! Not... destroy." Her words tore loose from deep inside her, voice raw.

"You can protect," said Teddy, patting Skye on the head. "Once you control your power, you can use it for good."

"Is that gonna make up for what we've done?" asked Skye, teary-eyed. "Storm might've been the only one who remembered seeing darkness shoot out of him when he became a Host, but what else could we have done to help destroy the Mortal Realm?"

Storm sighed. "Well, I'm pretty sure by now none of us are continuously producing pools of special darkness that summoned the Risen and enhanced them aside from the moment we got injected by those stones and became Hosts. I'm going to assume that somehow, that darkness might've continued to spread from those initially created pools, if we're seeing enhanced Risen like what I witnessed."

Skye subconsciously repressed almost all of her memories when darkness flooded her the night of the exams. They didn't know if Dr. Lycaste was behind it or if he was another casualty.

"There're silver linings! We sensed no other Hosts! It's safe to assume it's just us. Everyone else got ambushed on a mission and got turned. That narrows things down somewhat," said Teddy. "As long as we stick together, we can learn how to break the curse."

"Teddy's right," said Dove. "All curses can be broken. Stick together, find a cure, and use our inhuman power to destroy anything too strong for humans. I've always wanted to be a hero since I was a kid, and I know we can be heroes, too!"

They followed Storm toward the nearest warp point.

"You know... It's impossible to accept this still," said Skye.

"Shadow got his Gwymond Darkness powers from our great-grandmother, and I was supposed to inherit all those Farien abilities —enough to make my ancestors proud. I thought ninety percent of it didn't come because it was delayed somehow. I didn't know it'd never come."

Shortly after Skye was born, a faint light aura surrounded her. This was how aura users were determined and it was common to name offspring in relation to the first element that manifested—the one they'd be the most apt at. Slight Spiritual Power in her light aura followed by enhanced power by the stars was less than the bare minimum for a Farien—the very bloodline that emphasized so much pride in one's abilities.

Dove's face filled with sympathy. "Skye-"

"Being strong in all the elements, being more durable than I was supposed to be, and being stronger and faster earlier than I should've made up for what I went through when I was little. I didn't know it meant taking away my light and my humanity." The words choked in her throat before Skye could get them out.

"It's very unfortunate," said Teddy.

Those people took everything from them. Skye wondered why they were the ones selected. Why did *anyone* have to become a Host?

"No use in sulking. It won't help," said Storm.

"I'm sorry, Skye," said Dove. "None of us deserved this-"

Their Communicators beeped. The message said: *Risen attack on Odin. Erratic and with unlimited aura.*

"Near here," said Teddy.

They quickened their pace toward the warp point.

"I wish the radars could tell us what types are there. It doesn't help to say they're erratic and without limits when they're ALL like that," said Storm. "They shouldn't keep telling us what everyone already knows after seeing the Risen that way for decades."

"True," said Dove. "We still don't know why Risen don't need to feed on living things for sustenance like they did for the longest time, until last century."

If this started before we were born... then we're not the cause of that, right?

They arrived at the caution sign and vanished into the light.

Odin was one of the least developed villages in Eta Geminorum, opting to preserve Orwyn's history. It comprised farmland with pens for livestock that turned to debris. The rusted scent of blood stained the air. Fruit trees had fallen through wooden roofs and most ceilings were missing.

Corpses were present, and screams echoed.

Dark figures lurked, spreading throughout the village. Trails of darkness stalked their paths, emitted from their spiked wings. Some had horns and skeletal masks. Others had arms of darkness and instead of hands, their limbs split into six long, finger-like joints barely reaching the ground.

Storm retrieved his staff and closed his eyes, boosting himself. Steel platforms appeared and floated into the air, carrying the survivors. Dove spun her spatha, conjuring protective barriers of wind around each one. Her eyes glowed gold along with Storm's.

"Teddy, let everyone know we've got it under control," said Dove, scanning them. "No data available, but these gotta be Level 4s or 5s at least. Let's not risk the Marauders' lives."

"Gotcha." Teddy typed into his Communicator.

"Skye, stay back," said Storm.

"But-"

Dove gave her an apologetic look. "Please."

Skye hesitantly watched the trio disappear. She just wanted to help. To be of service.

Civilians remained protected in the air as Risen attempted to extend their limbs to envelop them with more darkness.

Corpses laid close to her feet with their limpless, lifeless eyes visible.

Did we... transform the Risen into what they are here?

Seven winged Risen emerged from dark voids surrounding her. Adrenaline rushed through Skye's veins as she clutched her axe, gripping it, preventing it from slipping.

I can at least protect myself, right?

Light shot out of her axe, and she boosted her speed, shooting more beams. They missed and hit nearby houses, creating more explosions. Flames, whirlpools, and sparks came out of her. Some hit, but barely did anything, leaving her with no choice but to evade or get slammed into the ground repeatedly as their claws grabbed her, piercing through her skin. Blood trickled down her lips, arms, and legs.

She attempted to break out of the bracelets, but a dark haze enveloped her.

Skye screamed in agony, blinded by darkness as it corrupted her mind.

You're nothing but a monster, screeched a voice in her head. Darkness increased as the voice increased in volume. *You exist to raze. You will never be a hero.*

With every negative thought, darkness spread throughout her body, stabbing through her mind and soul as well. It seared through her skin.

Skye heard footsteps along with explosions.

"Think positively! Think of your friends, Shadow, your parents! Astrid!" yelled Teddy.

Winged Risen disappeared and Skye expected to see delight on Teddy's face, but his eyes widened with horror.

The left side of Skye's body shrouded in darkness. Black spikes jutted from her elbow and the back of her calf. Her fingers felt thinner and longer, as if poking out of her glove. A second arm of darkness attached to her side with the same spikes and with a black, bony, claw-like hand. Skye's left arm was so thin, the bracelet slipped right off while the right remained.

"W-what's... H-happening?"

Teddy's voice was barely a whisper. "The darkness... It... transformed you."

Storm arrived and froze. "That's not... Gwymond..."

Skye's ribcage tightened. She shook her head. "N-no... It doesn't l-look like this... Is this... a Host thing?"

"It's never happened to me," replied Teddy.

"Me neither." Storm looked exhausted at the constant glow around his staff, keeping the civilians protected in the air.

A feminine scream was heard.

"DOVE!" She ran in the scream's direction.

"Wait!" exclaimed Teddy.

Maybe I can't be a hero... Maybe I'm taking part in destroying the Realm... Maybe I've failed until now... Please... let me save Dove.

Dove was on the ground, bruised with deep scrapes. Wind force fields covered the civilians buried underneath a fallen house. Dark voids surrounded her and more Risen with skeletal masks appeared, armed with blades.

One slashed straight through Dove, cutting through her clear shroud of defence. Blood spluttered from her chest.

"NO!"

With all her might, Skye's eyes glowed the most radiant gold she had ever seen, creating a shine so bright that it nearly blinded her. She broke out of the bracelet on her right wrist and unleashed every element at her disposal. Flames, gusts, bolts, waves, spikes, stalactites, blizzards, dark beams, and light beams flew out.

Skye directed the axe toward the Risen, but the elements blasted in every direction. Explosions occurred and gray smoke shrouded the entire village. It became too thick for Skye to see through, and rumbling occurred in the distance, along with more screams.

Village of Odin went silent as the smoke cleared.

Airborne platforms and force fields vanished. Not a single building was intact. Storm and Teddy glowed, shrouded by their durability shields.

Her heart lurched. "What have I... done?"

Inner remains of the corpses were blown up further ahead. Blood stains and fragments of bone littered every corner. Not a single, living civilian was to be found. Steel spikes severed several, and the entire area smelled charred.

Dove was alive and shaking. "Skye..."

Storm walked toward Skye. "I TOLD you to stay back! Do you KNOW what you just DID? YOU CAUSED A MASSACRE!"

"Storm-"

"She's dangerous. She's a walking time bomb waiting to create more unnecessary bloodshed. Clearly, taking her out for training will not work."

"She just wanted to help!" protested Dove.

Teddy remained silent, staring at her body made with half-darkness.

Pain was a hollowness inside Skye, a searing ache that struck deeper into her chest. Pain had been reserved for discovering her status as a Host. She believed that was the worst of it...

Skye slumped to the ground; face soaked with tears. Her cries echoed back to her face. Her sobs made her feel like she was going to drown in her tears. Perhaps that's what she deserved. A punishment of death. To repent for her sins.

Skye's eyes rested on the axe in her hands.

She gripped the handle. "I'm sorry."

Zephyr... Please live. Even if darkness swallows the world because of me... You better not die.

Dove gasped. "Skye, wait!"

With a small smile, she struck the heel of the axe against her chest.

Piercing sounds of clashing flesh and metal rippled. The sharp edge lodged inside her and blood gushed as she dropped to the ground. A searing pain spread first, followed by cold sweat. Pain crashed in waves as she struggled to keep her eyes open.

"Skye!" Within seconds, her lids shut.

⸱⸱❨⸱⸱

SKYE AWOKE in a cot in one of the medical rooms. Bandages wrapped around Skye and the darkness around the left side of her body vanished along with her third arm.

This isn't... Tartarus...

On her left was Dove, sitting on a stool. "You're awake!" She got up and hugged Skye, seemingly in perfect shape. "Astrid and your parents were just here. They had to step out to rest, but they'll be back soon!"

"How am I... alive?"

Dove's smile faded. "I should've told you this... back when we told you what you were. But, you already had so much trouble taking it all in as is back then..." She sighed. "And none of us thought it would come to this... but... you can't die." She moved the top part of her shirt, revealing a deep puncture wound by her heart.

Life only had meaning because it had an end. As a Host, there was no end in sight. Skye became trapped in a never-ending cycle of causing destruction to the Realm she dreamt of protecting. A child forced to watch those she loved die as she continued to destroy and live on. Forever. She had no choice but to throw her aspirations away. Being an Agent of service was beyond her reach.

"What are we supposed to do?" blurted Skye. "If I'm so dangerous and I can't die... how are we going to fix this? Are you going to lock me up? W-"

"Please, calm down." Dove's hands were on her shoulders. "You need a lot more training to control your power. Darkness from those Risen transforming your body was unheard of and locking you up won't help. We need to figure out how and why the darkness did that to you."

"But... I killed those people. And destroyed Odin." Her being burned with guilt.

Dove exhaled. "It was your doing, but we share part of the blame. We have to make sure you have the restrictions on you at all costs until you're ready."

"What about... the loved ones of those I killed?"

"They will break the news to them... But we have no choice but to tell them it was the Risen that did it. We can't have Agents appear in a terrible light."

"Right..." Although it didn't lessen her guilt, it relieved part of her. Skye felt the air rush back into her lungs.

"Giving up isn't the answer. Being heroes is harder, but not impossible. Once we break the curse, we can save the Realm. We made the Risen stronger, but us five can fight them all without dying. Giving up will not help when we need all the help we can get."

Skye sighed, trying to shake off more of the memories from flashing through her head. The bravest thing she'd ever done was live and continue forward, even when she wanted to give up.

13

SHATTERED DREAMS
LUNA

Twilight Treader was more apt than Luna had imagined. Evelyn had been rendered comatose from their previous mission, so Luna filled in on Recon work for the past weeks. As the backup Recon expert within Star Strike, second to Glacieus, they would've been fine. Exploring and keeping an eye out at Thet Wetlands was a C-ranked mission with nothing stronger than a Level 3 Risen.

Southern Thet had a plethora of non-tidal wetlands in its flood-plains along rivers and margins of lakes. Vascular plants dominated marshes, mostly used for medicinal purposes. Most engulfed swamps had far too many shades of green to where it was revolting and made Luna want to gouge her eyes out. At least it didn't rain this time—precipitation depressed Luna habitually.

Walking through swamps was a pain in the ass—they couldn't walk fast in areas not covered by aquatic vegetation, while wearing heavy, waterproof garb. They were almost out of the worst parts and the rest of the swamp-area comprised trails and what remained were wet meadows.

"Why does Thet gotta be so biggg?" asked Adriel. "Imagine the days when they had colonies. Crazy how they gained so much land in history-"

Luna groaned. "Stop. You sound like Zephyr."

"Ain't that a compliment?" asked Saylor.

"I'll take it. Not like she hands them out too often," joked Adriel.

"True." Luna stifled a grin as she observed water levels up ahead.

Out of the teams, Star Strike hung out the most with as kids, it was Twilight Treader. Luna had grown apart from them ever since she joined Unity Squad. This mission gave her a sense of nostalgia, and she fondly remembered pairing up with them for assignments or witnessing Shadow and Glacieus's pranks. Luna bonded with Senna and Saylor first over books, frequenting the bookstores alongside Blaze. Teachers often placed Luna's seat beside those two. Being around them felt like old times. Simpler times. Almost like they were as close as they once were.

Luna's Communicator beeped.

"What's up?" asked Adriel. "Is it some fancy, classified Unity Squad or A-ranked or clan stuff again and you can't tell us?"

"Nah. Stuff on figuring out teams to send to the Taonian Temples."

"Only one Dark Sphere in one of them, right?" asked Senna.

Luna nodded. "Our major leads right now, but Triple Strike has more classified info."

"Sheesh, this is confusing!" said Saylor. "You'd think there'd be more of 'em in temples!"

"Anyways, Dark Spheres are hit or miss in areas we'd most expect them to be in. At this rate, we're checking every nook and cranny of the world to find traces or clues."

The Recon, Tech, and Intel Departments had never-ending assignments and projects. Between figuring out how these Dark Spheres even worked, trying to decipher any leads for who might cause all of this, and trying to reconnect with the rest of the Mortal Realm, they hardly had time to breathe.

"Watch there be one here," said Saylor, ducking under a branch. "Wouldn't that be nuts?"

"I don't see it happening." Luna's senses became blurred because of prolonged, frequent usage of the past week. Her range decreased, but surely, she would've been able to pick something like that up.

"It's been the same stuff on our C-ranked missions. Would be cool if we'd contribute more to discovery!" said Saylor.

"Enjoy it while it lasts," replied Luna. "You'll appreciate the mundane, eventually." Anything B-tier or below had lower stakes, without surprises in mind.

"By the way, do y'all have any more suspicions on whodunnit?" asked Adriel. "My money's on former Thanatos people."

"ONE of the most common theories," said Luna. "Recent new suspect is Cerberus."

Senna faced her. "Well, we're on their home turf right now."

"Cuz they hate Lumière Inc.?" asked Saylor. "But haven't they always?"

Luna nodded. "They're a sad bunch for attempting to be their own Agency, just because they don't think we deserve to be 'running the world' since my clan originated from Eta Taurium."

"Why are we suspecting them now?" asked Adriel.

"Dark Spheres haven't been noticed until around the time word got out about Heracles, and the few times Specialists have encountered them, they seemed to mess with the Risen. It's possible they could've awakened powers unseen before with it... Something that could've created the Dark Spheres. Who knows what other creations they have that could've spread something?"

"No hard evidence for now, right?" asked Senna. "I'm assuming Thet Royal Garde is investigating until they need our help."

"That's all I know," replied Luna. "Higher-ups are dealing with the logistics. For now, we'll provide Thet authorities information as needed about Dark Spheres." She stepped forward, avoiding a deeper section of the water, and paused. More Risen. Fifteen of them near the wet meadows' entrances.

"You got your sensing face on," said Adriel.

"Well, today's going to be more interesting."

Once they stepped out of the swamp, skies were visible again, albeit pleated with cloud ripples. Hard winds swept Luna's layered hair across her forehead. Their day started out stone gray, and the water had been a bleak slate. The sun would fall over the earth's edges soon.

Level 3s were there, of course. The same Grindylow Risen she sensed—fifteen of them. They were human-like, with scaly skin covered in darkness, sharp claws and teeth, and disturbingly long, wiry arms and fingers.

Senna pressed her right hand to her earrings, glowing red. Her Beast form was lither than Blaze's. Although her flames weren't as vibrant or immense as Blaze's, she had potential to be a powerhouse.

Adriel's hatchet glowed black, and his signature flames of the same shade appeared. Grindylows tried to douse his fire, but it was futile. The Sylfiran blood inside him made it nearly impossible.

Luna closed her eyes, and white magic circles appeared beneath Twilight Treader, spinning around them.

Adriel speeded, striking faster than the Grindylows could keep up, releasing balls of black fire. Her whip extended, latching onto a few, granting Adriel leeway to land more direct hits.

A crash and clashing claws came from Saylor and Senna's direction. A Grindylow's limbs latched onto Senna, dragging her into a pool of water while another struck, sinking its teeth into her underside with a sharp twist. Red gashes and bite marks pierced her belly and areas above the apex of her heart. The wounds turned her red fur into more of a mahogany shade. She howled as the red aura around her shattered, reverting to human form.

"Senna!" Saylor shot the Grindylows, blasting them away from her while Luna rushed to her side, pulling her out of the water and moving her to the grassy patches.

One false move could've caused Senna to bleed internally. That girl was all muscle and fine bones. Luna's right hand glowed green, closing the wound while the left checked her pulse.

She'll be okay.

More explosions occurred and Luna no longer sensed the Grindylows.

Saylor hurried to Senna, clutching her hand. "Senna…"

Luna retrieved bandages from her Communicator storage, dressing Senna's wounds.

"Thank you, Luna," said Saylor with a worried frown. This was the first time Luna had seen him less than content.

Saylor cupped Senna's face and caressed it. "I'm glad you're okay." He pressed his forehead against hers. They exchanged smiles and the love in their eyes was so intense that even Luna felt something.

The sight reminded her of the way Zephyr and Skye looked at each other—as adorable as they were together, she wondered when they'd get their shit together and become a couple. Luna didn't know how much longer she could handle them blushing at each other since they were little and doing nothing about it.

Luna's thoughts traced to herself and Stream before she snapped out of her wishful thinking.

"Let's rest," said Adriel, putting away his hatchet. "Senna's in no shape to continue right now. We could use some rest, anyway."

"I'll be okay."

Saylor chuckled and stroked her hair. "You don't need to act tough, ya know."

Adriel and Luna built the campfire, letting the lovebirds have their moment. He handled their stew for the night. It was rich and coagulated with an umami aroma, filled with foraged herbs and mushrooms.

Adriel wasn't as good of a cook as Stream, but far better than anyone else on Star Strike. That wasn't much of an accomplishment.

"New recipe?" asked Saylor, taking a spoonful. A line of herbs rested near his lips. Luna wanted to give him a napkin and tell him to sit up straighter.

"Ancient recipe. Mom caved and gave me her Sylfiran secrets."

"We gotta go to Eta Sagittarium," said Saylor. "When we figure out how to portal again."

"Before or after we become Marauders?" asked Senna, sitting up.

Her aura replenished quickly as expected—that rare Morpher ability sure proved useful.

"Afterward! So, Luna! Do we got what it takes? To become Marauders at this rate?"

Luna finished chewing chocolates Saylor made earlier. "Yes, but don't let that get to your head. Plenty become as good as projected to be or better but take it for granted. And fail. Dream Teams never stopped improving—that's why all surviving members succeeded."

"Wonder how it'll go for a team never planned to be a Dream Team!" said Saylor.

Twilight Treader was the first case where an average team turned out stronger than predicted, thanks to Saylor. Everything here depended on their peaks. Predictions weren't always accurate, yes, but they usually were for determining a surviving team's success.

"Any premonitions?" asked Adriel, turning to Luna.

"Well, I think that-" Luna detected a dark aura signature in the distance. Resembling a dark void. Her eyes widened. "What the...?" A ball of light wrapped in darkness was there, in the shape of a human. "Someone stepped out of a dark void." Luna stood and so did Senna.

Saylor clutched her hand. "Senna-"

"I'm fine now. I can help sense what's out there." She transformed again.

"Then we might as well all go," said Adriel, putting away their supplies.

Shadows blended into the dark as they followed Luna and Senna's lead. The figure moved east and stopped, where more voids manifested and Grindylows came out. Another ball of darkness appeared, multiplying the hordes.

"I can hear a cloak blowing in the wind," said Senna. "Material smells unordinary. There're metals now... A lot of Risen combining with them."

"Grindylows are being drawn out of their hiding places... Toward the figure and the darkness they created."

Luna enhanced their speed once more, and they made haste, approaching a clearing.

Grindylows disappeared into the voids. Pieces of metal lodged inside them, and their limbs were now robotic. The cloaked figure followed the artificial-looking monsters.

Adriel threw the hatchet as the voids closed and evaporated, landing on the ground in front of where they once were.

"Dammit!" said Adriel.

Luna scanned the area with her Communicator. She peered at the clearing—nothing unordinary here. "Almost as if nothing happened."

"Did they... modify Risen?" asked Senna.

"I could no longer sense part of their bodies."

Adriel shook his head. "And how'd that person disappear into the void like that? And create it!"

"At least they weren't around town," said Saylor.

"There is one five kilometers from here," said Luna. "If their voids appeared there, we'd have to go half the distance where the nearest warp point is at and teleport there."

"We should start heading there, just in case," said Adriel. "We can backtrack later."

"When I said I wanted to make more discoveries, I didn't mean it like this," said Saylor. "Holding on okay, Senna?"

She nodded, reverting to conserve aura.

"Was that person a Cerberus member?" asked Adriel.

Luna shook her head. "No idea."

"If people are possibly modifying Risen... shouldn't that be enough for Celeste to intervene?" asked Saylor. "Help us mortals out?"

"That alone wouldn't be enough for the Gods to let her," replied Luna. "Mankind has done far worse, and it didn't suffice. Guessing Gods think we can still handle it all. It's weird, though. With the amount of lives lost and darkness around, you'd think they'd be here by now."

"Could they be busy with other worlds?" asked Senna.

"Guess we'll never know for now," replied Luna.

"We got a lot to fill Ev in on," said Adriel.

"Uh-huh!" agreed Saylor. "I should ask Dad how she's doin' soon. And if she's awake yet. Maybe if we stop by the town after our mission, I could get her a souvenir."

Luna mused on what it would've been like in the Devaux household. Her parents were hardly around, so her butler, Sebastian, primarily raised her. Did parents with both biological and adopted children treat either of them any less? What about in Evelyn's case where she wasn't taken in until five years ago?

A brother like Saylor would be nice. Having a sibling at all would be. And less lonely. Luna preferred not to stray away from reality but couldn't help imagining the scenarios. She envied Spark, Leif, and Glacieus for how many siblings they had. In the era of baby booms to keep populations up, Luna was the sole only child of the group.

"What kinda souvenirs would be in the farm town of Spinel?" asked Adriel.

"Heard their cheese is good," said Senna. "Ev's practically made of cheese."

"Good idea!" Saylor kissed her on the cheek.

"What kind should we get-"

"Watch out!" yelled Luna as darkness overtook them.

A silhouette emerged as a human, slightly smaller than Luna. It released a high-pitched shriek. Dark pulses spread, destroying every part it touched, razing the ground and trees. Tremors erupted as land ruptured, leaving crevasses.

Luna sped everyone once more, granting them time to evade. Activating her Mark of Lumière, she created platforms of metal, lifting her comrades into the air.

The silhouette remained unbothered by Saylor's blasts and launched a haze at Senna. Darkness flowed around Senna, destroying her Morpher crystals. It disappeared, reappearing behind her, grabbing her by the neck.

"NO!" Saylor struck the enemy with his gauntlet, freezing it in place.

"We have to retreat!" yelled Luna. "That thing's beyond a Level five!"

The ice shattered before Luna could call for help or make another step. A dark hand shot up behind Adriel and Luna, grabbing them.

Luna screamed, feeling her aura siphon. Her Marking disappeared. At first, all Luna could see was billowing darkness. It parted slightly.

The Risen gathered darkness throughout its entire being, more concentrated than before. Dark hazes surrounded the party.

"What the?" cried Adriel. "What do we do?"

This was the most amount of aura Luna had ever sensed in one area. The strongest. Most horrifying. One direct hit of pure darkness from this being, and she would've left this world. It was erratic, as if toying with them before it could finish them.

Light blue aura glowed in Saylor's hands, and he crossed his arms. Magic circles surrounded the silhouette, blocking its darkness from spreading. The haze faded as ice crept its way around the silhouette. Simultaneously, Saylor's aura drained.

"Saylor, NO!" screamed Senna. She ran toward him, but an ice wall stood before her. "What are you DOING?"

Frost traveled throughout Saylor's body. "Promise me, you'll become Marauders."

Adriel's eyes widened. "Stop! There's gotta be another way!"

"I love you guys."

With a final hand wave, ice covered the silhouette and exploded. Darkness shattered into scattered shards, staining the grass. All other forms of darkness disintegrated.

Luna and Adriel landed on the ground.

Saylor collapsed.

Senna caught him.

Frost covered every centimeter of him. A faint smile remained.

A tear trickled down Adriel's cheek as he and Luna scrambled toward their friend. "Saylor..."

Saylor's eyes fixated on them. "Take care of Ev for me. And each other... Keep moving forward." He didn't move again.

Senna sobbed as she cradled Saylor's lifeless body in her arms. The wrenching sound that escaped from her lips could travel kilometers.

Adriel fell to the ground in a disheveled heap as his grief pooled a flood of uncontrollable tears.

Luna had seen plenty of horrific things throughout her career, but the most she could get were moistened eyes. *Rest easy, Saylor.*

Tremors occurred, and Luna looked up. Shards combined, creating bigger pieces, forming into liquid darkness.

Adriel recoiled. "What...? How is...?"

"We have to go," said Luna.

The darkness expanded.

Senna attempted to lift Saylor's body.

Luna grabbed Senna's arm. "Senna. We can't."

"We can't leave him!"

"We'll die, too."

Senna hesitated again, and Adriel grabbed her other arm.

Luna sped them once more, releasing white magic circles onto the party, and they ran, gripping Senna as they dragged her toward the nearest warp panel. Her boots hit the dirt path. Adrenaline worked its way like an electric current through every layer of Luna's flesh.

Another shriek echoed in the distance.

"Its aura's weaker. It's slower this time." Luna activated her Marking, increasing the speed boosting spell with all her might. She pressed the "Emergency" button on the Communicator, signaling for help.

Sweat coursed down her as a shiver crept down her spine. Soon, she could no longer sense the silhouette, hoping it was a good sign.

Luna's lungs ached as they arrived in the thicket separating them from the statue of King Tyrell—the warp point. Her breathing labored, and she dared not to look behind her as twigs snapped from behind as they passed tree after tree.

Branches gripped the fabric of Luna's jacket like fingers, scratching her legs so hard she bled. But she didn't care. Yanking herself free and pushing away, she rocked back onto her heels and continued forward. Her heart thudded against her ribcage.

"What are we gonna tell Ev?" asked Adriel in a whisper. "She didn't get to say goodbye."

"None of us did," said Senna. "I can't believe it didn't die." The tears never stopped.

"Let the Marauders take care of it. Going after that thing will be suicide," said Luna, breathlessly.

She stumbled over a pile of branches, falling.

"Luna!"

Luna grit her teeth, brushing herself off. A wave of dizziness hit her.

Right as the stone statue came into view, her aura emptied. Within an instance, she succumbed to the dark.

14

HOMECOMING
LUNA

Luna's head pounded as the bright light crept through the windows, blinding her heavy eyes. The fragrant aroma of cinnamon glided from a burning candle resting on the fireplace in the familiar black room with white furniture.

I'm... home?

Her shelves lined with books, weapon racks, a vanity, sofa, coffee table remained dust-free during her prolonged absences. Out of all places to arise, home was the least expected—Luna figured she'd either be dead, in the Medical Wing, or barely alive by the statue.

It'd been months since she'd been home.

Zedler Manor had a similar structure to her cousin's, albeit more modern. Everything looked new with geometric shapes and gloss. Her parents embraced modernism over tradition, much to her chagrin. Monochrome tile filled the floors, and the walls were pure white. Every room was minimalist, save for her bedroom. Everything looked barely broken in, almost like nobody lived there... Which was partially accurate.

A woman with the same hair, height, and voluptuous figure stood in front of the bulletin boards hanging on the walls beside Luna's desk and computer setup across the room. Important notes and news articles remained pinned on the boards, along with team pictures.

"Mother...?" Luna barely got the word off her tongue.

Her turquoise eyes met hers. "Good, you're awake." The only actual difference was their eye color—Luna's was more of a blue with specks of green, reminding her of The Dancing Tides.

Luna couldn't remember the last time Elara Zedler had been in her room. Frankly, she was surprised her mother even knew where it was.

She sat on the bed. "We thought it'd be better for you to be on bed rest at home. And more comfortable."

There was a pause—first of many for the night. Luna braced herself for them. Her parents probably only bothered talking with her to feel better about themselves.

"How did I... get here?"

"Your friend. He collapsed as soon as he got you two to the Base's hangar from the warp point."

"Are they okay?" Luna didn't think her parents were attentive with what their only daughter was up to within the organization. Or at all. Out of the adults, if there was anyone who paid the most attention to anything she contributed to Lumière Inc., it would've been Sebastian. Ziel would be a close second, followed by Stream's moms.

Her mother remained expressionless. "They're recovering. And... we found your other friend's body."

Luna didn't expect to shed tears. She spent years bracing herself for anyone she cared about to die. Casualties were inevitable. Especially for non-Dream Teams or Marauders. Had it been Star Strike on the unfortunate mission, it would've played out differently. Star Strike would be free from most threats save for Level 4s and 5s, which they haven't encountered since Wellsprings Cave. Had a Marauder team been there, their odds of dying were far less. Twilight Treader was far more vulnerable.

Mother's face fell. "I'm sorry."

Luna did a double take. Elara Zedler never apologized, not even for accidentally calling her the wrong name several times. "Who's taking care of it?"

"Triple Strike's doing further investigation, but they haven't located that Risen. No signs of changed Risen, however. Or any hooded individuals since. Don't dwell too much on it. Please rest and recover for the time being."

How d'you go from forgetting my birthday to THIS, Mother?

They had jobs to do, ones with a role in determining the fate of the entire realm. It didn't justify everything, but Luna understood their busy lives. Even Zephyr's parents made time for their kids. If they weren't her parents, she would've called them out long ago. As brutally honest as Luna prided herself on being, even she didn't have the gall for that.

Relax days were necessary for all living beings—aura could only replenish itself when not in use periodically. Even Gods required extra time to recover if they exhausted their reserves too much, and overworking could diminish them permanently.

Her father came into the room. "You've done well with your recent contributions." He had the same golden skin, blue eyes, and tawny hair with slight stubble, always looking more youthful than the average parent, scarcely fitting the image of one.

Family reunion. Joyous.

"You've been the talk of the organization."

At least Mother showed slightly more care for my wellbeing. The bar is so damn low when they care more about their image than anything else.

Luna's eye color and surname were enough for portions of the public to treat her worse than Zephyr and his siblings. Since her mother wasn't the President, she'd take her father's name. Luna figured it'd be easier to distinguish between sections of the family tree, otherwise the amount of people with "Lumière" in their names would've been overwhelming. She was fine with it since most other clans didn't use the same last name.

Ignorant commoners believed it was "shameful" to not continue the surname and a sign of inferiority. Having eyes that weren't the exact shade of turquoise and not being able to produce glyphs added salt to the wound, apparently. It was most likely another lame excuse to slander the Lumière name.

Luna couldn't care less about what the public thought. Those who followed tabloids were superficial halfwits who had nothing better to do. The clan didn't treat families and spouses of the President's siblings any less. Everything was merit-based and not going by the surname hardly meant anything with them; Capala would've never cared about such trivial details.

Her mother let those people get to her, and it made little sense. As a result, she rejected most traditions out of spite.

If Mother had any ounce of logic, she'd focus more on what's pertinent.

Her parents spent the rest of their "family reunion" attempting to make small talk.

After exceeding the threshold for how many awkward pauses one could handle and more one-sided conversations, Luna thanked Celeste for their beeping Communicators.

"We can talk later," said her mother as they left the room.

Her butler appeared through the doorway shortly after with a tray. Her favorite black tea and hariberry sandwich cookies rested on porcelain plates fit for royalty.

"Sebastian!" He set the tray down on her nightstand and embraced her.

"It has been far too long since you have last returned home, Miss Luna."

"I'm sorry for the delay." Her only reason for coming home would be to see Sebastian and the other staff members.

"That is all right, Miss Luna. You came just in time for your favorite bookstore to be done with its renovations."

Luna smiled and sipped her tea. "Thanks for the reminder."

Her entire world revolved around the Agency and was proud of it, despite risks. She wondered what it would've been like to live as someone else. The life of a kid going to a school for their educational career was probably similar to what she'd seen in shows.

Even as a regular kid, one would live in fear of having their loved ones getting killed. Or having their homes destroyed. Nobody in Stream's family worked for Lumière Inc, either. It must've been hard to have family members stressing significantly more over their daughter's or sister's life as a Specialist. Others had immediate family members get killed…

If I was axed… would my parents care more about my death? Or how the public portrayed it?

Sebastian studied her face. "Is there anything you would like to talk about, Miss Luna?"

Luna looked into his kind eyes. In the past, she chose not to confide in him. She wasn't an imbecile anymore. "They spoke to me more in five minutes than they ever have in my entire life. In my room, of all places. What happened?"

"Master Ziel's words have finally gotten through to them after so many years."

Her mother and uncle have never been on the best terms—working together if needed, but nothing more. There was a one-sided brutal competition between them, and the animosity her mother held against the President only deepened when her uncle became heir instead of her.

Luna and Zephyr being on the same team didn't help. Her parents were never good at hiding things, and Luna knew pretty early on how her mother felt about it. All it did was make her want to be even closer to her cousin and help him the best she could. Whenever Luna became lonely, Zephyr tried to get her parents to let her come to their place, but they always refused.

It upset her as a kid, so her parents tried to compensate by letting her do almost whatever she wanted. "How'd Uncle do that?" She knew they were working more closely over the past few years. It was nothing compared to decades of disdain, however.

"It seems your uncle finally proved to your mother that he was worthy." She supposed the years of proximity would've helped. There had to be something else serving as the catalyst. "He convinced her to take a visit to your grandparents' house."

Their retirement home was in Thet. They must've made the visit during her five-month absence. "Terror can surely have an unexpected effect on anyone," said Luna, stiffened.

Tension and trauma can make people bond in more ways than one, even those who had long-term grudges.

"Including you, Miss Luna." Ever since, she hadn't been the same person who always prioritized people's feelings over everything else.

Luna remembered the day she stumbled upon her parents' reactions to the news, revealing how they had just lost connection to the other worlds. She had returned from Stream's house after hanging out with the other girls and was excited to see her parents. She'd never seen them panic before and her mother yelled about "Ziel's poor leadership," even though it wasn't his fault.

Beforehand, Luna only knew the "worlds were dangerous, and they were going to help save them" and "sometimes people died."

Guilt spread throughout her butler's face. "I should've done a better job to protect you before you joined the Unity Squad." She hated to think she was the one who caused some of his gray hairs to appear.

"It wasn't your job to protect me, Sebastian. I was the one stupid enough to take the plunge."

She found footage in her mother's study. Her classmates had been curious about their parents hiding things from them, but she was the only one who searched for answers. There were few rules, so she wasn't breaking any of them.

Luna saw a plethora of dead bodies, destroyed places, and an entire Base blown up in the footage, taking place in other worlds. The relatives she never met and wished to meet, died with no mercy.

Sebastian found her in the room. He cautioned her not to tell her friends about the incident, and it didn't take long for her to acknowledge how thoughtlessly she acted. She learned those lessons the hard way and committed to ensure nobody would commit similar mistakes. That was only the beginning of the nightmares that haunted her.

It was her butler who stood there for her. After every disastrous mission, every time someone she knew died, every time she witnessed a tragic event. This time was no different.

⋅∙❨∙⋅

HER PARENTS STAYED at the manor for the next few days. The same chit-chat remained, and Luna thought she was going to go mad. When she received word of Evelyn waking up from her coma, she decided to visit Garnet Hills.

Luna tore through the canvas of brown and green buildings and streets that pulsed with the daytime rush as Garnet residents went about their day. The neighborhood was in orderly fashion, and the rich scent of coffee beans emitted from the many shops that served the energizing beverage.

Had Luna been in the mood, she would've stopped by the chocolatiers. She and Stream used to visit all the time, sometimes bringing the other girls on Star Strike with them. Other times, she preferred to be alone with the brunette.

Adriel and Senna waited for her outside the Devaux Residence—a sturdy, two-story building with high arched windows, velvet drapes, and tasteful, gray stone.

Senna had bags under her eyes and her hair unkempt. Her eyes were bloodshot, as if she spent days in bed crying. Adriel was no better, looking paler than usual, if that was possible. If they weren't grieving, Luna would've handed them cosmetics to make themselves more presentable.

Adriel knocked on the door.

Mrs. Devaux opened it, giving them a sad smile. She looked like an older, female version of their fallen friend. Like Saylor, she always brightened up the room and brought cupcakes for their class as kids. She was the one who taught her son how to bake so well and was warm, loving, and what Luna imagined a mother to be, unlike Elara Zedler. "Come in."

Saylor's family lived regular lives, preferring to be out of the public eye. Their parents' worst nightmare came true, but for non-Lumière Inc. parents, they handled it better than most; they didn't curse the organization.

"Let me take you upstairs." She led them up the wooden staircase, toward Evelyn's room, and left, closing the door behind her.

Evelyn sat on her bed. "Oh, hey, Luna!" Her smile faded upon seeing their grim faces.

"Hey, Ev," said Adriel.

"Where's Saylor?"

Senna let out a sob.

Evelyn stared at them in disbelief. "Guys?"

"Ev…" Tears welled in Adriel's eyes. "I'm… sorry."

"Where's my brother?"

"He's… gone," choked out Senna.

Evelyn shook her head. "No. No, that's impossible. You're joking. It has to be a joke. Right?" She looked between her teammates. "There's no way. He was the strongest of us all!"

"He sacrificed himself to create a Frost Shell," said Adriel. "Used up all his aura as a last resort. To save us."

Evelyn's pupils narrowed. "That's a forbidden technique for Ice Affinitists. When'd he learn that?"

"I don't know," replied Adriel. "Maybe he had it up his sleeve this whole time. In case he needed to protect us."

"I can't believe it! I won't!" Evelyn curled into a ball, burying her face in her hands. Senna ran over to her, embracing her, and Adriel joined in. For minutes, all Luna heard were sobs and sniffles.

"Adriel…" began Evelyn. "What do we do… now?"

"I… I don't know."

15

LOSS
SHADOW

DESPITE ASTRO STRIKE'S EMINENT ROLE IN HUNTING AND DESTROYING Risen nests in record time, they had yet to find clues linked to the cause of the rising darkness. Ziel granted them an extra day to rest and praised them for their "exemplary work." Lightheadedness occurred at the end of each mission, and Shadow wanted to be spared from losing ANOTHER "Risen Bashing" contest to Spark and Leif because of burnout and weakened aura reserves.

"What are y'all gonna do for our day off?" asked Shadow, exiting the Base's hangar alongside his team. A group of Agent Trainees passed through, waving at them. Instructor Cross heeled the young teens, grinning at Astro Strike.

"Training!" said Spark. Leif claimed they could classify her as a new breed of monster for never showing signs of tiredness, amongst other things. He wasn't wrong. For someone who grew up under Silvatica's values of "work hard, play hard," Spark sure didn't follow the latter.

Leif crossed his arms behind his head. "Course ya are."

Spark practically shot bolts out of her eyes at Leif. "What's THAT supposed to mean?"

Aurora coughed. "Anyway, Leif and I were planning on shopping."

"Yeah! Could use some new threads outside of work with this sweet, sweet paycheck! Figured Rory would be the next person to go to for help since Stream ain't around!" said Leif, earning a dirty look from Aurora.

Shadow's eyes practically popped out of his head when he saw the balance in his bank account after receiving his first electronic statement. Luckily, Shadow didn't have to learn how taxes worked and all the other fun stuff that drove Dad nuts yet. It excited Shadow to swipe his shiny silver card with little of a second thought. Shadow had no qualms about whatever policies the Silvatican Council enacted in the capital city of Argentica—it wasn't like he understood them, anyway. Zephyr said it was a "later thing to worry about" when they became "real adults."

Shadow didn't want to be a "real adult." All he wanted now was to stuff his face with whatever baked item Cynthia had ready for the twins when they returned. His stomach grumbled at the thought of rich, decadent cakes splattered with hariberries. They were especially tasty during these warm months.

Twilight Treader approached the Base's entrance once Astro Strike made it outside.

Shadow waved. "Hey! Been a while!" He did a double take as soon as he got a closer look at his former classmates. Dark circles marked their territory on the trio before them. The sight of Senna and Evelyn with no makeup, hair tied back, and dressed like they'd rather lounge at home in sweatshirts made Shadow raise an eyebrow.

Maybe they woke up late?

Adriel nodded. "Hey..."

"Where's Saylor? Is he late again?" asked Shadow, glancing around for signs of his friend. Maybe he'd get a taste of Saylor's famous muffins soon, too.

Evelyn stared at Shadow, eyes moistening. "Saylor's dead."

Senna trembled as the last word spilled out of her lips.

Adriel clenched his fists, refusing to look Astro Strike in the eye.

Zephyr and Skye appeared expressionless, while Aurora's hands flew to her mouth.

Shadow's heart leaped to his throat.

This had to be a joke. A cruel one. It had to be.

"WHAT? T-there's NO WAY!" exclaimed Spark. "This is Saylor, we're talkin' about!"

"How did it happen?" asked Leif, voice cracking. "And... w-when?"

"We thought it was stronger than a Level five," said Adriel, refusing to look them in the eye. "And... it was our last mission from a few days ago. Luna was there. Saylor sacrificed himself to save us."

Shadow flinched at the emptiness in Adriel's voice.

"No..." said Shadow, lip quivering. "He was supposed to be a Marauder! He was supposed to be a hero! Alongside us! We were supposed to spar... one day." Tears slid down his cheeks.

Shadow thought of the pranks he helped Glacieus pull on Saylor, laughs they shared, muffins he baked, classes they endured. Saylor was a hero with an honorable death. Gone too soon. First of their class to leave the Mortal Realm.

Aurora sniffled upon seeing Shadow's state.

Skye wrapped her arms around them, patting them on the back.

Zephyr hugged them as well.

"Dammit..." said Leif, trying to hold it in.

Spark kept shaking her head, eyes turning red. "We were supposed to spar, too..." She looked away to hide her welling tears.

Shadow knew the risks of being a Specialist. He shoved worries aside all the time. Star Strike had little to worry about. Initially, Shadow thought it'd take much longer before any former classmates died. Stories from older classes about such tragedies weren't a foreign concept. It was more impactful when it was his friend and a classmate he'd known most of his life.

"Yeah..." said Evelyn. "It's... not the same without him. On the team. Or at home."

Senna exhaled. "The memorial service is coming up in a few days. They're announcing the news soon." Shadow couldn't imagine his teammate AND sibling getting killed. If the same thing happened to Skye, he didn't know how he'd take it.

"Is he... getting replaced?" asked Shadow. With casualties like this, the organization gave teammates and loved one's time to grieve in private before spreading the word.

"Malcolm from the year above had the rest of his team killed in the Retalia Invasion," said Adriel. "A powerhouse. That's what our mission is for today—getting accustomed to a new teammate."

"We should go," said Senna. "H-he's waiting for us."

Twilight Treader gave Astro Strike sad smiles and disappeared without another word.

"We encountered nothing higher than a Level three-point-five other than our first mission..." said Aurora, trailing behind Zephyr, Spark, and Leif.

"We would've been dead," said Zephyr. "If Skye hadn't shown up."

"Mhm. It's amazing how everyone else survived," said Skye. "It could've been worse... At least Luna wasn't killed, too."

Leif's posture tightened, frowning at her. "What are y-?"

Zephyr sighed. "Let's not demoralize ourselves any further. It happened. Nobody can undo that. They called for help but got unlucky."

"What if we get unlucky?" asked Aurora. Her voice quavered.

"It's different with us. We're a lot stronger than our first mission as Specialists," said Shadow, digging his nails into his skin so the tears would stop. Four white ovals appeared on his left arm where his fingertips were. They faded, leaving crescent indentations.

"Let's not get ahead of ourselves," said Skye firmly. "Anything more than a Level three-point-five is still risky for you, but I'm here to keep you safe. Star Strike is a top priority to keep alive."

Leif opened his mouth, but Zephyr silenced him with a look. "We shouldn't dwell on this too much. It won't help us."

Spark separated first, toward the woods for training. Aurora and

Leif headed east, in the direction of the shopping district and Garnet Marketplace.

"Wanna come over, Zeph?" Shadow needed him around. To stop moping.

"Sure. Though, I shouldn't stay too long or else Tandy will yell at me for not spending enough time with her."

The trio cut through Garnet Hills and traversed northeast, into Daybreak.

Shadow wondered how word would spread through the streets of Garnet City about Saylor's demise once the organization released the news.

They walked through the front door into the Hikari Residence, reaching the living room.

Cynthia sat on the couch with Mochi in her lap, scratching his belly and feeding him dog treats.

"Back, already?" Cynthia sprang up and hugged them.

Skye crouched down to scratch Mochi's head.

"Uh-huh. We owned those Risen!" exclaimed Shadow, forcing a toothy smile. He wondered how frequently Mom, Dad, and Skye witnessed tragedies, and kept it hidden so he and Cynthia wouldn't have to worry. "You shoulda seen us out there!"

Shadow turned on a game system and plopped himself on the carpet beside Zephyr as Skye ventured upstairs with Mochi tailing her.

"Whatcha up to?"

Skye stopped, turning her head toward Shadow. "Taking a call."

Shadow grabbed his Communicator, connecting it wirelessly to the console with the "Controller Emulator" app and selected *Monster Quest VI*. Once he pressed the "Start" button, the red user interface appeared on the electric screen.

"Wonder if the new software patch is out already," said Zephyr, reaching for an input device with two gamepads and a joystick. Zephyr claimed the "motion detection" was faster than emulated controllers and their holographic counterparts, but Leif and Shadow disagreed. Shadow supposed it was all up to preference.

Shadow loaded their latest save file, picking up on where they last played. "Heard they buffed Hero and nerfed Alistair!"

Focusing on slaying monsters, enjoying the game's soundtrack, and repeatedly mashing buttons kept Shadow's mind occupied. His best friend's presence soothed him as they stuck together in battles for video games and missions.

Mom poked her head into the room. "Ziel told me you were coming home for the night! Zeph, why don't you stay for dinner? Lukas is making your favorite!"

Another thing to distract myself with.

Zephyr's eyes brightened. Shadow assumed anyone could easily kidnap Zephyr with a pile of noodles. When they were kids, Skye joked about Zephyr being made of seventy-five percent ramen broth.

Once dinner arrived, everyone sat around the black kitchen table. Each person had a shiny lacquered bowl with Kadelathan blossoms painted on its sides. The aroma of hearty, rich broth brimming with spices made Shadow salivate. All ingredients in their meal came fresh from Kadelatha's eastern regions inhabited by the Hikari clan, amongst others, where their tea gardens, rice paddies, and bamboo forests thrived. Shadow wished the other half of him—the Farien—had half as tasty cuisine. Unfortunately, they skimped on seasoning and flavor, similar to Snowholt's regional dishes.

Shadow's helping became heaped with scallions and bamboo shoots.

Mochi remained underneath the table, eyes peeled for scraps that Cynthia usually dropped, thanks to her clumsiness.

"How do you like working with research and intel teams?" asked Dad.

"Definitely different from protecting regular civilians," replied Shadow, grabbing a clump of noodles with his chopsticks. "These guys understand how battling works almost as well as any regular combat Agents. These missions also take more time with observing and whatnot."

Mom nodded. "It's slower paced, yes. Rolf was never a fan of those kinds of missions. He was an impatient one, wanting to complete them ASAP."

"Really?" asked Zephyr, slurping his last spoonful of noodles.

"Definitely mellowed with age," said Dad, handing Zephyr a second bowl. "Always a hothead, but Anaïs kept him in line. Ziel was always patient, though it annoyed the rest of the team."

"Our team had a lot of quirks and oddities, but we worked well thanks to Ziel."

"Sounds like Zeph!" Shadow elbowed him.

Zephyr picked up a piece of pork belly. "Well, I have a long way to go before I catch up to Dad. He always makes it seem so easy in the stories he told us as kids."

Mom laughed. "Oh, Ziel always gets straight to the point with his anecdotes and whatever he says. I'd imagine details in those stories would've been nice!"

"Oh, like what?" asked Zephyr.

"He was dense for anything outside of being an Agent! I swear to Celeste, it took him forever to discover his feelings for your mother. Don't tell him we told you this, though," said Dad.

"No way!" said Zephyr.

"Sounds familiar!" Cynthia turned toward the twins, who cocked their heads to the side.

Shadow wondered why his best friend and sister looked flushed. Maybe they thought it was embarrassing, since people paired them together and joked about their future children in gossip articles. Shadow saw nothing wrong however, IF a romance happened. He would have an exceptional brother-in-law, hypothetically. One thing Shadow didn't understand was why his friends smirked whenever the "rumored couple" stood close to each other or held each other steady after exhausting missions.

Skye's Communicator beeped, and she glanced at their parents, receiving a nod from them. She brought her bowl and chopsticks into the sink, disappearing from the kitchen.

"Who's contacting her NOW?" asked Cynthia.

"Probably Aqua again," said Mom.

Shadow and Zephyr exchanged glances.

After dinner, the boys helped clear the table.

Dad washed and dried them while Cynthia put them away.

Mom retrieved a plate of hariberry macarons from the fridge.

As much as Shadow would've preferred something more "cakey," he loved the meringue-based confections that people mistook for "macaroons." They were mildly moist, filled with light orange buttercream and glazed with ganache.

Shadow and Zephyr walked to Skye's room, knocking on her white door.

"Skye! Do ya want any macarons?" Shadow paused, only to hear nothing. "Skye?"

Shadow entered the room, whose walls matched Zephyr's eye color. Skye's room for the past years looked as if it was hardly slept in. It was tidy, with panda plushies, white wooden furniture, a walk-in closet, weapon racks hanging on the walls, a bulletin board with childhood drawings, and Taonian seashells on her bureau. Everything was in its place except for her.

"She's gone!" said Shadow, returning to the kitchen.

There was always a warning ahead of time whenever Skye had another mission.

Cynthia looked at their parents. "Did she go out the window?"

"Oh, she'll be back," said Dad with little reaction.

"Maybe Aqua needed her for something quick. We'll set some macarons aside for her."

Shadow and Zephyr knew their nonchalant behavior too well.

⟨⟩

THE FOLLOWING DAYS BECAME A BLUR. Shadow skipped out on checking the news for a report of Saylor's death, passing the time by playing more video games. Before Shadow knew it, the day of the memorial service arrived. This was the first time in a while where neither of his sisters needed to wake him. Coincidentally, Cynthia sometimes pulled Skye's same stint of dumping a bucket of ice water on Shadow.

Shadow wanted to poke fun at the chocolate crumbs on Skye's cheeks at breakfast. The dreaded day, followed by vague details about Skye's disappearance and more instances of being away, made Shadow opt for silence. Dad's famous waffles tasted like sawdust, and the hariberry syrup Shadow loved felt like glue when it touched the roof of his mouth. It became more difficult to swallow food with each passing day as reality struck him and Shadow could no longer distract himself.

The sun rose to the Spirit World above, a luminous cluster of glares in an overcast sky when the twins went outside. Every step on the concrete sidewalk toward Garnet Hills felt heavier.

"Have ya been to a Specialists' funeral before?" asked Shadow.

Skye's face filled with sympathy. "Yes."

"Were they within Combat Squad?" Part of Shadow didn't want to know how many she'd been to. Or how many times she and Luna might've witnessed a friend's death.

"Some of them. You… get used to it after a while."

A looming sense of dread filled Shadow. "Right… Makes sense. Just like… seeing cities get destroyed and that kinda stuff."

Skye patted her brother on the back. "We're in this together… I know I'm not around much, but I'm here for you."

The twins came across the white picket fence that framed the Devaux's backyard. Matching Celestial Lillies lined the fences alongside rows of lit candles. A shrine took root in the center of the yard with a portrait of their fallen friend. Varying models of Saylor's fist cuffs hung on the shrine, accompanied by Agent certificates, trophies, a StrikeBall jersey, and dozens of photographs chronicling Saylor's brief life.

No casket, huh? thought Shadow. His insides churned at the sight. Shadow wondered if Saylor's parents requested their son's memorial be placed at the organizations' cemeteries for honoring heroes or elsewhere.

The rest of Astro Strike was present alongside some of their classmates and the twins joined them, seating themselves.

Twilight Treader sat on the opposite side with Saylor's family.

Zephyr's parents were there, said to be present for every funeral within the organization when possible.

Unfortunately, Nova Strike was preoccupied on another mission, and Shadow imagined how hard this would've been for Glacieus and Luna to deal with, considering how close they were to Saylor. Shadow assumed other colleagues had similar reasons for their absence. He imagined they'd drop by during the week if possible to pay their tributes.

A funeral director stepped up, front and center. "I would like to welcome you to this celebration of the life of Saylor Devaux, who entered to rest by the Fates. Saylor was a beloved son, brother, friend, classmate, colleague, and teammate. He heroically sacrificed himself to save his teammates on a mission and will be forever remembered as a hero who stood brightly in the face of darkness. Because of his deeds, let us have a moment of silence, praying for his rebirth as a spirit."

"May the stars and Celeste guide you to the Spirit World," said the guests in unison. Nobody understood how immortals judged mortals' actions and determined their placement into the Underworld or the Spirit World after death. Nor was there confirmation about the status of mortals reborn as spirits.

Speakers spoke more about Saylor's feats and worth of becoming a spirit. Shadow wondered what sorts of praise other heroes have gotten at their funerals. He wanted to live long enough to continue earning glory.

Songs about rebirth followed suit, aided by melodic choruses sung by choirs and accompanied by local Garnet Hills instrumentalists.

Shadow sat up straighter when Adriel walked to the front. Not a single dark circle was in sight, much to Shadow's relief.

"Saylor was the best close friend and teammate you could ask for. We met the night of the Qualification Exams and became inseparable ever since. He brightened every room he entered. Even though his happy-go-luckiness drove our team bonkers, he was always there for us as a shoulder to cry on, the glue that held everyone together, and Twilight Treader's star member. From obliterating Risen as a team powerhouse to being obnoxiously wholesome and sending baked muffins to anyone he could think of, Saylor was an enigma. I can only imagine how he'd brighten up the spirits in the Spirit World. The Spirit World gained a special spirit the night he saved us all. Our world may never be the same without him, but I will hold every memory of him close to me and keep moving forward, like he always reminded us to do."

Shadow sniffled as he rose to clap. The standing ovation mellowed once Evelyn took her turn, looking put together.

"Although Saylor and I aren't blood-related, he became more and more like a brother to me as we grew up. Eventually, we became adoptive siblings and my life changed forever. Saylor was the type of person who'd drop anything to take care of you. He would be your number one cheerleader, supporter, and someone impossible to not love." Evelyn wiped her face. "I don't have many words to express how heartbroken I am over losing family like this, and I don't know yet how life will be like without him, but I know that I have been incredibly lucky to have someone like him. I tell myself every day to 'keep moving forward,' just as he's always told me. So please… keep moving forward, everyone."

Shadow choked back a sob. He didn't need to turn around to know that his friends were doing the same.

Skye handed him a tissue, eyes darkening as she fished out another for Aurora and Spark.

The closing remarks finished, and Skye followed Shadow toward Twilight Treader.

Shadow nodded at Adriel and Evelyn. "Your speeches were fantastic."

"Thanks, Shadie," said Adriel. "I'm sure Saylor thought so, too."

"Do ya think he's watching over us?" asked Shadow.

"I know he is," said Senna.

"I also know he wouldn't have wanted us to mourn over him for too long," said Adriel. "Tomorrow and onward, we're moving forward."

"I'm glad," said Skye. "Time heals."

Once the twins said their farewells, they exited the yard in silence.

The heavy, suffocating feeling in Shadow's chest refused to soothe itself.

"How about... we stop by the Interplanetary District and get something from Magnolia Bakery?" suggested Skye. "My treat. Whatever you want, however much of it." Her golden-amber eyes brimmed with hope. Whenever Shadow became upset years back, Mom and Dad brought him there to cheer him up.

Shadow hesitated. "That's okay." In any other case, he would've beamed at the idea of spending quality time with her.

Skye's lips flattened into a thin line. "Oh..."

"Hard to think about food at a time like this."

"I understand... But you've hardly been eating. I thought going to Magnolia could help. Do you want to talk about it?"

Shadow looked at Skye, heart heavy. "I keep thinking about Evelyn's speech back there. What if I was in that same situation...? What if I lost you?" Skye took a step back, as if slapped in the face. "I-I don't want to lose my twin."

"Don't worry about me. I'm here to protect you." Skye embraced her brother as a tear rolled down her cheek.

PART II

ASCENSION

16

SPARKS FLY

ZEPHYR

AFTER THEIR TIME OFF, ZEPHYR'S FATHER SWAMPED ASTRO STRIKE with more missions over the past weeks. Some were harder than others, which kept the team busy from grieving too much over Saylor. Zephyr took it upon himself to check up on each of his teammates' wellbeing every night and his insides melted, seeing Skye continuing to take care of her brother. Skye was the same girl with the air of kindness that put others before herself—the one who could lessen Zephyr's worries upon seeing her smile. She may not have been around much, but she was always there when they needed her the most.

Zephyr couldn't stop beaming at her when the team waited at the Base for "The Rival Duo." As soon as Skye turned at Zephyr's gaze, she fidgeted with the turquoise bracelets on her wrists. They matched Zephyr's eyes alongside the walls in her room. When Zephyr first realized this, his heart thundered in his chest.

"Check this out!" said Spark, running over to them and gestured to her outfit, one that Zephyr had never seen her wear.

Spark's wardrobe comprised sleeveless hoodies and shorts. This one had a silver mesh top with a cerulean vest. The mesh had a black "X" crossing through the middle, and her black shorts had fringe at the hem and a white lightning bolt on the left. She paired it with silver, knee-high boots that lace up. Matching armbands and pieces of armor wrapped around her arms.

"Cute," said Aurora. "Just came in?"

"Nah! Stream had it done a while back! Felt today was the day to debut this thing!"

"Looks nice," said Zephyr. "Seems pretty lightweight, which is good for all the jumping and flipping around."

Leif strolled over with a piece of toast in his mouth. Crumbs fell and pigeons followed his trail, hoping for an early meal. "Yo!"

"Even Shadow's earlier than you," said Aurora.

"Would've been late! If Cynthia didn't stick a feather! In my nose." Shadow scratched his head. "Skye tried throwing plushies! But it didn't work." Everyone looked at Skye and she stood silently, awkwardly avoiding eye-contact.

Zephyr didn't notice how much he missed the team's old selves until more recently. He hoped Shadow could smile and joke around as much as he used to. Part of him speculated that Leif and Spark put up an optimistic facade to motivate the team to return to normal quicker.

"Anyway! Notice anythin' different, Leif?" asked Spark, striking a pose.

Leif licked jam off his fingers. "Ya got more strands down the side of your face!"

Spark whacked him upside the head. "Don't make me smack ya!"

"Don't tell me AFTER YA hit me!"

Spark pointed at her clothes. "Do ya notice now?"

"You got new gear just so you can beat me in today's Risen Bashing Contest?" Leif grinned, putting the key into ignition.

"Like Tartarus I did!" Spark grit her teeth, shooting him a look that said, *I'll show you, Underwood-Moreno.* "Don't make me carry you on THIS mission!"

"HA! Bro, nobody's carried me since my momma!"

"That's a lie!" yelled Spark.

Zephyr and Aurora practically had to drag the bantering pair into the Base. Father sent them a message the night before, summoning Astro Strike to his office. It was on the highest floor of the rightmost dome—one of the most secure parts of the entire Base.

Zephyr's pulse bounded as he entered an elevator with his friends. He did not know what his father wanted them in his office for, and he hoped it had nothing to do with their progress reports. The only one underperforming was himself. He still couldn't build up sufficient aura reserves but was at least able to improve in other areas.

Unless I'm getting overconfident again. . .

The President was an understanding man who did what was right and by the book. Aqua was a lot like him in that regard. Zephyr couldn't bring himself to think the same way.

"Welcome, Astro Strike." The President smiled at them upon arrival into his office. Holographic screens floated around Father as he remained seated at his desk.

President Ziel's circular room featured dark blue metallic walls and windows faded to opaque. The painted Lumière symbol in the center of the room contained a holographic projection table that remained hidden beneath when not in use.

"Good morning, Father," replied Zephyr.

"I've heard of your growth and am pleased you've worked well with various research and intel teams."

Zephyr braced himself for the President to say anything further about their progress. "They've been pleasant to work with and excellent examples to learn from."

"Perhaps you would like more challenging tasks. B-ranked missions would suit your current skill levels and larger team size and would help you grow as quickly. Now, this is entirely up to you if you wish to take these opportunities as you continue your quest to find clues."

More challenging tasks? Is this a way to push Astro Strike further?

Zephyr looked at his teammates, who either nodded or gave him a thumbs up. "We accept." He couldn't afford to look uncertain in front of his father or his team. The President knew what he was doing by giving them a new challenge—a test.

President Lumière showed no reaction; he expected them to accept. "We believe it's best to have you more involved with uncovering the mysteries, albeit in lower risk situations."

"I see. What would that entail, sir?" asked Zephyr.

"Instead of having you search areas for leads, you would partake in taking care of the Dark Spheres. We theorized Dark Spheres manifest in areas not necessarily just landmarks, but areas inhabiting massive amounts of aura ages ago. Luna found one at a temple in Taonia. We discovered these spheres can draw out aura and Spiritual Power released in highly concentrated amounts throughout history.

"Monsters in that temple are no stronger than a Level three or three-point-five, as with any other B-ranked mission, and this should not be a hassle for you, given Skye's role to protect you in case of emergency. Your aim is to escort researchers as they gather data and destroy the spheres once given the okay. Should you succeed, we will continue to send you on more missions of the sort within your ranking."

Zephyr wished his aura sensing ability was as strong as Luna's. She unsurprisingly found more than one Dark Sphere, and he was proud of her.

While Astro Strike ranked up, Nova Strike contributed more to the cause with intense recon missions and inventing gadgets. Star Strike's chances of finding much noteworthy as of now were low. The organization had been at it for decades... It could take months, maybe even years, to find out who was behind these occurrences.

"As you know, the desert is not one to mess around in. It was a place to teach residents of the kingdom how to survive back in the day. It may be a lower risk location compared to others with Dark Spheres but stay ever vigilant."

"Sounds reasonable, Father."

Even if these monsters had to be less than Level 4s, it didn't worry Zephyr much less. Level 3s had the broadest range of Risen with questionable criteria. Letting his guard down wasn't the move.

"We should stock up on panaceas and antidotes before we head off," said Skye.

"This was once a place revolving around a 'survival of the fittest' mentality for a reason," said Aurora.

"Ah, right! All the poisonous monsters! And ones that can petrify," said Shadow. "We'll take 'em on! As long as we don't get hit!"

"Even if we get hit, we got the medicine!" said Leif with a thumbs up.

"More instructions are being sent to your Communicators and they'll meet you at Gessu. Be sure to prepare as necessary before departing." The President wished them the best of luck before they left the room.

They stepped into the elevator. "Didn't think I'd be able to come with y'all on a B-ranked mission so soon!" said Spark with a dimpled smile as she readjusted her ponytail.

"Guess bein' a try hard for all them solo missions paid off," said Leif.

"Dude!" said Spark. "You're just jealous cuz I got more done faster!"

While they bickered, Zephyr internally planned with haste.

He mentally mapped most of it out, employing most of his methods for previous, successful missions.

His plans came faster—they had to be, since this mission was more spontaneous—a test of preparation efficiency. Major worries stemmed from what could've been inside the temple, given how strong the aura was in that area throughout history and protecting the researchers from them. Thankfully, their work with previous research teams put him at more ease.

"BTW, Shadie, can I look at your weapon before we get to Gessu?" asked Spark. Since Shadow's was the most customizable, it would make sense to maintain it more often.

"Sure. We went back and forth so much, I must've forgotten to take better care of it."

Spark gave Shadow a thumbs up. "Good thing ya got me here!"

"Except, I'm the one who designed the one he uses the most!" said Leif, smirking.

"No, it was you AND Stream! There's no way ya could've built the part that lets ya switch between staff and axe!"

"Doesn't change how my boy picked MY design!" Leif grabbed Shadow from behind the shoulders, making him grin a little.

They got off the elevator then, and Zephyr hoped they would be less loud by the time they walked into the lobby. Once again, he was wrong. Luckily, they'd make it out of the Base soon and toward the shops.

"But he picked MINE all other times!"

"Because ya spend so much time designing it and my cinnamon roll feels bad!" Leif put an arm around Shadow. "Zeph's one, too!"

"Next time, I'll make a design ya pick because ya like it better!"

"Don't forget all the times our clients pick ME to upgrade!"

Zephyr was sure the Knight and the Underwood-Moreno families had it so at least some of their kids were the same ages. Their families did everything together. He had no clue how the households ran a weapon shop together with all the bickering and turning everything into a contest.

For the sake of efficiency, Astro Strike split up within the Market District to finish their errands. Skye, Aurora, and Leif would get medicine and tools. The rest took care of food and weapons.

Zephyr's half of the team entered The Phoenix Forge, where Spark's mom greeted them. The display windows always featured their newest products and fanciest ones; this time, there were gun scythes and gunblades.

Spark led them past the shelves and glass cases of knives and toward the back room. "Follow me!" More shelves of weapons and maintenance tools filled the back room. Connected to the back room were the forge and the garage.

They came into the garage, and Shadow handed Diablos to

Spark. Spark pressed the button, inspecting the staff. "Yep, looks like we need to give the axe some TLC."

Spark cleaned the head of the axe with steel wool and acetone. Afterward, she wiped down the handle with extra fine steel wool and turpentine. She then oiled down the handle and head with boiled linseed oil.

"This is satisfying to watch," commented Zephyr. Everyone had the items to maintain their weapons, but nothing beat the treatment from The Phoenix Forge.

Spark took the axe over to the sharpening station. She clamped it to a bench and placed it under a wooden wedge, filing at the edge at various angles. The last steps were to run a sharpening stone over the edge with circular motions and run it over a piece of leather.

"Whattaya think?" Spark handed Diablos back to its rightful owner.

"Looks good to me. Thanks, Sparky."

"Just remember, it was *I* who did it! NOT Leif!"

Time to go to the next order of business: groceries. Zephyr felt like a dad when he kept having to pry all junk food out of Spark's hands. He was an adult and believed it was time to be a bit more responsible with his food choices, as appealing as some instant noodles were.

"Boss! The potato chips are on sale!" whined Spark.

Zephyr sighed, giving in. "All right, fine. You can have them IF you get more veggies." Her love of junk was because of how she was one of those kids who grew up eating dragon-shaped nuggets, if she wasn't at Leif's house for dinner. Mrs. Underwood-Moreno was a superb cook and a national treasure.

Spark threw a corgi-shaped Communicator charging case into the basket. "Oh, and this looked cool!"

"We're not buying things to buy things here!" exclaimed Zephyr, exasperated. He had to admit, it looked cute, just like Skye's panda case and Blaze's bunny one.

"What is THAT?" asked Leif, pointing at the charger case.

"Isn't it adorable?"

Zephyr facepalmed.

⸰⸱⸲(⸱⸱

RESEARCHERS WERE to arrive in Gessu in the afternoon. By the time Astro Strike teleported west, they were in the desert city early, which gave Zephyr extra time to plan.

Half of Gessu split into an urban environment with glass skyscrapers, and the other half was more suburban, with sand and an oasis behind the civilization. Wealthier classes dwelled in the urbanized portion, adorning silk and expensive jewels found hidden in the desert. No matter the class, most had the same mixes of tanned people with blonde hair and gray eyes or darker individuals with black hair.

Suburban side was quieter, preserving more of Taonia's ancient culture with its houses made of either steel mesh, clay, or recycled glass. More farms were present, housing camels, goats, and sheep. Wheat fields, along with areas for barley and lentils, covered the land in the distance, eternally golden by the constant sunshine.

"Man, it's extra hot this time of year!" said Spark as they passed colorful cacti planted on the streets.

A few chickens strolled around, pecking at the ground. Zephyr was wary of crossing paths with any scarpers—their poisonous tails and sharp claws were not a picnic to deal with.

"It's been a while since I've been here," said Aurora. Last time they were here was seven years ago, when their families took a vacation to the neighboring kingdom. "Come on! Let's go see what else has changed around here."

Zephyr fondly remembered the hole-in-the-wall eateries they came across on vacation. Taonia's flatbreads and cheeses were to die for. Somehow, the unleavened dough cooked by being buried in the hot sand and embers beneath fires.

He and Skye disappeared with Mother to sample from different ones to determine which was best before hitting up history museums back then. Skye wasn't the most enthusiastic about going,

as much as she tried to hide it, but went for his sake. Out of grati-
tude, he convinced everyone to visit the beaches north of the city.
Once succeeding, he helped her find seashells for her collection.
They were prettier than the ones at Garnet's beaches.

Skye put her hand out. "Wait, there's a-" Aurora tripped and fell,
not seeing rocks lying around. "Bunch of... rocks."

"And Gessu has taken in Stumbles as its next victim," said
Zephyr with a smirk.

"You okay?" asked Shadow.

Aurora got up and brushed the sand off her dress. "I heard that,
Zeph! And yes!"

"How come every time I'm around Rory, I get hit?" asked Leif.
Spark always joked about how it would be a "running gag" if they
were in some entertainment show.

Spark bonked him on the head lightly with her fist. "Beats me."

"Maybe Stream could help her. I'm sure they train models how
to not fall over on the runways in those giant heel things," said
Shadow.

Zephyr was pretty sure "those giant heel things," were "stilettos."
He found it peculiar how Stream had the courage to model a lot of
the Agent outfits and act as a "poster girl." Her moms and sisters
were models, so it made sense for her to do it sometimes, but she
never quite got over her shyness.

"Yikes! Aurora on a runway would get someone killed," said Leif,
shuddering.

"I HEARD THAT!"

Leif instinctively went to hide behind Shadow. "Shadow, help a
bro out, okay?"

"Ahem." Everyone turned to see the research team behind them.
Zephyr's ears got hot. How much did they overhear?

"Hello, Astro Strike," said the head researcher, chuckling. He had
black hair, brown eyes, and deep bronze skin. There were four of
them.

"Hey, there!" said Spark, waving at them.

Aurora glanced at her disapprovingly.

"Ahem... I mean... It's a pleasure to meet you all."

Leif winked at a female researcher, earning a venomous glare from Aurora, who hid behind Spark.

Zephyr wondered if it was possible to facepalm to the point of permanent injury.

The head researcher extended his hand out to Zephyr, who shook it, chuckling again. "I'm Dr. Caraway."

"Nice to meet you, Dr. Caraway," said Zephyr.

Everyone else respectfully greeted the team, and Zephyr got a closer look. Judging by the crests on their cloaks, it looked like they were all from the Gwynervan Base. Most of the research teams originated from there, and Dr. Caraway was the only one Zephyr was familiar with.

"We can get started," said one of the other researchers. "We just finished surveying the borders of the city."

Everyone transported to the designated Taonian Temple.

Zephyr noticed Skye almost tapping on the wrong button and stifled a laugh. He resisted the urge to fanboy over pyramid-shaped architecture in front of the researchers. The Taonian Royal Crest and other royal symbols scattered around the edifice. It looked exactly like what was in the pictures in the textbooks, and Zephyr was glad it wasn't like some other ancient, worn away buildings. So much has changed over the eras, including landmasses that shifted.

"The exterior looks fine. It won't be quite the same on the inside, however," said Dr. Caraway. "The monsters the inhabitants of the kingdom of Taonia all had to face back then are replaced entirely by Risen, today."

"It would make sense to have a Dark Sphere here," said another researcher. "These temples housed an incredible amount of aura and Spiritual Power. This one is more special than the others because it became the resting place of Taonia's Spirit, Aramis later in history."

"So, even though the Triad Spirits can't be summoned anymore, portions of their Spiritual Power remain dormant somewhere in their respective kingdoms?" asked Zephyr.

"Correct," replied Dr. Caraway.

"Aramis specialized in powering up the strongest element in the area, or whatever the user specialized in. If we waited any longer to eliminate this sphere, there's no guessing what would happen to how powerful this area was. Though, that's expected with the power granted by Celeste's sister herself."

"You sure know your stuff, Zephyr!" said Dr. Caraway. Skye smiled at this. "All right, whenever you're ready, open it up."

Zephyr retrieved his Communicator and pressed it against the door to the temple, and it opened.

Skye and Zephyr were in front, while the rest of Astro Strike walked behind the research team. The temple was dimly lit with torches hanging on the walls and had flames made of fire aura. Thick pillars made of stone and marble dispersed.

Scorpion and Snake Risen filled the area further ahead, and Zephyr sensed darkness and the fire element from their bodies. There was also a potent, dark presence, stronger than anything he had ever detected. He assumed it was the Dark Sphere.

Up above were staircases and beams made of stone that seemed to connect from one side to another. "Those Risen look ready to ambush anyone who crosses their paths. We have to take out most of them in this section," said Zephyr.

"How?" asked Spark.

"Strike them down from where we can't be seen. We can hide behind the pillars and attack when they aren't looking. Myself, Leif, and Aurora can take out some of them and Spark can rout the rest when the time comes."

For a harder mission like this, Spark would be especially useful, and it made Zephyr's planning easier. Spark backed up different roles, able to serve as a secondary powerhouse or a secondary protector. She was essentially a support unit who could use her skills and utility to bring the entire team together. Combined with her devastating affinity for the lightning element, thanks to her lineage, she was a force to be reckoned with.

The twins moved behind to protect the researchers while they observed the battles to come and recorded everything.

"Spark, now!"

"On it!" Spark grinned, and Zephyr could practically see the fire in her eyes. He'd seen no one so enthusiastic about fighting.

She jumped up, twirling her lance, and struck the air in a downward motion, unleashing a plasma type of shock spreading throughout the battlefield. Lightning bolts appeared from above the enemies, striking through them. The plasma chain multiplied, wrapping around more victims, and electrocuting them. This took out the rest of them in the entire section.

Under normal circumstances, those who could manipulate their aura into the forms of the nine elements would most of the time have an element they had an affinity for. Parts of the team matching algorithms involved elemental affinity, and the organization ensured there was a variety of specializations. Those who had a specialty would require a lot less aura for techniques consisting of the element they were best in. Steps above were Master-level or close to it and required even fewer—Spark's aura levels refused to budge.

"This section should be cleared for investigation now," said Dr. Caraway. "Hang tight for a few moments."

The researchers spread out.

Other Agents scouted the temple before they discovered Dark Spheres, so there was no need to bring any Recon Specialists to map out where everything was inside a man-made building. The researchers took snapshots with the Communicators of all the aura released into the air and examined remains of the Risen. Ice Tetra took more notes and pictures before gesturing to Zephyr to keep moving.

Past the entrance was a maze with magical switches that unlocked different pathways. Getting through it would've been a cinch due to all the information gathered from the Recon Specialists. It didn't seem like the Risen would want to destroy parts of the maze, either. Doing so would make it easier for intruders like themselves. They remained in formation in case any foes lurked in darker areas.

The group continued their way over to the next switch. "You aren't a finalist of the arena challenge for nothing," said Dr. Caraway.

Spark blushed. "Oh, you people know about that?"

Aurora gave her another look.

"I mean, er... It's my pleasure, sir—I mean, doctor! Dr. Sir."

Dr. Caraway seemed amused. "Yes, over at Briton, we always pay attention to the arenas held at our sister Base."

More variations of Scorpion Risen made themselves known as the teams went deeper into the maze, along with regular basilisks.

Zephyr created a ball of wind. It expanded and swept over to the Scorpions. They retaliated and fired pin missiles at him at speeds faster than he could dodge or create glyphs to push the missiles out of the way. As a result, the pins struck him in the arms and legs.

"Zephyr!" yelled the rest of his team.

Skye was about to move, but Shadow ran over to him first, pulling out an antidote from his storage. The others focused on taking out the enemies, while Skye remained in her spot to defend the researchers.

"Ugh..." Zephyr winced as a burning and stinging sensation spread throughout his body and sat down to the side. Nausea hit him and sweat trickled down his forehead.

Shadow untwisted the yellow bottle and poured it down Zephyr's throat. He pulled out the pins and lifted Zephyr's sleeves. The struck areas became blotched with purple. They would continue to spread until the antidote kicked in.

Shadow pressed the switch on his axe, switching it to the staff form. "Hang in there, Zeph." He pressed the staff against one blotch and green sparkles appeared from it, numbing the pain.

The Basilisk Risen looked like a darker, more terrifying version of a regular basilisk. It had a snake-like head, wings of a dragon, a lizard body, and the tail of a serpent. It was green and shrouded with darkness.

"Leif! Watch out!" screamed Aurora.

One let out a blood-curdling screech in Leif's direction and a blast of gray aura emerged from its mouth. In an instant, Leif turned to stone.

Spark rushed over to his side. "Leif! What the...? Leif! You dummy!"

"Spark! Watch out!" yelled Skye, as Spark was a hair's length away from getting turned to stone.

A crashing sound came from Skye's direction, along with Scorpion Risen hisses.

For a second, Zephyr thought he saw duplicates of each of his teammates.

"What do WE DO?" asked Spark, somersaulting to block hits with her shield as a blue magic circle appeared beneath Aurora's feet.

"We learned about them in class," said Aurora. "Get a panacea to Leif ASAP, don't get hit, and make sure they don't attack him."

Right as a whirlpool manifested from Aurora's spell, the ground trembled and more Basilisks emerged, launching blasts at the party, mostly toward Aurora.

"Aurora!" cried Shadow.

"Go... h-help them..." said Zephyr, head spinning.

Without hesitation, Shadow jumped into the fray, shielding Aurora with Diablos' head, only for a beam to bounce off and hit part of the temple's walls, causing part of the room to shake.

"They'll target longer-ranged units, right?" asked Shadow. "We just gotta not ALL get hit!"

Spark ducked to block another blow, shooting lightning out of her lance, killing one before it got to Leif. Three foes directed their next hits toward Spark.

Aurora nodded. "Spark, keep diverting their attention. You, too, Shadow."

"Gotcha!"

Shadow created threads of darkness while Spark continued with her jolts and bolts. Basilisks kept turning back and forth, as if puzzled. They directed most of their next rounds of attacks toward Spark and Shadow.

Aurora conjured more whirlpools to entrap the Risen and Spark stabbed the ground with her lance, allowing the water to conduct her shock waves, disintegrating them.

"Leif!" Spark sprinted over to his statue-like state and sighed with relief.

Aurora poured the bottle on him. "That was a close one."

"No kidding," said Zephyr. The pain decreased, and the blotches faded.

All the colors returned to Leif's body. "Whoa! I can move again! Not gonna lie, petrification was kinda cool!"

"Don't say that, ya dunce!" yelled Spark.

They didn't have any other mishaps with monsters for the rest of the journey through the temple. Zephyr sensed the dark presence getting stronger as they worked their way into the deepest part of the temple.

A floating platform separated the last area.

This was it: Aramis's lair. There was a pedestal and gravitating above it was a Dark Sphere. As they originally thought, there were even stronger Risen protecting it.

Upon spotting the party, they shrieked and morphed into a giant raven.

Nevermore Risen could spawn minions from their bodies and self-regenerate. The raven could also deal damage at a fast pace. With the six of them, however, it should be relatively straightforward, especially since it was a Level 3 Risen. A more tedious monster to deal with, but its defences were low once one got past its healing capabilities.

Spark and Leif were skilled with aerial combat, and Zephyr could use his glyphs to give himself and the others a boost. Aurora chipped away at its health with stone blasts while Leif could jump up and take care of the minions. Zephyr created a wind blast with his katana, knocking it against the wall.

When distracted enough, Spark leaped up onto its back and stabbed it with her lance, resulting in it crashing to the ground.

The four of them launched their attacks simultaneously, and it burst into nothingness.

The Researchers spread out throughout the room to do their thing. "Every time there's a Dark Sphere, the most powerful Risen, AKA the 'Boss,' would defend it," observed Dr. Caraway. "It's clear the sphere powers up all of them and helps create spawns, but we don't know how they are created."

"These spheres are a mere supplement to what caused them to become so much more horrifying over the past years," said another. "The data shows they're too weak to be accurate sources of the waves."

"It looks like we're done here," said Dr. Caraway. "One of you can destroy the sphere."

"I've got it," said Skye.

She drew her sword and stepped up to the pedestal.

Before she could strike at the sphere, a dark void appeared further from her right. A hooded figure in black robes emerged from the void. The figure released a bolt of electricity out of their hands with extreme speed, sending her flying backward.

17

CHANNELING

SKYE

SKYE LANDED ON THE GROUND, UNSCATHED ON THE OPPOSITE SIDE OF the pedestal. Pointing her sword at the figure, blasts of light burst out, forcing the figure to focus on evading. "Get them out of here!"

"Right!" said Leif. He and Aurora briskly escorted the researchers out of the room while Skye created earth walls to keep the figure away.

The figure skirted around Spark and Zephyr, releasing air thrusts to knock them to the side. They launched more bolts at Skye from different angles, and she disappeared and reappeared to evade. Electric bullets shot at her from the figure's fists, and she deflected the rest with her blade. A sword made of lightning appeared in the foe's hands and a battle of the blades occurred, clashing each time, and sending each other flying.

Clashing once more, the figure used their non-sword hand to shoot more bullets. Skye jumped to deflect them more. Whenever Shadow charged at them, the figure moved closer toward Skye.

Astro Strike needed as much information from the enemy alive. Skye couldn't make any guarantees, however. One false move toward her team, and she would've ended them.

Spark and Zephyr struck. The figure evaded their attacks with little effort and knocked them backwards in retaliation.

"Don't come closer!" said Skye, redirecting a lightning attack launched in their direction. Gold filled her eyes as she felt the surging power of her boost coarse through her veins.

Skye's durability shield coated her.

Spark and Zephyr hesitated and backed away.

A click came from Shadow's direction.

Shadow pointed his staff at the opponent. They would've been moving far too fast for Shadow to charge anything and throw it at the foe without hitting Skye.

A crackling sound came from behind Skye, and a giant bolt of lightning shot through her body. Before she could do anything, a chain reaction of electric explosions hit her and she crashed into a pillar, slamming against it and causing it to shatter.

"Skye!" yelled the witnesses.

Her body slowed and remained static. It seemed like the figure was only targeting her, so they would've been fine—she could tank twenty-seconds worth of direct hits before she recovered and could move again.

The figure appeared in front of her, and Shadow jumped in, blocking a hit from his staff intended for her. Shadow attempted to protect himself from more of their attacks. Eventually, the enemy moved at a pace her brother couldn't keep up with, almost getting hit a few times.

Skye recovered in time to redirect a hit that would've been fatal for her brother. She grit her teeth, ready to draw blood. "I told you to stay back!"

"I'm not gonna watch ya get hurt!" Shadow continued, switching Diablos to axe form.

"No-" Shadow threw the head of the axe and enveloped it with a light blue aura.

They grabbed the head and charged it with electricity, throwing it back at him. It hit the pillar next to him, causing chunks of debris to fall.

"SHADOW!" Her heart beat so violently she thought it would burst out of her chest. Skye boosted herself, speeding to his side, cutting through the chunks into millions of pieces before they hit.

Lightning struck Skye before she could feel relieved. Electricity spread within her body, rendering her catatonic once again. Shadow was about to slam Diablos against them, but electric bullets landed, paralyzing him.

Her body recovered faster than before. She caught him, disappearing and reappearing next to Spark and Zephyr, throwing her knives at the enemy, using her aura to tail him. Skye handed Shadow to them.

Skye disappeared and reappeared again, slashing at the hooded figure, bloodlust flowing through her. None of her blades could pierce their skin—adding fuel to the rage growing inside Skye.

Darkness manifested in Skye's chest, along with the all-too-familiar voice in her head. *Kill. Them.*

Skye drew the power from her stone, the power she loathed for so long, the power that wasn't hers to begin with, boosting her elemental powers with all her might. She spun, creating a fiery vortex, transforming into a star made of flames, enveloping their body. They created a ball of lightning, absorbing the flames. She did a spin kick in the air and punched the figure, slamming the foe to the ground, creating cracks.

Crashing fatigue crept into Skye's insides.

They created a storm of lightning bolts, enhanced with darkness. Skye and the knives returned to her side, creating earth blocks, protecting her. The blocks turned into the shape of a serpent dragon, knocking them backward. Skye glared at the figure and lifted her sword, charging it with a dark blue aura. They created a ball of electricity, also charging it up.

Blasts launched at the same time and hers overpowered the enemy's, causing most of their electricity to disappear and the impact hit them. They vanished into the dark void, but the remaining electricity transformed into a beam and hit her in the chest. She remained standing, albeit jolted back.

Dammit! Skye clenched her fists. *That should've been easy!*

"Skye!" Zephyr ran up to her and put his hands on her shoulders. "Are you okay?" Worry filled his turquoise eyes.

Despite getting hit by the beam, she felt no more sparks running through her body. "I think so."

Skye looked at Zephyr's hands on her shoulders and she felt the heat rush to her cheeks, and he turned pink as well, retracting them.

Spark treated an unconscious Shadow with medicine. "Dude! Who WAS that?"

"I don't know," said Skye, trying to mask the tension in her voice. "How's Shadow?"

"He's okay, just recovering."

Relief washed through her. Shadow was only paralyzed... Had it been more, Skye would've imagined her dark form emerging. And she didn't know what she would've done if Zephyr caught sight of that. She didn't want to see him react to her tearing apart the assaulter, limb from limb.

"Good. Let's destroy this sphere."

"Are you sure you don't want to wait a bit and recover?" asked Zephyr.

"I should do it before anything else jumps out at us," replied Skye. "I can take another hit from the sphere and drink an Elixir right after."

⸱⸱⦅⸱⸱

ONCE SKYE FINISHED DESTROYING the sphere, everyone retreated to an inn in Gessu.

Zephyr insisted on carrying Shadow on his back, despite his heaving bouts of exhaustion. There was a back room the innkeeper generously let them use for the time being for their call.

"He's an idiot," said Aurora, exhaling as they set Shadow down on a bed in the boys' room. "Why does he always want to be the hero who saves the day?"

Zephyr put the covers on Shadow. "It's frustrating. And

dangerous."

Skye wondered if Shadow's actions had anything to do with Saylor's fate, alongside his frequent need for validating praise.

They didn't stay long—debriefing with the President was next.

Astro Strike and Ice Tetra stood around Zephyr's floating Communicator in the spare room.

President Ziel's holographic image manifested above the device. "Keep up the wonderful work, everyone! As for the person in the hood, there's never been an occurrence involving such persons attacking. . ."

"Are there any further leads related to Cerberus or Thanatos?" asked Zephyr.

"Royal Garde and the Marauders are investigating Cerberus's headquarters in Thet. No other reports about sightings regarding Thanatos members have been made. However, this is the first time we've received word of lightning abilities quite like that," replied Ziel.

"Those were insanely strong!" said Spark. "Couldn't recognize some of their techniques. Could rival Typhon Electro's power!"

"If only we had someone like Electro with us," said a researcher. "Or the rest of the Typhons. If one can enhance an element with darkness... and manipulate lightning in ways unseen for decades... it could result from the Heracles Serum."

"All nations have been told to keep their eyes open," said Ziel. "They've granted us permission to conduct more thorough searches through civilization."

Why... did the person come after solely her? Skye set her suspicions on Cerberus for the time being. Skye took deep breaths, to not allow her emotions to consume her, taking Dove and Aqua's advice.

Scientists and apothecaries concocted remedies for the curse over the years—so far, they made medicines to quell the special darkness that manifested within Skye. Although it appeared far less frequently in times of Skye's distress, it wasn't completely effective.

Shadow entered the room after the President explained logistics for their next mission and signed off.

"What're you doing out of bed?" asked Skye.

Shadow gave her a thumbs up. "I'm fine. A little electricity won't hurt me."

Skye didn't have the heart to lecture him as of now. She hoped he'd take it as a lesson to not do it again.

"What about you, Skye? Those attacks weren't anything ordinary," said Zephyr, with a slight edge in his tone. "Do you need to rest or anything?"

"I'm okay."

"But-"

Leif had his arms behind his head. "C'mon, Zeph! They're okay! They'll catch z's when we're ready!"

Skye silently thanked him. Since their "spat" at Castor, such disagreements hadn't come up again.

"Hmm, I guess you're right," said Zephyr.

"Don't dwell on it for now," said a researcher. "Focus on recovering from the cumbersome mission."

After the meeting adjourned and a quick dinner, Skye decided to check inventory outside and get some fresh air. A drop of sweat trickled down the gutter of her back. Tying her hair into a high ponytail, she secured it with a turquoise scrunchie. Wind came in off the horizon, bringing in the desert's scent of sand, ruffling the stray hairs at the nape of her neck.

Skye rolled her shoulders. Her muscles were still stiff from her earlier battle and her forearms ached. She wanted to submerge her body into ice water at some point.

Spark popped up with Zephyr and Aurora. "Whatcha up to?"

"Checking on everyone's stuff."

"That's nice of you," said Aurora, holding a box of matches. "We're practicing our aura control! Swifty gave us some exercises to go through."

"Spark and Rory are," said Zephyr. "I'm observing since I need to rest up."

Spark used a lot of her aura in their last mission. Her stamina and endurance impressed Skye.

"Where's the others?" asked Skye.

"Gaming," replied the others.

"Why aura control?"

"Only thing stopping me from being a Lightning Master!" said Spark. "I could've countered whoever attacked us if I had better control."

Skye nodded. "Wish I could do more to help with that. Good on you for going to Swifty."

Skye's excessive aura reserves made aura control difficult. Aqua immensely helped mitigate the issue. It could never be as good as Aurora or Shadow's, however.

Aura control granted users the ability to manipulate shapes of the elemental techniques they used. Spark's bolts, currents, shock waves, and everything else were some of the most powerful displays of lightning aura she had ever seen. If she could shape it into more than a chain, Spark could become S-ranked before the others. Spark was at the top of their class for combat—the best secondary power-house and defender in decades. Technically, Spark was part of their enormous and convoluted family tree, albeit distantly spaced from the twins.

Every Dream Team had at least one Combat Squad member. The coveted position was a tossup between Spark or Blaze until Skye became a Host. Astro Strike needed another unit honed on the defensive side aside from Shadow, and Nova Strike thrived with Blaze's placement.

Spark would've been a far better mentor. At least her power's legit.

"Well, you're getting close to achieving your dream," said Zephyr sweetly.

"Course! I'll be on par with Swifty!" Marauder Swifty was the only other Agent who rivaled Spark with lightning specialization. "And hopefully, you'll one day agree to spar with me, Rory!" The two were both trained by Swifty at one point, so it made sense.

"Right..." said Aurora.

"Then, I'll take on Leif, Shadow, and YOU, Zeph!" said Spark.

The familiar fire in her eyes appeared again.

"Ready when you are," said Zephyr.

Spark pointed at Skye. "I got no chance against you now! But our fight when I become a Lightning Master'll be legendary!"

Skye smiled. "You can use what you've learned on me whenever I'm free."

You guys are going to go far. I'm proud of you all.

Skye's thirst for battling used to be unquenchable; it used to make her think she could conquer anything. Sparring classes were her favorite. It was one thing she felt competitive about. And was good at it. Everything else that had to do with being an Agent was mediocre to poor.

"When will that be?" asked Aurora.

"After Star Strike saves the worlds and kicks the Risen outta this century!"

"Always loved your enthusiasm, Spark," said Zephyr. "Definitely boosts morale."

"Sure hope so! Wasn't blessed with all this energy for nothin'!" said Spark.

Aurora sighed. "I sure hope it wasn't for nothing." Aurora and Spark grabbed a match. "All right, focus your aura on your fingertips."

"Okay!" Her hand glowed. "Dang it!" The glow remained around her hand.

"No worries, keep trying," said Zephyr gently. "It took me forever to get it to my fingertips." Skye wondered when Aurora walked him through the same exercise. Of course, she wasn't home enough back then to know.

"No biggie!" The match exploded and puffs of smoke appeared. "At least it destroyed nothing in the city!"

Skye's skin prickled. *Did she hear about the watermelons?*

"Speaking from personal experience?" asked Zephyr.

"Yeah. Accidentally set some kid's treehouse on fire!" said Spark.

Skye sighed.

Zephyr chuckled. "When is someone's treehouse NOT on fire

thanks to us?"

Spark elbowed Skye. "Or sheds!"

"Oh, I forgot about that!" Aurora snickered. "Skye and the out of control axe swings."

"Yeah! How'd it hit the same elderly couples' sheds EVERY TIME?" asked Spark.

Skye cringed. Glares from the elderly woman sent chills down her spine. Whenever that woman dropped off cookies at her doorstep, she'd give Shadow, Cynthia, and her parents chocolate chip ones, leaving Skye with the atrocious, revolting... oatmeal raisin ones... She was half-convinced it was a new form of child abuse.

The others laughed. They'd found it... funny? Skye supposed it was. Would the watermelon incident be considered funny later, too? After Aurora lectured her, neither she nor Zephyr brought it up again. She'd get dirty looks in towns or whispers. What mattered most was what her friends thought.

The bracelets she cursed herself for wearing back then... were mere shackles reminding her of her sins. She was selfishly glad none of her teammates used them for training or needed it. It would've been too triggering.

Skye looked up from inventory frequently to watch. The first training session she held was a disaster, but she hoped she'd gotten better at demonstrating and explaining since. It had been a while since they worked on durability, but they had time.

Spark yawned after a few more attempts. "Think that's enough training for today."

"Keep up the good work," said Skye.

The blonde grinned. "Thanks! Hands are numb and I don't wanna burn the inn down."

"Not the most desirable outcome, yeah," said Zephyr.

"I'd say! That was a good trainin' session!" Spark pointed her fist at Zephyr, who bumped it with his own. She walked toward Skye with her hand held high. Skye stared at it, slowly lifting her fist, and touching Spark's palm. "Yer supposed to gimme a high-five!"

"Oh." Skye raised her hand to try again but retracted it as soon as Spark turned toward Aurora to do the same.

Aurora grabbed Spark's arm. "Are you coming, Skye?"

"Actually, I was about to ask her about the plan for tomorrow," said Zephyr.

"Ya just wanted your alone time with her," said Spark, elbowing Zephyr twice. "Boss sure is sly! All right, see ya later, lovebirds!"

She and Aurora smirked at the pair as they strolled into the inn.

Zephyr scratched his head. "Wanna look it over? I should've asked you earlier, sorry."

She nodded, and they sat down.

His Communicator displayed the map for tomorrow's mission. He made a note of hazardous zones and speculated about where the Dark Sphere would be if there was one. Zephyr also listed the known monsters there and different battle strategies and formations, jotting them down on the screen.

"Your planning is solid," said Skye.

"Awesome." He put his Communicator back into his jacket pocket. They sat there in silence for a bit, and Skye noticed how bright the stars were. "You know…"

Skye could see a dusting of cinnamon freckles on his nose. It was faint, but she could only see it because she sat so close. Her heart stuttered faster as his gaze locked on hers and she fumbled with the miniature panda charm wrapped around her belt.

WHY IS HE STARING AT ME LIKE THAT? OH GODS! Do I have cookie crumbs left on my face? She wiped her chin, thankfully not feeling any stray crumbs.

"I appreciate everything you've done for us. Without you, I wouldn't have had as successful missions, and I really owe a lot to you." His deep, gravelly voice went quiet.

"That's nothing compared to what you did for me back then," said Skye in a whisper.

Skye noticed the spots of brightness in the dark skies. They were extra bright that night. Zephyr was the only one she wanted to watch the stars with.

18

SHRINKING VIOLET

LUNA

STAR STRIKE HAD SUBSEQUENT SUCCESSFUL MISSIONS. EVERYONE HAD a role in eliminating the Dark Spheres. Normally, this impressed most, but it hardly fazed Luna.

Luna paid attention to every weekly report. She told Skye about the average or below average performances of some of their teammates prior and could only hope the reserved girl would speak up to them about it. Nowadays, they were above average, so she believed she did. It was better... for now.

Times were too hectic for her to pay anymore attention to how Astro Strike was doing. Luna had been juggling her own training, ensuring Nova Strike's progress went well, searching for evidence on who was behind the creation of the Dark Spheres, and seeing what updates were going on amongst the higher-ups.

Blaze and Glacieus were at Pollux's Base, and Nova Strike was getting accustomed to where they could reunite with Astro Strike for bigger missions. Glacieus and Stream had more tasks for their respective fields before they could join up, but it wasn't an issue, since Dark Sphere eliminations didn't require them. Being busy helped, to an extent. She'd also check up on Twilight Treader and Glacieus on occasion.

"Luna?" She turned when she heard the sweet voice.

A brunette with a golden-bronze complexion and sapphire-blue eyes appeared. A pendant around her neck matched the blue streak in her straight hair. Her short-sleeved, silver dress with a high-low skirt had white stockings underneath, reaching her thighs, and paired with silver boots. Two cyan belts crossed her waist and trimming of the same shade lined edges of her sleeves and gray gloves that reached her elbows.

Stream was a style icon. A woman of glamor. A graceful woman with an eye for the finer things in life. She made Luna appreciate it all.

Luna smiled when Stream gave her a hug. Most of the time, she hated physical touch. Unless it was her. "Hope you're ready, Princess."

Stream smiled in a way that lit up rooms. Only Luna could call her that nickname. "I know I'll be safe with you around."

Luna wanted to spend time with Stream. Seeing her made Luna's breath come to a stalemate. Notes of longing struck a chord in Luna's chest, and she struggled to tone it down. This *wasn't* the time for distractions.

Their mission at Sevinnon Gorge, bordering Silvatica, would be an excellent training exercise for Stream. Higher-ups suspected the gorge to have a Dark Sphere because of its history of odd weather patterns and hosting Spiritual Power. Astro Strike went through the area last but found nothing noteworthy.

Once they were at the entrance of the gorge, Stream pressed a switch on her gloves and silver claws shot out of the knuckles.

Luna stepped forward with Stream following, and they stopped as soon as they saw a giant, poisonous Sevinnon Flytrap.

Stream retrieved a small capsule, and it floated.

An antenna poked out and Luna detected an aura from it, directing toward the plant, causing the capsule to glow. "Smooth," said Luna. "How long did it take you to build that thing?"

"From the ground up, two weeks."

Luna shook her head, amazed. "They should promote you

beyond Tech Specialist III already." Stream was already the youngest unit within that ranking and made the most contributions with creating their devices at her age.

"I don't think I'm ready to be working in the same rank as Blossom." The brunette checked her blinking Communicator and Luna peered over her shoulder, catching a whiff of jasmine and freesia. A diagram appeared on her screen showing graphs, listing the detected toxins and aura levels.

"Looks exact to me," said Luna. "Let's check the others."

They came across a noxious flower field soon after. Everything looked like a pretty arrangement of tulips to the naked eye, but monsters opted to hide within the petals. As soon as they stepped into it, the tulips enlarged themselves to the size of cattle. Stream set up the capsule once again, and the duo waited for the wasp monsters to fly out.

Stream summoned her water aura, and it covered her claws. Dodging a sting from one, she threw the other set, and they spun, creating a torrent. The edges returned to her gloves, and she leaped into the air and swiped at the rest.

"That was risky of me," said Stream. The tulips returned to their normal size. "One misstep and they could've stung me."

Expectations combat-wise for Stream weren't as high as others. If she didn't have strong DNA from the water worlds of Piscium and potential to be a solid support unit and quick fighter, being solely an Agent in the Tech Department would've been fine for her. They placed her on Star Strike and Nova Strike for a reason. When Stream wasn't busy building devices to help Lumière Inc., she played a similar role in battle as Luna.

"Don't be afraid to take risks. Use your judgment and one of us can help if need be." Monsters here weren't particularly threatening —the most they could do is inflict minor wounds.

"Looks like it's only gathering one section of the field and not all of it."

Luna perused the information. "Anything outside of a ten-foot span looks inaccurate."

"Exactly." Stream jotted this down on the notes app. "I'll have to do some adjustments to get it all regardless of distance."

"We should check the ivies next and see if you get the same issues."

More powerful monsters blocked their path when they crossed the river to get to another section of the gorge. This time, there were slugs and slimes, who were agitating to fight as soon as they got up too close and latched onto one's body.

She remained behind Stream, and a white magic circle appeared below her. Luna focused her aura on herself and Stream, targeting her. A red glow covered Stream's body, powering up her offensive attacks. Stream had the latent power to do the same someday.

Stream dashed forward, spinning around rapidly and she turned herself into a whirlwind of flying claws, charging toward them. It destroyed all but one slug that was attached to Stream's upper arm, sapping her aura, and she yelped in pain, slicing through it with her other set of claws.

Luna placed her right hand on Stream's upper arm, mending Stream's wounds with a green glow. She only knew two healing techniques. Sufficient for Unity Squad. It wasn't enough to be a primary healer like Shadow or Aurora, but Nova Strike could sustain themselves given this and Blaze's high defences. All teams had someone with at least one or two healing spells as an alternative to using items in a pinch.

Ivies hugged canyon walls up ahead. Stream went further into detail about what needed updates with her radar capsule. Sevinnon Fowl flew around, landing nearby and pecking at the ground.

Willow trees were next. These were more hidden, and a Golem blocked their path. It launched stone blasts at them. Stream attempted to block the blasts with her claws, enlarging them with metal aura.

Luna created another white magic circle targeting Stream. It soon covered the brunette in a white aura, increasing her defences. This happened conveniently right before a blast hit Stream, but barely affected her.

"Nice!"

"Keep focusing on the Golem."

Luna threw her whip, holding the Golem's arms in place with it like a lasso.

Stream powered up her claws with ice aura and slashed at it again, barely affecting it. A clear shield covered the Golem's body.

Stream retracted her claws and her gloves glowed black. She remained close to the Golem and moved her hands around, jabbing into different spots around its arms and body with her fingers. The glow around the Golem disappeared, and it attempted to shoot more stone blasts at them, but nothing happened.

Stream zipped through, jumping and back flipping as she continued to land more and more strikes on the Golem, causing it to explode into nothingness.

"Excellent," said Luna.

"That was a little freaky."

Stream gathered the same information as before in the willows. For smaller plants, Luna watched her nimble fingers type at swift speeds to adjust the settings. This was the same woman who could breach security systems in mere seconds during practice sessions.

Unity Squad trained Luna within the Tech Department as well—disabling systems and the sort was a skill useful for over one member of Star Strike. Although she had exceptional expertise, Luna was nowhere near Stream's level—she couldn't build and design gadgets. She was no prodigy like Stream.

The biggest feat Stream accomplished that day was blocking the aura points of the Golem. So far, it only worked on humans since monsters were always inconsistent with where their aura points were located. It was a useful skill to have, even if it seldom worked on more formidable fighters.

Hues of red and orange stretched far and wide, bold as the colors of Aurora's hair and Leif's vests sitting within the sky. Hotter months were approaching, and up above would eventually resemble a hariberry shaded crown before twilight seduced the stars into arrival.

Stream's aura levels depleted. "We'll continue tomorrow."

Stream sighed in relief. "Thank Celeste."

"You thought I'd work you to the bone?"

"I figured you'd come close since this is my only fighting mission for the week."

"Your reserves are growing faster than expected. You haven't used them a ton during training, it seems. Recently, at least."

Stream pondered as they continued their path. "Yeah... I spent too much time focusing on my solutions that I missed some hours."

"Gotta give your mind a break with exercise. Otherwise, you wouldn't be as worn down."

"I'll make it up to you. Promise."

"How about you partially make it up to me by getting in those missed hours and coming to our favorite chocolatier on our next day off? They've got extra-dark chocolate now with no sugar, which is great for your skin. So, you better come and eat up *this* time."

Stream grinned. "The things I would do for perfect skin like yours."

"What do you mean? Yours is already perfect. Like a princess." Luna's smirk increased when she saw Stream's cheeks burn.

Sugar used to be Stream and Aurora's worst enemy. They were the last people who needed to cut it out to maintain their figures. Luna was glad they weren't stupid enough to follow dieting tips most socialites swore by. Fad diets rose and fell quickly within Garnet City, just like fashion trends. As much as Luna appreciated those who took care of their appearance, some Garnetites pushed the boundaries of common sense.

Their laughs were cut short when Luna detected individuals near the entrance.

"Someone's here."

No forms of darkness had been recognized; these people must've strolled in.

Five wore the same tacky Cerberus uniforms with expandable bags strapped around their shoulders.

Some placed herbs in vials. Others looked up when the girls approached.

"Isn't it against Sevinnon policy to pass their borders and take their property?" asked Luna.

Stream remained hidden behind her, pressing a button on her Communicator. Luna didn't need to turn to see the fear in Stream's eyes. She resisted the urge to squeeze Stream's hand.

"We have permission, like you," said a sneering Cerberus member. Another held up a seal on their mobile device—the Sevinnon National Symbol. "We have business operating here."

"What are you doing with the herbs?" asked Luna. She was aware of other nations granting Cerberus access to their resources, but Sevinnon would've been the least likely to agree to it.

"What's this? ANOTHER interrogation?" The Cerberus member rolled her eyes. "What does it look like? We're trying to improve Heracles. That's it. We don't need you AND Royal Garde up our asses, watchin' every move."

Last Luna heard, they searched all Bases belonging to Cerberus. They found labs filled with flora and research pertaining to drug effects on aura. Nothing related to Mutations or Dark Spheres. Yet.

"I don't know why y'all treat us like we're criminals. Lumière Inc. has been more of an obnoxious nuisance than anything. So, can ya please leave us alone?"

"You wouldn't have been able to come here if it weren't for us, getting rid of the haze." Luna studied their faces and undertones, wishing Blaze was around to hear pulses to check for lies. "What does Heracles currently do? If you provide more info now, we'll hound you less later."

One sighed, eyeing Luna's whip. "You can detect auras, right? You got the eyes. Well, kinda." Metal covered him, turning into armor.

A shroud covered the interior of his body, rendering the metal aura more concentrated, stronger than normal. The figure in the cloak she encountered at Thet Wetlands didn't have the same effect.

"Try darkness." Darkness replaced the silver aura, hardening as armor—nowhere near the amount of darkness detected from the cloaked figure. "So, it makes it easier for you to manipulate your aura with that shroud."

"No sign of Alchemist abilities returning. Or anything of the sort," replied the man.

"What about manipulating Spiritual Power?" He shook his head. "Enhancing Risen?"

"Why'd we do that?" asked a Cerberus lackey. "Royal Garde asked the same thing about modifying Risen."

"Satisfied, now?" asked the female Cerberus member. "We don't have all the time in the world."

Piss off, woman.

Luna had to bite her tongue to prevent herself from giving the woman a piece of her mind.

There was no other new information Luna could extract for the time being. "Fine. Carry on. But don't expect this to be the last time we meet."

Stream followed her out.

"That was scary," said Stream, after a long silence. "But what they said... sounded true."

"We can't speak for the entire faction. But I know those guys weren't whoever was in the cloaks. Anyways, you recorded everything, didn't you?"

Stream nodded. "We can identify them easily."

"Good work."

Cerberus wasn't off the hook. Unknown variables remained. At least they had more confirmation, but it was another headache.

Luna let her mind rest before she went insane.

⁙

UPON ENTERING the inn and walking to the receptionist counter, Stream looked at her, expecting her to go up first. Luna motioned for her. "H-hi! I-I would like to get a double w-with... her."

Luna wondered if they'd ever share a bed. She found Stream's shyness endearing. Nervous flutters manifested within Luna's chest around Stream ever since they were younger. Unfortunately, her favorite cousin caught onto her feelings for the brunette.

Zephyr tried to give as much advice as any ten-year-old could like the sweet idiot he was. Of course, he knew little about relationships. The only one who ended up having relationship experience was Luna herself, but none of the sub-par guys and girls she dated before lasted long due to her hectic schedule. Glacieus was the only one she could confide in. Even though he only dated men, his impossibly high standards made his relationships end quickly. The organization encouraged relationships within teams and departments because of common experiences and schedules.

Their Communicators beeped not long after dinner. Two towering holographic images appeared before them in their room once Luna answered the call.

"Lunie! Streamie! How's it going?" Glacieus's grayish-green eyes twinkled when he called them by the hair-raising cutesy names. Much to her chagrin, others caught onto his habit.

"Don't call me that!" Luna snapped at the dirty-blond man-child.

Glacieus blew a raspberry, and she tapped her foot. "Is there a reason to call other than being annoying?"

"We have updates," said Blaze.

"We do, too," said Luna. "I'll go first."

"I see," said Blaze, frowning after Luna filled them in. "Doesn't rule them out. Cerberus could be divided amongst other possibilities. Maybe those with the special darkness abilities are the only ones in cloaks."

"Weird how they've always worn them whenever spotted. Maybe something to do with the darkness they create?" asked Stream.

"Would make sense," replied Blaze.

"Anyways, what's been going on your end?" asked Luna.

"Dawn Brigade thinks whoever's causing all of this crap has a hidden hideout," said Glacieus. "As in, hidden by a barrier. An undetectable Base or something underground."

"Anything visible in terms of a Base has already been looked into. With no more reported ex-Thanatos members and all known Cerberus locations searched, it's possible," said Luna.

"Who can make a barrier that strong?" asked Stream. "Do you think either has that level of tech?"

"We won't know, unless we figure out how to detect hypothetical barriers," said Blaze.

"That could take ages," said Stream, sounding defeated. "We only just learned how to detect gasses, but even those have a long way to go before release."

"Well, I think the undetectable idea sounds workable," said Luna. "We have a way to go before checking every centimeter of Eta Geminorum. Stream, once we're done with tomorrow, I'll have you go to Pollux. I have to see how Astro Strike is doing in the meantime."

Blaze sighed. "It'll take forever before we can take another step in fixing all of this." He seemed impatient and Luna couldn't blame him.

"They've been digging deeper into the Typhons' old prototypes with detection radars here at Pollux. Maybe we'll try something similar with barriers," said Glacieus, sounding hopeful. "Tech people here think Electro's last theories on how sensors can detect pulses and waves with the use of Mythril and Azoth might be onto something."

"Can't wrap my mind around how that stuff works," said Blaze. "It's still a longshot since his theories existed twenty years ago. And were mostly untested."

Out of Nova Strike, instructors trained Blaze the least within the non-Combat areas. Although he had virtually nonexistent skill in the art of Tech, his major strengths were within fighting and possessing heightened, Morphic senses. He and Stream had a decent grasp of Recon as well.

"Wait, what theories?" asked Stream.

"Blossom had the idea to check the Communicator found at the Labyrinth all those years ago again," replied Glacieus.

"Thought they checked everything when they first got ahold of it," said Luna.

Decades ago, the Labyrinth appeared for the first time in centuries. Once it spawned beneath the Mortal Realm's surface, it would remain for a century. Since it was linked to the Underworld, many believed it could lead them to figuring out how to stop the rise in darkness. It was the biggest risk ever taken. No Mortal in history had gone in without aid from the Gods.

Nobody heard from the Typhons again after the Labyrinth Expedition. Any rescue missions dispatched to the Labyrinth resulted in few returning alive. Until they had a surefire way to enter, leaders of nations and the organization agreed to block the entrance. The entrance teleported whenever unopened for more than a year and assumed a distinct form each time.

"He upped the security on that thing," said Glacieus. "Very hidden file, but that's all we found."

"I suppose that's some glimmer of hope," said Luna. "Typhons carrying us, even now." She knew she could count on the elite, even those who were no longer alive.

19

SNEAK ATTACK
SHADOW

TODAY'S JOB WAS A CINCH. THEIR TARGET WAS TO CLEAR THE RISEN nests around Port Kilia. Astro Strike located the nests and demolished them in record time. As soon as they wrapped up, they set out toward the port town to rest up for the night.

The next day, Astro Strike would take a ship to the Aquarius Islands. It was impossible to teleport there thanks to magnetic fields and other scientific mumbo jumbo Shadow couldn't remember.

Port Kilia was in northern Taonia, facing the sea on the western part of Solaria and southwest of Silvatica. It was Taonia's primary source of trade, part of the smaller, non-desert section of the kingdom. At Aquarius, they were to meet up with Ice Tetra again and Luna.

Little was on the outer edges of the port, aside from woodlands that served as a border between Taonia and Silvatica.

"Hey, Skye!" Skye turned to Spark as they passed through the trees. "You always use Excalibur. Was wonderin' if ya wanted an upgrade, dude!"

Excalibur never left Skye's sight, unless stored, always in tip-top shape. Skye always kept her knives on her as well—for killing Risen and for those trying to touch Excalibur.

"That's all right."

"If ya ever change yer mind, lemme know."

"Hmm. . . Modifying Excalibur wouldn't fit," remarked Zephyr. "Its two forms are iconic. Everyone recognized Seren Adnet, and nobody saw her without Excalibur in the news." Its default form had a white and gold blade with a gold, wing-looking cross guard, black grip, and gold pommel.

"Public would go nuts, too. With how often people talk about Excalibur," said Aurora. Excalibur was notorious for its ability to change form depending on how much Spiritual Power was used.

Shadow and Cynthia's healing abilities had Spiritual Power—a type of energy that belonged to immortals, being stronger than aura. It was more tiresome to use, but more effective, exclusive to bloodlines related to or blessed by Celeste or Celestria. Skye only had Spiritual Power in her light-based attacks. Thanks to their Alchemist blood, Leif, Glacieus, and Spark also had fragments.

Excalibur served as a family heirloom and unintended to be passed down. The twins had their fighting styles focused on axes, and the organization projected Cynthia to be a dual blade user. After Skye joined Combat Squad, she stopped using axes and used Excalibur instead. Shadow wasn't sure what caused the transition.

"Didn't yer great-grandma have a special sword, too?" asked Spark. "That katana? Both that and Excalibur had its crazy way to channel aura and Spiritual Power!"

Shadow nodded. "It got destroyed! During an insane battle!"

"Nobody in Eta Geminorum can recreate a blade like them," said Zephyr. "Craftsmen in Tau Geminorum were something else, but it's interesting how coincidentally similar some weapons were in other worlds. That, and some customs."

Zephyr continued his rambling about how cultures throughout histories of migration. Shadow quit listening. Watching leaves fall seemed more interesting.

"Now that I think about it, you people don't switch yer weapons enough!" said Spark.

Agents kept at least two or three spare weapons stored. Shadow mainly wielded Diablos but switched between Maimer or Braver.

"Welp, we don't need thousands of weapons like YOU, bro!" said Leif, tossing a chakram into the air and twirling it with his finger.

Before long, Shadow saw docks at the right hand side of Port Kilia with larger ships of every kind planted—including one's belonging to the organization, pulsing with the rush and hurly burly of trade. Waves crashed in the distance and gulls squawked.

The entrance was on the left side, paved with brick and had a "Welcome" sign. An inn stood across the street, neighboring a Panda Emporium. Blocks of houses and warehouses painted in a variety of colors screamed to stand out. Children ran, playing StrikeBall with wooden swords.

A tide of passerby flowed into the streets that held a sprawling array of shops and markets. Shopkeepers set up stands with free samples of desert crabs and coffee. Traders possessed pearls and other sea jewels. Faint scents of the sea came from piles of freshly caught fish with bright eyes.

"We should explore!" exclaimed Zephyr.

"I'm going to rest up," said Skye.

Zephyr nodded. "Take all the time you need."

Skye left toward the inn. Shadow assumed she was tired from the "mysterious missions."

Everyone else stepped onto the brick paths, slipping into the traffic of travelers and individuals dressed in brown robes who Shadow assumed were members of Taonia's nomadic groups.

"So, Port Kilia was a more recent addition after Taonia dismantled its isolationist policies way back when! Itself, Gessu's urban sections, and Taonia's capital, vastly differed from its desert towns. It became a recurring tourist spot, and their plentiful shops around the harbors are ones to look at!" said Zephyr, seeing if anyone was listening.

"Sea-salt ice cream?" asked Spark. She pointed at a chalkboard sign in front of a hut on the boardwalk, listing it as the "flavor of the day."

"It's famous around here!" said Zephyr. "Kinda salty at first but then sweet with a vanilla flavor. We could store some in our freezers for Skye when she's done resting."

"Aww, that's sweet," said Aurora. "She'd like that. I wonder if they have yummy cookies too."

Spark tapped her finger against her chin. "Never thought of sea-salt on ice cream. But, hey! I'll try it."

Once they got their treats, Shadow licked the blue ice cream bar, glad to have his appetite return after weeks and weeks of eating like a mouse. Salt coated Shadow's tongue initially, but his taste buds registered the sweetness afterward.

⋅ ⦂ ☾ ⋅ ⋅

BY THE TIME they retreated to the inn, the sun lined the horizon and the waters below. The sky filled with a variety of shades—blends of reds, oranges, and yellows.

Shadow followed Spark and Aurora into their room to deliver the ice cream to Skye.

"I need to extract that electricity from your body and look at the wounds you've had for quite some time now," said Celia, holding a med-kit. She stood next to Skye, who sat on her bed.

Zephyr and Leif poked their heads into the room. "Celia? What are you doing here?"

"Eila sent me to check up on her older injuries. Luckily, I came in time to discover the excess electricity running through her body."

"Electricity?" asked Shadow. "You mean... like what happened at the Taonian Temple? That was a long time ago!"

"Whoever did it was a Lightning Master and got the electricity to latch within her body in a dormant state, which would make it undetectable as long as it remained dormant," replied Celia. "Users can trigger the latched electricity and activate it to spread throughout her aura points and shut them off, which would knock Skye out for quite some time."

Why activate it now? wondered Shadow.

"Technique only Lightning Masters can use," said Spark. "An old technique... Nobody can use it anymore."

"Good thing I came. It only just activated. Had I arrived a day later, she would've been unconscious by morning."

"Sounds like a very lucky scenario," said Aurora. "How did it happen?"

Guilt spread throughout Shadow's body. It wasn't because of me, right? There's NO WAY I caused this!

"Before the hooded person disappeared, she got blasted in the chest by a super-charged bolt. Small, but dangerous," said Spark. "If only I had the control to extract it... or recognize a technique like that!"

Skye's skin looked lighter. She was almost... sickly. Seeing her draw blood for the first time as a Marauder back in Lastalia wasn't a peaceful sight to take in.

Panic seized in Shadow's muscles. "She'll be okay, right?" He internally prayed to Celeste that his sister was going to be okay. This would not be a Saylor situation. It couldn't be.

"She can't continue until I extract all the electricity and I'm afraid she won't be able to come with you to the islands."

Shadow released a breath. "I don't know what I would've done if I lost you, Skye."

"Right. . ." said Skye in a barely audible whisper. "Promise me you'll be careful."

Leif gave her a thumbs up. "Course we will!"

"Don't worry about us and focus on yourself," Aurora chimed in.

"I'll need to set everything up for the extraction," said Celia. "If you guys don't mind, it would be best if we had privacy."

After everyone got settled, they headed to the dining hall. Unsurprisingly, there were endless piles of shrimp, lobster rolls, and crab cakes. Leif went all out with five plates stacked high. Nobody knew how the man had an appetite rivalling Morphers and trash compactors.

"Yo, Shadow!" said Spark.

Shadow looked up from his plate of calamari, wishing he had some marinara. "Yeah?"

"Spar with me tonight, my dude!"

"Why me?" Shadow hoped she'd bring up how much stronger he'd gotten. Leif was always her sparring partner and she usually beat him nowadays. Spark single-handedly defeated her classmates in sparring games at age twelve.

"Good to practice against people with different fighting styles! 'Specially ones with great aura control!"

"Sure," said Shadow, sitting up straighter. Even if he lost, it's not like anyone else would see. Hypothetically, if anyone saw, it was a sparring match. Shadow wouldn't use his full strength. So, it wouldn't count if he lost.

Once my Gwymond power takes full shape, I'd win every time!

"Someone needs a life," said Leif.

"Hey! That certain someone realizes she has a much longer way to go before she becomes a Lightning Master! Next time anyone tries anything against Hikari like that, I'LL be the one to deal with it!"

"They were trying to target only Skye, weren't they?" asked Zephyr. "It's weird how they only activated the electricity now. Almost like... they were waiting for the perfect time to do it."

"Any new suspects?" asked Aurora, stirring the straw in her iced tea.

"Not that I know of," replied Zephyr. "Biggest suspect is Cerberus."

Lumière Inc. had an endless amount of things on their plate. Shadow had faith. This was why everyone trained for their entire lives before they became Specialists. With Star Strike rising, the organization had less to worry about.

"What confuses me is how the electricity remained undetected by the Communicators. I can understand how there are forms of aura that I can't sense, but the data should've been picked up, dormant or not," said Zephyr.

"Luna detected specific stuff back at the Gorge, yeah?" asked Spark. "If there're undetectable things here…"

"Maybe Luna didn't detect the same sort of thing at the Gorge," finished Leif.

"Heracles could have different effects on abilities depending on the bloodline," said Zephyr. "Whoever's recognized out in the open as a Cerberus member could be someone with toned down abilities to throw off suspicions."

Ugh, why's there gotta be so many possibilities? I just wanna rank up higher and get more important missions, already!

20

TORMENT

SKYE

I don't know what I would've done if I lost you, Skye!

"What's on your mind?" asked Celia.

She held Skye's left arm and pressed a suction cup onto it connected to wires that latched onto a medical stabilizer. Small currents absorbed from her arm and transferred into the stabilizer. The extraction process was the first step for the medical checkup.

"I guess I've been thinking a lot about my team... and what Shadow said." Shadow's words reminded Skye of what he said to her at Saylor's funeral.

A grim look appeared on Celia's face. "Everything you Hosts went through... the entire story... It's a lot, even for me to take in."

"We don't even know the entire story, yet."

"I understand why you prioritize their wellbeing over everything else, even civilian lives, now. But still I don't think you're justified." Celia sighed. "How much longer are you planning on lying to your friends and brother? And hiding an entire part of you from them?"

"Until they become Marauders. At least. Or if I fade away, sometime around then."

"The longer you wait, the more upset they'll be." Celia's words chimed a discordant note inside Skye.

Skye closed her eyes. "I deserve it, yes. But it can't be said. Not now. My duty is to protect them."

"Your call," said Celia. "It's not easy dealing with all of this at your age. Sometimes, I forget you're still a kid. Do you ever just... want to live life as a normal teenager?"

Let Skye take care of you.

Skye can handle all of it!

You can count on Skye!

Skye clenched her fists. "I'd be nothing if I couldn't be of service."

Skye was the one that contorted and curved, but never cracked. Azoth might've been the hardest material in the Realm, but even that could shatter with enough pressure. She was to hold all the pressure, the weight of being the last Host. The one to protect her siblings. The one to save Astrid.

Celia pressed a button on the stabilizer, increasing the pressure. "I figured you'd say that. Any new clues on how to break the curse?"

Skye shook her head. "At this rate, I don't know if we can find a cure. I've been prioritizing the search for that Undead Host and setting Astrid free." Just the thought of Astrid created a heavy stone in Skye's chest that weighed down her entire body.

The Undead Host that killed Saylor hadn't been seen since. Based on the information provided, it couldn't have been Astrid. It was a Host they hadn't encountered before. Somehow. They hadn't encountered an undiscovered Undead Host for quite some time now.

It surprised Skye that the Undead Host didn't destroy more than Saylor. They were unpredictable. Erratic. Capable of slaughtering Marauders. Nobody knew why Skye transformed into that revolting form of darkness or why she hadn't faded away yet. As an Undead, she'd be even more god-like, but completely out of control.

Celia nodded. "I understand." She removed the suction cup from its spot. "Your arms are good to go. Let's look at your back."

Skye braced herself for Celia's reaction to the new set of scars on her back and nerve damage, followed by destroyed aura points that needed time to self-repair. Thankfully, these fresh ones were on her hands, chest, and back. Most were from her battles against Undead Hosts.

The scars on Skye's hands were the nastiest—pitted and ridged. Some were discolored. Others, an angry pink or mellowed into splotchy shades darker than her skin tone. They remained gloved, and she avoided looking at them uncovered. She hated remembering how bony and claw-like they looked when darkness overtook her body. At least the others were more tolerable to look at, but they made her feel hideous, regardless. Skye dodged all mirrors for this purpose.

Whenever Skye imagined the hypothetical, yet impossible scenario of ever holding Zephyr's hands while ungloved, she'd wince at how disgusted he would get. Scars reminded her of what needed to be done and what she had been seeking for so many years, only to keep failing.

Skye had to stand stronger than Azoth. She lost so many already, and she refused to risk losing anyone else.

21

ISLANDS
SHADOW

SHADOW KEPT HIS COMMUNICATOR CHARGED—ZEPHYR REMINDED him the night before. Teleporting between islands back and forth was possible, but such a thing ate up so much battery. It drove him nuts. It also meant no gaming for a while. Which was even worse.

Shortly after getting ready, Shadow knocked on the girls' door.

Celia opened it. "Morning." She always looked full of energy, even on twenty-hour shifts.

"How's Skye doin'?"

"She's better—unconscious right now. She'll continue to be like that as I get to the next phase of the extraction process." Shadow's Medic exams went into detail about the scenarios for extracting elements from one's aura points. For Skye, it would've taken longer because of her high number of aura points and reserves.

"Keep me updated?"

"Of course. Your leader already asked me to, but your primary focus should be your upcoming mission."

Everyone else was at the dining hall by the time Shadow made it downstairs.

"It was weird... Almost like she wasn't breathing," said Aurora, stiffening as Shadow sat down next to her. "That was never mentioned to be a symptom in any of our medical texts."

Spark speared a piece of pineapple from Aurora's plate with a fork. "Haven't seen anythin' like aura points shutting, but it was terrifying! Celia told us not to worry, though."

Zephyr took a sip of hariberry juice. "There's a lot out there that we don't know about."

"If Celia's telling us not to worry, she'll be fine!" said Leif. "She's one of the best Medics."

"Leif's got a point," said Spark. There was a slight cut on her right cheek from their sparring match the night before.

Shadow put up a good fight but got overwhelmed by her lance-work in the end. Spark and Zephyr praised him for being able to go toe-to-toe as a protector facing up against a secondary powerhouse. Good enough for him, as there weren't any other witnesses. Next time, he'd win.

After fueling up, they set out for the docks. Ice Tetra stood by S.S. KAI. It was the same size as the other ships and made of Azoth, with the signature dark blue coloring. "S.S. KAI" pleated with silver was painted across the front.

"Imagine steering these in battle!" said Leif, marveling.

"Wait till Stream and the others get back to working on Project ASTEROID and finishing it!" said Zephyr. "I'll be like in the comic books!"

"Ya know it!" said Leif. The boys fist-bumped, leading Aurora to facepalm.

A staircase emerged from the vessel, unfolding itself and attaching to the dock. The party followed Ice Tetra up the stairs and onto the deck. They waved at the captain and helmsman, who left toward the bridge.

"We got the report about your sister," said Dr. Caraway. "It's a pity, but at least it'll be taken care of and it's better to do so now than later."

"Are you excited about joining Miss Zedler?" asked another

researcher. Shadow tried to remember her name, but it wasn't coming up.

Zephyr smiled. "Of course. It's been so long since I've seen her."

Luna was to meet them at the capital, Scorpio, and this was the first time Shadow had ever been to an underwater city. The rest of the Aquarius Islands were between being under and above water, which Shadow found cool.

A horn blared across the port, and the ship moved east, sailing across The Dark Waves.

"Look at the whales!" Leif pointed at the blobs floating around the surface. He bent over the railing to get a closer view. "If only Blaze was here to understand what they're trynna say!"

Spark giggled. "Yeah, like Blaze would get on a ship!"

"Pretty sure we'd have to strap him to the mast, so he doesn't panic and run off," said Zephyr, chuckling.

The incident occurred at Spark's birthday pool party, where Aurora slipped and knocked him into the deep end. The rest was history. Leif's brothers rescued the poor dude. Whenever they took trips to the beach, Blaze stayed as far away from the sea as much as possible, and Luna often teased him about it.

Honestly, Shadow missed life before being a licensed Agent. Years spent hanging out in their "Usual Spots" felt like eons ago. Their childhoods were far easier, and he thought exams would've been the hardest things to deal with in his lifetime.

The ship stopped moving, transforming itself into the shape of a submarine. Everyone was automatically inside. S.S. KAI dove below the surface. Shadow caught the sight of seabeds and coral reefs.

"Whoa!" exclaimed Shadow.

"So cool...!" said Zephyr in his fanboying voice.

S.S KAI moved faster than a jet, though it didn't feel like it. The sea floor in this part of the world looked tranquil. Schools of fish swam by, and Leif made funny faces with his hands at them.

Spark laughed and joined in.

"That's the dome that shrouds Scorpio, isn't it?" asked Aurora, pointing at the sea-green dome further away. It had a triangular pattern spread out entirely and gleamed from the rays of sunlight coming from the surface.

Dr. Caraway nodded. "It used to be guarded with monsters to keep out aura users back in the Era of Core Regeneration."

As soon as the submarine made it closer to the dome, a rectangular opening appeared and S.S KAI sped through. The opening closed as soon as the ship went inside the dome, transforming itself into an airship and soaring.

Architecture of most of the buildings in Scorpio was ancient—preserving its history. Terraced gardens, fountains, cobblestone streets, and villas complemented each other with their placements being strategically placed for aesthetics. The dome was translucent from the interior. Anyone could see marine life on the outside. Overall, it was a gorgeous city. Shadow felt claustrophobic about the idea of dome-living, however.

S.S. KAI made its way over to the loading docks, which looked more modern than the rest of the capital. Other ships designed for transport, cargo, travel, and battle were also stationed.

"Greetings, Ice Tetra, Astro Strike," said a familiar, husky voice. They had gotten off the ship and taken in the scene before them when Luna appeared.

"Luna!" said Spark and Aurora. They went up to her, arms spread, but Luna gave them a nod. This took aback Shadow. It'd been so long since they'd last seen each other. He thought Luna would've at least hugged them and told them how much she missed everyone.

Seeing Luna reminded Shadow of Saylor. Part of him wanted to ask Luna exactly what happened… Part of him didn't want to hear the gory details.

"Hey, Luna," said Zephyr.

The cousins smiled at each other.

She went up to Ice Tetra, shaking their hands professionally. "Nice to see you again, Ice Tetra," said Luna in a business-like manner.

Her presence felt powerful, able to command an army. Luna's

outfit also seemed put together. She had a white scoop neck that had thick straps with cut off shoulders and slits down the sides. A gray undershirt peeked underneath. Her red skirt (Shadow was pretty sure it was called a "tennis skirt") had a silver chain attached to the top. The look was complete with black boots, red gloves, and a red and black Lumière symbol on her left chest.

"Good to see you, Miss Zedler. It's a pleasure working with you and Astro Strike. They've always been impressive in our missions together and having you around would only make for a more phenomenal experience," said Dr. Caraway.

"Glad to hear," replied Luna. "I scouted between the neighboring islands to see what I could sense. We should figure out our strategy to take down the Dark Sphere."

This type of Dark Sphere had been unheard of. Spiritual Power and aura absorbed to create it came from the Alchemists who went rogue in Astra's era. It didn't have a guardian, and there were reports on how it was indestructible.

"I think I should see this sphere for myself to get a proper sense of what a Dark Sphere made of Spiritual Power from Alchemists would feel like first," said Zephyr. "That also gives Ice Tetra a chance to observe firsthand as well for anything. Sounds good to you?"

"Should be the first move, yes," replied Luna.

The Dark Sphere was on the central island, Antares, and they teleported to its entrance from Scorpio since they were within range of the nearest warp panel. Here, it was above the water and seemed like an ordinary tropical island with palm trees and white sands.

Not a single Risen was in sight and they walked at a moderate pace, allowing Ice Tetra enough time to capture the current state of the island.

"Any updates on new Dark Spheres?" asked Zephyr as everyone followed the Lumière clan members.

"As you would've guessed, there was one Dark Sphere in Cordelia Castle's dungeons. Like the one in Thet," said Luna. Starla de Cordelia was another of the twins' distant ancestors and a

Daughter of Light because of her contributions to two Solarian Wars. When they were younger, Skye requested stories to hear about Starla's princess adventures the most around bedtime. "Athos's power was dormant in the dungeons."

Athos, Aramis, and Porthos were the Triad Spirits that the royal families of Cordelia, Taonia, and Thet could summon, respectively. Celeste blessed and entrusted them to keep peace within Solaria. Nobody nowadays had the abilities of the spirits because of intermixing and bloodlines mutating.

Zephyr motioned for Luna to continue. "I see."

"Risen showed up, mutated," said Luna. "Same kinds with metals attached to parts of their bodies. Saw something similar in my mission with Twilight Treader but got a closer look this time."

Twilight Treader. Others winced.

"We're doing our best at Briton to investigate them further," said Dr. Caraway. "There's so much to unpack here."

"Indeed," said Luna, crossing her arms. "Hopefully we can learn how to trace Mutations soon." Something was off about her ever since she became a Specialist two years ago. Zephyr brought it up first, and Shadow thought he was exaggerating. No matter what, he thought the old Luna would return when Star Strike was fully functional.

There were no visible Risen by the time they got to the Dark Sphere, which was close to an abandoned Assassin's Keep. Shadow waited for Luna to comment about Zephyr's improved sensory capabilities. Or Shadow's OWN improvements, but nothing came.

Zephyr closed his eyes, focusing. "I can feel the same aura and Spiritual Power. It's too far away for me to get the exact coordinates, but it's on two other islands, each opposite of this one. That's where all the Risen are at, too."

Spark twirled her lance. "No Risen here, but they're overflowing other islands? Wacky. So, they're powering up now?"

"There hasn't been word of them invading civilization yet," said a researcher. "We can't get through both islands in one day but taking down the swarms in one by tonight would prevent any attacks from occurring."

Leif threw a chakram into the air and caught it. "Where we goin' first?"

"Graffias for today," said Zephyr.

Everyone took out Communicators and teleported, hiding out of sight behind palm trees. Sunlight harshly stitched itself onto the skies. Shadow regretted wearing a black hoodie as sweat trickled down his forehead. At least he had short-sleeves and cooling fabrics embedded into his clothing. Otherwise, he'd feel like roasted Sevinnon Fowl on a stick.

Within a heartbeat, they arrived at their designation.

Shadow had never seen so many Risen in one area. He could barely see the grass and grains of sand. Graffias was an island for training and civilians were unlikely to be around. Part of Shadow hoped there might be some to save. To show Luna and the others what he could do.

Luna locked eyes with Zephyr. "Orders, Cuz?"

"If we tried to take on all of them, we wouldn't have the stamina or aura to do much tomorrow," began Zephyr. "There are Risen that have the same mix of Spiritual Power and aura as the Dark Sphere, and it feels like they're intertwined by some thread made of Spiritual Power. Do you feel that, too?"

"Yep."

"So, take out those Risen and see what happens?" asked Leif, squinting from the sun in his eyes.

"Hmm... They're hidden within the waves. If I can get in range, I can mark our targets with glyphs. Though this might drain a lot of my aura. Aurora, you can connect your aura to mine to power up my reserves to some extent."

"I've never done an aura transfer before," said Aurora, stiffening. "That's risky! What if I hurt you?"

"Your aura control is enough to transfer to one person fine," replied Zephyr. "I can tell based on what I've seen so far."

Spark pumped her fist into the air. "Show 'em your control, Teach!"

"Your speed would be especially useful here, Leif," said Zephyr.

Leif twirled both chakrams on his index finger. "Aw, yeah! Leif Meister back at it again!"

Aurora closed her eyes. A white link appeared and attached itself to Zephyr.

It amazed Shadow how fast Zephyr came up with plans. On missions, Zephyr looked like he was calculating everything at once. Trying to determine the best outcome. This happened in their Star Chess matches as kids. Zephyr thought ten steps ahead of everyone and was nearly unstoppable. He'd only slip up whenever he underestimated the opponents and got cocky.

All visible Risen looked the same and Shadow scanned them. They were "Bearers," resembling Phantoms with curved horns that reminded him of rams, red eyes, and fangs.

They were scary-looking, but Level 3s, as shown by the scanners. A breeze for them...

As soon as they saw the party, each Bearer duplicated.

"We'll have to clear a path," said Zephyr. He created a few glyphs, larger and with a brighter wind symbol than before. They rose, and he used one as a launch pad, slicing through Bearers. Zephyr landed on another glyph, sending him flying in the opposite direction to slam Galeforce against more.

A clear glow appeared throughout Leif's entire body to block orbs of darkness launched at him. Shadow's defensive barrier automatically shrouded him for protection.

Shadow twirled Diablos in staff form, sending orbs of Gwymond Darkness flying at him back at the Risen.

Three glyphs appeared underneath three of the Risen within the crowd, and Leif made motions with his chakrams, summoning stalagmites from underground that crushed the targeted Bearers.

"Leif! That was your first time using the shield all the way!" Zephyr patted him on the back.

Spark shook her head. "Course ya activated it first! Guess I'll find something to learn before ya one of these days."

Dang, Leif! Welp, least I did somethin' great, TOO!

Shadow had to make up for getting knocked out at Taonia. He could've had whoever was in the hood and saved everyone. Minor slip ups happened. No big deal. All heroes made mistakes—Celeste, Lumina, everyone. He'd bounce back several steps forward.

"Dark Sphere feels slightly weaker now!" called out Luna.

"All right, we'll just keep on doing the same thing!" said Zephyr in response, side-stepping and skewering another Bearer.

Geysers appeared from underneath a group of Bearers from Aurora, blasting them into the air. Zephyr sent a glyph to one, forcing it toward the geyser, and Shadow created a whirlpool that disintegrated more.

"We're done with this area," said Zephyr. "Keep trying to defend and keep away from them until we get to the next section."

Shadow guessed that another team would take care of exterminating the nests once they dealt with the sphere. He couldn't wait for the day when he was S-ranked and could annihilate two entire islands full of Risen in one go. Either way, he patted himself on the back for handling Level 3s so easily. Their fights against Level 3s grew shorter because of their growth as warriors. Others were impressive, but his chains and orbs of Gwymond Darkness had to impress Luna the most.

⁘⁙⁘

"I noticed some missteps you guys made in battle," said Luna as they waited at Graffias Rainforest. Ice Tetra wanted to survey the area before proceeding and Zephyr and Spark disappeared to collect water.

Shadow thought he misheard, but Aurora's pretty, minty-green irises widening said otherwise.

"Sorry, I'll do better next time... What did I do wrong?"

"Your techniques looked almost the same as they were the last time I was around. They should be sharper, more precise, and should cost less aura. I thought you were working on refining your spells these last months."

Aurora avoided looking at their second-in-command. "I've been busy working on that, my aim, not having to rely on everyone else so much for protection, taking less time to cast spells, and my durability shield."

"It definitely shows that training like that will not work for you. You need to focus on one thing at a time," said Luna, spitting her words like bullets. "At least you're aware of what needs improvement, but you'll get nowhere if you keep bouncing back and forth like that."

"Hey! Skye mentioned nothing about that with Rory's training!" said Shadow, frowning. He expected praise for ALL of them at least.

"This isn't the academy. Nobody should monitor you all the time and tell you what to work on and how. You're Specialists now and should be competent. You should be far more aware of your performance and how to improve." Luna appeared expressionless, with no warmth.

Shadow was in disbelief over what his ears detected.

Leif cast Luna a glance. "We'll get the hang of it. Give us time and we'll adapt."

"You two have been slacking off with training. I can tell that much. Given the time you've been certified, you should be more wary and master a lot more."

Shadow did a double take. "What?" He hated the gnawing feeling stirring inside him.

Luna shook her head. "Well, now that I think about it. . . Skye's to blame for a lot of this, too. Part of it is on YOU guys, but if you're like this, then it's also because of an incompetent mentor not doing her job properly. What in the name of Tartarus has she been teaching you?"

"She's helped! A lot!" said Shadow, flaring up. "Training us! And guiding us!"

"Obviously, she's not doing it enough. She's supposed to protect you and guide you. But she's also supposed to be a mentor. All she's done in that regard is hinder you."

Shadow ground his teeth, feeling darkness creep up inside. "You know what, Luna? I don't know what happened to you or what changed you, but you're being way too harsh! We're your friends and there's no need to talk to us like that!"

Luna didn't flinch. "I'm being honest. On the job, you guys are my colleagues and choosing to sugarcoat things because of our shared childhoods won't help you."

"You could AT LEAST BE LESS HARSH about your criticism."

"It's not being harsh, it's being honest. I'm not Skye and thank Celeste I'm not. Otherwise, you'd all be stuck where you guys currently are, like any other Agent." She paused once again, recollecting her thoughts. "Anyway, I should go tell Spark and Zephyr what they need to work on, too." She got up and left toward the river.

"What happened to her these last months?" asked Leif, knitting his brows.

Aurora sighed. "I-I don't know…"

Luna had been gone for years, returning home sporadically during her time in Unity Squad. She always hung out with them, teased them, and told them about her adventures, which often left Shadow in awe. Shadow hated change. He wasn't a fan before, but it was becoming less desirable.

22

WEALTH AND POWER

LUNA

"You're doing well, Spark," said Luna. Turning her bolts into the shape of an orb was an obvious enough indicator of Spark's training.

"Really?" Spark filled a canteen with purified water and added another purification tablet into the section of the river. It fizzed, dissolving into the gentle currents. Spark grabbed another empty canteen from her storage compartment, twisting the cap off.

"You're where you're supposed to be." Swifty had the same capabilities at Spark's age. Their growth rates were very close, but Spark was to surpass her in terms of elemental mastery.

"Wow, I'm... Shocked!" Zephyr chuckled at the pun.

A smile tugged at Luna's lips. Luna missed Spark's jokes, as stupid as most of them were.

Upon receiving word of the incident in Taonia leading to Skye's condition, Luna was unsurprised. If Cerberus truly hid their abilities from being detected, it wouldn't faze her, either. She became desensitized to the perpetual, expanding pile of the unknown. Luna couldn't say the same for the others.

They have no idea, thought Luna.

No Marauders had died for a prolonged period. Now wasn't the time to get overconfident. It didn't matter how many of them survived if the Mortal Realm got destroyed in a few years. None of it mattered if they didn't find answers soon.

They failed most of the time to protect assaulted cities thanks to more lives lost than saved. With each destroyed area, lives lost, and Risen growing, darkness would spread even more. It amazed Luna that the Balance between light and darkness in the world hadn't gone haywire and caused Eta Geminorum to self-destruct. Every time it came too close to happening, either too much light OR darkness, Celeste aided heroes, albeit with limits. Rest of the Gods dictated how much Celeste could help.

No signs of Celeste intervening in Eta Geminorum gave mixed signals. Gods could've believed the mortals could save the realm on their own. Or they stopped giving a damn after the last time the Realm was in trouble—Celeste included. Luna forced herself to believe in the higher-ups within the organization, but every passing day, every new discovery made it more difficult to latch onto that faith.

I'm tired of this shit-

"Luna?" Spark waved her hand in front of Luna's face. "Helloooo!"

Luna pulled herself out of her thoughts, pinching herself to stop thinking about it. "Spaced off for a sec. What were you asking?"

"What other feedback do ya got for me?"

She paused, recollecting what she had to say. "You realized you're not as close to being a Lightning Master as you think. It humbled you. Motivated you to keep preparing as much as you can. And to not stop improving. Well, I think that's a good mindset to have. It'll prepare you for the long run."

"Okay! Gotcha!"

"What about me?" asked Zephyr.

"As for you, I've seen no one do that with their glyphs before. You know, the ricocheting?"

Zephyr scratched his head. "Hmm. . . It came up on a training day. I went along with it ever since."

"Well, I think that if you utilized more of it and experimented, it could be pretty useful. Also, glad to see your sensory abilities are where they should be."

"Yeah, I was getting concerned about that. What about everything else?" His urgency gave Luna all she needed to know. If Zephyr was a true leader, he would only show these signs to a few, if any.

One of the first things she noticed was how Zephyr presented himself. He gave off the poise of a leader and looked the part. That facade shattered as soon as he asked for her approval for strategies. People who still sought for approval when making leadership decisions were only those who weren't ready for a higher position.

Children of the clan were hand-picked by the current leader for higher positions of power. They groomed their training regimes for them to take on a set of trials that determined their worth. Trials only took place after passing screening tests.

"Anyways, your leadership is fine, Zeph. Keep up the aura reserve building and all other stuff and I'll check up on it again soon."

"Heh! So Boss is on track for a higher position several months from now?" asked Spark.

It took Aqua nine months to earn her Lieutenant General position. Such a title granted her the ability to order Combat Agents and Medics. Eila became third-in-command within the Medics, six months after graduating from Garnet Academy. Everyone projected it would take nine months for Zephyr to pass and try his hand at the trials to be like Aqua or a Commander.

Non-clan members had a unique process to go through for the titles, but there were many exceptions and had the same amount of rigor. There was no one-size-fits-all method to determine hierarchy within the organization, but they prepared all Lumière children for their entire lives for these chances of gaining more honor.

"Missed having you around, Luna." Warmth covered her, but not to where she'd hold back on any future remarks if she saw him committing any unacceptable mishaps.

It was best for Zephyr to figure out when would be the best time to stop asking for approval. Most important lessons she learned through Unity Squad were on her own and by doing, not by having someone tell her about it. It would only make sense to apply that logic here.

"Makes the team more complete now," said Spark, grinning. She stated before that Luna was the "glue that held them all together." Perhaps it would carry on into adulthood... If they'd make it till then. If the Mortal Realm wasn't destroyed by then.

Luna saw the charts and graphs predicting the Realm's demise. Two to three years was what they had left.

All of Luna's trainings methods were intended to prepare them for the worst—something she wasn't ready to witness yet.

Skye, Aqua, Fang, Ambrose, Calypso, Sunny, and Zetta were the strongest Agents. All went through periods of adversity to get where they were at, and such experiences powered their unwavering resolve. Her friends wouldn't rank up with half-truths. Luna knew they could withstand the strongest Risen—she at least had faith in that regard. They would be the last line of defence, preventing the Realm's destruction.

Skye's mission information throughout most of her youth was vague, but Luna could only imagine what she'd see. Luna trusted her uncle and the higher-ups and respected that whatever information they chose not to disclose was for a good reason. The fact Skye pressed onward to become the Agent she was now, despite the shortcomings as a little kid, earned Luna's respect. As an Agent, at least.

Given her experience, Skye sure as Tartarus had no excuses for being an inept mentor. Leif, Shadow, and Aurora committed rookie mistakes that wouldn't have happened if Luna was around. Helping them train and protecting them was the bare minimum. If they didn't understand how to improve themselves properly or have the correct mentality as a Specialist, they were doomed. Especially during their peak growth periods, where they had to take full advantage. Otherwise, they would not hit Marauder level and be key in stopping the Mortal Realm's destruction.

Once Skye rejoined the party, Luna had to confront her. Now was the time to keep focusing on becoming a Marauder and for Zephyr to earn a title. Star Strike got more involved with uncovering the overarching threat earlier than expected, but their primary focus was advancing up the ranks and experiencing all that came with being a Specialist.

"Let's head back," said Zephyr, putting away filled bottles, stepping over mud puddles.

Graffias Rainforest was a tranquil place to get lost in. Because of the astronomical amount of rainfall it received, they had the longest rivers in the world, fed by countless streams, tributaries, and creeks.

Shadow and Aurora stiffened when they saw Luna arrive behind Spark and Zephyr.

Their reactions were exactly how Luna predicted. Any twinges of guilt needed to be set aside. Survival was more important than how her friends could handle the truth. They had to get used to it and toughen up for anything.

No pain, no gain.

"Ready to go?" asked Dr. Fern. Her wise, green eyes shined behind the rims of her thick glasses.

"Yep. We'll stick with current formation," replied Zephyr as they passed a collection of streams.

Everyone resumed position, and Luna stood behind Spark and Aurora. When a swarm of Risen came into view, Aurora's aura focused to her fingertips before casting it into a spell. It was slower than before, however.

Why is she hesitating? That could cost her in battle.

Leif showed techniques unseen before that she imagined didn't take long for him to figure out how to use effectively. Years back, he was the only one who could keep up with Spark during sparring class. His aura had been used far too wastefully, however, a sign that he hadn't been training enough. Earth aura barely cost him any to use, thanks to having Earth Alchemist blood and distant relation to the glorious hero, Stryder Bancroft. He was also lucky to have an exorbitant amount of aura reserves, but this wouldn't work for an A or S-ranked mission.

Having natural gifts was a blessing and a curse. If he'd been working hard, he would've earned Luna's praise.

"Last of them up ahead," said Zephyr. Luna felt his aura getting low. His resilience improved, and his reserves would never match up to the rest of Star Strike. They could only build up so much, but there were silver linings.

"Lemme at this one!" said Shadow once they came across the last marked Risen.

Shadow spun Diablos, creating dark chains wrapping around the Bearer. He struck, swinging with momentum. His passive shield protected him from retaliating strikes, preventing so much as a scratch from getting inflicted.

"Check this out!" Shadow grinned. Gwymond Darkness surrounded him as he twirled Diablos' handle once more. Such darkness was more potent than the regular kind, stronger and a darker ebony, capable of taking more forms and transforming the user. The same dark glow appeared around the Bearer and extracted darkness from its body. Luna sensed its aura getting drained as its body minimized in size. Shadow slammed the hilt through the Bearer's chest, disintegrating it.

"Everyone see that?" Shadow's hands were on his hips, gauging reactions. A stupid grin plastered onto his face, making Luna want to roll her eyes.

"Nice!" said Spark and Zephyr.

Leif shook his head. "Show off!"

And nothing to be so proud of, thought Luna. *Way to let it get to your head.*

Shadow held himself back from his true potential. He outsped Bearers in terms of blows and movement on the battlefield, but chains of darkness were verbatim as what he could do five months ago.

Where was the signature, dark hand that Lumina Rayne tore armies apart with?

Leif, Shadow, and Aurora were supposed to surpass her in fighting capabilities. Why didn't they use their full potential?

"Excellent work, everyone," said Zephyr. "I can feel the sphere weakening to half its strength."

"You guys have any updates on your fancy theories and all that jazz?" Luna shot Spark a look that told her to "be professional." Spark put her hand to her mouth. "Oh! I mean... What's the status of the research theories?"

Professor Fern laughed and appeared unfazed by Spark's unintentional insolence. "Well, this sort of thing hasn't appeared in other areas with Dark Spheres concentrated with Alchemist Spiritual Power. The invisible links binding souls of Risen to the Dark Spheres are a fresh add-on, almost like an experiment."

"My guess is that whoever caused Dark Spheres to appear in the first place may try to place them in the same spots again, but with these add-ons," said Dr. Caraway.

"Still dunno why someone would do this on purpose," said Shadow.

"Best not to question it anymore," said Luna. "Just gotta expect the unexpected."

"Agreed," said Zephyr, eyes bleary. "We can discuss more of it after we get some rest." Everyone took out their Communicators and transported back to Scorpio.

"How far's the inn?" asked Spark as they headed toward the depths of the ancient city, exiting the only completely modern section of Scorpio.

"Few streets north," replied Luna.

Scorpio could've been a tourist attraction if it didn't focus so much on being hidden from the public eye. The dome drifted around in a circular motion around the archipelago. It fluctuated between integrating technological advancements into its culture or preserving ancient tradition with its buildings.

They passed by Scorpites adorned in odd blends between traditional and modern fashion—nightmare-fuelled clashes between robes and denim as they approached Scorpio Marketplace.

Why doesn't someone tell them how hideous they look? It'd save my eyes from bleeding.

Aquarius' Government was something else, but they at least agreed on working with Lumière Inc. without complaints, so they weren't all bad. Luna didn't know a ton about their foreign policy. If she wanted to invent a new form of torture, she'd ask Zephyr.

"What is he doing HERE?" asked Leif, pointing at the panda at a market stall.

The panda waved at them in response, and they waved back.

"Beats me," said Zephyr. He gave the panda a high-five, and the creature giggled.

Socialites and other fancily dressed individuals strolled about with their obnoxiously large sunglasses, resembling giant beetles. Some had fake nails longer than Stream's claws, which seemed more like a fire hazard than a fashion statement. At least their darker skin wasn't from fake tanning and their darker hair looked natural, like the rest of the civilians.

According to Eila, they often gossiped or threatened to sue businesses for miniscule problems. Or made contests out of how much of their spouse's money they could blow in one spree on their trips around the world. Nowadays, it was far worse than before and had been that way ever since Gold became a universal form of payment, where one didn't have to wait days to exchange different currencies at the bank. The whole point of making everything universal and interplanetary was to make trade easier... NOT promote shallower impulsivity.

No wonder their spouses wanted to leave them.

Scorpio was one of the most expensive places to live in and loaded with people who were... loaded. There was some nonsensical social hierarchy and over importance to stand out.

Luna didn't want to, but she recalled an event four years ago where Lumière Inc. hosted a charity gala. All proceeds went toward reviving the fallen capital city of the kingdom of Orwyn. There was a grace period where Risen attacks had halted, and it gave them an opportunity to rebuild.

She came home after a mission with Instructor Vine and her Unity Squad classmates. Her parents were around for the first time in forever, and she was a lot more excited to see her friends and Sebastian. Zephyr was going to be at the gala along with Eila and Tandy, and she was looking forward to seeing her other cousins, too. Luna's only additional wish was to see Stream, but their reunion would've had to wait.

"Finally," said her mother when she came downstairs after getting ready. That was the first thing she had said to her after not seeing her parents for at least four weeks. Or was it three?

There wasn't much she could do with her layered hair besides tie a section into a small side ponytail. She had on a little black dress with short kitten heels and put on red lipstick, smokey eyeshadow, and mascara.

"Ready to go?" was the first thing her father said to her. Sebastian led them to the car, opening the door for Luna in the backseat. A vehicle was unnecessary but arriving in style in an automobile with heated seats and a fridge was apparently all the rage. It was stupid.

She watched Sebastian put the keys into ignition, driving past the over the top, garish, and bizarrely decorated manors in Aurum District. Feathers were in season. And chunky gemstones. Attached to the roofs...

Celeste, kill me now.

They arrived at the Base's Event Hall minutes later. Thankfully, Luna's eyes didn't fall out of their sockets from the horrific sights she'd seen.

The cool air was crisp, and Luna felt like a moron for forgetting to bring a coat. Garnet never hit frigid temperatures, but it wasn't warm in late autumn.

"Here you are, Miss Luna." Sebastian put her matching black coat over her shoulders, which made her smile.

Ladies and gentlemen in fine dresses costing thousands and suits made of the best textiles in the entire nation of Silvatica strolled through the Event Hall entrance. Some wore kimonos and gowns, showing the contrast between cultures of Kadelatha, while others had Taonian silk.

Caterers carried trays of food and drink, and the golden ballroom looked overtly glamorous with the chandeliers and vases of white peonies. Champagne flutes, triangular glasses with an umbrella and a piece of fruit, along with random mushroom appetizers and other ridiculous nonsense considered "fancy" were there.

"Elara, you came!" Uncle Ziel and his children were behind him.

Zephyr came up to Luna and looked very uncomfortable in his suit and bowtie.

Tandy followed him over, reminding Luna of how a baby duck follows its mother.

"Of course, I did," said her mother with a hostile air around her. "What kind of person would I be if I didn't show up at one of my dear brother's events?" The temperature of the room dropped at least twenty degrees.

Her uncle's friendly smile remained, despite this.

The sheer noise of the room drowned the rest of their conversation out as the adults walked away, leaving the children to fend for themselves.

"I hate this stupid neck trap," said Zephyr. "I feel like I'm getting choked."

"I'm sure Skye'd like to see you in it," teased Luna.

This made Tandy and Eila laugh, and he went all shy with embarrassment, putting a finger to his lips as if anyone overhearing didn't already know.

Could he be any more obvious?

They spent the rest of the night going to the auction and avoiding shallow guys who hit on her. Most were sons of proprietors who barely had to work a day in their lives. Some thought of fighting as "barbaric" and looked down upon her clan, but those forms of ignoramus wouldn't have stepped foot in Garnet.

"I've never been on a date with a Lumière before." A teenager winked at her. He reminded her of a praying mantis. His teeth were so bleached they looked blue. His tan was so fake; he looked like a tangerine.

Ugly AND a dumbass? Sure haven't dealt with that a million times by now.

Luna sighed. "And with a line like that, I'm sure the number will stay the same."

Zephyr covered his mouth, trying not to burst out laughing.

Eila and Tandy exchanged looks.

Zephyr fist-bumped her once he left, red in the face.

"You woke up and chose violence," said Tandy, amazed.

All went well, until a revolting banshee of a woman spoke. That's all it took. Luna could handle unsolicited flirting from any gender, go on deadly missions, and prepare to die at any moment. What she couldn't handle was this. . .

Luna overheard shallow conversations among old money folk daily. She could tell who had inherited wealth and did nothing with their lives vs. those who earned it by hearing if they spent more time talking about their hair than what was important.

Her dress was long and sheer, with slits on either side and sleeveless. Judging from her blonde hair pulled into an elegant twist, ridiculously long lashes, and blue eyes, she was from Thet—a noble, guessing by her style of dress. Her beauty mark didn't make her beautiful.

"President Ziel put in all of this effort for a kingdom who had it coming, didn't he?" Her face was flushed and held an empty goblet. "There are barely any good vacation spots there!"

Zephyr made an about face. Tandy and Eila glared at her.

A woman with permed blondish-brown hair, high cheekbones, an abnormally long neck, and a fake nose stood next to her. Her light blue eyes and ball gown-like dress made her look Cordelian. "Exactly! He could've chosen to raise money to help Burgundy instead!" She sighed, gulping down the rest of her drink. "I guess I won't be going to my favorite vacation home next summer."

Luna clenched her fists, blood boiling to the point of eruption. "SHUT UP!"

Eila let out a gasp. More eyes were on her now.

"YOU HAVE NO DAMN CLUE WHAT YOU'RE TALKING ABOUT!"

"I beg your pardon?" Both turned toward her.

Luna trembled as she fought the urge to hurl every insult into their faces. Her eyes stung, and she forced herself to not shed any tears. "People have DIED trying to protect those cities and ALL YOU CARE ABOUT IS A DAMN VACATION SPOT? A city that ONLY HAD ONE AREA DAMAGED compared to one that was COMPLETELY DECIMATED. You don't know what IT'S LIKE! To be out there! Watching people you know get killed! To have family-"

"Luna, that's enough." Instructor Vine was next to her, sounding soothing, like cool water on a burn. "You needn't say more."

The small crowd who overheard remained, despite how exponentially loud the room was, staring at her.

"Luna…" Zephyr's voice was incredibly gentle.

They saw the bodies.

A species of mutated Risen plagued the area, able to create a haze that unleashed a rotting, flesh-eating sickness. It consumed anyone without enough aura to protect themselves. She and her colleagues had to stay put as Vine went to collect any survivors and fend off the monsters.

Explosions followed suit and debris fell against her, knocking Luna unconscious and separated from everyone. She tried to scream but could barely make a sound louder than a whimper. Corpses were present, and Luna woke up, surrounded by them. Rotting limbs, half-eaten flesh, and purple lips were everywhere. Faces hardly looked human, being swollen like maggots.

It took everything inside of Luna to get up, stop shivering, and look for the others. She had to push the images out of her head and eventually came across Vine… he was a former Marauder… but even he couldn't save the group of survivors around him from being hit by the haze emitted from the demonic-looking thing's breath with one eye and scales.

It moved faster than him, teleporting behind the group Vine was trying to protect. Blackish-purple spews shot out, forming into the gasses. It spread throughout their bodies, starting from the bottom. Splotches appeared, chewing away at their skin, boring holes as they screamed in agony. Eye sockets were last, and eyeballs dropped to the ground, with bloody roots still attached.

Luna had nightmares every night since then, and the only one she talked to them about was Vine. These ignorant ingrates had at least heard about the casualties, yet miraculously lacked empathy. There weren't a ton of witnesses who overheard, and Luna was glad more didn't hear her uncontainable outburst. Instructor Vine calmed everyone down and swept it under the rug, which maintained the Lumière image. If word reached the rest of her family and spread out to the public, her parents would have punished her for once.

"They were being ignorant, and you were the one only making sense," said Zephyr softly. He followed her outside once the commotion died down. "You could at least imagine what those people who lost so much had to deal with." His voice sounded soothing, and her blood pressure decreased somewhat. But not enough.

She neglected to mention that they were staying overnight at the capital when it got attacked, along with all the gory details. She ended up in the wrong place at the wrong time one too many times now.

"They seriously had to be such fuc-"

"Luna. Listen to me."

She shut up, taking deep breaths to avoid popping veins.

"Once we're all certified as a team, we'll make it so we wouldn't have to do these charity galas anymore. We'll save those cities and make sure they'll remain standing, no matter what!"

"I dunno about that. I know if I ran into those two, I'd let them get killed. We'd be better off if half these people were gone."

Zephyr sighed. "Don't say it like that…"

"This Realm is messed up. Accept it, Zephyr."

Star Strike was the "Beacon of Hope," an ambitious Dream Team with the largest cast of descendants from notorious heroes. The Agency devoted the most amount of funding to them in hopes they'd become one of the strongest Dream Teams, like the Wings of Order. They were "The Indomitable Dream Team," and the first Dream Team since Dawn Brigade conceptualized, which explained all the hype. Luna believed in all of it before that time at least.

23

DIVIDE
ZEPHYR

IF THEY WEREN'T IN AN AQUATIC DOME, IT WOULD'VE BEEN DARK BY the time Zephyr woke up. He knocked out as soon as his head hit the pillow, and he never had such a proper nap ever since certification. It was refreshing and a relief.

He rubbed his eyes and left the room, where he found the others outside of the inn with targets set up. Zephyr thought he was seeing things when he saw Leif standing in front of one.

"Luna yelled at me for playing my game," said Leif, answering his silent question. "She gave me and Shadow a lecture about how we needed to train more." He and Shadow were together while the girls were on the opposite side of the space, luckily out of earshot.

"She yelled at you guys *and* lectured you?"

Shadow's expression turned sour. "It was weird. She said something about how I needed to 'actually pull my weight.'" Zephyr had never heard him sound so bitter in his entire life.

"And went on about how Unity Squad prodigies often relied on pure talent, only to struggle reachin' mastery level with their fighting styles. And I'd be put real far behind or whatever," said Leif.

Zephyr's eyes narrowed. "I see… That's… a lot. No idea why she'd say it like that, but she knows more about preparing to rank up more than the rest of us." Luna had always been honest and had less of a filter as they aged, but she never criticized them before as far as he could remember. The most she ever did was express her opinions without holding back.

"Guess it won't hurt to train a bit more," said Shadow. "Not all of us wing it like you, Leif. Hate to admit it. But I wish I could pull it off."

"What's the point? I can already do everything fine!" said Leif. "So, what if I use more aura? It'll take less the more I use it in battle!"

Zephyr shrugged. "I mean, it couldn't hurt to practice a bit. You'd at least be doing it with us. Even Aqua spends almost all her free time training."

"Strange how they don't talk a lot 'bout what happens post-certification," said Shadow.

"True," agreed Zephyr. "They say to train five days a week, but never said how long."

Leif frowned. "Five days, if ya need to."

"Maybe it's up to our own judgement to figure out how much we need," said Zephyr. "They're pushing us into the water and telling us to swim without explaining how."

Zephyr set up training bots, ready to practice his swordplay. He remembered his lessons with Skye, where she gradually gave more descriptive explanations with pointers. Zephyr missed hearing her voice and having her around. It'd only been less than a day, but it felt longer without her. Celia sent him a message earlier about how she was being purposefully knocked out for sixteen hours so Celia could finish the rest of the extraction process.

Zephyr hoped to be by Skye's bedside by the time she regained consciousness. The crestfallen look on her face when she found out she had to stay behind made Zephyr's stomach turn to knots.

"How's training coming along?" Zephyr turned, seeing Dr. Caraway behind them.

"Wouldn't be so bad if our veteran teammate wasn't being a pain," said Leif, groaning after throwing his chakram at the target for the umpteenth time.

Dr. Caraway chuckled. "When I was a student at Vigor, they forced us to hone our skills during mandatory training sessions for four hours a day."

"Four hours?" Leif scrunched his nose. "At Garnet Academy, we had sets and reps! But how long didn't matter if we did 'em."

The wise researcher inspected the training yard. "There's been much debate over what is best for the development of combatants. Mortals mutate so much to where it becomes a matter of trial and error. It doesn't hurt to train at least five times a week, however. Especially during your peak."

"Do you miss your combat days?" asked Zephyr, swinging at a bot's arm.

"There was something invigorating about slaying monsters and saving lives, but it became more and more tiresome to draw out so much aura as I aged. I miss it, but I also appreciate the transition for what it is. Making discoveries and watching the newer generations succeed is as invigorating to me."

Humans in combat exhausted a vast majority of their aura in their thirties and forties, depending on the person. By that point, it was too risky to put them in fighting positions for treacherous missions.

"That's why we have to make the most of it as much as we can," said Zephyr.

"Your weekly missions consisting of tracking down missing persons and accompanying older Agents on rescue missions and taking down only the fodder on nest extermination missions are long gone and left for the Trainees."

After training, Zephyr got a hold of his cousin to talk about the plan for the next day. He already memorized the layout of Sargas. It was similar in size to Graffias, and he also remembered the locations for which Risen was soul-bound to the Dark Sphere.

They seated themselves on the comfy, cream-colored sofas in the rec room. It felt extra toasty thanks to the crackling embers in the fireplace. Perfect for discussing strategies.

Luna took a sip of black tea. "Sounds good to me." She had that serious demeanor and cool tone that only diminished when they left the docks. "Never destroyed a Dark Sphere but shouldn't be too bad."

Having Luna around lessened the paranoia, and he needed to stop relying on her or Skye like a crutch to feel less anxious all the time. The migraines he used to get didn't help, either, or he appreciated medication more than ever. He had a nagging fear of impending doom for "expecting the unexpected." How was his father able to do it? Did Aqua have this many internal conflicts eating her alive?

Asking for reassurance wasn't necessary most of the time anymore for both battle strategies and how they handled mission logistics. At first, he only did it because he was paranoid about pulling dumb moves after overlooking any critical details—he hadn't missed one in subsequent missions in a row. He wanted a second pair of eyes.

"By the way... did anyone say anything about me and the screening tests?"

"I don't know. Well... I think Uncle will let you know when the nine-month period hits."

Zephyr studied her body language and the undertones. Luna's eyes darted a minuscule amount. She knew.

The old Luna would have told him everything she had heard, even if classified. If only Spark were his cousin—he would've found out in seconds. Either way, he had no choice but to respect it.

"It would look bad if you asked Uncle about this."

"I know. There's something extra to think about if I become an Enforcer."

"Worry about your missions and how to qualify to become one. A lot can change in these next seasons," said Luna. "You could slack off and get stupidly cocky for all I know. If you keep doing all the good things, you wouldn't be far off from Aqua."

"Yeah, I don't plan on getting cocky." The nine-month mark since he became a Specialist felt like ages away.

Zephyr didn't want to think about the new plethora of things to worry about IF he became a Commander or Lieutenant. There was the idea of making larger scale decisions that different parties might not approve of, and it was already weird to come up with plans that Luna or Skye might dislike… Oh, Celeste… He was already thinking about it.

Perhaps he needed a fresh approach and could try worrying and overthinking less. His responsibilities were going to pile perpetually from here on out.

"Anyway, does herbal tea help you sleep any better?"

"More or less."

"Wonder if Blaze has any more ideas in terms of remedies. Maybe Stream has something up her sleeve."

The way Luna smiled after saying the brunette's name made Zephyr smirk. He refrained from teasing her about "her Princess." Knowing his cousin, she would've had some retort about him and Skye to "just kiss already."

"Speaking of which, how is Nova Strike doing?" It wouldn't have been long before Zephyr would lead both teams.

Naming when referring to different teams for combinations of groups of team members was confusing, but he wasn't the one who came up with the names. He never found out who did it. Everyone rolled with it.

"Still going off the theory that these irritating people have a secret hideout. No genuine leads, but they have made progress with the search. Glacieus thinks the samples from the Mutations could make it easier to trace the sources."

The secret hideout, if it existed, could take ages to figure out. If the attempts to reconnect and communicate with the other worlds and learning how to travel out of them were continuing for what seemed like forever, Zephyr could only imagine the timeline for figuring out how to disable shrouding barriers.

"We need to have patience. There have been no reports of places getting decimated for a while now, right? At least, I didn't hear about anything."

"Nah, just as sporadic and unpredictable as ever. That's not your priority now. Your priority is rising as a leader and helping Star Strike hit A-rank."

"Makes sense. I just hope to be like Capala, Aqua, Dad, the Marauder leaders, and Mercury." Zephyr sighed. "I have so many people to look up to. And so many to be compared to."

"You'll get used to it. Though, the day you get a portrait hung on the walls, you better not dress in a tacky outfit."

Zephyr laughed. "Of course not. I'd be suited up like Mercury. Hopefully as successful as him too."

Luna raised an eyebrow. "You want to be considered for VP like him, too?"

"Well, I didn't mean that. I meant with his leadership abilities, the way he kept himself always composed, the person you'd want on your side because he'd do anything to achieve his goals and power through it. All of Typhon Strike are worth looking up to." Agents never forgot about the Typhons and their contributions to the organization. They had classes dedicated to informing Trainees about their legacies and who they once were as people.

Zephyr recalled all the essays he wrote about Mercury during his school days. His classmates groaned whenever they had to watch his presentations throughout the years on the man he admired. Others often presented about their ancestors. Annually, each class would perform in a play about a legacy whenever Hero's Day rolled around.

Luna drummed her fingers on the armrest beside her. "Stream and Spark looking up to Electro makes sense aside from his ego and feelings of under appreciation. I get the worship toward the other two."

"I want to say we're on the right track to being like our predecessors, but right now, everything's so hard to tell."

"If you start getting cocky, I *will* slap some sense into you. All this hero worship we're taught to believe in sometimes backfires. We need to stop getting complacent."

EVERYONE (INCLUDING Shadow) agreed to wake up early the next morning so they could clear the next island. Today's island exploration was easier since it was basically a round two. Zephyr was less fatigued by the time they finished destroying the soul-bound Bearers, and he sensed the drained Dark Sphere, which should've been penetrable by now.

They returned to Antares. Luna walked up to the sphere after activating her durability shield. It looked the same as it did earlier, but it didn't feel that way. She retrieved a knife from her pocket and slashed through it. An explosion followed suit, and she winced slightly when it hit her.

"What's the move, Boss?" asked Spark.

Luna gave her a look that said, "Really?"

"First, we'll have to go back to Port Kilia to check up on Skye."

"And we have to figure out how we're splitting up," said Luna. "There are two areas to investigate that might have Dark Spheres and Uncle wants to see how we'll fare when split into halves with each side being led by someone who can sense auras. One side will go with Ice Tetra and the other will work with the Sirens."

"Which one of us knows how to fix sirens?" asked Shadow.

Aurora rolled her eyes.

"The research team, not the alarm," said Zephyr with a snicker.

The warning alerts that blared from their Communicators cut everyone's laughter short: *Ambush on Port Kilia.*

Zephyr miraculously didn't have a pounding heartbeat like he did back when Lastalia and Castor were under attack. Tremors erupted throughout his body, but he was at least able to think more clearly than those times.

Aurora's hand flew to her mouth. "Oh, no..."

"Port Kilia? What in the world?" yelled Spark.

Leif's eyes drifted. "It's just like Cas-" He stopped himself when he saw Shadow's distress. This time, Zephyr doubted he'd get into another unresolved morality debate with Skye...

"We have to go back there right NOW!" cried Shadow. "Skye is there and probably unconscious! What if-?"

"We need to stay composed," said Zephyr calmly, glancing at Luna, then at Spark. "You too, Spark. We'll teleport to Scorpio and take the ship as quickly as we can."

Without a second thought, they hurried over to the nearest warp spot and teleported back to Scorpio's docks. S.S. KAI remained in its spot.

Shadow paced back and forth within the submarine and at that rate, he was going to bore a hole in the floor. His Communicator was in his hand and Skye's holographic image remained floating above his screen along with the phone icon.

Aurora's Communicator almost slipped out of her hands. Celia's picture floated above her screen. It kept ringing.

"Why's nobody picking up?" yelled Shadow. "Why'd we have to be where WE CAN'T ALREADY TELEPORT?"

"Shadow, we're all worried," said Luna, sounding gentler than before. "Knowing Celia, she's probably evacuating your sister and herself and helping anyone she can."

Zephyr put a comforting hand on his best friend's shoulder. "There will be other Agents around to help while we're on our way and the captain is doing everything he can to get us over there as fast as possible."

He practiced worrying less—a gradual, but hopefully effective process. After conducting research the night before, he discovered mindful meditation and was willing to take a shot. So far, the breaths he held and exhaled soothed him, along with reminding himself of how Ava and Luna operate during these times.

"Exactly!" said Leif. "Since when did those two not be able to bounce back?"

Shadow exhaled. "I just..."

"You don't want to lose her. None of us do, but if Celia was with her this entire time, she should be safe," said Zephyr.

Star Strike's attempt at comforting Shadow poured down the drain not long after S.S. KAI returned to ship form and sailed above the surface. Port Kilia was in the distance, and all Zephyr could make out was a ton of smoke and buildings that were charred or singed completely.

Spark gaped. "The whole port... burnt down like that? But how?"

"We'll find out soon enough," said Dr. Willis. Docking at the port couldn't come sooner.

Spark and Shadow dashed down the stairs, almost tripping over each other. The entire town smelled like ashes, and something was off about what Zephyr sensed... Risen always composed of either pure darkness or mixed with another element. What had released into the atmosphere felt like nothing he had ever detected.

A tremor of shock rolled through Zephyr as he tightened his grip on Galeforce.

"Oh, Gods!" Spark gasped at the remains of the boardwalk they visited earlier. The boardwalk was now a pile of debris and bodies were littered everywhere. Not a single Specialist was present.

"That's the..." Shadow's voice sounded shaky when he pointed at the lifeless man in the familiar red and white striped uniform. "He was alive forty-eight hours ago, handing ice cream to us..."

"Let's go," said Luna. "We can mourn afterwards."

"C'mon, Spark," said Leif, grabbing her wrist.

"How can most of you be so okay with seeing all of this?" asked Spark as they walked through the rest of the town. Pain contained in her gasps.

Dr. Fern always sounded wise and logical. "Usually by the time a Specialist has served for a year, they statistically would have witnessed such an encounter at least once. It exponentially increases each year."

"It feels a lot worse when it's a place you were at..." said Aurora.

"Ya know, I never watch the news," began Spark. "Hated hearing about what the Agents couldn't save. It's discouraging. After spending our entire lives hearing all that crap about how we were indomitable, I believed it." Shadow looked at her with under-standing in his eyes, and so did Aurora.

"There's a lot that needs to be fixed with this organization AND the media," said Luna, taking the words out of Zephyr's mind.

"Living in a naïve, idealistic echo chamber does more harm than good."

"Their intention was to have everyone keep believing in the organization's aim, no matter how much bloodshed and reconstruction that had to be done," said Dr. Caraway. "The organization is how it is because of history and public perception. President Ziel has done as much as possible to fix it, but it's going to take more than him to mitigate."

Zephyr had always had the utmost respect for his father. It was even more so now. Every head of the organization had a new set of troubles to face, depending on the decade. The organization was very much capable of conducting questionable acts for the sake of saving the Mortal Realm.

No living human had been found by the time they returned to the entrance.

Zephyr glanced at the inn that was halfway torn down. He couldn't see any corpses...

"So... Skye and Celia aren't here... Otherwise, we would've found their remains... right?" asked Shadow. Aurora pulled out her Communicator once again to contact the Medic.

"How were they able to destroy the town so quickly? Gotta be a record," said Leif.

When Capala founded the organization, she predicted that the Risen could destroy cities in a few hours. Most didn't believe her.

Luna crossed her arms. "Well, these Risen were modified. I can imagine a lot stronger than what we've seen before."

"Mutations, huh? I see... So, that's what I sensed," said Zephyr. "But how'd someone control an entire army of Mutations?"

"These people can create Dark Spheres, manipulate areas with Spiritual Power, create Mutations AND order them around like that, create voids, AND have unique variations of Dark Spheres?" asked Luna, hand to her forehead. "Goodness. . ."

"What's the next move?" asked Shadow.

"We'll split three and three. Aurora and Shadow, you two will have to be in separate groups for sustainability. Same goes for Spark and Leif," replied Zephyr.

"One group for Maxia Forest, the other for the Silvatican Mountains," chimed in Luna.

"Shadow and Leif, you'll go with Luna to Maxia Forest. I'll take Spark and Rory. Once we're done, we'll meet back at Garnet," said Zephyr.

"We'll accompany you to Maxia Forest," said Dr. Caraway to Luna.

"Awesome!" said Leif.

"Guys, I got an update from Celia!" said Aurora. "They've evacuated everyone to Gessu and Skye's still asleep."

Shadow sighed. "Thank Celeste."

"She's going to be very confused when she wakes up," said Leif.

Spark lightly smacked him, stifling a grin.

24

WRATH

SKYE

Skye advanced through Cordelia Woods, making a quick pit stop before rejoining her team. It hadn't been long since she recovered from the electricity she should've never been hit with.

Triple Strike wouldn't have been badly wounded if Skye was around. She was supposed to be there the other night to help them find the Undead Host that killed Saylor. And others.

Skye would find that Undead Host. And kill it. Once and for all.

I've taken lives, by accident or otherwise. Someday, Astrid will be my next kill.

The more Skye thought about Astrid, the harder it was for her to do what she failed to do for the past years.

The day she first almost killed on purpose was the day the Hosts and the Wings of Order infiltrated one of Thanatos' Bases. They split up: Skye, Dove, and Aqua in one subgroup, everyone else in the other. Each assigned a half to investigate.

They were in Snowholt, by the glaciers. Thanatos' Base was underground, close to where INDRA, a now defunct organization, once operated. The thick masses of perennial ice would've gleamed if it wasn't near twilight.

Skye treaded carefully, hoping to not slip into any open

crevasses, mustering every bit of strength she had to stay focused on the mission, no matter what information attained.

Nuckalavee Risen came into view.

Snowholtians lived in constant fear of these creatures resembling a vile hybrid of man and beast. Its skinless body had a surface appearing raw. Black blood coursed through its veins when unshrouded by a dark aura. Every movement caused their sinewy muscles to writhe, and their gaping jaws spewed darkness.

Skye stared fear and death in the face countless times. After the Odin Massacre, little fazed her. Every thought of the sight of it razed her soul less and less.

Dove swung her spatha, creating precise, metal needles exploding upon contact.

Aqua twirled her lance, generating slices of water, severing their limbs.

Skye threw the head of her axe, allowing it to engulf in star-shaped flames and spin, creating crashing heatwaves. Parts of the flames melted more of the ice than desired.

What would've terrorized an entire town was gone in seconds. The sheer power and tenacity of two Hosts and the strongest human Agent... was immaculate.

"Your control's gotten better since last time," said Aqua, putting away her lance.

"Still not perfect."

"At least you're not training until collapsing anymore," said Dove brightly. "You've progressed faster when you're not burnt out."

Skye sighed. "Why do Hosts get burnt out like humans? Of all things?"

"Let's not dwell on it too much, okay?"

Truth be told, Skye should've felt happy to have both her Agent mentor and Host mentor on a mission with her, but she wasn't. Aqua was only there in case Skye's power went out of control.

Skye glanced at her wrists. Even after growing out of the bracelets, she was a liability. A walking time bomb... like Storm said. He wasn't as hostile anymore, but Skye wouldn't exactly consider them to be friends, either.

The waxing moon shimmered upon them. An airship glided through the skies, as predicted. Thanatos stole it from one of Vertbarrow's military factions, with blood-red adorning its prismic shape and triangular wings that directed forward with claws at the end. Laser cannons and four diffusers connected to its board engines.

With a nod, the girls activated their speed boosts, jumping on top of the ship.

Dove slipped through the door, knocking out the Thanatos members with swift punches to the side of the neck. Aqua moved the unconscious pilot and drove the air vehicle toward the red marker on the holographic map.

"This should bypass the security just fine. Especially if Blossom's disabled most of the security by now on their side," said Dove, after creating a rope of aura that trapped the Thanatos members and hiding them in the storage compartment of the ship.

Skye couldn't keep her eyes off the Thanatos grunts, armed with gunblades and mini-cannons. Their uniforms included gray trousers and long sleeves with a black flak jacket. Black buckles lined the waist and thighs and one wrapped around the upper arm, where the scythe-shaped crest marked its territory.

Were they there the night of the exams? Anger grew hotter inside her. Her fingers felt bonier and longer. Darkness consumed her left arm.

Dove put a warm hand on her shoulder. "You'll make it worse if you let your rage overtake you. While we're still trying to deduce if they're tied to the Risen and Hosts, you need to breathe."

"Don't let your emotions cloud your resolve," said Aqua. "Focus on intel and if necessary, capture them for interrogation."

Skye exhaled to quiet the unease roiling inside. Darkness decreased.

The airship plunged toward a range of snow-capped mountains. A metallic, rimmed tunnel opened underground, near the mountains' sides. Lights lit up their path as they made their descent. Ahead was the hangar, which held more ships.

Androids patrolled the area, coined, "Thanatos Guard-500" or "TG-500." The soldiers appeared slim and humanoid, clad in white armor with charcoal gray robotic workings underneath their joints. When alerted, their helmets glowed a red light over their black visors. Rifles slung across their backs.

"They move in a pattern," said Dove, checking her Communicator. "Zetta said most of 'em guard, while the humans do their thing. Their tech isn't advanced enough to detect much aside from line of sight and a certain level of sound."

They crept out of the ship, observing the patterns of the TG-500's.

Dove pressed a few keys. A holographic image appeared in front of them, with moving red dots showing their pathing. The hangar included a fuel storage, weapon storage, an aircraft system controller, and generators. TG-500's patrolled in front or beside them or near the entrance to the inside of the Base.

Aqua went first, hiding behind a pile of oil rigs, narrowly avoiding an android's field of view, motioning for the others. Skye and Dove hurried, stopping by a generator adjacent to the rigs. A TG-500 strolled a mere four meters away.

Weapon and fuel storage sections were next, with the Hosts crouching by it while Aqua dashed to the controller. She shot aura into the air sixty degrees, creating a mini burst of wind. A red light appeared on the visors of the two TG-500's guarding the entrance to the Base, and they walked in the wind's direction, pausing. Skye and Dove sped through the automatic doors with Aqua in tow, as the TG-500's returned to their positions. More robots stood in front of them, lighting up, leaving Dove to shoot them with an electric pistol, draining their battery and causing them to collapse. Aqua grabbed the bots and stuffed them into a closet nearby after pressing her Communicator against it to breach into it.

The halls were tunnel-like, with closed, circular entrances that had a standing lock with a card slot and fingerprint scanners. They ventured into a corridor split into four paths, each blocked. A Thanatos member from the right corridor, toward the upward one, and inserted a card into the slot.

As it opened, Dove activated her super speed, knocking the guy out cold and taking his key while Skye and Aqua followed. Dove moved the member's body off to the side, behind one shelf, trapping him with another rope, and shut the door.

Shelves lined the walls. Blades with crests belonging to the Thet, Taonian, and Cordelian royal families in one, another with Balancers from Gwynerva and Vertbarrow. Medallions and other ancient heirlooms from clans such as the Clarimond and Astalli looked dull in display cases.

"How much Gold is this worth?" asked Dove.

Skye's eyes found purchase on a shuriken from the Hikari clan. Maybe from a raid, after Kadelatha's rural villages bordering its capital city of Magneria got destroyed by Risen. Mini-barrels attached to it, accompanied by a compartment with a grappling hook.

"Modifications like these cheapen the value," said Aqua, glancing at a Lumière training glove with a keypad control attached. "If they want to earn funds or overpower us, 'corrupted people,' you could achieve the latter, but not with equipment like this. This looks copied from our outdated tech."

Dove sighed. "You'd think ex-Agents have better ideas for how to turn against us."

Aqua led them to the west wing. Sounds of weapons clashing and knives thrown echoed through the halls. Large windows lined the rooms, leaving the girls to stoop and catch glimpses. Children, presumably aged 10 to 14, sparred with each other, wielding similar aura-draining gloves and modified heirloom weapons. One had a blaster, replacing an amputated arm with a red core and switches. Skye wasn't much older than the eldest kids in the room.

Once making it to the end of the hall, Thanatos members popped in.

"Halt!"

Dove glowed white, unleashing a barrier, rendering the area soundproof.

Skye created strands of light aura to tie them up, pinning them to the ground.

One shrieked in pain as the rope seared through their uniform, and melted the floor, leading Skye to stop her aura.

Aqua slammed the back of her lance onto their backs, knocking them out.

"Sorry," said Skye.

"Good try," said Dove.

"Find somewhere to hide them," said Aqua. "There's gotta be another storage area."

Skye lifted half of the Thanatos members. "We could try that room at the end of the hall."

They unlocked it, revealing an area with beds separated by curtains and carts with medical supplies.

Dove inventoried the room while Aqua and Skye placed the unconscious Thanatos members within the sheets. "Just like any other rest area. Should be good."

The eastern wing had one door on the right. TG-500s flashed and grabbed their rifles. Some had red blades jut out of their wrists. They aimed at the girls, firing and dashing, swiping blades at them.

Dove disabled each one with her gun. She created a gust of wind, sweeping the disabled TG-500s and carrying them into the room with her after Aqua unlocked it.

The room was more spacious on the inside, with a generator in the center and lines of pods with TG-500s surrounding it and attached to it with cables. Tools were strewn about, along with blueprints for other android models and prototypes. A holographic monitor displayed data Skye couldn't comprehend. Skye tried to help Dove with her investigation, but there wasn't much she could do. She was awful at Recon and Intel gathering.

Before Dove could get to the monitor, the door opened.

"Haven't you already destroyed us enough?" asked a Thanatos

member, arriving with an ensemble behind him. "First you take over every world, sabotage our work, and now this."

His voice sounds familiar, thought Skye. Flashing images poured throughout her head. *Could it be... from the night of the exams?* Skye studied their faces. It was unclear, but it didn't stop the raging darkness building inside her.

"We're doing what we can to bring back peace!" said Dove.

"How is peace gained by having every world obey you?" asked another. "We're man enough to break free from your corruption."

Aqua frowned. "Attempting to exterminate my clan isn't the answer. We asked if you'd work with us. Negotiated. Warned you. We have no choice but to stop you by force." She drew her lance, dodging bullets from a rapid shuriken.

Skye caught the shuriken thrown at her, along with chains from the blasters. *They dare use my clan's weapons against me?*

Vacuum waves and knives spun in a circle around her. The impact of the waves destroyed parts of the walls as the room crumbled. With a hand wave, the hilt of the knives struck, disarming her targets, and knocking them against the pods, shattering part of it.

More clashes of metal occurred, and Aqua gasped, leading Skye to look up from her own fray. A chain wrapped around Aqua's neck, coming from the aura-draining glove. Mark of Lumière activated. Blue aura enclosed her, sapping out of her and into the chain. Aqua turned pale and sickly as her body trembled.

"A counter for your bloodline," said a Thanatos member, lips curled. "Finally."

Aqua collapsed.

"AQUA!"

One lifted her gunblade, about to stab Aqua through the heart. A familiar rage raised the hair on the back of Skye's neck. Darkness enveloped Skye.

Destroy them, said the darkness in her head.

Skye gathered metal aura and snapped her fingers, creating multiple slabs and slammed them against the Thanatos members, sending them crashing against walls. With a hand wave, Skye used one slab to crush the gunblade. Half of Skye's body shrouded in darkness, and she made full use of her third arm to grab Aqua's assailant by the neck, choking them.

Aqua's assailant gagged as her eyes watered.

Every piece of conjured metal burst into shards, leaving cuts on Skye's victims' limbs and stomach, painting the walls with splattered blood. The metallic, rusted stench left its own stains. Its vile pungency smothered and suffocated Skye. It was sickeningly sweet, like at Odin.

Retribution.

Knives emerged and Skye flared with bloodlust. She aimed, and the blades whirled as they multiplied, about to land a final blow.

Dove boosted herself, letting tempests of wind loose, driving Skye's blades away and surrounding the enemies. "That's enough."

"Skye. . .!" Aqua sounded hoarse as she stared at the blades and splattered blood.

Aqua was the one who trained Skye. She was a family friend. Zephyr's eldest sister. A high-ranking Specialist. The strongest human. And she was afraid of *Skye.*

Skye dropped her weapons, hearing them clang against the floor.

Dove shot small sparks out of her fingers, leaving the Thanatos members in a paralyzed state, and knocking them unconscious.

"Skye, what were you thinking?" asked Aqua, getting up.

"You almost died," replied Skye. The darkness faded.

Farien Principle Number Four: Never act out of aggression unless for the greater good.

Skye pondered whether the Farien Principles were relevant anymore. She was a monster. Why try to act like a hero? But… she wanted to uphold the principles—if she did horrible things out of her own volition, the least she could do was make up for it when possible.

Aqua sighed. "What you did was… completely against the moral code of an Agent."

Skye put her hands up in mock surrender. "It's not like I would've killed them for no reason! Your life was on the line!"

Dove walked up to them. "Killing can only be done as a last resort if there are no other approaches. There could've been other, peaceful ways to stop them. Your intentions weren't wrong. Just... don't do that again."

The anguish in Dove's eyes and her words made Skye look down in shame. "I'm sorry."

Skye reached for her fallen knives with trembling hands. Her blades were honed to fatal sharpness, capable of gliding through sections of human flesh as if they were paper. The hilts ran ice-cold against her fingertips as she reattached them to the straps around her thighs.

Dove's Communicator beeped, leading Skye to nearly drop a knife. "Zetta said they've found the locations of the other Thanatos Base. That's going to be where they're mainly operated. No association to Risen or Hosts seen so far, even in the files they searched."

Relief washed through Skye. Remorse took root inside her, colliding with the growing residue of shame and guilt.

"We can head back now," said Aqua, avoiding Skye's gaze.

Skye couldn't tear her eyes away from the unconscious Thanatos members.

It'd been a long night—it started rough, went smoother, got rough again, smoothed again... and now this. She almost killed several people. On purpose. But it was to save someone she cared dearly for.

Am I becoming a monster? Inside and out?

"Skye. We have to go," said Dove gently.

"I... I almost killed them."

"Skye, look at me." Dove held Skye by the shoulders. "You saved Aqua's life. We can worry about this later." She grabbed Skye's hand and led her out the door.

After the Odin Massacre, Skye swore to not take another life. She forgot about that promise that night. Unfortunately, her next kills were out of her control once more.

25

REMEMBRANCE

SKYE

OUT OF ALL THE PEOPLE TO BE HER NEXT KILLS, THESE WERE SKYE'S least unexpected. Skye was almost at the grave now. They thought it was fitting to place it on the edge of one of the highest cliffs, overlooking Cordelian Woods, even though they had no corpse to bury.

The day it happened, Dove, Teddy, and Storm had fluctuated power for months. Their mission was to destroy the hordes of Level 4 and 5 Risen dispersed around the grasslands of Cordelia.

"Teddy!" cried Skye as he stumbled.

Storm and Dove caught him.

Skye held in a sigh of relief.

Sometimes, they lasted weeks without rest. Others, they barely unleashed aura without collapsing. Every time it happened, Skye and the others sensed the weakening states.

"Thanks…" said Teddy.

Skye shook her head. "Why does this keep happening? You were doing fine this morning! And… why doesn't it happen to me?"

"No idea," replied Teddy.

"I have a feeling it's related to how only you can turn into that dark form," said Storm. "Must've done something to your stone the night of the exams."

Skye looked at him. "If only we had clues."

With Thanatos disbanded, no more leads were present. Skye's voracious hunger for answers and a way to break the curse triumphed. Her friends didn't deserve this. Dove especially suffered the most from the fluctuations—her smile lost most of its brightness and her skin no longer had that shimmering glow. Dark circles made its mark under her eyes, but she kept smiling.

"We'll find something, don't worry!" said Dove, cracking a weak smile. It became more difficult for her to put up a convincing facade as time passed.

We'll be heroes together, Skye. Don't you worry!

I'll be fine! Don't worry about me!

Skye, wipe that worry off your face! We'll figure it out! And end the curse!

Teddy stood up, brushing himself off. "C'mon, we got a mission to finish before it gets too dark. Then, we can finally go home and sleep!"

"We all could use some," said Dove, elbowing Skye.

Skye grinned sheepishly. "Hey! I get at least four hours these days!"

"Way better than zero." Dove wiggled her finger in disapproval. "This kid thought she could function, only to faint the most amount of times I've ever seen anyone do in my entire life!"

Storm smirked. "There's a reason why she's never been the 'Brains' of whatever team she's placed on."

Skye grimaced. *Ouch.*

Teddy smacked Storm on the shoulder. "Don't be rude!"

Skye snickered. "Okay. You're not *wrong.*"

Crashing occurred further north, interrupting their laughter.

Everyone followed the noise, past the rock formations and vegetation. An army of Level 4 and 5 Risen emerged from piles of dark voids. They weren't anything the Hosts hadn't fought before, except this time, there seemed to be more darkness around them than usual.

Teddy boosted himself and shot bullets out of his gunblade, activating his super speed. He moved faster than Skye could see, slicing through the air, creating fiery diagonal lines. They combined, transforming into magma pillars and a heat wave that burned through the Level 4s dark flames.

Swinging his sword, an enormous, violet, circular pattern appeared below Teddy, and he raised his weapon into the air. Layered circles of electric aura rose, and a violet lightning bolt struck the middle. Asteroids made of aura rained down upon the enemies.

Level 5s unleashed blasts of darkness strong enough to wipe out an entire town.

Storm's eyes turned golden, and he jumped in front, tanking every hit with his durability shield like it was child's play. Spinning his staff, he stabbed the ground with it. A hyperresonance swept through the battlefield, generating chain reactions of explosions.

"Don't overdo it," said Storm. Raising the staff into the air, he summoned thunder clouds producing lightning.

"Can't let you hog all the fun!" said Dove, emitting a glow from her eyes. Wind rushed out of her hands, transforming into a horse. Mounting it, she grabbed her spatha, throwing it over her head as she whacked and struck Risen once her ride was in range, also taking all explosions directed at her without trouble. Pointing her sword at a Level 5, a twister shot out of it and the horse grew wings.

Raising her fist, Skye slammed it into the ground, creating a massive crevasse, swallowing more whole. She snapped her fingers, allowing the crevasse to glow brown and revert. "I got it under control this time!"

"Proud!" Dove gave her a thumbs up. She looked radiant, as if she consumed thousands of energy supplements and her aura reserves completely replenished. "Lemme handle the rest!"

Dove zigzagged toward the remaining army. Golden circles appeared on the ground, forming a constellation, and bursts of light exploded. Millions of hands of darkness tailed her, and Dove created a mirror made of water aura, ricocheting the attacks. She disappeared, transforming herself into a humongous light arrow, filling the sky with magic circles and meteor storms fired from them.

The light was so strong; it blinded Skye. Once it faded, all enemies disappeared.

"How's that! Piece of cake, right?"

The Hosts caught Dove as she fell.

Dove's hands turned transparent and crystallized fragments emerged from her body, rising above the surface. Orbs of darkness floated from her palms.

Skye gasped. "Dove! You're... fading away!"

Dove's expression was unyielding, even as the transparency and darkness spread to her upper body. "I'm sure it's nothing to worry about."

"You've always told me not to worry!"

"What's... going on?" asked Teddy, eyes widened.

"You used a lot of aura back there," said Storm. "Maybe you're just... I-I don't know."

Dove's body continued to fade. "Skye, what did I tell you about wiping that worry off your face? I'll be fine! Promise!" She cupped Skye's face with her hand.

"I can't feel your-" Darkness covered Dove's body.

More crystals and orbs appeared, and Dove vanished into nothingness.

"DOVE!" screamed Skye, standing up, eyes wet. "Where'd you go? DOVE!"

"She's... gone," said Teddy. He wrapped his arms around Skye. "I'm sorry."

"Gone? Gone where?" asked Skye. The ground seemed to drop below her feet as a sob tore out of her throat. "No, it's impossible. It can't happen. We're Hosts. That's... No, that's not... How is that possible?"

Storm joined their hug. "I... I don't know."

Skye thought all the consequences that came along were temporary effects of the curse. That damn curse. It could happen to any of them somehow... But why Dove? And... why Astrid, too?

It all brought more questions than answers. The remaining Hosts pursued their search. Skye would do anything to bring Dove back. She owed it to her.

⋯ ❧ ⋯

THEY VENTURED to a cave in Vertbarrow, weeks later. Supposedly, the cave had a powerful Risen, a Level 5 or Undead Host. In the past, when they destroyed Undead Hosts, they'd see visions of individuals in their previous lives, before or after defeat. It always started off with a humanoid silhouette. Darkness would disappear, revealing their identities. Nobody recognized them, however.

At the end of the cave, she stood.

Dove was as radiant as the sun. The smile, the damn smile on her face, only reminded Skye how loving and genuine she was.

Skye stared at the image before her. Tears of joy dripped from her eyes. "Dove...?" She ran over to her, arms open. "Dove! It's you!"

"Wait!" called Teddy.

Dove struck Skye in the abdomen with her spatha and pulled it out.

Gore gushed out as Skye gasped. She was about to strike again when Storm created a temporary barrier, pushing Dove away.

"She's an Undead Host," said Storm. "We have to put an end to her."

"No, it's me, Dove!" Her voice, her smile through the pain—everything was the same. How could Skye... destroy her? "Did you forget me... like the others?"

Skye hesitated. "But there's no darkness around her! She's more real than the others! It... It must be Dove! Not... an Undead!"

"Dove wouldn't attack us," said Teddy. "It's another illusion."

Skye missed the days when they didn't believe illusions existed.

Darkness shot out of Dove's palm and wrapped around them.

Storm and Teddy boosted themselves.

Skye's head cascaded with memories: when they first met, when Dove cradled Skye after revealing she was a Host, training together, the time she comforted Skye after the Odin Massacre, when they stopped Thanatos. All the smiles, hands on her shoulder, all the times she told Skye to "not worry."

Explosions occurred and Skye felt another blade strike her left side as she slammed against the cave wall, snapping her out of the illusions. Blood dripped down Skye's lips.

The stars aided Skye that night. Unfortunately, that wasn't enough.

Storm and Teddy fought toe-to-toe with Dove, moving so fast that Skye couldn't track what was happening. Dove landed a punch on Teddy, breaking his durability shield and ugly, cracking noises echoed. The cave would've been destroyed if not for Storm's barriers.

Faster. And stronger than us.

The enemy flipped between appearing as Dove and the familiar, humanoid silhouette.

Dove gripped Storm by the neck, squeezing it. Darkness surrounded Storm, suffocating him. Skye sprang forward, holding Excalibur, shooting blasts out of it. She was still getting accustomed to wielding the sacred sword, but felt it was essential to use.

Skye grimaced, both from attacking Dove and from blood loss. Her head spun.

Dove released the most potent forms of darkness Skye had ever seen. They hit Teddy, covering his body with darkness, draining him as he writhed. Excalibur glowed, transforming to its other state, meant for creatures of darkness.

Skye boosted herself and shot photon blasts of light at Dove, using some to form into an exploding chain. A black claw materialized, trapping Skye.

Orbs of darkness cast at Storm. He dodged them, using a burst of wind from his hands to shoot him up and create a meteor, slamming it onto Dove. Storm grabbed her. Dark hands crept from below, wrapping around his body and neck. He snapped and engulfed himself and plunged into flames. The hands around Skye disappeared.

Skye raised Excalibur, readying her strike.

As she almost landed it, Dove smiled again, and she hesitated, stopping her attack. Two dark arms ejected, throwing them backward.

"Why'd you STOP?" yelled Storm. "She could've been down with that hit!"

Skye flinched. "I'm... sorry. I can't... do it."

Teddy covered himself in metal aura, breaking free. Turning himself into another gunblade, he and his own weapon floated in the air, blitzing through Dove in an "X" pattern. The hands vanquished again.

Activating his super speed, Storm grabbed the blades and stabbed Dove through the heart, crossing his arms. All darkness evaporated, revealing Dove with her body transparent.

"Thank you for setting me free," said Dove.

"Dove... it's... you?" asked Teddy.

She nodded. "My soul was trapped and tormented in that dark body."

Storm and Teddy's eyes glistened.

"I'm glad it was you who killed me. I don't think anything else could've been done."

Skye went toward Dove, trying to hug her, but to no avail. "Dove... I'm so sorry!" She felt nothing once again.

"I told you not to worry." A smile lurked at her lips. "There're more souls to release, including Astrid. You need to focus on them next."

Skye choked back a sob. "I tried... I thought this was something we could undo... part of the curse. But... we failed you."

"Wipe those tears and keep moving forward. We're counting on you to break the curse. It's too late for us, but... it's now up to you. Promise me you'll do this for our sake. For me, Astrid, everyone else we've lost."

"We will," said Teddy, wiping his face.

"Set them free and become heroes." Dove smiled once more, as she faded into light. "Goodbye, everyone. I'm glad I got to meet you all. Never... forget me."

The light disappeared.

Teddy comforted Skye as she wept, soaking his clothes with her teardrops.

Storm sniffled, sobbing. The three of them stood huddled, keeping each other warm.

· · ·❨· ·

UNFORTUNATELY, only Skye was left to keep the promise.

When Storm's time came, Skye had to deal the killing blow.

Teddy was by her side that time. Eventually, Teddy had to be finished by her as well, and she was the only one there... to comfort herself. By the time he passed, Skye realized how alone she was. As the last Host. She wished she could see her old friends once more, but her heart pumped for reasons unknown.

Those were some of the hardest memories for Skye to think about. Every anniversary of someone's death triggered them. The excess darkness flooding her mind didn't help...

Skye retrieved a bouquet of Celestial Lillies from her Communicator storage. "Hey, Dove." She placed them on the tombstone. A light breeze brushed a few of the petals.

The one who attempted to take care of her, check up on her, and be there in her time of denial was Dove. Dove was the reason Skye and Astrid accepted their fates and without her, they wouldn't have moved forward. Dove was the hero Skye wanted to be but couldn't be. The one to be of service.

Skye's throat closed as tears welled in her eyes. "You hated seeing me cry."

Wipe those tears and keep moving forward. She brushed them away, sniffling. Dove's words carved a wound in her chest.

Skye could barely breathe. Her heart and head ached. Guilt tangled inside her. She was ashamed of the mess she made and regretted the lives she'd taken and almost taken. She was ashamed of the lies, coverups, and everything else she'd committed that dishonored the Farien name. But she would conduct those acts again to save her friends. She would do *anything* for her friends.

Skye clutched Excalibur, allowing her most prized possession to strengthen her resolve.

26

MARAUDER AND THE BEAST
SHADOW

SHADOW HALF-EXPECTED ANOTHER LECTURE FROM LUNA BEFORE going to bed when they teleported to Sapphire for the night. He imagined Zephyr would've loved to tour around on the Mythril-powered trams that connected all districts in the city.

"Good night," said Luna, disappearing into her room at the inn. They investigated areas outside of the enormous Maxia Forest. Luna's senses got fuzzy. She also had migraines from overexposure. Therefore, they had no choice but to call it for today. And continue tomorrow. It wouldn't hurt to skip training this time since they were all exhausted, right?

Leif turned on the electronic screen and retrieved a bag of potato chips and fruit snacks. Last time Leif produced a snack pile from his Communicator, Luna snapped at him for chewing too loud.

"Wow, they got your spikes down!" said Shadow, pulling out an orange fruit snack in the shape of Leif's head.

"They even got Aurora's hair clippie thingies!" Her fruit snack form was lavender, like her favorite color.

When they had to stock up in Sapphire, one of the first things they saw were the fruit snacks. They nearly laughed themselves to tears. Shadow sent a picture to the group chat and Zephyr and Glacieus got the biggest kick out of it. Star Strike posters and keychains were one thing, but FRUIT SNACKS? Kadelathans and Thetians were their biggest fans outside of Cerberus.

It was a light-hearted break from all the nonsense that went on for the week. Right now, the most stressful thing was Luna being on their case. Especially now that they were alone with her. Unfortunately, her tendency to act more like a manager than a friend to them extended.

"Here come the Garnet Phoenix's and the Gessu Griffons!" called the announcer.

Cheers came from the audience as the StrikeBall teams came out to the field.

"Phoenix's were to take on the Lastalia Chimaeras tonight. . ." said Shadow sadly. He thought StrikeBall would've been the least affected by all the terror. One of their star players got killed during the assault on the fallen city. Rest of the team was on standby.

Reconstruction would've taken forever. There were too many places and buildings to rebuild. Lumière Inc. could only do so much while the rest was up to the governments.

"Yeah… I wonder what they're gonna do about Castor's team. It's in better shape, but they lost their stadium and equipment."

⋯ ⟨ ⋯

THEY RESUMED their investigation at the spot they left off the next day. Shadow didn't mind having Luna as a leader. What he DID mind, was Luna ignoring how much more powerful he'd gotten. Almost as if she purposely avoided praising him.

Whenever Shadow asked Luna about how good he was doing, she got dismissive.

"Stay up front, Leif."

"Could use yer boosting spells to speed this up, ya know," replied Leif. "Not used to all this fighting in a row!"

It was a Level 3. Ones with defensive abilities were the few Leif couldn't one shot. Instead of focusing his power into one hit, Luna wanted him to practice his precision, so he'd use less aura.

"You don't need it."

"Dude, this is gonna tire me out more!"

"Not if your aura is trained enough." Leif scowled, about to argue.

"How's the sensing coming along?" asked Shadow, hoping to change the subject.

"There's definitely something in the forest, but it's fuzzy. There's something else out here too, but I don't know what it is."

"Then let's check out what's over here since it's closer," said Dr. Caraway. "I have no clue what you could sense if it's so unclear."

Luna led them to a clearing that was along the outskirts of the forest. The only noteworthy thing was a golden shrine with the Thet Royal symbol on it. "A Spirit Shrine? That's what I was sensing this entire time?" She facepalmed. "Gods, I'm an idiot. Sorry, everyone."

None of her clan could distinguish the difference between Spiritual Power or aura when sensed. They appeared the same, sensory-wise, so it wasn't her fault.

"Not all for naught," said Dr. Willis. "We have updated intel on the area, and you cleared the nests."

On their way back to the warp panel, the all-too-familiar warning alert blared. This time, their Communicators read: *Assault on Nara.*

"Again?" asked Leif. "Ugh, gimme a break!"

I WON'T let this turn into another Lastalia or Port Kilia! I'll be the hero! I'll show Luna that I'm astounding!

Shadow was out of breath by the time they got to the panel and teleported to Nara's entrance. While it had some modernized-looking skyscrapers, there were traditional Kadelathan styles for residence and shrines. Curved roofs supported by posts and lintels, moveable screens and sliding doors, were present within most of the wooden houses. During times of peace, cranes often perched on tops of most buildings.

Risen dropped from voids in the skies like raindrops. Shadow cringed at the crimson willows that had been knocked over. At least no buildings were damaged... yet.

Lumière battleships flew above, and Agents jumped down, landing beside them.

"We'll take care of Ice Tetra while you guys keep moving!" said one of the team leaders.

"Make 'em count, Luna!" cheered another Agent.

What about ME? I'm Shadow Hikari, for Celeste's sake!

A Beast Risen resembling the silhouette of a regular Beast Morpher was in the distance, lunging toward a young boy.

A little girl wasn't too far behind.

The Beast was likely going to target her next.

Shadow chucked the head of Diablos, knocking it aside.

Reinforcements came into the alley as Diablos' head returned.

"Leif, get the children out of here!" ordered Luna, holding off the reinforcements, allowing Shadow to run over to the girl and block another hit with Diablos' handle.

"C'mon! We'll get ya outta here!" said Leif to the boy.

"Don't fear him! He won't bite and he's here to help!" said Luna, keeping the remaining reinforcements in her line of sight.

"Okay, crazy lady!" The boy climbed onto Leif's back.

"Crazy lady?"

The Beast was faster than Shadow, annoying him to no end. There were too many close calls, almost getting the girl hurt in the crossfire. He hated to admit it, but he needed Leif to return as soon as possible. Luckily, they were close to the entrance.

Leif sprinted over to him and the girl. "I'll get you to safety!"

"You'll protect me, too?" The girl choked back a sob.

"Of course!" She climbed onto his back, and he departed back to the entrance.

Shadow, switching Diablos to staff form, jabbing the Beast's belly.

Luna came over to Shadow and wrapped her whip around the

Beast, tossing it into the air. Shadow spun his staff around, generating a record amount of dark orbs, blasting it into smithereens.

"Took you awhile," remarked Luna.

Shadow seethed, gripping Diablos. *Did she NOT see what I did? It takes A LOT to do that with Gwymond Darkness!*

The alleyway was empty, save for rotten orange peaches that fell from crushed fruit stands. An explosion occurred up above.

"What the?" Shadow heard Leif behind them.

A Lumière battleship plummeted from the skies, emitting smoke. The trio ran out of the alleyway toward the falling ship, making it to the concrete streets. A raging inferno shot up at heights higher than the skyscraper, decimating hordes of flying Risen.

Before the ship could crash, someone stood before it, catching it with their right hand. A mane of black and caramel hair flowed from the impact. The figure used their free hand to grab a sword to shoot blasts of light aura at a flock of Risen swooping down below.

Shadow bolted toward her. "Skye!"

"Shadow, wait!"

A pile of Risen appeared before him, blocking the way. Before they made another move, the same flames exploded. Standing before Shadow was none other than his teammate in Beast form.

Leif and Luna caught up.

"Whatcha doin' here?" asked Leif.

"I'll explain later," replied Blaze.

Luna frowned at Shadow. "No more charging in like that."

Skye set the ship down. Only the backside had damage.

Agents emerged with minor injuries. "Thank whoever created the concept of barriers," said one of them. "Thank you, Skye and Blaze."

"Any major casualties?" asked Luna.

"Nah, we got the barriers up in time before the flocks exploded on us," said another Agent. "Pity that we couldn't do it on the entire ship, but at least we're in one piece."

"Still annoying to have one less ship for evacuating, though," said an Agent. "Anyway, we should go."

Shadow embraced his twin. She froze for a split second, smiling and hugging him back. "I was so worried about you!"

Skye raised an eyebrow. "About me? I was more worried about you guys."

Leif gave her a funny look.

"I'd love to stay and chit-chat, but we have to check out the rest," said Luna.

They passed other Agents evacuating civilians to the surviving airships. Nara wasn't as large as Lastalia or Castor, so they scouted at a faster rate. Shadow recognized teams of his former classmates. He hadn't seen them since the graduation ceremony.

Shadow caught sight of the half-torn up verandas and fallen bonsai trees. Vehicles and stone bridges had missing portions. Nara River would've been gleaming and filled with sparkle, but the water was murky and littered with debris.

Massive chunks of a falling building crashed from above. Blaze shielded Leif and Luna from the debris on one side, letting it bounce off his body while Skye raised her left fist above her head to cause a chunk the size of a house to shatter into nothingness.

Luna nodded. "Nice job."

Shadow felt a flash of irritation. *Is it THAT hard to tell me that, too?*

In the next section, hordes of airborne Risen appeared.

Skye jumped and landed on top of another skyscraper to take care of them.

Screams pierced the air.

Shadow dashed toward them.

Two clusters of civilians were present in this district, trapped between ruined statues of the Gods and Level 3 Beowulves. They were similar in physical appearance to their lower leveled counterparts, but larger and with jagged claws. These were as easy to kill as any other Level 3 but dealt more damage than most.

One cluster was closer to them, but with six people.

Luna and Blaze headed toward the further away one, which had twice the amount of victims, leaving Leif and Shadow behind.

So, they think I can't handle the harder one to save, huh?

"Ugh!" Luna winced as a Beowulf slashed her right arm, leaving a nasty gash.

Shadow charged, barrelling Diablos' head onto the Beowulf, sending it flying away from Luna. Gathering his Gwymond Darkness, he spun Diablos, creating a silhouette of himself instead of orbs. He and the silhouette mirrored each other, both landing blows against a handful of Beowulves. Before he could finish them, Luna lodged metal shards into their bodies.

Shadow was about to complain about taking his kills, but he heard more screams.

Leif stood alone, encircled by Beowulves. They knocked several civilians unconscious. Beowulves multiplied, leaving Leif struggling to hold them off, getting slammed against a statue.

As they were about to land fatal blows on the civilians, a hatchet with Sylfiran flames spun, knocking them away. Trails of needles appeared, pinning the enemies. A Beast Morpher slashed her claws against the Beowulves.

Twilight Treader.

Instead of signature gauntlet blasts showing up, a guy with red hair and brown eyes struck with his katana. He stabbed the ground, creating crevasses that swallowed the remaining Beowulves whole.

Malcolm. Not Saylor.

"Just in time," said Adriel. "We'll evacuate them."

Leif got back to his feet as Luna and Blaze arrived. "Thanks, guys."

Once Twilight Treader disappeared with the civilians, Leif turned to Shadow. "Why d'ya leave me alone? They would've been killed!"

"I thought you could handle it!"

Luna glared at Shadow as if she wanted to bury him alive. "Well, obviously he couldn't. Blaze and I were fine."

"You were hurt!"

Skye landed beside them, jumping off a nearby building.

"We all know you wanted the praise and glory and show off. Don't pull that shit on me. You wanted to play hero-"

Skye raised her hands. "Luna, that's enough. I don't have context, but I'm sure Shadow had good intentions."

Leif groaned. "Course, YOU defend him. You think he can do no wrong."

Skye frowned. "What's *that* supposed to mean?"

"Guys," said Blaze. "Save this for another time."

"He's. . . right," said Luna admittedly. "We've got more pressing things at the moment."

"Castor all over again," muttered Leif, leading Skye to bite her lip.

They surveyed the rest of the district. Aside from shattered streetlights and scattered signs ripped into shreds, there was nothing noteworthy here.

"Rest of Nara is clear!" said Adriel.

Shadow turned, seeing Twilight Treader behind them. "No reports of deaths for the time being. Not a ton of damage had been dealt overall to the city, either. Compared to other ones, at least."

"Glad to hear," said Luna. "We can head out."

Star Strike walked alongside Twilight Treader.

"Those were your flames that filled up the streets, Blaze?" asked Senna.

Both Morphers reverted to human form.

Blaze nodded.

"It'd take me a year to conjure up flames that formidable."

"Goes to show how like the rest of Star Strike, Blaze was at the top of our class," said Adriel to Malcolm.

Shadow found it hard to get used to seeing him as part of Twilight Treader.

Malcolm glanced at Star Strike. "Makes sense. Even if Star Strike wasn't at the top, wouldn't they have gotten extra training to get there?"

"Something like that," Blaze replied.

Special treatment brought levels of resentment and envy within their classmates, but most of them got over it by gradua-tion. Whenever Zephyr felt guilty about the favoritism, Blaze and

Luna reminded him what it was for. It made perfect sense to Shadow.

"What brings you here?" asked Senna. "Heard you were with the other half of Nova Strike."

"They're currently working with the Wings of Order, so it was best to summon Blaze here for the sake of getting accustomed to Star Strike. He's also going to be invaluable for our trek through Maxia Forest," Luna replied.

Blaze readjusted the chain around his neck. "I was going to meet them in Sapphire tonight when the alerts went off."

"Damn. Boggles my mind how y'all are working with elite teams already. At B-rank," said Adriel. "Crazy how we're technically the same rank, too. Not too far behind y'all!"

"Oh, yeah? We'll see!" said Shadow.

"They're not too far behind," pointed out Luna, eying Leif and Shadow in a way that made him uncomfortable. Something told him another lecture was brewing.

They arrived at the entrance's warp panel.

"Welp, guess we'll see ya later!" said Adriel. "Sometime, we gotta compare our skills side-by-side, Shadie!"

"Sure!" Twilight Treader waved and disappeared.

"So that was Malcolm. Glad they're doin' better."

"Time heals," said Blaze.

"Right," agreed Luna. "They'll fare well. Malcolm's a formidable powerhouse. Anyway, we should get back to Sapphire. Long day ahead tomorrow."

"Are ya comin' with us, Skye?" asked Shadow.

"The others are in the Silvatican Mountains, right?" Shadow nodded. "I'll join them."

"I was about to suggest that," said Luna, sounding stiff. "Minimize risks."

Skye waved and disappeared into the light.

"All right. Once we're back at the inn, we need to talk," said Luna, pointing at Leif and Shadow, who exchanged looks.

⸱⸱⸱◗⸱⸱

THE JOURNEY from the warp panel to the inn to Luna's room seemed like an eternity. Every step along the pavement, the lacquered, wooden lobby floors, and freshly vacuumed carpet felt heavier. Shadow wanted to get it over with. He twiddled his thumbs as he waited for Blaze to handle changing their room to a triple.

They were going to get a tongue-lashing. Worse than previous ones. Luna's icy demeanor told Shadow everything he needed to know.

Blaze gave them a sympathetic look before Shadow and Leif followed their leader into her room and shut the door behind them.

She eyed them. "I was gonna have this talk tonight, regardless. But more needs to be addressed than thought." Luna tapped keys onto her Communicator. "Open what I've sent you."

Shadow skimmed over what she sent—a report. Of his performance. Graphs and charts showcased Shadow's current stats and growth rates. And his expected rates vs. actual ones. Luna wrote a comment, stating he was doing "slightly above average."

Leif skimmed the report. "Isn't this good?"

"For the average Specialist, your results would be fine. For you, it's not gonna look good amongst the higher-ups if this continues. You both fluctuated too much between 'good' and 'slightly above average' which is NOT what we should see at your peak period. You should be between 'good' and 'outstanding.'"

"What's 'good' in your eyes?" snapped Leif.

"Not needing my boosting spells to kill the Hawk Risen at a faster pace than you did back there. And being able to take down more than a Beast Risen on your own. Twilight Treader being around today, was a nail in the coffin. They're not far behind you. They're not even a Dream Team and they're like that. Obviously, it's an indicator that you're not working hard enough. And are incompetent by Dream Team standards."

Leif cocked an eyebrow. "We've trained these past days, except for yesterday! We're tryin'!"

"You should've done that earlier and for more than an hour, and I shouldn't be the one to tell you how long you need to train for each thing you need to master. If you aren't meeting the high standards for Star Strike, then you're only going to be a liability. Otherwise, you can join a different team."

Shadow and Leif looked at each other, speechless.

"Performance isn't the only thing. You need to have the mindset of a Specialist. And always trying to be a hero, hogging the glory, and trying to look good, isn't it." She glowered at Shadow. "You're prioritizing that over the state of the Mortal Realm. You don't care about saving lives."

"Not true!" sputtered Shadow. "I-"

Luna put up a hand. "Spare me. Being a Farien and descendant of Celeste and hyped up as a member of the Dream Team for your entire life has gotten over your head. It's made you deluded and your excessive pride is a hindrance. We were all stupid to not see it earlier. You keep asking for praise, but all that won't make things better. It'll make it worse."

"Star Strike having all those successful missions inflated your ego. Guess what? None of that means shit if the Mortal Realm gets destroyed in three years! Maybe we'll save it by then, but who the Tartarus knows? All I know is you're never going to be a Marauder if you keep being a dumbass."

Shadow wished he could snap his Communicator in two. "You know what-"

"Learn to be a Specialist. Or quit. Being here for the wrong reasons and being insufferable will turn you into dead weight. Or dead. Like Saylor." Leif gasped. "But at least Saylor had a noble sacrifice. If he didn't sacrifice himself, we would've been slaughtered. He didn't do it for the sake of appearing 'heroic.'"

Leif and Shadow stood speechless.

Rage consumed Shadow, but he couldn't find the words.

"No lame excuses? Gods, this is giving me another migraine." Luna rubbed her forehead. "Well, if you have nothing else to say, you can leave. Take in everything I said and put it to use. Or else there WILL be more consequences."

Blaze looked up from his book when they sulked into the triple. "Heard what happened. Walls are thin."

"How much longer is she gonna to be up our asses?" asked Leif. "And demoralizing us?"

"She was like that with Nova Strike when we became Specialists."

"Was she ever completely tactless with you guys?" asked Leif. "Is she less patronizing toward you since you guys are closer?"

"Critical, yes. Tactless, no. She never told us what she's seen on missions, but it's hardened her a lot." Blaze set down his book on the nightstand. "She never held back on pointing out my mistakes, either. I'm not justifying anything, but perhaps she's on your case to prevent another hardening outcome with Star Strike."

"Hardening outcome?"

"Like what happened to Twilight Treader. Gap between B, A, and S-rank is questionable. As a Dream Team, we'd be in far harder and riskier missions when we get there. Luna's seen a lot. She's doing what she thinks is best to ensure we stay alive… If the Mortal Realm doesn't collapse."

Shadow missed the wise-cracking, softer Luna who made jokes all the time. Hearing the belittling made it feel like a dark cloud permanently hung over his head and dragged him down.

"It'd help to be encouraging," said Leif, softening. "Instead of attacking us."

"She'll come around," said Blaze. "Though I can see her point. She's right about prioritizing the Realm. And fully using our peak periods so we can minimize the odds of dying as much as possible."

"I guess." Shadow shrugged. Her accusations rang in his ears, stabbing him repeatedly. "But is it true? All those things she said about… me? Caring about things for the wrong reasons?" He looked at Leif, who avoided his gaze.

"Think of the big picture. Maybe some priorities need to be

reassessed. You can enjoy whatever those are after we save the Realm. If we save the Realm," said Blaze.

27

WALLS
ZEPHYR

ZEPHYR ASSUMED THE SIRENS WOULD BE AS PLEASANT TO WORK WITH as Ice Tetra. They were a younger team of Briton Researchers but seemed more "hip" (no offense to Dr. Caraway, as cool as he was). They had to cover the areas east of Garnet City and work their way up to the Silvatican Mountains.

"Nice to meet you, Cornelia!" said Dr. Schnee. She told Star Strike they could ride on her back in Dragon form for quicker transport. "We were cheering for you at the Vigor tournaments! We have errands to run in this town, but I'd love to hear more about your experience later."

"Sure thing!" replied Spark. Sometimes she took an extra second to realize she was spoken to whenever anyone used her real name. At the Academy, even professors called her "Spark."

Frelia was a small, suburban town with a giant clock tower in the square. The inn, followed by a Panda Emporium, was right next to the tower. It was cozy with a mystic air and brick buildings, built after the Kingdom Spirits era in opposition to the spread of technology around the world. One could find only basic electronic devices.

"So, this place preserved the ancient history of Silvatica! Well, the good parts at least," said Zephyr.

"I swear ya become more of a nerd each year," said Spark, retying her ponytail.

"You're not wrong."

"It's okay, Zeph! We still love ya! Not as much as SOME OTHER people, though!" Spark elbowed him repeatedly.

Frelia's only inn was tiny and mostly booked when they came, so they had to share an extra-large room. A screen wall separated his bed from theirs, and it seemed as if every centimeter of spare space was utilized effectively. Somehow, a brown sofa fit through the door.

Aurora rummaged through her storage, pulling out a hairbrush. "Ugh, I have this annoying knot in the back."

"Whatta knotty problem!" said Spark, earning an eye roll from Aurora and a chuckle from Zephyr. All her puns were great, as much as the others groaned at them.

His Communicator went off and the holographic call icon popped up along with Celia's profile. "Wanted to give an update on your teammate," said Celia. "She's home on bed rest."

"Currents were that bad?" asked Spark.

Spark had never seen Skye sustain injuries during Astro Strike's missions. People frequently painted Marauders as invincible and almost impossible to harm. Given her admiration of the Queen of Blades, her surprise then and now was understandable.

"Couple days. And it's more than currents. She sustained nerve damage and demolished reserves."

"Demolished from what?"

Celia hesitated with the same expression adults had when they realized they've said too much. Zephyr recognized that look from his mother and Lukas. "It's classified."

"What? What's classified about that?" Everyone else shot Spark a look.

"Thanks for the update, Celia," said Zephyr.

She nodded and her holographic image faded before Spark continued badgering.

Lukas and Seren hadn't brought up anything about Skye disappearing that night after dinner. Whenever anyone asked about where she went in the past, they always said, "destroying stronger Risen." Over the years, Zephyr learned how to detect a change in pitches of their voices from Blaze.

Spark tapped her chin. "Eila wouldn't let that slip. When'd that happen? No way it happened back in Taonia."

"Maybe when she disappeared after dinner the last time I was there. Maybe even earlier, like when she went on day missions without us," replied Zephyr.

The longest anyone could survive with discarded aura storage within their bodies was three weeks. Medics trained in the art of removal surgery to prevent fatalities and it was partially why the organization encouraged Agents to retreat to Base weekly if possible—exhausting aura was disadvantageous for reasons other than causing fatigue. Power-wise, Skye was within the elite, but she wasn't around long enough to have built up stamina and resilience of aura levels like the rest.

How many times has she recklessly used her boosts?

"Why didn't she tell me about her destroyed reserves?" asked Aurora. "She's keeping things from us... just like our parents. You know, I thought these months of seeing her every day would've been different. She'll train with me outside of missions and is so sweet, but she won't let me in."

Zephyr's mind went down a rabbit hole, and he thought back to her tortured screams whenever he spent the night in Shadow's room. It was the most painful thing for him to hear, and more memories overflowed.

"Zephyr! Where are you?" A shuddering Skye looked back and forth for him, as if a Risen was going to pop out and attack in the woods by her house.

"I'm here!" Zephyr was behind her. They were the seekers in their hide-and-seek game. "Take my hand."

She grabbed it, squeezing tightly, and he felt a sweet feeling pool in his chest.

Skye feared anything that might've hidden Risen at six, even though Garnet City was the safest place in the world. She insisted on coming with them—being alone kept her mind clear enough for flashbacks to creep in.

"Thank you, Zeph... Sorry for being needy..."

He gave her pigtails a playful tug. "Stop apologizing!"

Either she apologized for "being needy" or trained hard enough to "stop being needy." Sometimes she'd leave classes early for appointments where they'd repeatedly expose her to captured Risen. Zephyr had asked why they would do something as dangerous as that and Skye stuck with it no matter what, citing that it could help her become the hero she always dreamed of. The hero of service.

They were at the manor in their training yard. Zephyr sat down after failing to convince Skye to take a break.

She struck the dummy with a golden glow in her eyes and sent it flying across the yard. It was strange to see her be able to use her aura to enhance her strength at eight years of age. He remembered seeing Instructor Cross gape at her for doing that during a sparring match, as if her data files didn't list it being possible.

She wobbled, and Zephyr ran up to her to put his arms on her shoulders before falling over. He walked her over to the seat next to him, plopping her down. "You don't need to push yourself like this."

"I have to. I have to serve my bloodline. And no longer make everyone worry."

Her power grew exponentially. For the next three years, he saw her precious smile again, where her eyes glimmered like a golden topaz. She radiated joy, like any other blood of the Farien, basking in few powers granted from the Goddess herself. Skye's dream of being a hero was on the horizon.

Until... it shut off like a light switch shortly after joining Combat Squad at age eleven. Walls built around his Skye. She said very little and showed very little. Times when he waited for her to return, wanting to be around her, only for her to stay cooped up in her room like a caged bird. Questions never ceased fire, and along with that came answers that hardly doused an ember.

"We should continue being patient with her," said Spark in a whisper. "As for the 'secret mission' stuff, maybe it's too dangerous for us to know for now."

"I understand if this was another Thanatos situation, but it's affecting Skye's wellbeing. They could tell us at least an extra detail without risking an information leak," said Aurora. "All we ever get is 'it's some strong Risen' and I'm really hating those words."

"Weren't there Agents who spied for them?" asked Spark. "And people who bugged the Communicators?"

"Yeah. Declaring different levels of classification was a precaution," said Zephyr. "But this is different. The way they act when hiding stuff related to Skye's missions is the same as how they act regarding the night of the exams and all the other stuff related to it."

"Like I said, maybe we'll find out when we become Marauders!" said Spark, giving Zephyr a thumbs up. "If Aqua, Eila, and them are in on it, everything'll be okay."

"You're right, Spark," said Zephyr.

"You hungry? We can start whippin' somethin' up!"

The girls insisted on cooking the past few days, so Zephyr had no choice but to watch Spark pull out the portable cookware that looked too new and unused. By the end of this week, it'd all be burnt, and Zephyr kicked himself for not placing a bet with Leif.

"Crap, I forgot to defrost it!" Spark pulled out the chicken from the freezer storage and it looked like a part of an igloo. "I could use fire aura!"

"VETO!" The word had never flown out of Zephyr's lips so fast.

"Aurora, do ya have your hairdryer?" She handed the pink tool to Spark.

Aurora took out a can and something that didn't look like a can opener. He had little room to talk about cooking, but he at least knew better than to attempt. "Oh, wait… this is a meat tenderizer. Don't JUDGE ME, ZEPH!"

If only their cooking could kill Risen.

"Guys... we can get food downstairs."

"Too late!" said Aurora.

"We got this! As soon as I figure out how to turn up the heat..." Zephyr couldn't bring himself to look at the rest of the disasters about to unfold.

"Wait, is THIS the right temp?" asked Spark, staring at the bubbling pot of oil.

"Put your finger in and find out," said Zephyr jokingly, earning a glare from the girls.

"Use the Communicator's thermometer."

"Forgot that was a thing."

The rest of the process was painful to watch, perhaps a new form of torture. The chicken was already dead when they bought it, but if a second death was even a thing, Aurora and Spark murdered the "cooked" chicken. Zephyr wasn't sure what was worse: eating a practical pile of ashes or getting food poisoning.

"Okay, so it's a little burnt! No biggie!"

There's a fine line between a volcanic eruption and a brûlée.

Zephyr had to choke everything down when his time of dying was about to arrive. There was no actual chance of dying of food poisoning or anything—just no flavor and odd rubbery and slimy textures.

After "dinner" it was time to figure out what to do for the next day. Once finished, he'd meditate. After taking more advice from Luna, he learned how to do it effectively and looked forward to it.

Trails and plains areas would take two days to get through, and they were simple days as long as Aurora didn't use up too much magic. Last stop was the Silvatican Mountains and was harder to plan for. Their best option was to conserve their aura until they got to the mountains and rest up in Ciela the night before.

Zephyr wrapped up, mapping out his plan and left the inn.

He took a seat in the grass off to the side, straightening his upper body. Bringing attention to his breath and sensations in his body, he relaxed. Zephyr chose a focal point, following breaths as they went in and out, returning his attention to it once his mind wandered elsewhere.

⋯✦⋯

TWO DAYS FLEW BY, along with Zephyr's meditative practices. He felt more refreshed after each session, which carried onto the following day. His thinking resumed its pace before they became Specialists, and there were fewer worries about bogging them down. Accurate tests of his new habits had yet to come, however.

After their mission, the party explored Ciela once they finished checking into the inn. It was near the entrance, where a sprawling selection of shops and markets had their elaborate displays of flower-themed displays and stickers.

Ciela's architecture was like the last town. Cielans painted its tidy streets in cheerful colors, reflecting the tulip gardens of pink, yellow, and red hues that adorned districts, emitting sweet, floral aromas. During the Summer Solstice, flower merchants visited Garnet City and decorated festivals to honor the Gods.

In the town square, a massive tree sat in its center, rumored to have existed since ancient times when Gods once walked alongside mortals. It shined gold, its branches extending at its peak during times of the brightest sunlight. Only Cielan natives knew the magical tree's true name.

On the opposite side of the tree, Cerberus members handed out fliers to passersby. Zephyr recognized two of them: Remi and Wren. Boxes floated in the air, amplifying voices of themselves and those within range. A recruitment sign as a hologram buzzed and flashed. It read: *Save the Realm, Eta Geminorum-style.*

"The heck?" asked Spark. They remained hidden by the tree.

"That's right!" cried Remi. "We're saving the Realm the ethical way! No enslaving children and controlling their entire lives! Cerberus members are adults, joining out of choice!"

"That's baloney!" yelled Spark, gritting her teeth. Zephyr stopped her before she jumped in and let them have it.

"'Enslaving'?" exclaimed Aurora. "We could've left whenever we wanted!"

"Can anyone sign up?" asked a Cielan.

"Anyone can interview! You just gotta have the right attitude and morality! Once you're in, you can take Heracles and unlock your true aura potential or enhance overall physical abilities for our non-aura user friends!"

Wren retrieved a vial containing a clear liquid with the Cerberus symbol on it. "Allow me to demonstrate!"

This works for anyone? That wasn't mentioned before... What did they change with this new iteration of Heracles?

Wren consumed it, not spilling a single drop. After wiping his mouth, a white glow covered his body, internally and externally. With a snap of his fingers, he levitated into the air. A trail of light followed his path as he glided. He spun, releasing photon blasts.

Remi waved her hand, and blades of flames appeared, attempting to stab Wren. A durability shield stronger than Zephyr had ever sensed manifested, taking the form of a screen of light, destroying the blades upon contact.

A massive pillar of metal appeared before Remi and she launched it at Wren. He struck it with a finger, shattering it into pieces.

The crowd applauded.

"Anyone interested? Register with one of us!" Wren landed on the ground and took a bow. "We'll be here for a few more minutes but contact us for more questions!"

"Flight abilities haven't been seen in ages. I wonder how they changed their formula," said Aurora as they walked toward the inn.

"I'll make a note of it," replied Zephyr. "If they can bring back flight... who knows what else Heracles can do..."

"Man! This is confusing!" said Spark, hands on her head.

The sound of boots landing from one cement roof to another interrupted them.

"I thought I'd find you guys here," said a velvety voice. She landed in front of the trio, jumping off the highest building.

"Skye!" Aurora pounced on her, giving her a hug.

"How long ya been searchin'?" asked Spark.

It was her turn and Zephyr almost went for it after. He hesitated a moment too soon.

"Got back from helping the others with Nara."

"So, you saw Shadow!" said Zephyr. "Well, I'm glad you're with us."

"You won't be busy tonight again, will you?" asked Aurora.

Skye shook her head.

"Perfect!"

Aurora remained close to her side, as if Skye was going to slip away at any point.

28

NEMESIS

SKYE

Skye turned her friends down when Aurora asked if she wanted to cook with her and Spark. Luna messaged her, requesting to talk. There were other matters for Skye to attend… as always.

Luna's picture popped up from her Communicator. "There's a lot that needs to be addressed. Things that need to change."

Skye messed up a lot… But what was it this time?

"You haven't acted like a proper mentor. Not even close." She gauged Skye's withdrawn reaction. "Shadow, Leif, and Aurora aren't where they should be because of you. You of all people should know better and if it were up to me, I'd assign the job entirely to myself."

"I see…" Luna was probably right. "What have I done wrong?"

"First glaring thing I see is a lack of proper training. I'm assuming you at least had training days. Aqua did that, and I figured you weren't stupid enough to NOT follow that. You didn't push them further and let them do their own thing after work."

"Right… I know it's different for everyone and the last thing I wanted was to give them the wrong type of training or advice. They know themselves better than me."

Luna shook her head. "They need to take full advantage of their peak periods to hone their skills. Even if you don't know how to train them for certain techniques, have them get someone to train them. If they have enough aura, push them. I know you've pointed out things they've done wrong occasionally, but that's the bare minimum. Do whatever it takes so they succeed."

Maybe they could have their durability shields mastered a lot earlier if Skye spoke up. Amongst other things.

"I know why you're so soft on them. You want to protect your childhood friends and brother, but this'll hinder them."

Going after the bandit tribes was Luna's idea to expose them to the ugliness of the real world, and Skye originally disagreed. Luna was the one who was glad to hear that they experienced dealing with Lastalia and Castor.

Skye detested seeing Shadow like that, and Zephyr and Aurora. But… it was going to come, eventually. This was inevitable, and they ripped the bandage. She didn't think the dreaded day would come so soon and that she would be the one to witness it.

I can't always be around to save them. I need to accept that.

"That's all I had for the first thing. You also need to make sure they have the right mindsets as Specialists. Especially Shadow."

This had to be about Nara. "Shadow's dangerously reckless. You've been around him long enough to know that and his stupid tendency to look good or be the hero. Stop defending him and get him to stop this madness. Or else one day, he could get himself killed or the rest of us."

Skye almost objected, but thought back to Taonia, when she thought Shadow would learn. She should've called him out on it. "I'm sorry. I've made mistakes, and it hasn't helped them as much as I thought they would."

Luna nodded. "We have to have Star Strike's best interest at hand. That means getting it together." If Aqua wasn't busy with ten million things at once, Skye would've asked her for advice.

"I will. From here on out."

"I'll hold you to it." Luna's image vanished as the call ended.

"Skye?" She jumped.

Zephyr was behind her. "Dinner's ready!"

Skye followed him into the inn, retracting her hand before it accidentally brushed against his. If their hands touched, Skye would've tripped up the stairs.

When they reunited earlier, she saw his face soften as soon as she came into view. All he did was make her forget about her missteps. Zephyr came up close to her after Spark's hug, as if he was going in for one, and she detected the sweet scent of amber. Skye was glad he didn't hug her because she didn't know what she would've done.

"I should warn you about the food," said Zephyr.

There was a very... strange scent that hit her as soon as she entered the girls' room. Was it burnt rubber? Burnt gasoline? Burnt tires? Why were those... stenches... in their room?

"It's ready!" Aurora was stirring a ladle in a portable pot. Wait... was the foul smell coming from that? "I may or may not have forgotten to cook the rice first before pouring it in, but it should be extra crunchy!"

Skye didn't think any of those words were meant to be in the same sentence for cooking rice. As a half-Kadelathan, she had credibility. Cooking was not her area of expertise either, but she was pretty sure that was one way to give Dad a heart-attack.

Skye would've liked being in Nara for a longer amount of time. Or visit in the future. She wished she was better connected to the Kadelathan half of her. Those with mixed blood sometimes rejected their heritage due to past discrimination. The twins were the only descendants of Celeste with mixed Kadelathan blood. They were more "exotic-looking" and tended to be gawked at in parts of the world with less diversity.

Spark plopped a pile of... whatever it was on a plate and handed it to Skye, bringing her out of her swirling thoughts.

I think this is what they call a "dumpster fire."

Zephyr said nothing, remaining stoic, but looking pale. Were they planning on doing this the whole week? Poor Zephyr.

"Dig in, everyone!" said Spark, shoveling in a spoonful. Her eyes went buggy, and she gulped, trying to get it down. "Uh... how is it?"

"Not bad," said Zephyr, trying not to stutter.

Skye grabbed her chopsticks and picked up a pile of... rice? And very wilted spring onions stuck to yellow pieces that resembled goo.

This seems like an interesting, yet uncool way to die.

"How is it, Skye?" asked Aurora. "You haven't had what I've made before!"

Skye's taste buds picked up a lot at once and calling it a flavor would've been too generous. The "flavor" tasted like they ran it over by tires. Mochi could do better, and he didn't have hands.

"It's... decent!" Skye forced a smile and put another pile into her mouth. This time, the texture felt like sand and parts of it lodged in her throat.

Aurora beamed. "Aww, okay! You can have seconds!"

Skye thought she had enough cookies from Cynthia to last her a while... but her rations might've ended up exhausted a lot sooner than desired.

⁙ ⁙❨⁙ ⁙

THE THOUGHT of how Skye would never take breakfast bars from the inns for granted ever again crossed her mind a few times as they ventured through the northern exit of Ciela where the trail continued.

Monsters inhabited the trail, and there were plenty of dead ends to go around. Thanks to Zephyr's mapping, it didn't take long to get through. Entrance was up ahead, and this was where Skye had to get a lot more cautious than before.

A silver barrier covered the opening of a mine.

"Aura signatures feel similar to Port Kilia after its destruction," said Zephyr.

"A connection exists, yes," said Dr. Schnee. "So, they could get through the barrier blocking the Ciela citizens from stronger monsters that dwell in the mines."

Zephyr pressed his Communicator against the barrier. The device absorbed the silver energy, causing it to disappear. An artificial-looking Risen ran up to them once they entered. It looked metallic, with mini-cannons attached to it. Standing on its metallic hind-legs, its arms resembled a Beowulf's and the head of a chimaera rested on its shoulders.

"What in the world is that?" asked Aurora.

Skye stepped forward, putting a hand in front of the party and the Sirens. "Stay back."

One strike with Excalibur and it exploded.

Dr. Schnee walked up to the sharded remains of the mutation and collected them in vials. "We'll be putting these under further observation later."

"These remains are discarded firearm magazines," observed Dr. Chen.

"There's more up ahead," said Zephyr. "It's infested with them, but if they planned on destroying it, they would've ambushed Ciela by now. A Dark Sphere is here for sure."

"Why would they target Port Kilia? There aren't any high concentrations of aura or anything around that area," said Dr. Schnee.

"We'll have to keep exploring," replied Dr. Chen.

"Sounds good to me. I'd like to see the Queen of Blades doing more of her swordplay up close in action," said Dr. Schnee, smiling.

Skye scratched her head. "Thanks... Hope you, um... enjoy it." She liked the name better than "Queen of the Fists," which was the same title they coined for her maternal grandmother. It was an honor, yes, but that title should have remained with one woman. "Demonic Embrace" belonged to her mother, and it could've potentially passed onto Shadow when his term as a Marauder came.

Silvatican law enforcement set traps throughout the mine. It was a common spot bandits tried to intrude upon for jewels and gems that could've been harvested. Other materials, such as Orichalcum, were present, which were used to craft weapons like Zephyr's katanas and Skye's knives.

More Mutations detected the intruders and ran toward the party. Guns appeared, attached to their bodies, and fired at the party. Glyphs appeared in front of Aurora and Zephyr to blast them away with the gusts of wind.

The hems of Skye's skirt blew from the impact as she stood in front of the Sirens. Concentrating her metal aura, she allowed her knives to float next to her in the air and move to protect them. She moved her hands, having all six blades knock away any stray bullets, hearing what sounded like a fangirl squeal from Dr. Schnee.

Spark created an electric chain from her lance, and it attached to four of the Mutations, shocking them all at once with a snap of her fingers. The Mutations spun around, repairing the cracks, and they were as good as new. "What the-?"

"Try attacking it with a spell after Spark lands an attack, Rory!" said Zephyr, blocking explosions.

A brown magic circle appeared beneath Aurora.

Spark did a spin-kick and twirled Reaver in a circular motion, generating electric waves latching onto the Mutations and zapping. Before they could self-repair, stalactites shot through them.

Skye turned and saw the Sirens recording and making a note of their observations. With a hand-wave, the knives returned to her belt. Tethys and Hyperion were due for maintenance. She liked the naming ideas Leif came up with, which was why she named hers after moon phases in Tau Geminorum. Her great-grandmother's home world used stardust gathered from the phases to power up themselves. This was fitting, given how most materials made to craft the knives originated from their sister world.

"Over there!" pointed Zephyr. "Anything more artificial-looking is a lot harder to sense."

More mixes of Risen were spotted. Some had horns, while others possessed venomous fangs, like the Snake Risen back in

Taonia. For a mission involving undiscovered monsters, those three did exceptionally well.

Luna took good care of them.

They arrived at the Dark Sphere in the deepest section of the mine. As usual, it had a guardian and this time it was a Level 3 Serpent Risen.

Spark jumped on its back and impaled it, killing it through electrocution with ease after Zephyr created a glyph for her to use as a launchpad. A durability shield shrouded half of Zephyr's body when the serpent spat out venomous blasts as it died.

"Awesome!" said Dr. Schnee. "You can destroy the sphere, now."

Skye slashed at it, tanking the explosion that followed suit. A black bag was behind where the sphere was. Something the size of a body was underneath it. "Guys, over here!"

"Oh, Gods!" said Spark when Dr. Chen pushed the bag over, revealing a dead man wearing a white coat.

"This is fresh," deduced Aurora.

Dr. Schnee pulled out the bag's contents. Tools and vials filled with metals and gems made up a pile on the ground.

Skye's eyes remained on the body, and her throat tightened. A blood stain was on the man's chest, revealing a deep gash where the same type of metal as the Mutations was lodged within it. A Cerberus symbol rested on his front pocket.

Similar to Dr. Lycaste. . .

"Cerberus. . ." said Zephyr. "So, they bypassed the barrier..."

Scattered bits of darkness formed inside Skye's chest, and her left hand trembled. Clutching her left with her right hand, she looked at Zephyr and exhaled to calm herself down. She mustered everything she had to restrain herself.

Please don't detect anything. Please don't detect anything.

"Why would they get killed by their own creations?" asked Aurora.

"That Guardian Risen was real weak, too!" said Spark. "Weaker than what we've dealt with!"

Dr. Chen examined the corpse. "Perhaps he was collecting materials for Heracles. Cerberus wouldn't have permission to gather from this mine, given how the area has been shut off."

"We'll further examine the materials collected and how they may be used," said Dr. Schnee, scanning the area with her Communicator. "That said, there's not much else here and we can head back."

29

DEFEAT

SKYE

Skye sat alone on a stump after setting up camp. Sirens told them to relax for the night as they examined the evidence collected. They were to return home soon for their reports.

Was that man there the night of the exams?

Risen killed the group of people who injected the stone into her body and turned her into a Host—their bodies were present as she collapsed. Their faces were distorted, before darkness overtook her mind, soul, and body. Her head hurt as she struggled to remember what she repressed for the umpteenth time, thinking the sight would jog her memory.

We'll find more answers... I'm sure of it.

She looked up, seeing Zephyr watch with horror at Aurora, using a hammer to mash vegetables on a cutting board.

Skye walked over to him, handing over the bag of cookies she was clutching. "Thanks."

He smiled and took one.

"Do you want to... help them out? They protested whenever I tried to say something. Maybe you can help make it more edible."

Since when did Spark eat vegetables?

Spark said a few choice words when she opened the portable

oven and poked at an unseasoned chicken breast with her finger. The sight of the white meat hurt Skye's soul.

WHY DO THESE PEOPLE NOT USE SPICES?

"I'll do what I can." Skye could use the distraction.

"If it's at least a little more edible, it works."

Skye walked to Aurora. "Mind if I help?"

Aurora's eyes brightened. "Of course!" She handed Skye the hammer.

What is this for? Skye took the hammer, but also retrieved her knives. Zucchini and tomatoes were on the cutting board, and she waved her hands, allowing them to float up once again. Another hand gesture, and the knives diced them into bits and pieces.

This isn't so bad! Cooking's fun!

Knives sliced and diced again, only for the cutting board to snap and the pieces to turn into the size of a grain of sand.

Nevermind.

Skye struggled not to break almost everything she touched when her power skyrocketed as a kid. Obviously, if it happened regularly, it would be an absolute disaster. Fortunately, it was only a cutting board this time.

Dinner wasn't good, but swallowable, even though it was difficult to scoop up microscopic pieces of "cooked" produce. Thankfully, Skye had plenty of cookies to go around. Otherwise, she would've had to eat a box of the spawn of the Underworld for dessert and Skye shuddered when she found out that the dried, foul, sad excuse of a snack was all Aurora purchased for "sweets."

"Spark, where'd you put the raisins?"

Hopefully, in the trash, where they belong, Skye thought.

Their nightly training came afterwards, and Skye felt more inclined to pay attention the entire time—she needed to put more time into it. Durability training was first, then sparring and spellcasting.

Skye sat down on a stump to spectate the match between Spark and Zephyr.

Spark may have been stronger, but Zephyr was the epitome of how fighting smarter worked. He knew her attack patterns and read her next moves with ease. A black glow surrounded Zephyr—the same color that appeared in Aqua's Marking. He knocked Spark onto the ground with a side-step and jab combo and avoided most of her blows.

Sweet feelings pooled in Skye's chest, and she couldn't stop smiling.

"Whoa!" exclaimed Spark, staring at the glow. "Is that...?"

He helped Spark back to her feet, beaming. "First sign of the Marking unlocking... it'll come. Maybe a month from now."

"So cool! Ya got another trick to it? Besides growing aura reserves?" asked Spark.

"You gotta drink a little human blood each day," said Zephyr. Skye and Spark stared at him, dumbfounded.

"WHAT?" exclaimed Spark. "You're kidding!"

"Maybe."

"Okay, but do you ACTUALLY?"

Zephyr shook his head. "That was my joking voice."

"They sound the same," replied Spark. She fist-bumped him. "Either way, ya did well back there, Zeph!"

"Zeph used his observations of his opponents to win. That's a way to defeat human opponents in battle," said Skye, jumping up from her spot and walking toward them. "Human fighters tend to have patterns and other habits. Limps, breaths taken, shoulder positioning when they're about to strike with their weapon, stuff like that. You haven't fought many human enemies in the past, but it's something to keep in mind once that comes." Now was a better time than any if Cerberus was the culprit. "Knowing these signs can help you predict their moves and blindside them."

Zephyr ran his fingers through his hair, shattering Skye's focus. "I see. Skye, you usually glare at your targets before releasing your stronger attacks. I twirl Galeforce whenever I'm almost out of aura and use the last of my glyphs."

"Huh... Never noticed mine!" said Spark.

"Not uncommon. I figured most wouldn't know," replied

Zephyr. "You twirl your lance as well before using specific techniques. There are a few others."

Spark crossed her arms behind her head. "Gotcha! Makin' a note of that!"

Skye nodded. "Yeah, I'll help you guys with this sort of thing."

"Ugh, still the same results as yesterday!" groaned Aurora as she looked through the data after launching a fireball at a target.

The others cast glances in her direction.

"You're fine, Aurora," said Zephyr, sounding gentle. "It'll take longer than a day."

"Ari would have improved this spell in a day," said Aurora bitterly. "If only I was as competent as my family."

Spark sighed. "We've told ya five times now! Yer as competent. Ya got the best aura control in years!"

"Even Luna thinks I'm not! Ari should've been placed on a Dream Team. Not me."

What did Luna tell her? She wouldn't have insulted their friend like that. As abrasive as Luna was, she would never go that far toward Aurora.

"I don't think Luna thinks that at all," said Zephyr. "What she told you might've been a lot, but there's no way she'd question what Dad decided twelve years ago."

"Your potential and competence was discovered back then, and you can't see it if you keep comparing yourself to your predecessors," said Skye.

"Exactly," said Zephyr. "You're too focused on them to realize what you can do."

"Mhm! If I kept comparing myself to Lightning Alchemists and the King of Lightning, I'd go nowhere!" said Spark. "Skye isn't Lumina or Seren and Zeph isn't Capala! We make our own legacies here!"

"Spark's right," said Skye. "Just know that... I'm proud of you, Aurora."

Aurora's eyes widened. "That means a lot coming from you,

Skye. Thank you." She turned to Spark and Zephyr, who both grinned. "Thanks to you guys, too."

Skye nodded at Aurora. "No problem."

Aurora rubbed her eyes. "I think I'm going to turn in soon."

"Me, too," said Zephyr, yawning. "Night!"

Spark put her arms behind her head. "Guess it's you and me! Mind lookin' over my aura channeling?"

"Sure."

Spark conjured static in her hands and demonstrated the waves, allowing it to travel up and down her body. The static turned into a current and didn't electrocute her. It traveled inside her aura points and back out.

"Can I see your aura control?"

Spark allowed the static to turn into one chain, then two, then four. It kept doubling until there were too many to count. Moving her hands, she combined them into one giant chain and then into the shape of an enormous lightning bolt.

"How was that? Pretty awesome, right?"

"Impressive, but you don't need to widen your stance as much; it takes up more aura. You also don't need to flick your wrists as much." She created the same static that turned into a chain without the wrist flicking and at a smaller stance.

Spark pressed the scanner, and it showed the before and after snapshots of how much aura Skye used. It hardly budged compared to Spark's aura gauge. "Ohh, so I'm not being precise enough!"

"No."

Spark's demeanor remained unwavered. "What's up?"

"Can you change the sizes of the chains?"

Spark shook her head.

"Mind showing me again?" The master-to-be shot the chains out of her hands faster than Skye could catch on to spot a difference. "Can you do it slower?"

Spark drew lightning into her hands. It remained at her palms as they turned into chains.

"I see it now." Spark motioned for her to continue. "I don't think you're drawing the aura to your fingertips. You need to practice more with that and when you do, all of what I mentioned will be easier."

Their practice continued until midnight. Skye opened her Communicator to make a note of Spark's progress.

Spark yawned. "Probably going to bed soon."

"Sounds good. Nice work today." Spark raised her hand and Skye reciprocated, lifting hers a few centimeters, but pulled it back when she realized Spark was punching the air.

Spark tilted her head, puzzled. "Was that supposed to be a high-five?"

"Uh... Yeah."

Spark flashed Skye a toothy grin. "Don't worry! We'll get it next time!" She stretched and put away the bots and training dummies. Giving Sigurd a twirl, Spark stashed it away with other lances Skye didn't recognize.

"Ya comin'?"

"I was going to take a walk."

"Night, Teach! See ya in the mornin'!"

Skye waited for her to leave before disappearing in the shadows.

She had to keep searching for the Undead and fighting, where she became one with the near silence. Skye no longer questioned when she'd be able to rest. She'd been fighting throughout her entire life.

The Communicator detected a Risen, Level 5 or higher, near the mountains.

Skye sped up the cliffs.

No sensors or those with sensory abilities could detect the type of darkness inside of Skye or other Hosts or Undead and it messed up their data readings. Any Level 5 detected could've easily been an Undead due to them having the same amount of aura.

Some Marauders grew impatient with thinking an Undead was around, only for it to be a Level 5. Their time spent wasn't for naught—any Level 5 spotted should be erased. Thanks to their efforts, there hadn't been many instances where Level 5s have attacked cities as of late.

Summoning her Spiritual Power through light, Excalibur glowed white along with the Farien symbol on its hilt, transforming into its other form. This form was reserved for the most formidable Risen, used sparingly due to how exhausting it was to use it.

"Gotta be 'round here, somewhere!" said a voice from further up the trail.

"It came this way, right?"

Skye crouched behind a large rock. Her posture tightened, gripping Excalibur.

Five Cerberus members entered at a brisk pace—the same people from Emerald Forest. Wren floated in the air with a trail of light following him, looking around. Mabel had a recording device tailing her.

"Should be close," said Wren, glancing at his mobile device.

"Can't believe this thing's been killing everything in its path," said Mabel. "Where'd it even come from?"

"Course Lumière Inc. covers everything up," said Remi. "All they do is lie and make themselves look good. Buncha phonies."

Skye's jaw clenched. *What are they...?*

A puddle of darkness appeared before the Cerberus members. The puddle transformed into a silhouette resembling the shape of a human. Smaller than Skye. It tore out a high-pitched, ear-splitting clamor.

Small size, high-pitch... That's the... Host who killed Saylor!

The feminine voice was contained with anguish, as if enduring years of torment. She sounded young, perhaps not much younger than Skye herself.

How long had her soul been trapped inside, tortured by the darkness?

Dark pulses discharged, and Wren attempted to block the Undead's hits with a barrier, only to get hit by the blasts. The barrier shattered into fragments of light.

"Wren!" screamed Mabel. Water bullets sprang out of her gun.

Others launched arrows of wind and fiery explosions. One created a blade of metal and threw it at the Undead Host.

Dark hands arose from underground, grabbing each member of the group.

Clutching Excalibur, Skye charged in, shooting beams of light at the Undead.

The hands evaporated, releasing Cerberus members from its grasp.

"Retreat," said Skye.

"And let an Agent bathe in the glory?" asked Wren, as Skye blocked a dark pulse with Excalibur, its edges glimmering in the moonlight. "I don't think so."

Skye released a breath of frustration. "I'm saving your lives!"

A Cerberus member moved at startling speeds, his knives slicing in tandem.

The Undead Host responded, dodging on instinct. Skye had to not release more blasts out of Excalibur, to avoid hitting Cerberus members in the crossfire.

"Like we'd let an Agent do that," said Knife Guy.

Skye glared and stabbed the ground, creating ropes of Spiritual Power, latching onto the Undead Host's aura points. She poured as much of her energy into it as possible, hoping to exhaust its reserves, boosting herself to maximum power.

Mabel cut through the night, unleashing a barrage of bullets with a spark of fire in her eyes. The Undead Host raised its arms, shooting out its own bullets of darkness, searing through her.

Her flesh melted upon contact as she tore out an ear-splitting screech. Darkness consumed her, disintegrating pieces of bone. The wind reached out for her, scattering Mabel's remains, now covered in darkness, into ashes.

"MABEL!"

The man with the knives dashed toward where Mabel once stood, like the fool he was, running straight into another blast from the Undead Host. It struck his neck, severing his head. Red liquid ruptured, splattering in puddles.

"NO!" yelled Wren, quivering.

Enhanced by the power of the stars, Skye boosted herself and slammed her fist against the Undead Host, sending it flying toward a mountain with an impact so hard it shattered. Swinging Excalibur, vacuum cuts of light exploded onto the Undead Host, causing it to create a shield of darkness.

The Undead Host disappeared in a liquid ooze of darkness, reappearing before Skye. A dark sword appeared in the Host's hands and dozens of blows exchanged. Clashes of light and darkness occurred. As soon as Skye had an opening, she stabbed its sides, razing part of its reserves. The Host grabbed Skye by the neck, slamming her onto the rocks multiple times. Shards of darkness struck through her as she struggled to boost herself once more.

Skye's screams echoed, rippling toward the stars and moon. She gasped as an enormous, dark claw gripped her body. A bright jab of pain stabbed her arm. A spiked blade of darkness protruded. Blood dripped. Another struck, lodging into her thigh. Several more whirred at her. Skye felt every ache and scar of the last year in her body.

Wren, Remi, and the last Cerberus member charged at the Undead. All it took was one beam of darkness before they disintegrated into ashes.

Not again. . .

Another beam launched at Skye, and she collapsed.

Skye succumbed. And failed. Again.

The Undead Host withdrew its darkness and disappeared into a void.

Remains of blood and ashes stained the earth before her. Next to the lone severed head was the floating recording device.

Hands shaking, she crawled toward the device. Every bone and muscle in her body throbbed as a wave of fatigue overtook her. Skye remained relentless, taking everything she had to force herself up to grab the piece of tech.

Realization hit her.

What if the Host's at camp?

Heart palpitating, she limped forward, clenching Excalibur and the device. She retrieved an Elixir from her compartment, chugging it as droplets escaped her lips, praying for its effects to kick in soon. Every bit would help.

Using the last of her speed boosts, she quickened her steps, nearly fainting. She ignored the agony and trails of blood seeping out of her as green sparkles spread throughout, lessening some of the suffering.

Skye supposed there were few silver linings. Next time she encountered the Undead Host, it wouldn't be as strong. And she would be smarter about her boost-usage. She targeted areas holding most of its aura reserves. When Twilight Treader and Luna encountered it in the past, she imagined Saylor destroyed some of them.

There was much they didn't know about Hosts: where the stones came from, how the power manifested. All was left for the Marauders to investigate for now. Anyone else would've been slaughtered.

She'd periodically check her Communicator for any radar sightings for Level 5s and onwards, despite having it slip out of her hands a few times.

By the time camp was in her sight, Skye was crawling and out of breath.

Spark and Aurora were peacefully asleep in their tents.

Thank Celeste.

30

NIGHTMARE
LUNA

LUNA HEARD A KNOCK FROM THE OTHER SIDE OF THE DOOR.

She sprang up, realizing they weren't under attack. Cold sweat covered her. "Coming!" Turning on her bedside lamp, she walked to the door.

Blaze stood in the doorway. "You screamed in your sleep." Red streaks in his dark brown hair stuck up, reminding Luna of a porcupine. "Wanna talk about it?"

As much as Luna hated having to rely on someone, it would be almost impossible to go back to sleep for the night if she didn't talk it out. Sleep-deprivation was dangerous, and she didn't want her last moments in action to be because "she didn't get enough sleep the night before."

He crossed his arms and leaned against the wall, ready to listen. Blaze and Glacieus were the only ones she spoke to for this sort of thing. "In my dream, I was with my Unity Squad colleagues once again. A year ago, or so." Luna thought she blocked it out of memory.

She was a B-rank Specialist. Missions at B-rank for Unity Squad members involved accompanying Recon or Intel Specialists and serving as their assistants. The amount of fighting they could do was limited.

"We were looking for a spot to set up camp, and we stumbled across an open area in the middle of nowhere. At least… that's what we thought." She stopped short, shuddering as the last sentence came out.

"An illusion?"

"It led us into a cave, and nobody realized it until the illusion temporarily faded away. I sensed something was up, but we were too late."

"Your senses were burnt out from the mission."

"We were in Maxia Forest earlier, trying to collect intel on unidentified Risen that was detected. There was an outbreak, and we needed info before any of them invaded Thet or Kadelatha." She paused. "Risen teleported to the clearing and cast an illusion before the sensors could notify."

"I remember, now. I also remember how hard it was to believe that illusions returned."

"Few knew about its return. Insanely powerful back when rare bloodlines could create them. Risen creating illusions were unheard of until then."

The ability died out. With the shift in the laws of nature, scientists hypothesized it was impossible within the last two generations once the last person who had the ability passed away.

"Remember when I first heard about it? Took forever to believe."

Since they've disappeared until recent years, few believed in their existence unless they experienced them themselves. Illusions coming back seemed almost as far-fetched as her clan being able to create portals from their aura again or Alchemists being able to do even a quarter of what they could do centuries ago.

Blaze studied her face. "You've been very unlucky." If all of this was because of the Fates trying to test her, she wanted to give them a piece of her mind.

"Also, I hadn't dealt with a Level four Risen until that point. Beforehand, my classmates would escape and let someone else handle it. Obviously, when you're trapped in an illusion, that happy course of events doesn't happen."

Pure darkness enveloping someone's head was one of the most perilous states to be in, being second to pure light. Few bloodlines were immune to either of the most powerful elements.

"What'd you see?" Blaze knew better than to show pity.

"First, my parents. I was in this... dream world, some kinda alternate universe. They were a lot like Sebastian, and I also had siblings. Then... I watched them get blown up. Again, and again." Like what she saw on tape. . .

Thinking about what could've been had given her more migraines than any state of sensory overload caused. The faces of her brothers and sisters... were a lot like hers. It even showed her family with Zephyr's, happily together like in a sitcom.

"Luna! Please!" her illusionary baby brother cried out for her in agony. He crawled toward her, blood dripping down his chin with the lower half of his body blown off.

She reached for him, mustering up as much healing aura as she could. "Sol... I got you!" She didn't. He had mere seconds left.

"Am I... gonna... go away?"

"No," she sobbed. "You'll live. And become the President. Like you've always dreamed of. And I'll be your VP."

Luna didn't know where their names came from or the sounds of their voices, but it sounded so real. Whenever she dreamt, she could deduce her state of slumber right away. Watching life drain from their eyes as they succumbed to their wounds didn't feel like a dream.

How did I feel so much about what didn't exist? I am weak.

"Keep in mind that it doesn't feel like a mere nightmare when you're dealing with an illusion. Your thoughts are uncontrollable and with darkness, it all turns into extreme negativity. Everything happy was torn from limb to limb and you slowly suffocate. What was minutes felt like an eternity."

"What was next?"

Luna faced the window, staring at the full moon. Her throat got heavy. "Star Strike became number one. We almost saved the Realm... One battle away, and I thought Stream got mortally wounded. Instead of helping Zeph win, I focused on healing her."

"So, she wasn't on the verge of death... And when you threw feelings into it, it cost Zeph the battle and Mortal Realm was destroyed," finished Blaze.

"I watched mistakes unfold again and again, too. And her death."

One of the late Combat Squad Specialists had a mind strong enough to break out of the illusion and kill the Risen, almost dying in the process. Illusions created by pure darkness were not a punishment Luna would wish upon anyone. The Balance and Celeste were essential for these reasons and beyond.

"You've never told me this."

"You had a lot on your plate."

Blaze paused to digest his thoughts. "At least they're off your chest now. Is this the first time you've had nightmares about the illusions?"

Luna nodded. "I don't know why they're appearing only nowadays. I wonder what the next miserable mission will pop up and be unforgotten... I need to read or something to keep my mind off it until I fall back asleep."

"Tap on the wall if you need me again." He left and closed the door behind him.

She took out the book about a fictional retelling of the Geminorum-Piscium Wars. People liked to romanticize those wars the most. Women loved the enemies-to-lovers trope Luna often disapproved of.

It only took one page before her eyelids drooped and Luna knocked out. She braced herself for more nightmares, but there were none.

···)(··

MORNING CAME, and Luna met with the others before warping to the spot closest to where they had left off at Maxia Forest. The

Agency set panels all over the place since the forest was so massive and easy to get lost in.

Maxia Forest was enchanted, and Luna had never been the lone unit to track auras in such a giant area with so many forms of concentrated aura before. Trees, shrubs, and critters here had higher amounts of aura than usual. Therefore, it was far more challenging to find anything amiss, if there even was one.

Luna could've gotten help from other clan members, but she wanted to serve as the sole sensor type for this mission. For an area like this, she had to concentrate harder to get more specific readings on the surrounding aura, which used far more energy.

Blaze closed his eyes. "Wildlife is purposely hiding here." When they entered the forest, Luna chose to not activate her sensing power to conserve aura. With Blaze's help, they could finish the mission twice as efficiently. She could last a lot longer by not having to use so much of her sensing power for what Blaze could also detect in nature through scent and sound.

"Explains why we haven't seen any," said Shadow.

"For Section Seven, there are only deer and rabbits. And I can hear large wings flapping with no identifiable scents from their bodies," said Blaze.

"Hawk or Eagle Risen then," said Luna. "Any reads on what they could hide from? Any metals?"

"Nothing unordinary."

Dr. Fern jotted it down. "Section Seven is clear." Prior to their mission, Ice Tetra sent in a request to the forest's neighbors to have it blocked off for their investigation. Their responses were almost instant, and Luna felt she should've had more of a role in the query. So far, there were no violators.

They followed Blaze's Beast form toward Section 9, avoiding spores that burst out of glowing, purple mushrooms. Thankfully, none of them got hit, or else they would've fallen asleep for at least half an hour. A path led them to the entrance of their designated section, and the trees were so tall that it blocked the sunlight.

Maxia was special in a way, where it changed its physical form every century. It was going to irritate Luna to no end if they ended up trapped between talking trees. Interestingly, even the talking trees remained silent and let the party pass into Section 9 with no repercussions.

Arriving at Section 9, Blaze closed his eyes again. "All wildlife here. No monsters or Risen."

"Weird," said Leif. "No Risen today, huh?"

He and Shadow seemed especially stiff around Luna recently. They had barely said a word to her, and she would've confronted them about it if there wasn't a pressing mission to focus on. She tried not to overthink what happened the other day. What she said had to be done, no matter how much they didn't like to hear it. Someone had to tell them. It was for the good of Star Strike. And the organization.

"Let's head onto Section eleven and thirteen," said Luna. Dwelling on their team "drama" was pointless now.

Two crossroads led to those sections—left to 11 and right to 13. Nothing was in 11. Floral monsters remained hidden from view, but they weren't aggressive unless provoked. Otherwise, nothing abnormal was detected.

On the way back to the crossroads, Blaze froze. "A group of people are in Section Thirteen."

Luna gripped the handle of her best weapon, Executioner.

31

TYPHONS

SHADOW

Section 13 mirrored 11. This time, there was a miniature Dark Sphere. Surrounding the sphere were four individuals in black cloaks.

A Hawk Risen soared above the sphere and attached to it were strings of potent-looking darkness. Each figure's hands contained dark orbs that had the same strings attached to both the bird and sphere. As soon as Star Strike and Ice Tetra stepped in, they stopped their magic.

Blaze remained in front and on guard.

A man waved a hand, and the Hawk Risen merged with the sphere. It enlarged three times its normal size, and the four disappeared into dark voids.

Leif and Shadow struck. Their attacks barely dealt damage, nothing more than a nuisance to the hawk. Leif charged up his chakrams with light and tried to jump onto its back but got slammed in the air by beams of darkness. He would've crashed onto the ground, if not for Blaze catching him and shielding him from the remaining beams.

Mark of Lumière appeared in front of Luna, matching the symbol on the backside of her coat. It faded, and she glowed silver.

Lashes cracked from Executioner, releasing lines of silver aura. The lines transformed into walls of steel. One line traveled toward Ice Tetra and a Golem made of metal emerged, ready to guard. Walls separated Star Strike and the enemy from Ice Tetra.

The hawk's wings became shrouded in darkness, and it swooped toward their leader. Luna blocked it with Executioner and attempted to absorb the aura from its wings, only to cause an explosion.

"Luna!" yelled Shadow, feeling adrenaline kick in.

Blaze stopped him from moving.

The smoke cleared. Luna remained unscathed, thanks to the clear glow covering her.

Shadow sighed in relief.

Blaze pounced onto the hawk's back, unbothered by the blasts. He unleashed a fiery breath, hitting its backside, and it crashed into the walls.

Leif used this opportunity to cut off its wings, and Shadow lit up the head of his axe with light and beheaded.

Luna stared at the sight before her, dumbfounded. "How did I fail to absorb its aura?"

"What was that?" asked Shadow.

Luna deactivated the Marking, wobbling as if she were to faint and fall over. The white symbol faded from her irises. She snapped her fingers, and everything conjured disappeared.

Ice Tetra came over.

"It was like those other times, too, where they disappeared like that," said Luna. "Other encounters. It felt like any other form of darkness, there was just a lot more of it."

"We'll inspect the battle footage later," said Dr. Caraway. "I can't believe such a powerful aura exists. The way they controlled the Guardian back there was baffling."

"So, they could even control the balance of the forest to an extent," observed Blaze. "Cerberus or whoever this is."

"You deserve to rest," said Dr. Fern. "We'll look into it some more."

LATER THAT NIGHT, Shadow braced himself for another heated series of verbal attacks from Luna. She stared off into space and turned in early, instead.

Shadow sat on a log, watching Leif and Blaze lay down firewood, tinder, and kindling within a circle of rocks. A small ember emitted from Blaze's fingertips. Red sparks danced in the breeze. Smoke twirled toward the skies.

Luna's words swirled through his head. Now that Shadow had downtime, it gave him more opportunity to think and reassess.

Have I been a good Farien?

Mom taught him and Skye to do the right thing, to follow the Farien Principles. He was a descendant of Celeste and a member of the Farien. Shadow was built to use his unique gifts to service others. These concepts were instilled into him from the day he was born, by both his family and the organization. Being a hero was all he knew. Even if he didn't want to be, he was born into it. Dishonoring the Farien and the Hikari wasn't on his agenda.

If that's true... then I wouldn't have done what I did back there at Nara.

When Luna was in trouble earlier today, he cared for her safety. He didn't rush in for praise. Or did he? Was he so horrible to where he cared more about his image and fame than lives? More than the wellbeing of his friends?

At first, Shadow assumed Luna was in the wrong... Based on Leif and Blaze's responses, Shadow questioned himself. Did Zephyr, Aurora, and Skye secretly think the same about him?

He thought of the times he asked for validation of his skills, when he believed he was better than his teammates, when he envied his twin due to living in her shadow.

I need to stop trying to be a trophy on a pedestal.

All that pondering made his brain heavy. He needed to stop. For now.

Blaze and Leif were both on their Communicators. "Whatcha up to?"

"Checking on the juniors," replied Blaze.

"You instructed some, didn't ya?" asked Shadow.

"Never pictured Blaze being a teach," said Leif, eyes glued to his screen. His fingers rapidly moved as Shadow heard shooting sounds from his device.

Shadow didn't either. It seemed like the quiet ones ironically ended up in the positions of teaching or mentorship. He thought of Blaze as a patient instructor. Maybe he'd grow up to be a wise old mentor with a long beard.

"I'm picturing you rewarding 'em with bunny-shaped candy and cookies! Like the ones you'd pack in your lunchbox."

Blaze readjusted his jacket collars, turning as red as the streak in his hair. The sight reminded Shadow of the time he discovered Blaze's collection of bunny plush toys.

"I want some!" said Leif. "Wait! Don't tell me ya gave 'em to yer 'children!'"

". . . I did."

"Still got some?" asked Shadow. Bunny-shaped candy was to die for and came in five fruity flavors. If the Gods ever had their own food or needed it for sustenance, Shadow imagined it'd taste like that candy. Only Blaze mysteriously knew where to get it.

Blaze grinned. "Have to earn it."

"I'm your teammate!" whined Leif.

"No exceptions."

⋯⟨⋯

BLAZE WAS up before the others the next morning. Even at their guys' nights, he'd always be the first one awake. Shadow didn't want to make any false generalizations, but it might've been a typical Morpher habit.

"What's the move?" Leif asked Luna.

"Considering having us return to Garnet since Ice Tetra is

heading to Briton soon, but something else came up. I've been in contact with other teams who have information to disclose."

"So, we'll discuss our findings together before we head home?" asked Shadow.

Luna nodded. "There's a lot to discuss right now with Triple Strike and Dawn Brigade."

"Wow... Triple Strike and Dawn Brigade?" Shadow hadn't met the team members, save for Lucia and Swifty.

"They'll be waiting for us at Terran's inn."

There was a bit of backtracking that had to be done after they bid farewell to Ice Tetra. Shadow was too excited to pay attention to his surroundings upon arriving at the new town.

Luna led them toward the inn. Dawn Brigade was already staying there, and Triple Strike was nearby, so it was a suitable spot.

It seemed less professional to meet in a room designed for parties and other fun events. It was thrilling to meet such incredible teams and take part in exclusive meetings. May not have been the real thing, but close.

Luna knocked on the door on the ground floor of the inn and walked in.

Nine sat at a long table.

"Welcome," said a woman with short, curly auburn hair and green eyes, who Shadow recognized as Elena, leader of the Dawn Brigade.

"General Elena, General Sunny," greeted Luna.

Sunny sat between her triplet sisters—Swifty and Sully. All were petite, had tan skin, and were blonde with cerulean eyes. The only way to tell them apart were their hairstyles and colors; Sunny had low pigtails and wore red, Swifty had a ponytail and wore yellow, and Sully had a bun and wore blue. It took Shadow years to learn the difference.

Many underestimated them because of their small size. Shadow knew better than to misjudge, since Aurora was the same and was as terrifying. "We've heard a lot about Star Strike lately," said Sunny. "You've done so much in such little time, which is expected!"

"Been paying close attention to you guys," said a man with brown skin and greenish-blue eyes. His hair was the same shade as Elena's and Shadow recognized him as Iyar—her younger brother. "Not gonna lie, I was skeptical about such a big team, but you've pulled through so far."

"Iyar! What did I tell you about saying stuff like that in front of everyone!" scolded another man with jet-black hair and a matching beard. He had one blue eye and one green eye. His name was Ambrose, and he was Iyar's boyfriend. Rumors circulated about their inter-party romance, and fans went wild when they confirmed it.

"Oops," said Iyar. "Anyway, it's nice to meet you." They added him to Dawn Brigade after his team got killed before his Marauder days.

"Forgive him," said Sully. "He's just jealous he doesn't have a team with two Celeste descendants, two Lumières, and all the other big names."

"He has at least ONE Celeste descendant and that's good enough," said Lucia with a huff. Her light brown hair was the same shade as Mom's, but that's where the distant family resemblance ended. None of Mom's siblings or first cousins had Lucia's blue eyes that matched Lumina's.

"Can you imagine what Star Strike would be like when Shadow reaches max power? Two identical twins with all that at their disposal would be nuts," said Oscar—the scrawny guy with messy blonde hair, glasses, and stormy-gray eyes.

"They're FRATERNAL, Oscar!" corrected Sully.

"Details," said Calypso, Dawn Brigade's last member and strongest. Her two-toned violet and lavender hair tied in a loose braid stood out. It served as a pleasant contrast to her fair skin, freckles splashed against her cheeks, and ebony eyes.

Elena frowned. "Guys, can we PLEASE get back to the subject here?"

For two legendary teams Star Strike idolized, they sure knew how to act like bickering in-laws. Then again, since when had the

Agents acted exactly like how the media portrayed them to be? Zephyr, as much of a geek as he was, was never on-screen. And they always saw Shadow as a ditz, oddly enough.

"Other half of Star Strike is back at Garnet, meeting with Wings of Order and Trinity Trio," said Elena. "Everyone in this room has recent news about Dark Spheres or sightings of people in dark robes or cloaks. I want you to explain what you've found."

Elena looked at Luna, gesturing for her to begin. She didn't miss a single detail and provided her own theories and speculations. Luna had her "professional voice" once again, sounding like a manager reporting to a higher-up.

"Controlling the Risen and creating the spheres themselves, huh?" said Ambrose. "No form of darkness a mere mortal can possess can do all that. At least, such a thing has been unheard of."

"Never heard of an absorption technique to fail before from a Lumière," said Swifty.

"Right," said Luna. "What information do you guys have?"

"Numbers of Risen didn't dwindle at all over the course of these past twenty years. It was impossible to happen naturally. Them being strong enough to bypass barriers of the strongest cities was icing on the cake," said Calypso.

"And they destroyed even the strongest barriers," said Oscar. "No Level three to four Risen that attacked it would've been able to break through Lastalia's. Therefore, a breach must've disabled them."

This was news to Shadow. Barriers protecting at least some towns and cities made all of it sound even worse. Another classified secret? Shadow wasn't sure why it wasn't publicly known.

"I never thought Thanatos was behind this," said Elena. "Back when they were still in power, they changed pre-existing stolen tech. I don't see them having the technological capabilities of creating such barriers to hide themselves or breach any. Their expertise was in weapons and robots, not security."

"Them being able to create Dark Spheres would've seemed far-fetched, too," said Iyar. "Creating those and evading all of us nearly every time? No offense, but they wouldn't have been that competent."

"Dark Spheres are only there to power up the Risen. Nothing more," said Ambrose. "Whenever a Dark Sphere appeared, the number of Risen didn't change. Most of the time, random Risen teleported to gain a boost in power."

"Looks like Level fives have never guarded the spheres. The most that's ever done so has been a Level four, and they take time to increase in power," added Calypso.

"So, that leaves Cerberus as the culprits," said Shadow.

"Based on newer information, we don't think it's Cerberus," said Elena.

Luna's expression didn't falter. Blaze did a double take.

"Then WHO did it?" asked Leif.

"There's been reports of Cerberus members who got slaughtered by the same Risen who got the Twilight Treader kid," said Iyar. "It's difficult to track, but we now think it's responsible for far more deaths than what we've seen or heard of. That thing goes on and off grid so easily. Extremely erratic."

How have they still not killed that Risen? Just WHAT ELSE can that thing do?

Calypso tossed her braid over her shoulder. "We have footage from that encounter—a recording device. Thanks to the other twin."

"Skye reported that?" asked Shadow.

Oscar nodded. "Some encounter on an evening stroll. My guess is these clips were supposed to be a promotional stunt for the public." Pressing a button on his Communicator, a moving image shot out of it as a hologram.

A black screen emerged, and a voiceover said, "Heracles is new and improved!" An image of a silver flower with a glow appeared next. It had seven petals, aligned in the shape of a star, curling at the edges. They shimmered, illuminating the black background.

"Celestial Perennials are one of a kind! The most aura ever seen in a plant!" A Cerberus scientist popped up on the screen, harvesting a bouquet from a greenhouse garden. More images depicted other herbs resembling what Shadow saw at Sevinnon Gorge from a previous mission.

"Heracles is composed of all natural ingredients," said the Cerberus scientist, holding a beaker of the clear serum. "It can unlock any member's true potential."

Images of Cerberus members in action appeared, killing Risen. Shadow recognized Wren, Mabel, and Remi.

"Watch our best healer work his magic!" said the voiceover.

A Cerberus member stood, shooting a cluster of green sparkles out of his staff. It traveled at least a kilometer, healing a cut on his comrade.

"We can also change elemental forms!"

Another touched a block of earth, transforming it into metal.

The hologram blacked out. "There's some rather... gruesome parts at the end," said Calypso. "Skipped those."

Shadow's heart sank. "Is Skye okay?"

Oscar nodded. "Minor injuries... but the thing got away."

"They omitted the fact they were using gems from the Silvatican Mountains. Which I know they don't have permission to do so," said Iyar. "Other half of Star Strike found a dead body belonging to Cerberus. Probably snuck in illegally and got unlucky and killed by Mutations that also breached the place."

Luna shook her head. "Hypocrites."

"So, if it were them, why would they get killed by Mutations AND a Risen they enhanced? A Risen they knew little about to begin with?" asked Lucia. "You might think, 'maybe they got out of control'. . . but according to Skye, they were purposely searching for that monster to kill it."

Leif blinked. "What about the weird stuff they did to the Risen those other times?"

"Never confirmed they were attempting to power up the Risen," said Iyar. "Could've been just messing around with their enhanced powers."

Shadow's face fell. "So, no more suspects?"

"Not quite." The General glanced at Star Strike. "We think it's the Typhons."

"Typhons?" sputtered Shadow. "That's insane!"

Luna and Blaze stared at the teams like they suggested something as outrageous as Mochi trying to take over the realm with his fellow household pet accomplices.

Blaze cocked his head to the side. "How's that possible?"

Shadow scanned the Marauders for answers. "Why'd they turn against us? Even if they were alive?" His teammates worshipped the Typhons, and Shadow couldn't believe what he heard.

"I expected your reactions," said Ambrose.

"Wings of Order speculated it first, and we thought the same thing. Zetta pitched the idea and almost all the things he speculates end up being true," said Calypso. Zetta was a master of Recon and Intel—a top student for a reason.

"If Zetta and Clay are onto something, it's a whole 'nother story," said Iyar. "And it makes sense. If anyone were to have that level of tech, it'd be the Typhons."

Elena took out her Communicator. An image of one of the hooded figures popped up, near woodlands. Another showed the side profile of the figure with the same build and height, hood off, knocked to the side by Ava's talons.

Luna gasped. "No way…"

Shadow peered at the wisps of silver hair and a red eye. "That's… Mercury."

Oscar clasped his hands. "They escaped before Trinity Trio could get more evidence."

Dawn Brigade's leader pulled up a profile image of a man with the exact hair and eye color. His coat had the Typhon's symbol—a hooked serpentine. In both images, the man looked the same, even though at least twenty years had passed in between.

Luna glanced at Elena. "How does he not look any older?"

"As one of the most powerful masters of darkness, it's possible he used it to prevent himself from aging," said Calypso.

Elena shook her head. "I can't imagine Ariadne doing any of this. She was 'Lumiére Inc's Sweetheart.'"

Were they up against the Typhons? Shadow barely accepted "expect the unexpected." His sister sustaining injuries like what he'd seen before, yes. A destroyed city, yes, but... Typhons causing this poison?

Swifty crossed her arms. "Lots of us women looked up to her. But if Electro is doing this, then Ariadne would follow. And if Electro is against us... it's not looking good."

Shadow remembered the Lightning Master as the dude who created the original security systems for the Base. It evolved since then but was ground-breaking at the time.

"Even Ursula turning against us is hard to believe," said Oscar.

"She was the one who wanted to bring back old bloodlines, right?" asked Leif.

Oscar nodded. "Emphasized pride in being who you are, yeah. Didn't have the best attitude in the world but earned plenty of respect for her legacy."

"Mercury is clearly alive, unless an illusion or cruel trick is being played," said Iyar. "If they're here, they gotta have a Base of operations. Only they would stay hidden for so long."

But illusions don't exist in our world anymore. How's it POSSIBLE?

Ambrose glanced at Star Strike. "Guessing President Ziel wants you to help us stop them. Once we find where they operate."

Star Strike was possibly going to work alongside the Marauders already? Becoming part of the elite was something he and Skye had dreamed of for so long.

Blaze ran a finger through his hair. "Dream Team or not, isn't it early?"

Elena shook her head. "If Ambrose's prediction is correct, it'd make sense to happen soon. Star Strike already contributed so much. Also, you have a Marauder who can continue to guide you and her spot gives you an extra leg up."

I should feel happy for Skye... Right? They all seem so modest.

"Also, Zephyr and Luna are putting the teams in good shape," said Calypso.

"Zephyr's got so much knowledge in his hands. Might not be as strong as the rest of his clan, but he's in a satisfactory spot by Dream Team standards and his tactics make up for it," said Oscar. "He's on the right track if he's picked to lead the organization one day. And we all know how good Luna is doing. You're ready."

"I don't know about that last part about Zephyr," said Iyar.

Ambrose looked like he wanted to silence him again.

"To command an interplanetary organization one day, it might be better to have someone more similar to Ziel."

"Always thought Zephyr was too idealistic and didn't have the proper mindset of a leader of an organization," said Sully. "A team is one thing, but an entire interplanetary organization? He's smart, I'll give him that, but it takes so much more to lead a company."

Data for projections of one's future abilities were recalculated monthly, sometimes more frequently. It wasn't always fully accurate, especially when the unexpected came up. The Agency projected Aqua as best pick for heiress, but toward the end of Zephyr's educational career, the two got far more in-depth reassessments. Zephyr became a close contender, and it was only a matter of time before Ziel announced his pick.

Such an announcement led more to talk and compare the two. Hearing the news stunned Zephyr when it first came up the year before.

Shadow sat up straighter. "Not anymore. A lot can change! When you're thrown out in the moment like I've seen him. He will pull through! You gotta give him a chance!"

That was pretty Farien of me, right?

Luna remained calm and opened her mouth to object. "Well, I think that Aqua's better suited to lead on the battlefield. You'll just have to wait and see how experiences will positively affect Zephyr. We'll need a leader who can challenge tradition and question everything which exemplifies who he is."

"She has a point," said Calypso. "President Ziel leads in a way very similar to his uncle and father. Aqua is also said to be a lot like Ziel and we know how the 'sticking to the book' approach to leading an interplanetary org can backfire over the last forty years."

Luna kept her gaze on the doubters. "Zephyr's investigative mind and tendency to try different strategies and approaches works. If the Realm's still intact, we don't know what it would be like another twenty years from now, and I think we need someone like that. Who knows what kind of long-term effects would occur, should we stop the Typhons and their spread of darkness. Plenty of other problems will still exist that we need to fix."

"They thought it was impossible to lose the ability to transport and communicate between worlds, but here we are now," said Ambrose.

PART III

ASSEMBLE

32

BRITON AND VIGOR

SHADOW

BEING SEEN WALKING ALONGSIDE DAWN BRIGADE AND TRIPLE STRIKE into Garnet City's Base felt like an honor. Shadow would've boasted about it but considered otherwise.

This is good for Star Strike. For the Mortal Realm. Not just me.

Shadow had never seen so many insanely powerful teams in one conference room before. It felt official, like he was a higher-up. The other half of Star Strike was sitting at the long table by the Wings of Order. Across from them was the Trinity Trio.

Aqua smiled. "Looks like we can start soon."

Shadow moved toward the other half of his team and sat down.

Spark waved to Blaze as he seated himself beside her. "Been a while!"

Zephyr gave the Beast Morpher a fist-bump and Aurora nodded at him.

Automatic doors opened, and Shadow expected to see the President walk in. Instead, Stream and Glacieus stood as tall and stylish as usual, reminding Shadow of models on a runway. Both were known as the most attractive members of Star Strike, stealing the hearts of many.

Luna had a look of delight on her face as she and Stream locked eyes.

Leif put his arms behind his head. "We've got the whole team."

"No kidding!" said Shadow with anticipation.

Glacieus and Stream took the remaining seats and all ten of the Agents were together for the first time in years. This time, they were reunited as Specialists. It was a historic moment to remember. If reporters were here, they would've gone berserk. Fans would've flooded the room, demanding autographs and pictures.

"Miss us?" asked Glacieus.

Blaze smirked. "Not really."

The blond's prideful grin faded, and he pursed his lips. "Well, Glacy didn't miss YOU either, Blazie!" With him, Leif, and Spark around, it was going to feel like a party. A very loud one.

"Glacieus! Not in front of the elite!" said Stream. She looked over at the Marauders, hoping they didn't overhear, but nobody paid attention. "I missed you guys."

"We did, too!" said Aurora. "And I love your dress!"

Stream always looked glamorous. Luna gushed about her "willowy" and "swan-like" body-type before in the past—not that Shadow paid attention or anything. He didn't even know what "willowy" meant. Stream didn't look like she slouched or drooped. Since when did models do that?

"Did you miss me, too, Rory?" asked Glacieus. "You're much nicer than that one, so I figured!" He pointed his thumb at Blaze.

"Of course," said Zephyr. "We've all been waiting to have everyone here! It's been what? A year and a half since all of us were in the same room?"

Luna grinned. "Sounds about right."

Star Strike probably felt as nostalgic as Shadow. There were three most important days to remember as an Agent as recited by Instructor Cross: your first mission as a Specialist, your first mission as a team of Specialists, and the day you become Marauders.

President Ziel's entrance cut their reunion short. As soon as he came in, the room went silent. Everyone watched him sit at the head of the table.

"Greetings, everyone." On duty, President Ziel looked proper and refined with his tailored black suits. Outside of the job, others would've found it strange to see him in anything casual. Shadow had the liberty of seeing him in swim trunks on vacations his and Zephyr's families took as kids. That certainly was a comedic sight.

"Greetings, President Ziel."

"First, we would like Elena and Sunny's side to report what they've found," said Aqua.

Generals provided a condensed version of their earlier meeting in Terran. Anyone who wasn't present beforehand listened intently.

"Thank you for the information," said Aqua. "Now, we'll give our side."

Ava was up and mentioned more of the suspicious sightings, including the dead body that Zephyr's group found in the Silvatican Mountains.

"We'll move onto the matter concerning Mutations," said Fang.

"They can absorb energy and life steal, but they seem beta-tested. That's what the attack on Port Kilia was for: an experiment and their way of powering up the Mutations," said Ava.

"Mutations and Dark Spheres are tied to the Typhons, confirmed," said Fang. "Ruling out Thanatos and Cerberus entirely for those and we can officially list them as red herrings."

"Very well," said Ziel. "Excellent observations and work done. Finally, we've tracked down who has been causing this."

"There must be a link between their powers and how they survived the Labyrinth," said Zetta. "Eventually, we'll have to circle back to get into it."

"We will have more luck finding where they operate and learning about their power and perhaps any additional information about the Labyrinth," said Ziel.

Shadow wondered how Ziel seemed so unbothered by the Typhon theories. He worked with them for several years. Many were his friends and were acquainted with the Candor's and Hikari's.

Shadow glanced at Zephyr, who managed to look equally unfazed, despite looking up to Mercury. Supposedly appearing stoic ran in the family. The other admirers of the Typhons appeared less than nonchalant with Spark shaking her head and mouthing *"No. . ."* and Stream's face falling.

The President gestured toward Star Strike. "Nova Strike, you'll work with Marauders to locate their Base. We should finish up the latest iteration of the barrier detecting tech soon and we can expedite the process with Stream's combined help with Blossom."

"Astro Strike, you'll train at Gwynerva. Guessing from how long it can take to locate such a Base, your training should be wrapped up just in time. If not, the practice will be beneficial for reaching A-rank."

"You'd be killing two birds with one stone," said Ava. Spark giggled at the subtle pun. It took Shadow a second too long to understand.

"Infiltration missions are some of the most difficult, so Skye shall be the one to help you along with Agents stationed at Briton," said President Ziel. "Since we've found our most likely cause, it's time to prepare to stop them once and for all, bringing our strongest teams together. Astro Strike is dismissed."

Astro Strike got up. Shadow wanted to stay close to the door to listen in, but Aurora dragged him away.

"Man, wish we could be together to help!" said Spark as soon as the door shut.

"Same here!" whined Shadow.

"Glacieus is going to be closely working alongside his brother once again, huh?" said Zephyr. "They'll do well."

Having Clay and Glacieus in the same room was interesting. Shadow had never seen them together before. Nova Strike and the Wings of Order working alongside each other was an interesting dynamic. Shadow imagined what it would be like to work with Cynthia's team.

"Exciting to work with 'em once they find the Base," said Leif.

"Definitely another way for Dad to test how well we can do," said Zephyr. "We gotta make the most of these training sessions. If that future mission will truly involve stopping the Typhons."

"Staying at Vigor will make it feel like we're in our academy days again," said Aurora.

"Never thought of that!" said Shadow. "So, we'll stay in dorms! Cool!"

So, this was what it was like to be a Trainee and live in a place where a Base didn't exist. At least they would get a taste of it throughout the next couple of weeks or however long it'll take.

"Yeah, I'm looking forward to it," said Zephyr. "If they're the ones who trained Stream and Glacieus in Recon and Tech, then we're in expert hands."

If Shadow remembered correctly, Vigor was the school dedicated to weapons, combat-training, and the Medical Department. Meanwhile, Briton did the Recon, Intel, and a ton of tech work.

"Yer lookin' forward to more fanboying," teased Leif.

"Uh-huhhh," said Zephyr. "Admit it, man. You missed my fanboying."

"I'll admit it reminds me of stuff in history classes that I don't wanna remember," replied Leif.

Shadow had to take Leif's side on this one.

"How d'you remember? All you and Shadow did was sleep," replied Zephyr with snark.

Shadow side-eyed his best friend. "Yeah, yeah, whatever!"

Not long after the meeting, the President dispatched Astro Strike to Gwynerva. He instructed everyone to not exhaust their aura reserves, leaving their only time of recovery for nightfall. Most of their training would be stealth-based. They would use not much aura at all, unless for sparring practice and practicing techniques.

∙ ⚫ ∙

GWYNERVA WAS an island south of the Aquarius Islands and north of the Gemini Desert. Before Lumière Inc. was founded, students for the schools ended up serving Gwynerva by joining their army or government. Agents who were citizens of Gwynerva reported to the nation's ruling council.

They teleported to the docking bay that was split into aerial and aquatic for either type of vessels. Further in the distance were two sister schools—Briton on the left and Vigor on the right, connected by bridges. Either side had linked towers, and both buildings resembled a mix between a castle and a school. Several impressive aqueduct-looking structures and archways had architecture that resembled Lastalia's arches.

A pretty boy with messy black hair and blue eyes approached. "Hey, there." His athletic build resembled Zephyr's but was a tad shorter. He looked close to their age and seemed friendly.

Spark ran over to him. "Yo, Tristan! Long time no see!"

Leif fist-bumped the guy. "How've you been, man?"

"You know each other?" asked Shadow.

Tristan smiled. "Met on a paired mission years ago."

"Met up again when we transferred here last summer," said Leif. "Now that Shadow's around too, we gotta play Strike Ball."

Spark turned to Shadow. "Yeah, this kid's offensive game is gross!"

Tristan chuckled. "Definitely down for a rematch." He sized up the team and his gaze pinned Skye like the tip of an arrow. "Good to see you again."

He reminded Shadow of the way people would check him out. Of course, Shadow didn't realize they were until Zephyr brought it up, and it took years to identify that look. If he received attention from multiple genders, then it would make sense for his twin to get the same responses.

Skye fidgeted with her bracelets. "Hello, Tristan."

Leif put his arms behind his head and smirked. "Small world, eh?"

"She's saved my life before. She's as strong as she is beautiful, you know." Shadow heard playful light in Tristan's words.

Spark and Aurora exchanged grins when Zephyr stiffened.

It was rare to see him turn statue-like, and it puzzled Shadow why he was like that now of all times. Maybe Zephyr was looking out for Skye, like an older brother would! He didn't have to, but Shadow found it cute and endearing.

"Um... thanks."

"I'll show you where you'll be staying for the time being." Zephyr loosened up, and they followed Tristan toward Briton's courtyard. Engraved square hedges wrapped around it and a wide collection of bricks with names of notable alumni.

Students with a variety of skin tones and hair colors were present, reminding Shadow of Garnet Academy. The Caspian Continent's most diverse nation seemed to be Gwynerva.

"Whoa, Astro Strike!"

Both boys' and girls' uniforms comprised gray suits, a white undershirt, gray tie, and white gloves. The male version had white trousers, while the female contained white stockings and gray boots. Garnet Academy uniforms looked similar, except the color scheme was black and dark blue.

"Can I have your autograph?" A girl came up to Shadow and Zephyr. She had pictures of glorified versions of the two in her pockets... which was odd.

Shadow's ego crawled up his spine. He tampered it down, resisting to give life to it.

Think of the greater good. Not your glory.

"Oh, Celeste! It's Cornelia!" exclaimed another. He dashed over to Spark and fumbled in his Communicator storage for a pen and a notepad. "Could you sign this, please?"

Spark took the items. "Call me 'Spark!'"

Others came up to Leif, Aurora, and Skye, asking for the same thing. Leif grinned and winked flirtatiously at the ladies, Aurora looked surprised at the much younger fans, while Skye gave a small smile when posing for pictures with them. Skye notably had fewer fans than the others. Some gave her funny looks.

Maybe I should talk to Skye about all this.

More groups came, and Tristan raised his hand. "All right, you can ask for pictures and autographs after Astro Strike gets settled. Please remember to not disturb them during training sessions or else there will be consequences!"

Tristan had to repeat himself as they walked into the long corridors after entering the school from the far western side. The interior of Briton reminded Shadow of a library. Not a lot of modern technology has been seen yet. Shadow assumed it'd be used more within non-Academy sections of the giant Base.

Two open doors sat across from each other in the hallway, revealing two cozy sets of bunks in each room. Four desks—two on opposite sides of the room rested adjacent to the walls. A large window sat in the center of the northern wall, with gray curtains and matching bedspreads. All fabric had the Briton symbol—a tree outlined in black.

"Hope you don't mind bunk beds!" Through the window, they could see Vigor. Its flag was also black with a shield crest lined with gray.

"Always wanted them as a kid," replied Zephyr. Their sleepovers would've been more fun with them, Shadow had to admit. Better late than never, right?

Shadow recalled the times he and his twin wanted bunk beds. The times they made their own "Communicators" out of paper, tubes, and tape. The times they pretended to go on missions, using their crafted concoctions and used Shadow's bedroom as the "inn" they'd stay at after a long and tiring day. Those days were simpler times. Happier times.

"I'll let you guys get settled. Call me if you need anything," said Tristan with a wave.

Once finished, Shadow knocked on the girls' door. Last time he barged in, Aurora threw a hairbrush at him, screaming to knock first, because she was "changing." For a mage claiming to have little physical strength, she almost gave him a black eye.

Spark opened the door. "Yo!"

Aurora and Skye sat on one of the bottom bunks. "I need to talk to Skye about somethin'."

"Okey!" Spark remained standing by the door.

A moment of silence passed. "Alone?"

"Oooh! Sure, sure!" Spark grabbed Aurora's arm. "Let's see what they got at the dining halls!"

Shadow plopped down beside his twin once the girls left. "Have I been a good Farien?"

Skye looked off to the side. "Is this about what happened at Nara?"

Shadow sighed. "Lemme guess. Luna had a talk with ya, too."

"What'd she tell you?"

Skye nodded along as Shadow provided his explanation.

"I see. Well, there are some things... I've noticed you've been doing that. . . I should've called out earlier. I can understand where Luna and Blaze are coming from, though I can't believe she said it like that. But... they're right."

Shadow glanced at the spotless floor. "Why didn't ya tell me what I did was wrong?"

"I'm sorry. It was stupid of me. I didn't want to upset you... and I thought you'd learn on your own. *I'm* supposed to teach you how to think as a Specialist. You wanted to be a hero... be recognized and seen as extraordinary."

"Like all those descendants of Celeste, Mom told us about. In storybooks. Save the Realm and be seen as a hero. Just like them."

Skye blinked, processing her thoughts. "You've taken it too far... If you keep being reckless like that, it's going to put yourself and others more in danger. Wanting a prize in a war is killing yourself at a faster pace, for the wrong reasons. Follow orders, otherwise you'd do more harm than good."

"I'm trynna do the right things for the right reasons, now! Honest! I wanna get better!"

Skye put a hand on his shoulder. "That's a start. Being aware. You have to crawl before you can fly and take advantage while you're still on the ground." Her pools of golden-amber moistened. "I know you'll be a better hero than me."

Shadow stared at her in disbelief. "What? Skye, look at YOU. You've done all these great things. When we were kids, I thought we'd be equals. Honestly, I got jealous when ya surpassed me. Got more used to it but feels weird sometimes."

Her expression was unreadable, and she looked away again. "I want you to know that I'm proud of you and to never stop improving. You know what to do with that information. Your power will come. It'll last longer than mine. I know it." She sighed. "Honestly, I wish it didn't happen—the spike in my power, I mean... I missed out on a lot."

"But you get to be a hero, for the right reasons! Earlier!"

"I'm not a hero that little girls look up to like Aqua."

33

BALANCERS

ZEPHYR

"Shadow and Leif, you should train," said Skye as they exited the dining hall.

Leif groaned. "Really can't catch a break here, eh?"

"Your eyes can get a break from those screens," Aurora pointed out.

"You're startin' to sound like Stream," replied Leif.

"I'll take it as a compliment." As long as Aurora didn't cook like Stream, they'd be spared… They would also be safe as long as she didn't accidentally fall while holding a sharp object. Though, if Zephyr said that out loud, he'd get smacked. Again.

The training areas were behind Vigor, and it seemed like the arenas were closed at the moment, much to Spark's chagrin. Aside from the amphitheatres that held tournament matches, most of the outdoor sections resembled Garnet's Base.

Specialists came up to Spark. "Mind sparring with us?"

"You're Team Night Fury, aren't you?"

One girl gaped. "You know us?"

"Course!" said Spark, retrieving Astrotearer from her inventory. "Now, let's spar!" She followed Night Fury into one of the sectioned off battlefields. Weapon racks and bleachers were off to the side, and it looked like they already had an audience. The day Spark ever turned down a request for a sparring match was the day Tartarus froze over.

Everyone else ventured toward the training dummies and targets.

Zephyr reached for the barbells and watched Aurora create a phoenix out of flames while Leif struck dummies with his chakrams.

"What should I work on?" asked Shadow. His battle stats emerged from Skye's Communicator. Snapshots from different months of her twin's training were visible and some of them, such as strength and Spiritual Power, were verbatim.

"They should be at least slightly higher by now. I want you to practice your light aura," said Skye. Her constructive tone sounded like Luna's but felt gentler. "Let's practice until your aura levels hit halfway."

Shadow nodded. "Okay."

Shadow didn't grin as broad as usual when his fangirls raved. Instead, he gave a small smile and thanked them for their compliments. Seeming almost... modest.

The past weeks changed everything. New experiences and revelations could trigger such growth in an individual. When Zephyr first heard the earth-shattering news about Mercury, it took everything out of him to stop himself from losing his cool. At the same time, the only people Zephyr could've imagined were capable of giving the organization so much trouble were their own. If the Typhons were behind all the poison, he wanted to know why. He had to accept it.

Zephyr wishfully dreamt about meeting Mercury alongside his other ancestors. Unfortunately, one of his wishes would come true.

Tristan appeared, looking proud. "Looks like Spark is giving everyone a whooping!"

"Yeah, they all want to test themselves against 'Thunderbird!'" replied Zephyr. He got a closer view of their new acquaintance. Tristan's white and gold streetwear jacket and jeans stood out against the students. He was attractive, which explained why a handful of students and Specialists gave the lad longing stares and fawned over him. He reminded Zephyr of any typical participant in love triangles in fictional stories.

Of course, he has black hair and blue eyes. Of course.

Whenever Tristan gazed at Skye, Zephyr's muscles tightened more from that than the weights. This was a pity, considering how pleasant Tristan was to be around. It's not like he had any justifiable reason for feeling this way—he seemed like a good guy. Zephyr blamed his young adult brain.

Tristan came up to Skye. "So, it's been a while." He stood *uncomfortably* close to her.

Skye tensed up again. "Yes."

Aurora looked like she wanted popcorn and Shadow drank from his canteen without a care in the world while Leif smirked.

"If you're free tonight, I can show you around. Think of it as a VIP tour of the best spots in Gwynerva." Tristan's voice was low and soft, like he was cooing.

Zephyr almost dropped both dumbbells.

Skye hesitated. "I'm afraid I'll be busy with preparations. Sorry."

Tristan was unfazed. "No worries. Another time, then."

Her Communicator beeped as if on cue. "I have to take this." She abruptly disappeared.

Tristan walked up to Zephyr. "You're in love with her, aren't you?"

Zephyr's cheeks burned, and Aurora squealed. "Huh?"

Shadow spat out his drink. "Who? Zeph? Nah, it's not like that!"

"It's obvious with the way you look at her," said Tristan.

"It's not like that," replied Zephyr. "We're family friends. Close family friends."

Tristan winked. "If you keep denying it and don't make a move sooner or later, one of us might swoop in."

Zephyr never knew the exact night when he started thinking about Skye until he fell asleep. The nights where he thought about what he did to make her smile, wishing he would've taken a photograph and kept it in his pocket. Having her around, day-by-day, only made him realize how much he'd been starving, how much he ached for her.

Whenever their eyes met, her irises glistened like melted honey, and her pupils dilated. Only around him would the shade of coral flood her face. Whether she recognized how she felt for him was up for debate. Ever since she put up those walls, he couldn't tell what she was thinking, unlike when they were younger.

He didn't want to stand in her way by admitting how he felt to anyone but himself. If word got out, it could trouble her. Even if she was aware of her own reciprocation, Zephyr was sure there was a reason she held back.

What matters is that she's happy.

Zephyr put away the weights, sitting down to close his eyes. He shoved away thoughts of the woman he loved—they had other matters to focus on. His deepest wishes and desires came second, though he wasn't sure how much longer he could hold his own feelings back.

He focused on experiencing the environment, sitting up straight, and resting his hands in his lap. Breathing in through the nose and out of the mouth helped. His anxiety quelled somewhat, but it never fully faded on riskier missions. Eventually, he'd have to accept how part of it will always remain. He'd learn to mitigate it enough to operate with minimal worries, one day at a time.

His mind wandered to his training performance the past weeks and what was yet to come. During sparring matches, the best strategies appeared against Spark, like how Zephyr sparred against new challengers before graduation, but also different, like he combined instinct with a sprinkle of caution. He needed to apply his methods for subsequent training sessions and on missions.

Balance.

·∴·☾·∷·

THE NEXT MORNING, Zephyr woke up Shadow and Leif before they had a chance of being late. This time, no plushies were harmed nor buckets of water. Instead, Zephyr strategically brought up waffles from the cafeteria to their room, allowing the aroma to do the waking. Zephyr wondered why he hadn't done that earlier, given the frightening amount of sugar both Shadow and his twin consumed.

The girls waited for them with Tristan outside of Vigor by the time Shadow finished scarfing the stacks of crispy goodness down his throat.

"You'll be on your own from here on out. Figure out how to get inside of Briton and reach the top of the tower. I'll be on call if you need any hints, contact me."

Bots and a mixture of students and Specialists scattered, guarding Briton. Since this was their first time, it wasn't a fully accurate simulation of an infiltration mission; it would get incrementally harder depending on how well they fared.

Their task was to take out everyone standing guard and not let one escape to prevent them from calling reinforcements. There was a threshold for how many units could spot them on the inside before it was "game over". A time limit also existed.

"Stick to the plan!" said Zephyr, zipping into the fray, creating cyclones, and sweeping people into the air. Most who stood in his path were close-ranged fighters.

Zephyr observed the fighting styles of brawler-types and those who preferred to kick with the greaves on their boots. Their moves were predictable with their tendency to attack during every opening, allowing Zephyr to evade with a minimal effort out of instinct. He took advantage of their frustrations and overuse of aura by continuing to dodge and strike on guard.

Act, but don't get cocky.

Gauging tells came naturally to Zephyr, thanks to his tendency to observe and calculate. Reading new opponents came with ease and Skye commended him on his efforts. Some Trainees released a breath whenever they unleashed an elemental attack, like Spark.

Leif separated from the group and zoomed through, knocking opponents out with one strike each. Spark summoned a thunderstorm and merged with lightning bolts to confuse more students while Skye grabbed Aurora and disappeared in a flash of smoke. Meanwhile, Shadow created earth walls that made it difficult for anyone to cross the party.

They blocked the main gate off, as Zephyr expected.

A hidden entrance had to exist somewhere. *But where?*

One window had a lock that could only deactivate with a switch.

Conveniently, Shadow destroyed a bot with his axe that dropped a remote and Leif finished the remaining guardians.

"Shadow! The remote!" It opened.

All foes had been taken out before the five-minute mark had been reached; they passed this level with flying colors.

Before everyone stepped inside, Zephyr created six glyphs, and one remained underneath each party member. Doing so would let them make less noise, as advised by Skye the night before.

Inside, Specialists patrolled. They blocked sections off with walls that hidden switches could only dismantle.

Everyone spread out, hiding behind walls.

A Specialist came up close and Shadow created a silhouette that teleported next to her and struck her to the floor. One almost saw them by arriving at the other side of the wall, but Leif trapped and muffled him against the wall with metal cuffs.

When clear, they hurried to one office after confiscating a key card belonging to an unconscious Specialist.

Hidden within a desk drawer was a list of codes along with a switch. A wall disappeared, allowing access to the opposite side. They rinsed and repeated, proceeding onto the next level, which had more walls and switches that had to be activated in specific orders.

Second round took them ten minutes, and the third took fifteen. Both were within the designated time limit, and the only ones who spotted them got knocked out. They called no reinforcements in time.

Why did I underestimate myself for months?

"Don't step past the boundary lines," said Skye once they reached the last level and knocked out the guards at the entrance. Zephyr didn't detect a single soul.

"What boundary lines?" asked Shadow.

Skye pointed off to the side and pressed a button on her Communicator, revealing laser barriers that crossed, filling up a hallway. Zephyr didn't want to risk it to see if they were real or not, as cool as it looked.

"A Recon Specialist would've spotted it before me, but at least this makes it easier to see. I'd imagine touching them will activate some kinds of traps and trigger an alarm." Zephyr's memory wasn't as good as a Recon Specialist, but he memorized the layout.

"How are we gonna get through?" asked Spark.

Skye pointed at her and Zephyr. "Use that aura ball transformation—what I taught you in training."

"Oh, snap!" said Shadow. "Y'all learned how to do that? Cool!"

Spark and Zephyr turned into balls of their specialized elements and disappeared through the openings of the lasers. A switch found purchase in the non-lasered portion of the hall. Once deactivated, the rest of Star Strike joined them.

Hidden Specialists ready to ambush were scattered throughout the level and their team almost got caught up a few times. They cleared it within the time limit and found the last room at the top of Briton Tower.

"Finally," said Tristan. He stood in the battle room along with four others whom Zephyr recognized as his teammates. "One last step: five of my team versus five of you."

Skye stepped off to the side to spectate.

Zephyr assessed Team Raven Mist. Three members weren't present—they must have selected their best combatants for this session. Tristan's teammates comprised a mage, healer, defender, and a martial artist. They were also B-ranked.

Let's see how well we do with more instinct.

"Whenever you're ready," said Zephyr.

Tristan lunged after Leif with his spiked ball on hand.

Before Zephyr could do anything else, the martial artist, Laken, punched him with his fist cuffs. Zephyr activated his shield, which took some of the damage, but still threw him against the wall. His cheek stung from the blow. Skye cast him a concerned glance from the corner of the room.

Tristan and Laken lacked the ability to manipulate their aura. Therefore, they had no choice but to make up for it with regular, physical attacks or use Balancers manufactured from the BSC Tower to emulate aura-based techniques. Zephyr was glad that the organization provided such opportunities for individuals like themselves. It would be beneficial to fight against opponents he couldn't sense.

Laken evaded much of Zephyr's strikes and jabs. He moved as if gliding on the surface of water. It was more difficult to predict what he could do, so Zephyr waited and tired him out.

Glyphs of various sizes scattered throughout the battlefield. Zephyr ricocheted back and forth between platforms, landing bursts of wind onto Laken. He moved in distinct patterns and routes. He feinted left, slipping past Laken, conjuring a glyph behind him.

Laken looked down, realizing he'd gotten juked into standing on a glyph.

With a snap of Zephyr's fingers, the glyph enlarged. The one behind Laken, along with others, came together, ensnaring him.

"Nice!" said Laken.

Zephyr ducked when Tristan launched a blast of artificial light aura at him.

"I gotchu!" said Spark, spin-kicking Tristan and disarming him.

Leif threw a chakram to block shards of ice from hitting her that were conjured by Raven Mist's mage. "Ya owe me!"

Spark created a current, only for the opposing defender to block it with his mace. "What? But how?"

"We've studied enough of your fights," said Tristan, smirking.

Their mage created five balls made of fire and Aurora retaliated by dousing the flames with bubbles.

Shadow stood in front of Spark, tanking a hit from Tristan and twirled Diablos' staff form, generating a cyclone.

Leif flung a chakram, and Zephyr attached a glyph to it, powering it up. The spiked disk spun toward the healer, forcing the mage to move toward a glyph behind her. It spun, trapping her into place.

Zephyr created an enlarged glyph for the defender. While everyone was trying not to get hit by Shadow's technique, Leif shot an icy wind from his chakrams, knocking the defender into the rotating glyph. Spark kept Tristan distracted by forcing him to dodge her bolts and electric currents. Aurora conjured a flame phoenix that flew toward him, pushing him into the glyph as well.

Only the mage remained. She created a miniature meteor storm as a last line of defence. Spark and Leif leaped above, destroying each one before the hits could land. Shadow's platforms of light knocked the mage into another glyph.

With one more enlarged glyph that sandwiched Raven Mist, Zephyr moved his hands so the wind symbols could slam them onto the floor.

"Well, that was fun," said Tristan, getting back to his feet.

Laken walked up to Zephyr and shook his hand. "Don't worry, the next session won't be child's play."

34

COVERUP

SKYE

DETECTING SENSORS, SNEAKING, AND OBSERVING TERRAIN WERE nothing new for Star Strike. The difference between here and their academy days was this was more advanced. Skye's team adjusted, and she could see their peaks coming through.

"Not bad for your first sweeper mission since graduation," said Amber as everyone exited Briton. "Y'all act and think super fast."

Skye could see how Raven Mist was so successful with a Recon Specialist like her around, followed by their expert combatants. Her strategic placement of undetected drones to gather info from the shifting terrain was unmatched for her tier. Amber was notably glued to Tristan and frowned whenever students fangirled over him. For someone so petite, she was certainly menacing.

Skye had the privilege of witnessing her team's powers grow. Everyone followed her advice and constructive comments. Finding the balance between critical and considerate remained troubling, however.

"Zephyr, your fighting back there was something else! I can imagine how powerful you'd be with the Marking unlocked. No generation has anyone with the same combat abilities when activated, right?" asked Tristan. "Except for overall enhancement?"

"Mhm!" replied Spark. "Never know what yer gonna get!"

"Seems like an easy way to win fights," commented Amber.

Zephyr put his hand on his chin, thinking. "Not necessarily. Some can counter it, like any other bloodline abilities. It can't be used as a crutch since it burns far more aura, too."

"Huh, guess it makes sense," said Amber. She was one of the Maizin. Outsmarting the opponent and usage of earth mastery would've been the way to win fights.

Balance as a concept existed everywhere. Dangers lurked for Lumière members who over relied on their gifts. There were drawbacks for higher levels and Skye was far too familiar with them...

Being able to see Zephyr grow and unlock the Marking somewhat compensated for missing out the past six years, before they stopped training together. Without Zephyr around to cross blades with her, Skye felt incomplete. Instead, her sparring partners were her Combat Squad colleagues. Last Skye heard, the surviving few were trying to hit S-rank, spending most of their time outside of missions in tournaments in parts of northeastern Solaria. Aside from stopping Thanatos, she hadn't seen them around.

"Can we take off for the night?" Leif asked Skye.

She observed everyone's more than halfway empty aura levels. "Sure."

"Cool! StrikeBall time!" exclaimed Leif, fetching a ball from his storage. Shadow retrieved his StrikeBall Axe.

"Wanna play with us, Zephyr?" asked Tristan.

"Nah, I'm lousy at it. Also, I keep getting the rules mixed up." Skye didn't get the rules either, even after all those games Star Strike attended seven years ago to cheer on Leif. And spend time around Zephyr.

"Bummer. Well, catch y'all later!" Tristan smiled at Skye and left with the StrikeBall participants and Amber.

"I lagged back there with my spells!" exclaimed Aurora. Skye wondered what triggered her higher bouts of self-deprecation ever since she rejoined the party.

"Hey. It's stronger than before," said Skye. "Try lighter breaths when you release the spells." Earlier, Skye contacted Swifty about everything she needed to know about spell-casting, hoping it'd help Aurora.

Astro Strike had come so far since starting off as E-rank Specialists. She was proud of them. Skye knew they'd become the very heroes they wanted to be. Better heroes than her.

Fans approached them. Fresh faces kept appearing as older students returned from their weekly missions.

A handful of kids oohed and aahed over Spark, revealing her assortment of lances, spears, and javelins after receiving requests. Some wished to see Skye's weapons as well—the fans that liked her still and weren't turned off by rumors and other slip ups that occurred the past five months. They wanted to try her blades out, but Skye had to put her foot down for once with Excalibur.

"You're as quiet as they say, Hikari," said a male student. "Why?"

Skye winced whenever her clan name was pronounced as "HIH-CARRY."

"Don't be rude, Bob! And it's HIH-KAHRI!" cried a female student. "Sorry about that. Some of us at least have manners."

Bob shrugged. "Everyone's got a story, ya know."

"Every team has some kinda strong, silent type!" said Spark, pulling out her shields. "For Star Strike, it's her and Blaze."

Zephyr chuckled. "I think Blaze better suits the category of 'Gentle Giant.'"

Being known as the "Strong, Silent" type was an upgrade from how the public used to perceive her as "cold and unfriendly" just because she didn't speak as much compared to Aqua when on camera. All personas were what she envisioned as a child, but one was more irritating than the other.

"I like your hair!" said the girl.

"Thanks... I, uh... grew it myself."

Zephyr chuckled while some gave her funny looks.

Skye wondered how Stream dealt with all her admirers.

"You're kinda weird, you know, Hikari?" said Bob, butchering her name again. "But I guess it works. You fight well, so it makes up for it."

How rude! How would YOU feel if I called you "Boob" instead? Also, WHO names their kid that these days?

Once the crowds dispersed, Skye followed Spark and Aurora back to their room.

Experiencing dorm life was an interesting change from camping out and going to inns. Bunk beds and lofts seemed fun and reminded Skye of how she and Shadow wanted to share a room when they were four. Their house had five bedrooms, so it made little sense to double-up, according to Mom.

Skye checked for messages from the Marauders as she leaned against the wall. Nothing. She heard Aurora's melodious voice from the shared bathroom, singing a tune Skye couldn't recognize.

Spark's legs crossed as she casually sat on the bottom bunk.

Blaze's holographic image stood in front of her. "Don't worry about giving me an upgrade. If it takes too much time, I can buy a new stone."

"Nah, it's okay. If I can figure it out, I'll be one step closer to learnin' how to craft 'em!"

Skye had never seen anyone build a Morphic stone, but it probably was the most difficult because of the materials capable of reacting to a shapeshifter's DNA.

"If you insist."

Glacieus' holograph popped up, squeezing Blaze out of the way. Gentle Giant side-eyed him in response. Their dynamic was always entertaining to watch. Despite being opposites, they seemed to hang out a lot ever since they were little.

"Hi-hi!" He waved at the girls. "You should upgrade *my* weapons, Sparky!"

"I've got cool bullets. Would ya want those, Glacy?"

"When would I not want spiffy bullets? BTW, where's Rory?" Glacieus waved his hands around as he spoke and enunciated his words—he tended to exaggerate his gestures and motions. He often burst out into song and his flair for the dramatic amused Skye.

Aurora came out of the room with a towel wrapped around her head. "Right here."

"Yay! Time to gossip!" exclaimed Glacieus. "How are the two boys in your lives doing? Any updates in the love department-"

"Glacieus, now isn't the time for spilling the juice!" said Blaze, exasperated.

Glacieus rolled his eyes. "It's not 'juice,' Blazie. It's called 'the tea.' Gods!" Slang was hard to keep up with these days. Especially with how it varied per region.

Aurora frowned. "For the record, nothing's happened! Well... not yet."

The "tea-spiller" turned to Skye. "Uh-huh! Uh-huh! What about you and Spiky?"

"Spiky" could've referred to either Zephyr or Leif. And Blaze somewhat.

"Who?" Skye wanted to play it safe.

"Progress has been made," said Aurora, beaming at Skye.

Progress for WHO?

"What about Stream and Luna?" asked Spark, smirking.

Glacieus waved his hand. "Our leader's got it WORSE!"

"Runs in the family," muttered Blaze, glancing at Skye. "They have ridiculously fast heartbeats around each other." Skye supposed even he couldn't resist partaking in gossiping. Though, she still couldn't figure out what was going on. As usual.

Spark stroked her chin. "Interesting! Guess when they're ready, they're ready!"

"Ready for what?" asked Skye, earning a facepalm from the others.

Glacieus snickered. "Skyie, I dunno how you and Shadie can be so clueless! Your brains are wacky! If only you could see how much Zephie lo-"

Blaze covered Glacieus' mouth. "Hey, don't ruin it for them."

)•(

SKYE WAITED for the others to drift off before sneaking out to continue her search.

Moonlight crept through the windows, and Skye slid off the top bunk. Aurora was curled up in the bottom one and shivered. Skye assumed she must've kicked her blanket onto the floor.

Before Skye tiptoed out of the room, she put the covers over her sleeping friend. Nobody was around, making it easy to exit and teleport.

She zigzagged into the forest, keeping her eyes peeled for what the Communicators detected.

All Marauders were trying to find the Typhons or were on duty to eliminate god-like Risen. Wings of Order were on call for the night and checking for any Undead Hosts or Level 5s. If Skye finished her duties here early enough, she'd back them up; better to be safe than sorry.

Past nights had all been Level 5s, and their spawn rates and late detections were still a mystery. Perhaps they would find answers from the Typhons.

Typhons. . .

Like Clay said earlier, thousands of possibilities emerged. The idea of the Typhons possibly causing most of the suffering made Skye's blood run cold.

Who else would've been able to break into the Base and remain undiscovered for so long? And that darkness they possessed... it couldn't have been a coincidence, right? But... if Dr. Lycaste was part of the Typhons, why would they kill their own kind? And... who were the other people in the room with her that night?

Skye disagreed with having Star Strike come with them to infiltrate the Base. Orders were orders. She had to accept the risks and exposure they were going to face by now. The President's word was final, and she had to have faith in him. After all, he'd been so kind and accommodating throughout her entire life.

All she could do was ensure their safety, and she prayed to Celeste every night, hoping the retribution she faced wouldn't extend to everyone else.

A cracking sound of a branch snapping caught Skye's attention. Excalibur was tightly in her left hand and one of her knives, Lynx, was in her right. Every final blow she landed on an Undead or Level 5 was with Excalibur. After all... it was all she had left of Astrid.

Standing in front of her was a Phantom Risen. If Skye hadn't known better, she would've mistaken it for a Level 3 and attempted to paralyze it, but it seldom worked on anything Level 5 or up. They always looked weaker than Level 3 and 4... Almost to trick mortals.

Phantoms were humanoid, like many Level 4s, but never reached their colossal, titan-like sizes. This Risen was tall, with long arms reaching the ground and bony fingers. Its face resembled a human skull that had a low-hanging jaw and eyeless sockets.

Phantoms could land hits with forces strong enough to send Skye crashing through a line of trees.

All the damage dealt on her strengthened her in the end. She couldn't die so easily, and so long as she still breathed, it was never over. Even if every bone in her body was broken, she'd keep going. No matter how broken she was, she'd fight her way through with Excalibur drawn. Skye never stopped fighting.

Skye summoned her Spiritual Power through light, and Excalibur glowed white along with the Farien symbol on its hilt, transforming into its other form. It didn't take many charged stabs to destroy—she had to take it down before it unleashed any bone-chilling screams that could petrify an entire town.

"No sign of Astrid?" Skye turned and saw Aqua behind her. For the longest time, it was hard for her to even say Astrid's name.

"Just a Phantom. This one was weaker."

"Maybe weakened somehow beforehand?" asked Blossom. She, Zetta, and Clay came into view.

"What'd you guys find?" asked Skye.

"A Reaper," replied Clay.

"And the Typhons?"

Aqua shook her head. "Getting much closer to searching every corner of the globe. Only Cordelia and Kadelatha are left."

"What about Nova Strike?"

Clay smiled. "In good hands."

"Still paired with Dawn Brigade?"

"Yes," said Clay. "We've got a long day ahead tomorrow and you better rest up."

Wings of Order were notorious for going weeks straight without sleep. To any non-Marauder, this was astonishing. Most of the elite teams could hardly go through a single week nonstop. Their reserves were that plentiful along with their stamina and resilience but were detrimental to their performance for aura usage. Therefore, it was better to not take the restless approach.

Skye's stamina and reserves were growing. Hopefully, she could reach their level of tenacity before it was too late. Maybe the stone affected her growth rates for that as well. She just hoped she could collapse less.

It didn't take long after Skye and the Wings of Order parted in opposite directions before she heard a shrill howl. Darkness shrouded and blinded her, and she clenched her fists, activating her shield.

"Who are you?" shrieked a feminine voice.

The same Undead Host she encountered around the Silvatican Mountains stood.

Gotta be a lot weaker this time around.

Darkness around the figure disappeared, revealing a teenager with mousy brown pigtails. Skye's stomach knotted, seeing pain in the Undead Host's gray eyes.

The dark aura swirled around Skye, and images flashed through her head, chronicling the girl's life. Even though Skye saw every major event in the girl's lifespan, it only lasted for less than a second in real time. Being able to see it all as a Host was another conse-quence as of the curse. As if being a Host wasn't already nightmarish.

She was from Thet, a distant relative of the royal family. Her parents were killed in a Risen attack, leaving her to care for her little brother. One day, her Host power went out of control to protect him from Risen... only for her power to slaughter him.

She never knew she was a Host.

The girl attempted to take her own life by stabbing herself through the heart as retribution, only to no avail. Just like Dove and Skye once did.

She isolated herself, wandering forests. Her wish was granted only when she faded away some time after... like Astrid and the others. All traces of her existence disappeared from this world, along with anyone who had memories of her.

If only she knew other Hosts... then there would be at least someone else who could remember her.

Skye readied Excalibur.

Dark pulses emerged from the girl, dealing strikes that could instantly kill any non-Marauder.

Skye dodged them, landing a slice through the girl, and landing on the opposite side, creating explosions of light.

"It hurts. . ."

Darkness around her shifted again, and Skye found herself in an illusion, seeing the girl at a younger age alongside her brother. They were both knocked to the ground in a pool of blood.

It's not real. She's an Undead Host, and I have to end her. Don't listen to her.

"Please... Miss... why are you doing this?"

"H-help... Us..." said the little boy.

A sharp thrust lodged into her abdomen, and she heard her barrier shattering before feeling the pain crash through. She winced, forcing herself to not black out.

Skye's knives floated around her, circling and cutting through the children, shattering the illusion. Their screams rang in her ears.

She was back in the woods. The girl held a sword made of darkness and their blades clashed in rapid succession.

Skye summoned the glow in her eyes. Golden light shrouded her, and she soaked in the power it granted her, aided by the stars. This time, she would use it wisely. Pace herself. Utilize the terrain.

Skye did a backflip, disappearing, and reappearing behind the girl, moving her hands, and allowing the knives to pin her onto the ground. The girl multiplied into several copies of herself surrounding Skye. She stabbed the ground, creating a massive crevasse, allowing it to swallow mirages. With a jump, Skye rebounded off the tree to her right, flicking her hand to throw another blade. Using her metal aura, she charged the blade from afar, slashing open the Host's calf. Darkness flowed out of it, as the girl howled.

Turning herself into a fiery star, Skye swirled around the battleground, knocking the Host into the air and punching her to the ground, creating an earthquake from the impact. Potent arms of darkness shot up from underneath the ground. As Skye dodged, an additional arm shot up and wrapped around her neck.

Skye's screams rippled through the woods, trembling as her aura drained. The arms projected her into the air, high above. Explosions of darkness occurred, sending her crashing down upon the trees, collapsing an entire section of the woods.

Right as the Host was about to land another hit, Skye boosted herself again. She disappeared and reappeared, creating a burst of wind from her hands. A meteor manifested, and she slammed it onto the Host.

Dark, solid platforms floated beneath Skye, levitating her. She stabbed Excalibur through one platform, using part of its pommel to swing and throw herself onto the Host, landing a punch that emitted a sound wave, ripping more of the ground.

Skye charged her water aura, striking the air with Excalibur, creating a blue serpent made of water that swirled around the foe. She lifted Excalibur into the air, generating blue sparks, and they struck the sky, raining down as lightning bolts, allowing the water to channel the electricity and explode.

With a last strike, Skye jumped and landed on the opposite side of the girl, causing more explosions. The girl fell to the ground as the darkness faded away from her, leaving her with her human form.

Skye approached the girl, who was now practically transparent as her soul vanished from this world.

"Thank you."

Skye nodded. "What's your name?"

"Eloise."

"I'll remember you, Eloise. You can rest easy now." *You, too, Saylor.*

Skye stayed with Eloise until her body disintegrated. She closed her eyes, allowing for moments of silence out of respect for the dead.

Nausea hit her like a truck.

Her fingers brushed near the traumatized side of her body, and they were wet. During the ultimate moments of their battle, the girl must've lodged the blade deeper into her. Skye had to have been too focused on ending her to notice.

Despite the agony, Skye's head filled with other thoughts.

She wondered why she was the only one left—in this world, at least. And why... she hadn't faded away yet along with where her dark form came from. They all thought the time would come soon after Teddy, but it didn't.

Every time before it happened, the Hosts mentioned feeling themselves getting lighter and other Hosts sensed their power dwindling. None of that happened with Skye yet... Did it have something to do with Dr. Lycaste's experiment? She was the only Host they knew who'd been ambushed on an exam night and was the last turned into a Host.

Staying alive was a double-edged sword. On one hand, it gave them extra time to destroy the remaining Undead Hosts—there were hardly any around within the past year.

Once she faded away like the others and transformed into an Undead Host... her existence would disintegrate from every non-Host's memory—the ultimate consequence of the curse—a discovery Skye took a lifetime to accept.

It still stings to think of that one time when Aqua asked me, "Who's Astrid?"

Even with Skye gone someday, Marauders remembered the existence of the Undead. They still knew Undead were the most dangerous forms of Risen they ever had to deal with. Their memories were tampered with… as if under the influence of illusions.

I don't think Eloise knew what she was creating as a Host. Perhaps… it was for the best.

They were the mortal version of Dark Spheres, except mostly unkillable.

Except… why did almost all traces of them disappear? Everyone remembered every known Dark Sphere and what guarded them, even after destruction.

Excalibur was all Skye had left of Astrid… and it only existed in this world still, because it belonged to their mother. Nearly every trace of her disappeared or became replaced with an illusion that only the Hosts could tell were fake.

When Astrid's time came, Excalibur was left behind and Skye picked it up, vowing to never part with it. She had Excalibur as her weapon of choice, to avenge her sister.

I won't fail again to find you and put an end to you, Astrid.

Skye remembered the sound of Astrid's tortured screams as an Undead Host—the last time she heard her sister's voice. The mere sight of her figure made Skye drop Excalibur, unable to raise her blade any further against a former source of light in her life.

Skye made a promise to the Hosts: to keep their situations concealed from the vast majority to not fuel the fear that already existed. It was for the best until they got more information and figured out how to end the curse and suffering. Even the Hosts' loved ones had trouble believing they had a sibling or child who no longer existed, with little to no evidence they could see.

She promised Astrid that she'd protect Shadow and Cynthia. Until they were ready.

Once Skye arrived at the Briton Courtyard, she searched for an area hidden from plain sight to address her wounds. A collection of trees caught her eye, and she moved toward them, about to reach for bandages from her Communicator storage.

Zephyr ran up to her from the shadows, wide-eyed. "Skye?"

It was only then when she realized how much blood she lost.

I think I've broken the record for the amount of times I've been stabbed in a year.

He gaped at the blade lodged into her. Blood soaked her top, and she kept it in place to not worsen it as she felt more redness cake beneath her undershirt.

Her vision blurred as she lost her footing. A sturdy pair of arms caught her.

Zephyr clutched her against his chest. "Don't worry, I got you."

35

CRUTCH

ZEPHYR

"THAT WAS A LOT OF BLOOD," SAID AURORA, WIPING SWEAT OFF HER forehead and putting away her tome. Skye laid still on Zephyr's bed with bandages wrapped around her waist, legs, and arms. Green sparkles remained, covering her. "She should be fine."

"What were those scars on her body?" asked Spark.

"Scars?" asked Leif. Shadow returned with a pitcher of water and cups, setting them on the nightstand beside the bunks.

Zephyr and Leif averted their line of sight when Aurora undressed Skye. Zephyr's cheeks burned, and he wanted to slap himself for feeling that way. She'd been stabbed, and he mostly thought of how perfectly she fit in his arms.

"Yeah. Tons of 'em. All over her chest and backside," said Spark. "What'd she run into?"

"No idea," replied Zephyr.

"So... what exactly happened again?" asked Aurora. "I'd like more context besides Leif barging into our room and dragging us over to Skye knocked out and left to bleed all over Zeph's bed."

"Wouldn't have happened if Shadow didn't take so long to wake up!" Leif side-eyed the older Hikari twin.

"Anyway," began Zephyr. "Insomnia kicked in, so I took a walk.

Before long, I ran into Skye, practically covered in blood."

"So, you carried her..." Aurora's lips curled into a smile. "That's... kinda romantic."

Leif sniggered. "Bridal-style, too."

Zephyr scratched his head. "She's lighter than I thought."

Aurora and Spark smacked Zephyr upside the head. "ARE YOU CALLING HER OVERWEIGHT?"

"That's a low one, man!" exclaimed Spark.

"No, no! I meant... I thought she'd be heavier because of her..." Zephyr gestured to Skye's chest. "I should... stop talking..."

"You're ruining the romance," warned Aurora. Stream coined Skye and Zephyr's pairing name as "Zephkye." Such a thing carried into the media like wildfire.

"What romance?" asked Shadow. "It's like the time Zeph carried ME! Huh... Funny how that works. Zeph carrying both Hikari twins at one point!"

Everyone else facepalmed.

Zephyr heard a tossing sound.

Skye tried to sit up but couldn't lift her head.

"Skye!" Aurora rushed to her side. "Stay there!" She held Skye's head up, grabbing a cup of water from the nightstand, letting her take sips.

"What happened?" asked Shadow. "How'd your shield break?"

"Went for a walk. Ran into the monster who killed Saylor and those Cerberus people."

Aurora's jaw dropped. "Again?"

Back at the Silvatican Mountains, Zephyr and the girls were shocked the next morning when Skye held the recording device in her hands, with nicks and cuts all over her.

Skye's eyes looked dull with pain. All Zephyr wanted to do was hold her again and stroke her hair, the soft strands she used to tie into pigtails that he liked to tug on when they were kids. Once Skye was bundled into his arms, he needed her there again. He yearned for her touch. He was starved from it and didn't realize how much until then.

"Killed it this time. Saylor and I weakened that thing in earlier battles."

"So… it was a Level five, right?" asked Leif.

Skye hesitated. "Something like that, yeah. We don't really know. . . much about them."

"Well… I'm glad Saylor was avenged," said Zephyr. Something told him she wasn't revealing everything to Astro Strike. As if she was holding back breaths.

"Maybe we'll find out more when we find the Typhons' Base," said Shadow. "And put an end to what they're doing!"

"Think we can do that?" asked Aurora. "How many are we up against?"

"We have to try!" said Shadow. "With us and the Marauders, we sure can!"

"It's all the more reason to train as much as we can," said Skye.

"They can't evade us forever!" said Spark. "We were made for this! Saving the Realm! Can't understand why Electro would do this, but whatever the case, gotta stop 'em!"

"Agreed." Aurora turned to Skye. "How are you feeling?"

"All right." Skye lifted her arms slightly, staring at the rolls of white gauze encasing her. Color drained from her face as panic flared in her eyes.

"Rory and I bandaged ya up! We saw the scars! No idea you had so many!"

"Just you two…?" asked Skye.

Aurora nodded, and she exhaled.

Zephyr wondered if there were more disfigurements scattered around her thighs and other parts of her body she had always covered up. Some faint scars around uncovered areas within her arms and lower legs were only visible in certain lighting. He recalled the times when Stream mentioned having to design her outfits with accessories such as belts, straps, and bands, and how Skye kept insisting on always having some of them on whenever Aurora suggested removing them when they turned in for the night. They seemed uncomfortable to sleep in.

"When d'ya get all those?" asked Spark. "What kinda monsters did that?"

"We should let her rest," said Zephyr, changing the subject as Skye hesitated to respond and winced. "We all need to go back to sleep, too."

Raindrops fell from the outside, splattering against the windows.

Aurora yawned. "Yeah, let's go. Do you want to stay here, Skye?"

"Wait... who's bed is this?" Skye looked around, knitting her brows.

Spark chuckled. "Zeph's! He's the one who carried you here!"

"Oh, okay. Wait, WHAT? It wasn't too much trouble for you, right?" Skye diverted her gaze from Zephyr, flushing, being absolutely adorable. "I thought I'd be heavy."

Zephyr put his hands up. "N-no! Not at all! You're pretty light!" He was glad this at least distracted her from the subject concerning her scars.

"Excalibur and my knives would weigh me down, though."

"That's... not what I meant."

Her head cocked to the side, reminding Zephyr of Mochi. "What did you mean?"

"Don't worry about it," said Zephyr, scratching his head. Spark, Aurora, and Leif laughed. "Anyway... if you want to stay in my bed... I can take the floor."

Zephyr tried to shove any suggestive thoughts as much as possible. Now was NOT the time to be thinking about Skye, partially clothed, in his sheets. His hands brushed against her curves when he set her down. He felt the soft brush of her hair as well.

"I can... be in my bed, thanks."

Zephyr nodded. "I'll help you get back."

Throughout the past five months, Zephyr knew many parts of the old Skye remained. Her warmth, kindness, determination, and selflessness shined, but were more hidden beneath the surface. Their training together only led to Zephyr wanting to spend more time with her outside of it, and so did Shadow and Aurora.

36

THORN ON MY SIDE

LUNA

"Whattaya mean, 'oatmeal is just breakfast food?' I like it, so I WILL HAVE IT FOR DINNER!" Glacieus reminded Luna of a kid whining for candy at the junk food aisle in a grocery store.

Maybe Stream has string cheese and a juice box for him, too.

Weeks passed since Nova Strike reunited and began their aggressive search for the Typhon's Base. Luna didn't know how much longer she could take, both not finding anything and Glacieus's current oatmeal obsession.

"Fine, you can have your oatmeal, but you better add some fiber," said Stream in a scolding manner, wagging her finger at him like a mother would. "And no more yelling in the inn!"

"This isn't an inn! I didn't get A MINT ON MY PILLOW!"

Now, he resembled one of those short-haired socialites who asked to speak with a manager or threatened to sue. Luna was forced to rescue some once from a sea monster and thanks to all their complaining, she almost wanted to let them drown. Or drown herself to no longer have to bear their nasally voices.

Stream facepalmed. "GLACIEUS! Keep doing that, you won't get any brownies!"

Glacieus shut up. "Yes, ma'am."

Luna wished Stream learned how to bake her confections several years prior. Living next door to that "child" for most of their lives seemed like a handful. Though, Luna would've graciously consumed anything Stream made.

They just arrived at the inn in the middle of nowhere, and Glacieus was already causing a ruckus, humming and breaking out into song as usual.

Luna and Blaze were conversing, trying to tune out whatever nonsense was being argued about while Stream made dinner.

"Are ya sure Dawn Brigade doesn't want your cooking, Streamie?"

Stream blushed. "What if they don't like it? What if they think I'm trying to tell them to go on a diet by serving them healthy food?" She stirred the pot of hearty soup, and a savory aroma filled the room.

Stream insisted on cooking. She conducted research on what was served at this inn and claimed none of the excessive saturated fat and other mumbo jumbo was good for them. If it was anyone else spouting this nonsense, Luna would've scoffed. But this was Stream. Her Stream. And she would've gone along with whatever Stream said.

"Doubt they'll think that," said Blaze reassuringly. "Either way, up to you."

"I think I'll pass this time. I don't know them well enough..." She brought out another pot and a box of oatmeal, and Glacieus clapped.

"You'll get used to it, Princess," said Luna. "They're chill."

"Don't forget the maple syrup! And peanut butter! And NONE of the zero sugar BS!" Glacieus made a retching sound with his throat.

⋯⟨⋯

SUNLIGHT ARRIVED and Stream was already up with her hair and makeup perfectly coiffed. She wouldn't be caught dead without it, especially in front of people she didn't know well. It helped that her cosmetics were smudge-proof and hair products seemed invincible.

Luna didn't know what the big deal was. Stream was drop-dead gorgeous, regardless. Some of her outfits made her look so good, it made Luna's chest hurt.

If Luna had an extra time, she'd touch up her appearance as well. Most of the time, it was for the cameras and any random publicity.

Blaze and Glacieus waited for them downstairs. Despite Luna wearing heeled-boots, the boys still towered over her and even Stream. They were the tallest Star Strike members, though Glacieus was leaner.

Glacieus wore a new outfit: an olive, collared vest with brown accents at the bottom over a white long-sleeved shirt with brown and black pants. His sleeves reached his elbows, hemmed with olive while the brown of his pants only reached to his upper thighs, leaving the rest black. An olive bracelet framed his wrist, which matched the accents on his brown shoes.

With palettes, Glacieus's clothes were olive, brown, and black. The greens made his eyes appear brighter, and it seemed like a common pattern for Star Strike's outfits to coordinate with eye or hair color. He looked mature until he opened his mouth. Though Luna would take his outbursts over most people's quirks.

"Good to go?" asked Elena, coming down the stairs. Her attire always made her look like a royal soldier, thanks to the pauldron and other armor pieces covering her arms. Most of the media dubbed her as "The Knight." Rough, but also gentle. Some also used the title "Silencer."

"We are," replied Luna.

The rest of the Dawn Brigade followed.

"Everything charged, Stream?" asked Oscar.

"Y-yes," she squeaked.

"Heh, cute," said Calypso.

Stream smiled a little—she was the least shy around the Water Mage. Both had ancestry from Piscium and specialized in water aura.

Once they were outside, Stream turned on the blue tracking cube. It floated into the air, emitting waves of light, remaining by her side. The waves shifted red if barriers were detected.

"Looks like it booted up faster than before," said Calypso.

Stream nodded. "Made some slight adjustments last night."

Luna found it ironic to think that they were using the Typhons' own theories against them. Questions over whether it could detect their Base had no answers yet.

Glacieus held a remote, controlling his long-distance drone and gathering a bird's-eye view of the terrain further ahead. What one could've missed should've been detected by another on any normal Nova Strike mission.

Ambrose and Lucia armed themselves with knives and staves respectively, standing in the back. The Combat Quad protected the Unity Squad Duo. Elena had her trusty halberd, Iyar never seemed to run out of explosives, Calypso was the most powerful mage Luna had ever met, and Oscar kept his scythe strapped to his backside.

All three had unconventional weapons of choice which made for unpredictable outcomes for fights. "Assassin," "Priestess," "The Knight," "Detonator," "Sorceress," and "Grim Reaper" could each individually defeat Nova Strike in a match.

Dawn Brigade stopped in their tracks once they arrived at a path that split into two before it continued straight forward.

"We'll check the left," said Elena. "Meet here when done." They disappeared, not putting any extra time to waste.

Nova Strike passed the outskirts of a village, technically not belonging to either Kadelatha or Cordelia. Any plots of land that weren't part of any nation or kingdom were a gray area, mostly for farming or travel. Produce and other goods shipped to anywhere of their choosing.

Luna turned to Glacieus. "Do you see them?"

If Spark was the one who never seemed to be lethargic, Glacieus looked like he had too much sugar in his system at almost all times, save for on duty. Currently, it was almost as if a switch turned off inside him and replaced his "jokester grin" with a stony-face.

He glanced at his screen. "There's six, two kilometers away. Hidden."

Radars would've shown the same thing, but Glacieus could spot something off about them. Through sensors, Mutations were untraceable still, which was another headache to deal with.

"They lack strength. Take them out before they attack the village." There could've been more groups out of Luna and Glacieus's range along this path.

Glacieus removed both tonfa pistols from its holsters. He powered them with ice Spiritual Power and pulled the trigger, shooting six bullets, each at a different angle.

No more Risen were at those coordinates.

"Snapped their necks," said Blaze, amazed. Glacieus was the most outstanding marksman seen since Blossom. His aim and range were second to few and Luna wasn't sure if he was better at that or Recon.

Luna's hunch was correct—more groups of six showed up kilometers after the previous encounter. Still no sign of Mutations or barriers, however.

A miniature swarm came out of dark voids to ambush when they arrived at a woodsier place. Stream inched closer to Blaze's side with her claws protracted. Nothing came up from the scanner at the porcupine-looking shadows, but it had the aura of a Level 3.

"Judging by their hands, they can climb trees," observed Glacieus. "Needles shoot ten meters max." He dashed up a trunk, freezing one and blocking another with a tonfa.

Glacieus threw both tonfas, allowing them to return to him like a boomerang with his aura. He charged them with ice aura and a mini-blizzard swirled. A wall of ice appeared in front of Glacieus, separating Risen from him and Luna. He shot it, crumbling it into thousands of shards, pelting it. Snapping his fingers, the shards combined into a boulder, steamrolling the enemies.

Stream spun at the same time as Blaze. A vortex of water formed out of Stream's claws, and she released it while a fireball formed between Blaze's front claws, combining it with the vortex, causing any Risen hit to disintegrate into steam. A blue spiral appeared around Stream, and she cut through twice, with oblique lines forming an "X." Water appeared in the "X" and moved toward enemies, pushing them further away. Blaze leaped into the air, doing a flip, and landing the final blow with his claws, eliminating the last of them.

"Good work," said Luna. "Should be the last of them unless more randomly show up."

"At least they were only Level three," said Stream.

Dawn Brigade was already back at the fork, for Celeste knew how long. Luna hoped they weren't being too slow and dragging them down. Regardless, the elite team knew what they signed up for.

"Nothing?" asked Lucia.

Glacieus handed the footage to her.

"Zilch on our end, too," said Ambrose, peering over her shoulder.

"There's three areas we haven't covered yet," said Elena.

"We should stick together as much as we can," said Iyar. "That way, we don't have to spend so much time looking over everyone's footage."

Calypso turned to Nova Strike. "Besides, it's more fun with you guys around. Gets boring with these same people repeatedly, every day."

Ambrose side-eyed her. "Welp, you're stuck with us, either way."

"What say you, Elena?" asked Oscar.

A light breeze brushed strands of auburn hair from her gorgeous, chiseled face. "We'll go with that," said Elena.

Part of Luna continued to feel awe at working with Marauder teams. There were thrills involved with partaking in missions like these. Luna imagined what it was like to be a Marauder. Nearly all elite teams were in their early to mid-twenties, at the most formidable they would ever be in their entire lives. Newer genera-tions of potential elite teams were being watched as they spoke. One day, Luna will play the role of Elena to an extent. Whether she could appear wise and adept was up for debate. Becoming like Dawn Brigade's leader was more attainable than bothering to reach Aqua's level. She wasn't her or Zephyr and was okay with that.

Fates had control over what happened in one's life. Nobody knew how much they had, and much was up for debate. Luna believed they predetermined most and instead of fighting destiny; it was better to swim with the tide. Ultimately, the most legendary figures possessed specific prowess, allowing them to be blessed by Celeste to save their respective worlds. Celeste could only give some advice and temporarily grant them extra power to be used wisely, but mortals couldn't utilize much of it.

Laws for immortals were stupid and convoluted. If Celeste wasn't here, then the Gods must've believed the mortals could save Eta Geminorum on their own. If Celeste came, the organization would pick Wings of Order and Dawn Brigade to save Eta Geminorum and stop the Typhons. Star Strike was just there to help.

"You're nothing like your brother," commented Iyar.

"I'll take it as a compliment," replied Glacieus. His voice stiffened; a regular occurrence whenever his family was brought up. Stream silenced any Star Strike members who asked about it.

"Oh, please do," said Iyar. "It's refreshing to find a Thorn who isn't a Medic for once. Gets kinda boring to have the same thing running in the fam, ya know."

Media scrutinization and gossip often revolved around the extended Thorn family. Biological members of the family were descended from Khione Aldaine, a comrade of Astra and renown Ice Alchemist who was notoriously skilled with healing arts.

"Yeah," said Glacieus. He looked as if he wanted the conversation to end.

Comparisons between Glacieus and the Medics were most likely infuriating to hear about day-to-day growing up. At least on duty, Specialists would be away from all the rumored drama. Must be tough, constantly having siblings to be compared with.

All of it made Luna think of her mother in a more sympathetic, but still unjustified light. Maybe that's why she was an only child. . .

"Which area are we covering first?" asked Blaze, attempting to change the subject.

"The river," replied Elena.

Lucia and Ambrose's drones were like Glacieus's. They were more complex to use with larger amounts of configurations and settings that were beyond Luna's level of technical expertise. Once Glacieus became A-ranked, he would receive better equipment that matched up to harder missions requiring it.

"Keep your drone between these coordinates," advised Ambrose, pointing at Glacieus's screen. He obediently adjusted the joystick, allowing his device to fly higher.

"Ambrose and I will keep searching closer to the ground," said Lucia.

Lucia was ridiculously good at healing, which stemmed from her Farien ancestry. Her other strengths lied in intelligence, observation, and stealth, which made the squad a better fit. In terms of combat, she was not one to mess with, as she strategically took advantage of appearing weaker than her teammates. Ambrose was more of a battler, among the Veglos. When time called for it, his knife-throwing was unmatched, and his magic was potent. His recon skills were higher than an average Unity Squad unit.

Some Specialists could've easily partaken in other roles, but it was too late now. Luna didn't know the rationale behind each Dawn Brigade member's positions but trusted her uncle's thought process.

⁙

LUNA HEARD the rippling water by nightfall. They had to stop before it became too dark to see well enough. She felt lightheaded from all the sensing, even after Nova Strike requested a break twice already.

Cobalt River extended around fractions of southeastern Solaria. Those lands were unclaimed and had been since Thet relinquished their colonies. The closest warp spot was a statue of Starla de Cordelia, standing kilometers away.

Elena glanced at Nova Strike once they arrived on the riverbed. "Let's rest for a couple."

"Sounds good," replied Luna, shutting off her power.

Blaze reverted to human form, sitting beside her in the grass.

The ribbon-like body of water to Luna's left was deep. Frothing currents swept through, and the sound of ripples emanated in the form of steady rumbling.

Calypso waved her hand, solidifying droplets from the river into a cylinder shape. Twirling her fingers, the liquid purified, and she absorbed it into her skin. A blue glow surrounded her, and Luna sensed her aura levels replenishing.

"Looked like you guys needed a break," said Oscar jokingly.

Stream turned adorably pink. "Oh... Sorry!"

Oscar waved his hand. "Don't worry about it. Reminds us to take a breather, which we are supposed to do more often, anyway. You kids are doing better than I thought."

Blaze's thumb grazed the smooth surface of the red crystal in his palm. "Thought we were dragging."

"Not at all," said Calypso. "Extra pairs of eyes and senses are super helpful here. Even if it takes more time, we're covering ground much more thoroughly. Plus, it gives us more time to see what y'all can do, firsthand. Especially excited seeing how your power changed over these weeks, Stream."

"I'm glad," replied Stream.

"Based on what I've seen the past couple of days, your power resembles your birth father more," said the Water Mage.

"As predicted," said Luna.

The Calderón's were friends of Stream's late parents, adopting Stream when she was a mere infant and Luna was grateful to have Stream on their team. Her moms told Luna and Stream stories about their mission days, and they treated Luna as if she were one of their own.

"Piscium sounds like a pleasant set of worlds to visit—way cooler than Taurium or Sagittarium. Argentum Island would be a must see," said Calypso. "Where our ancestors lived."

"Long ways to go before that's possible, IF it's still possible," said Iyar.

Calypso shrugged. "You never know."

Iyar shook his head. "We don't even know if the other worlds are intact."

"And we don't know if they're destroyed, either."

If Eta Geminorum lost a little more than half its original cities by this point, what were the odds of the same or worse happening to other worlds? With how long it took the organization to find leads or make progress toward their cause and how they still found no Base belonging to the Typhons, Luna believed they would fail in three years. IF it took three years for Eta Geminorum to be destroyed along with the Realm. It could've been sooner.

There's only so many more cities to get destroyed and lives lost. How much longer before the Balance goes haywire?

It didn't surprise Luna that some Marauders had doubts. She wondered if Aqua secretly grew apprehensive as well.

Ambrose did a double take, looking at his Communicator screen. "Guys, check this out."

"What is it?" Everyone surrounded him.

"Not a single Risen has been in sight," said Ambrose. "Wide-open space, far from warp panels and tiny sensors hidden in the trees a kilometer away." He pointed at them on the display.

Stream reactivated her cube, and it spun, flashing red. "I can't believe this worked."

37

STARS AND NOVAS
SHADOW

"G REAT HAVING Y'ALL HERE." SAID T RISTAN, SHAKING EVERYONE'S hands near the schools' main warp panels.

"Thanks for the help," replied Zephyr.

"Next time we play, won't go easy!" said Leif.

"Looking forward to it," said Tristan. He winked at Skye, pointing his index fingers at her and cocked his thumb in a way resembling a handgun. "Hope to see you again soon, Gorgeous." So, he was hitting on his little sister all along! She didn't mind, so Shadow didn't.

"Uh… sure," replied Skye, scratching her head and attempting to reciprocate the hand gesture. Zephyr tensed, and Amber frowned again. Everyone else looked content.

Whatta weird mix of reactions.

Ice Tetra and the Sirens patted Star Strike on the back.

"Good luck, Astro Strike," said Dr. Caraway.

"We're rooting for you," said Dr. Fern.

They vanished into beams of light. Briton and Vigor were fun while it lasted the past three weeks, but it was time to get back to work. Shadow felt like he was back in school again, but without homework and written exams—the much more fun version.

Nova Strike and the others were in the familiar meeting room, waiting.

As soon as the door closed behind them, all eyes glued to Aqua as Astro Strike took their seats. An image of a tan fortress came from her Communicator. It was shrouded by a clear barrier and in a flat, plain area.

"Our scouts kept an eye on the Base for a week," said Aqua, arms crossed. "Nobody's gone in and out at all." She nodded at Glacieus, Lucia, and Ambrose.

"Could be teleporting in, for all we know," said Lucia.

"We should consider a sweeper round with one or two teams to scout ahead before calling in the others," said Clay. "Those not part of the round can stay at the scouts' camp. At a distance we can ambush from and out of range from the sensors, depending on how long they take to disable."

Aqua nodded. "We can't brute force this without knowing HOW to stop the darkness from rising first and the source of their power beyond the Labyrinth. We'll divide into three phases: one to sweep through to survey the terrain and disable security systems, another to send remaining Marauders and Star Strike in to gather more intel, and a third to send in reinforcements as needed."

"Phase Three should only be with a full-scale battle," said Zetta.

"Triple Strike can infiltrate for the sweeper. We're the lightest and quickest," said Sunny.

"You'll need backup," said Tiamat. "Once infiltrators get in, there'll be some way to disable the sensors."

"We can back up Triple Strike," said Elena. "Best way to avoid being seen as much as possible is to gather information before we stop them. Kinda like what we did with Thanatos back in the day."

"As soon as you get the updated data, send it over," said Ava. "Trinity Trio is the most at risk with being seen due to our sizes."

"Especially me," said Tiamat. "If only it was possible to shrink instead of enlarging."

Iyar paused. "Didn't even consider that. Yeah, that bites."

"Sweeper mission would be the easiest part," said Elena. "We're up against unknown powers here. Who knows what else Typhon Strike can do in battle."

Aqua nodded. "As for Mutations and other Risen, we'll have to plan according to what we find in the sweeper before conducting a deeper search."

They dismissed everyone for any preparations. Seemed stressful but having all ten members of Star Strike once again lifted Shadow's spirits.

Their first stop: Garnet Marketplace.

Stream double-checked everyone's shopping lists, making sure nobody was missing anything. There were a lot of medical supplies to pick up, especially after Astro Strike burned through half of it from the exponentially harder training sessions in the past few days. They also had time to kill after waiting for Leif's parents to maintain everyone's weapons.

"I missed you guys!" exclaimed Glacieus as Star Strike waited for Blaze and Aurora to purchase Potions and Ethers.

Luna tapped her chin. "Last time we were all on a mission together was at eleven?"

"It's sad how we were all apart from each other for so long," said Zephyr.

"Of course, if YOU GUYS DIDN'T BETRAY US BY TRANS-FERRING TO OTHER DEPARTMENTS, WE WOULDN'T HAVE THIS PROBLEM!" yelled Leif, pointing at Nova Strike and Skye. It was only a matter of time before Leif and Spark got hyper whenever Glacieus was around.

Glacieus blew a raspberry at Leif. "HMPH! WELL, WAH WAH WAH! SOMEBODY CALLED THE WAMBULANCE!" Passerby stared at the commotion and a lady almost dropped a watermelon.

"Quiet down, you two! You're going to scare away the customers!" scolded Stream.

"She has a point," said Luna.

"Heh! Some stuff never changes!" Glacieus eyed Skye and Zephyr standing close to each other. "Except you two! Looking closer than ever! Y'all lovebirds have that gaze when you look at each other!"

Spark and Leif grinned. Luna smirked.

"You guys!" said Zephyr with a reddened face. Skye turned away.

"Someone's in looooove!"

"Glacieus!" said Stream. "There's no need to keep pointing out the obvious!"

"CAN A GUY GET ANY HELP HERE?" yelled Zephyr. The same lady from before dropped her watermelon this time.

"Heh, heh! No!" said Glacieus.

Shadow looked at his best friend and his sister. *What's with those two?*

Aurora and Blaze came up to the others. "Finally done! What's the next stop?" asked Aurora, putting away bottles in her inventory.

Next up, was figuring out possible battle strategies, as advised by the first and second-in-command.

Star Strike scattered into groups in the Lumière Inc. Training Yard.

Shadow stood beside Glacieus, Stream, Spark, and Skye, wanting to catch up with the former two.

Zephyr and Luna monitored everyone's data from a few meters away while the others chattered, figuring out their plans.

"Not sure if we'll even end up having all ten of us fight together, but you should have strats for it," said Luna.

"Agreed. All right, so we've identified seven types of Mutations so far." Zephyr pulled up images. "If we put Glacy here and Spark here..." He pointed at different positions on the screen.

Were they even considered B-rank anymore? Shadow heard nothing official from Zephyr yet, but all eight had to be pretty darn close to A, right?

Everyone's been doing so well. I'm... proud of 'em!

"Inside the Base is going to be scary," said Stream. "Who knows what else is there!"

"We've got Marauders on our side, Stream!" said Shadow. "We've got this."

"If you're grouped with me, stay close. Our safest option is to stick together," said Skye.

Spark gave them a thumbs up. "Or me!"

Stream smiled. "Thankful for you both. I'd feel safer with either of you around. And Zeph's guidance. But this is the Typhons we're talking about, the original Dream Team we've all aspired to be. Can we even win against them?"

Skye faced her. "We will. You need to have faith."

Glacieus patted the 'scary ones' on the head. "Sparky and Skyie are terrifying! With them, we can kick butt!"

Spark stood straighter. "We're the scariest!"

"Aurora's scariest when mad enough," muttered Shadow.

A mischievous glint appeared in Glacieus's eyes. "HEY, STUM-BLES-" Shadow covered his mouth. His loud friend emitted muffling noises as he tried to wrestle Shadow's hand off him.

"Do you BOTH wanna get killed?" asked Stream.

"Please don't anger her," said Skye, in a feather-light whisper that floated past Shadow's ears.

"Not the move, man!" said Spark.

Stream sighed. "Better not to be killed now, BEFORE the mission. I'm sure I'm not the only one scared of what these Typhons can do. . . We're going against the likes of Mercury... and Electro!"

Spark's optimistic expression remained unwavered. "We gotta be ready! For anything! Didn't think Electro would be part of any of this, but it's less surprisin' if ya just expect anything to happen!"

"That's true..." replied Stream. "But can we even do anything against his tech? Finding the Base is one thing... but what about everything else?"

"This is what the Fates have destined us to do! They built us for a mission like this! To put an end to the misery!" Spark put her hand on Stream's shoulder. "Better to rip the bandage off and go for it! Accept whatever gets thrown at us!"

"Exactly!" said Shadow, nodding along. "With Marauders on our side fighting these battles together, we'll be unbeatable! We're not split up, scattered around the world! This time!"

"Uh-huh! If it's anyone stopping 'em, it's us AND the Marauders!" Spark pumped her fist into the air. "A test of what Star Strike can do at this level!"

"Ever notice how since Star Strike came into play, the Agency's made more discoveries? Either a coinkydink or we're just that awesomesauce," said Glacieus.

"Or Fates had something to do with it," said Luna.

Shadow jumped when he saw the other half of Star Strike behind him.

Please, Celeste, Shadow thought. *Have mercy on your descendant and not allow Aurora to hear anything I said.*

"We gotta adapt to whatever gets thrown at us. Whether Fates or being a Dream Team has anything to do with it," said Zephyr.

"Trust your instinct," advised Luna. "If all else fails for this mission."

Leif put his arms behind his head. "Except we won't fail."

"Best be prepared to," replied Luna. "We can't rely on the elite to help us all the time. Or anyone, really. If there's a technique out there that you still haven't mastered, use something else. Please, use your head for this mission."

"True," said Leif. "Did ya guys think we'd be here with the elite already?"

"I thought most of you would be," replied Aurora.

"Honestly, I didn't think the Agency would even make it this far," said Blaze. "But Eta Geminorum isn't destroyed yet at least." That stung.

Stream fiddled with her necklace. "I'm surprised at how much progress Lumière Inc. made in months, compared to the years spent with nothing new."

Luna paused. "Well, I think that we've had our share of losses. But miraculously, better than bad recently. I don't know how much longer it'll be like this, but we should embrace it while we can." That also stung.

Since when were they so pessimistic? Did something happen to Blaze and Stream, too? Shadow was glad to see Glacieus acting the same. Never in a million years did he think Zephyr would start having doubts and think like a pragmatist.

"With that being said, eat and sleep properly before we leave," said Stream. "The last thing we want is to feel sluggish and fatigued."

"For sure," agreed Zephyr.

Stream looked at the less responsible ones. "Make sure everything is charged, properly stored, and you have everything you need."

"I'll be watching you two!" Aurora said to Leif and Spark.

Spark grinned. "Okay, Mom."

"I'll watch Glacieus and Skye'll monitor Shadow," said Stream.

"I'll make sure Zeph gets enough sleep with what I can think of," said Blaze, facing their leader. "Your heart rate should not be that high."

"I appreciate it," replied Zephyr.

Skye glanced at him, eyes tight.

Zephyr has had insomnia since they became Specialists. Shadow didn't know what the cause was, but it worried him.

Blaze sighed. "It's going to be a long couple of days."

Maybe they weren't ever going to revert to who they used to be. Maybe it was time for Shadow to accept change. And to accept how they weren't invincible. It might've been dangerous, but he felt ready to take on the challenge.

"We've done what we can to prepare for the worst," began Zephyr. Everyone's focus diverted to their leader. "Marauders made it clear how there's only so much time we can afford to spend worrying about the what-ifs and risks. That's why we gotta learn to trust ourselves and our decisions to react to the unknowns."

38

BREACH
ZEPHYR

Maybe it was the experience. Maybe it was the herbal tea Blaze gave him that put him in a soothed state akin to the effects of certain drugs. Or maybe it was meditation. Regardless, Zephyr felt ready.

Despite lingering concerns, Zephyr tried not to let it overtake him. What he said to motivate his team was easier to preach than practice; he was going to put in his all to set an example.

Electronic tents scattered and shrouded beneath barriers. They assembled a separate tent larger than the others in the center, serving for medical purposes. Top Medics were on call with airships on hand, stationed at Garnet's Base, ready to come once Aqua gave the command.

All Marauders were one big, happy family—much like Star Strike. Outside preparations and duty, Zephyr never got a glimpse of what they did until now, save for his eldest sister, who spent her free time studying architecture and ruins. Little did anyone know how she was "almost as nerdy" as Zephyr with history.

Blaze spoke with his former mentor. Stream and Blossom paralleled them. Glacieus kept himself across the area from Clay—something Zephyr would talk to him about if he wished. Mostly everyone else was mingling, though it looked as if the less social ones were only listening.

"What're you doing?" asked Aqua, walking toward him.

Zephyr shrugged. "People watching. And reflecting."

She had an eloquent, dignified air, resembling their father. "Don't reflect too hard. We know what happens when you overthink."

"Can I ask you something?" She beckoned for him to continue. "How do you feel about working with us?"

"Who wouldn't be proud?"

"Your idea or Dad's?"

"Both. You might not pay attention to the press much, but they're going wild over these team ups. They'll see multiple strong teams in a room together, and that's enough to hype things up, even if there's no information about what they're doing."

As soon as he dropped a bomb, a pile followed suit. "Did you ever feel nervous, being watched all the time?"

"We all did."

"Were you ever afraid to make mistakes with Dad and the others watching?"

"Happened to all team leads. Create errors, fix them, and learn," she replied. "Prepare to take risks, but don't get overconfident."

"I wish I knew earlier. Everyone made it seem so easy." They seated themselves in the grass toward the front of his tent.

Sympathy appeared in Aqua's eyes. "Wish we did a better job of warning you earlier. Every Dream Team had an obnoxious fuss over them, but yours was more extreme."

"Maybe not giving me a warning was necessary," said Zephyr. "Best thing was to keep trying until I figured out what worked no matter how crazy the solution."

"You're better at keeping a facade than the rest of us," stated Aqua. "One of the many reasons you're better suited as an heir. Same goes for the way you think." She patted him on the back. Now, she resembled Mom. "Little more than a year ago, I saw the pieces you held. You needed to bring it together and adjust."

"A few times, I thought you were insane when you said I'd be a better heir. Others probably did too." Dawn Brigade and Triple Strike had slight hostility around him for tenable reasons. Not everyone was going to approve of him—a fact he knew but had to learn to accept.

"And now?"

"You'll see." Zephyr stood. "I'm going for a walk. Might help me get more sleep."

"See you later."

Shadow and Aurora remained by the exit, sharing one of the snack mixes Shadow brought with him.

If Rory's stuffing her face... that's not a good sign.

Aurora gulped her handful. "You know, you've been... acting smarter than usual. It's nice."

Shadow grabbed another handful and poured it down his throat. "Trying somethin' new!" He grinned at Zephyr. "How's it goin'?"

"Trying to relax more. It's a beautiful night."

"Skye just left, too." Aurora smirked at Zephyr. "Maybe you should catch up to her."

Zephyr shrugged. "Guess we're all trying to destress."

Aurora's smile faded. "Yeah... For our biggest mission yet. Years of little progress led up to all this happening so quickly at once. Is it too good to be true? Can we stop them, this time at least?"

"Expect the unexpected," said Zephyr.

Shadow swallowed the last of his snack. "And give it all we got!"

Zephyr patted them on the back. "Exactly." He waved and ventured out.

Being in the middle of nowhere came across as peaceful, contrasting the liveliness of Garnet. Zephyr went camping a few times in areas like these when younger—a change of pace from the Hikari's backyard. Tandy enjoyed the quiet because of the peaceful sounds of nature—something Blaze also appreciated.

He barely got to see his younger sisters with his cycle of coming and going. Zephyr tried to remember to bring back gifts for them from his travels. This was a tradition Aqua started and Eila continued. Lumière kids all being in the same room was rare, so his older sisters wanted to have something to remember themselves by.

Zephyr trekked along the dirt path for a kilometer.

Stars that night were sequin-silver, like scattered moondust. Beyond them was the Spirit World. Capala, Lady Garnet, and others had to be up there. Would the reborn keep memories of their past life?

Skye tended to stop and gaze at the stars. And the sun, as if she were to glimpse into the Spirit World. Zephyr wanted to find her and cherish the state of wonder. Together.

A dark void emerged before him, releasing an Eraser.

It wielded a mace. Its aura was more potent than the first.

His glyph boosted his jumps enough to dodge every blow. He lacked the raw strength to cut through it—the most he could do was hold off additional strikes.

Once the opening came, he pressed two buttons to notify Skye. He'd wear it out, play defensively, and observe until she arrived. He wasn't Aqua for combat, and that was okay.

Having the most balanced traits in the party had its drawbacks with defences, along with possessing weaker durability shields. He had no choice but to evade, like when sparring Spark. His instructors growing up frequently emphasized how being a skilled combatant didn't mean having the highest power. Most of his solo victories back then and now were about reading opponents.

The Eraser charged its mace. An upcoming beam so thick would be difficult to avoid. He fired his katana, enlarging it.

"What the?" A glyph appeared under his feet with an ebony Lumière symbol. A thin shroud of electric-blue aura covered his body. He cut straight through the beam seconds quicker than normal and landed a larger vacuum wave that sent the Eraser flying across the path. A glyph the size of a boulder materialized and spun, trapping it.

Skye appeared. Her jaw dropped. "That's the…"

His aura depleted at a higher rate, as expected. Recklessly spamming his newfound power never crossed his mind—it was a death trap waiting to happen, ready to strike as soon as fatigue hit him. Was he Zephyr Lumière if he threw away his ability to strategize in favor of this?

"Lemme fight with you."

Skye grabbed a knife and nodded. She and the Eraser were at full power this time.

He stabbed the ground, and a flock of wind birds swarmed around the Eraser.

It launched millions of needles, and Skye deflected them. The shroud enhanced Zephyr's shield. The buff had limits; it couldn't protect him from most of Eraser's attacks.

Excalibur blocked almost every blow attempted on Zephyr. A glyph propelled Skye into the air, allowing her to jab her blades through the Eraser. Zephyr created a tempest and a second after, an electric chain wrapped around the Eraser, sapping its aura.

A tornado swept the Eraser into the air. It threw its mace at Zephyr, but Skye caught it, crushing it into dust with her hands. Dodging its fists, Zephyr slashed at its side. The Eraser doubled over, releasing screeching sound waves. Skye grabbed Zephyr and disappeared with him, reappearing away from the attack. Another massive glyph grew out of Galeforce, and birds of wind exploded onto it.

The two dodged explosions from the Eraser, landing on opposite ends.

Both grabbed their blades, striking it simultaneously as they lunged diagonally.

An "X" made from light and wind respectively, appeared around the Eraser. Their aura attacks detonated, shredding the Risen into pieces.

Zephyr focused, and the enhancements vanished, feeling woozy but satisfied. "One more thing to train, huh?" He could only imagine the strategies and flexible possibilities with this at his disposal.

Skye's eyes shined. "A momentous occasion."

They retreated toward camp, alert for voids.

"I was hoping to catch up to you."

She hardly contained the delight on her face. "Oh. . ."

"Stars are shining brightly tonight. You always wanted to see them like this at Garnet when we were little."

Skye did a double take. "You... remember that?"

Zephyr smiled. "I remember every moment shared with you, Skye."

She tucked a loose strand of hair behind her ear. "I do... too..."

"I don't know what's going to become of this mission... but I'm glad it's by your side. As it should've been. Always."

Skye touched Zephyr's wrist, sending a jolt down his spine. "I'll keep you safe. I promise. With every bit of aura I have, I'll protect you."

Arriving at camp, Skye stood outside Zephyr's tent.

Zephyr gestured for her to follow. "Gotta break the news."

Glacy and Shadow looked up. Their hyperactive friend wanted to mix things up and hear "the juice." Whatever that meant. Last time Zephyr heard, it was called "spill the rice." When he tried to use it in front of Tandy and Suzie, they laughed at him for being "old."

"I unlocked the Marking."

Glacieus squealed, and Shadow cheered. "I wanna see!" Zephyr showed them, and their volume increased, leading him to wave his hand to get them to settle down.

Aurora and Stream had similar reactions, reminding him of fangirls.

Only Luna and Aqua were next.

Aqua appeared smug as Skye and Zephyr entered her tent. "You have the brand, don't you?"

"Felt it once you got within range," chimed in Luna with the same expression. Teacups were in each of the women's hands. Teatime never looked so sophisticated. "We'll see what comes next."

Luna's absorption ability manifested as soon as her brand did. Previously, it could only weaken one's power levels. Siphoning to enhance her own aura and physical strength came much later.

Aqua smiled. "Use it wisely."

Newer generations of the clan knew better than to abuse the

Marking. Older members committed mistakes where they overused it to the point of forgetting other skills. Others became sickly from excessive aura depletion and, in rare cases, spamming it could decrease lifespans.

Mark of Lumière was a symbol of worthiness and wisdom. There was an ancient statement about how "one was not complete without the Marking." Unfortunately, half the clan believed in outdated superstitions and beliefs.

༺ ☾ ༻

THE SUN barely rose when Zephyr heard the signal. He dragged Glacieus and Shadow out of bed, ignoring their whines.

Everyone stood in the center of the campgrounds.

"No Typhons have been spotted—just Mutations. They turned sensors off, but it's best to avoid destroying them unless they catch you," said Aqua. "Use this opportunity for a deep search—find the information necessary to stop the rise of darkness and defeat them. All electronic doors should be unlocked, thanks to a discovered control panel. Any other types of entrances should be entered with minor issues, should everyone have the gadgets and techniques on hand."

Aqua forwarded diagrams to everyone, listing everything spotted within the first sweep through the Base. Parts were missing, but they had more details on the layout than expected, such as hidden passageways. Now, it was easier to determine which group should cover where.

"Star Strike, you'll take on the east and west wing of primarily the second story, unless you find hidden levels," said Clay.

Zephyr peered at the map, memorizing the layout. It was designed similarly to a hospital or a school. Labs, atriums, and rooms with non-electronic doors were shown on the diagrams. Those would've been relatively easy to get into, given Specialist training in breaching. West side was more spread out with more

Mutations positioned. Its eastern counterpart had more rooms stretching endlessly down the hall.

Your tactics are fine. Be cautious, but don't overthink it. Or get cocky.

"Aurora, Luna, Shadow, Glacieus, and Spark will go west. Rest of us will go east," said Zephyr. "Each side gets a tankier unit and someone with Recon and Tech mastery."

Spark stretched her arms. "Wouldn't your side need a healer?"

"Your side'll need more sustain. In an open area with more chances of enemies, it works. Ours requires fewer battling and more stealth with how narrow the eastern wing is. For either case, we'll need someone who can switch between long and short ranges in battle." Zephyr nodded at Glacieus and Leif.

"A riskier strategy, but faster and more effective," said Luna. "It works as long as nobody on your end gets critically hit. Leif's speed and endurance works well here, and Blaze or Skye would be good for taking damage."

Luna's side also worked better with Glacieus' higher defences for aura attacks for certain Mutation types and Blaze's smaller size compared to the Trinity Trio worked for their assigned area.

Aqua walked toward Star Strike. "There's no turning back from here on out."

Aurora looked as if she was afraid to screw up, and Luna looked tense and grim, like she was bracing herself.

Everyone else appeared determined. Without another word, everyone went their separate ways in iterations.

Zephyr had to have faith in every one of his teammates. They all had roles to play with their own set of strengths and weaknesses.

Time to find the truth about you, Mercury.

The campsite disappeared on the horizon, hidden by trees. They had a kilometer before arriving at their destination. Silence cleared his head, giving him more room to mentally prepare. He could cut the amount of tension around him with Galeforce.

An open space was in front of them, past Cobalt River.

With a button press, the rectangular, concrete, and steel Base became visible. Its three stories and industrial design aligned with square, tinted windows made it simplistic, not concerned with embellishments to look elegant.

How long has this been here? Decades?

Safe, hidden entrances were marked green on the maps thanks to the Dawn Brigade. Zephyr waited for the rest of his team to tiptoe through the doors placed on the side of the Base, covered by barriers created by Luna and a force field emitted from Stream's device.

They weren't fully undetectable, but movements made by them had noise suppression unless deactivated somehow.

Zephyr's eyes scanned the area, calculating everything at once as they entered the plain, white halls. He detected further ahead auras belonging to the Wings of Order.

His heart stopped for a split second, waiting for anything to jump out, but nothing came forward. Zephyr motioned for his team to continue.

Everyone spaced their entry and varied their pathing as instructed earlier.

No alerts went off—Stream would've indicated otherwise.

Blaze and Skye set a good pace. Skye kept one hand on Excalibur's hilt. Her muscles contracted and had been since dawn.

Mutations were around, but their movements and patterns were predictable, making it easy to avoid their line of sight. They were ninety percent robot, leaving the team to rely on Blaze's hearing and other senses. Even when unshifted, he fared well. Stream could pinpoint their exact power sources and shut them off by powering her claws and shooting them into the designated parts like a needle.

This is almost too easy. . .

Surely the innovators behind Lumière's modern security prototypes would keep their headquarters well-guarded by more than weaker Mutations.

The first room they came across had an electronic door that opened once approached.

Inside was an ensemble of cots and charging stations. Laminate floors cracked in corners, showing signs of wear and tear.

Zephyr and Blaze peered through the closets and drawers, which were empty, save for bunches of dust.

Skye and Stream opened another door in the room, revealing a bathroom.

"This place hasn't been inhabited for a while," said Blaze with barely a whisper. "Few weeks, judging by the dust."

"Guess they gotta rest somehow," said Leif. "Maybe they got other rooms like this?"

Zephyr shrugged. "Makes sense. Since there's nothing else here, we can leave."

They headed toward the next spot, which was filled with shelves of medicinal supplies. Clothing racks rested beside the back walls, along with spare weapons.

Blaze eyed the glass bottles and untwisted their caps. "Typical Potions and Ethers."

Stream sifted through lab coats zipped inside garment bags. "No black cloaks here."

"Figures," said Zephyr. "I wonder how similarly they're structured to Dark Alchemist robes—there's only so many ways you can infuse clothing to grant immunity to effects of darkness and even that is almost impossible for any non-Alchemist."

"Weapons look old, too," said Leif, picking up a mini-cannon. "This model's outdated by twenty years."

After Stream took snapshots of the room, Zephyr motioned for them to continue.

At the end of the first corridor was a flight of stairs. Close to it was an elevator—its lights remained blinked.

What kind of generator do they have? How'd this place get built beneath our noses for at least a few decades? How long have they put up this facade that allowed so many to admire them?

They paused in every corridor, ear out for patrols. It was hard to not jump at every sound that filled the atmosphere—metallic pounding and twisting of machinery.

A door with a traditional lock was next with a deadbolt.

Stream released one blade on her gloves, and it thinned, sliding beneath the door. A clicking sound followed suit and Stream tugged at the handle. They stepped inside, shutting the door behind them gently.

On the other side of the lock was a metallic hand. Stream pressed a button on her gloves and the hand reverted to its default form, reattaching to her fingers.

Desks and filing cabinets were inside. Stream had her spinning cube scan everywhere.

"History notes," said Stream, checking her Communicator. "Archives on different bloodlines and their abilities that had been lost and trends with how laws of nature shifted throughout different centuries for Eta Geminorum."

"Guessin' they went with what Ursula wanted." Leif peered through desk drawers holding office supplies as they waited for the cube to finish scanning.

"Not sure how that ties into them purposely spreading darkness," said Blaze, scratching his head.

Zephyr perused the yellowed documents in cabinets. "They did a lot of research on this stuff back in the day. If it's just lying around here like that, they probably have electronic copies."

Stream scrolled. "There's some stuff on the rise of Nothingness in Tau Geminorum that led up to darkness naturally rising a lot those eighty years ago."

A file detailed Capala's visions and predictions for what was to become of the Mortal Realm versus actual measurements of darkness levels detected from sensors in the Mortal Realm. Both datasets were similar until years dating twenty years or fewer from the present. Numbers exponentially increased after that point.

"Looks like they don't have any current data listed on levels of darkness," said Zephyr. "Nothing past the last fifteen years."

"Did they stick strictly to digital data?" asked Blaze.

Stream's cube flashed white, indicating all information from the files in the room had been successfully scanned.

"Let's go," said Zephyr.

In the next set of corridors, there was one other door with a traditional lock. Charging stations—most likely for the Mutations were visible from tall windows for the rest of the rooms with electronic doors, with Skye being the only one too short to see.

Zephyr sensed flashes of lightning, fire, and water traveling at speeds of sound waves. *Triple Strike.* They were in good shape.

The swarm of unease inside him lessened, but he didn't know how long it'd last.

"Just dates from when different species of Risen from decades ago were first discovered because of the shift," said Stream, upon arriving in another office and checking her device once scans were complete. "Nothing on the exponential growth or Typhons' powers."

These rooms looked barely inhabited, more so than previous ones. Dust strewed the corners, accompanying dozens of cobwebs. A spider crawled about, finding solace amongst the unkept walls.

Leif took a step forward, and a tile beneath him illuminated.

Trembling occurred. Stream latched onto Skye with sheer terror flashing onto the brunette's face.

The door behind them shut, and a hidden staircase revealed itself up north.

Skye went first, and the rest followed, tip-toeing their way in.

Blaze tilted his head, looking for any traces of sensors.

A robotic-looking Mutation stayed suspended beneath the staircase.

Leif trapped its arms with a chakram, and Stream attached a drill to its backside, pulling up a holographic interface, temporarily disabling it.

"You'd think they'd have something other than old-fashioned locks and weaker Mutations around," said Zephyr. "Or at least someone here."

"And be around here more often," said Blaze. "The place is hardly used."

"This can't be the best they've got," said Stream. "Maybe they have more than one hideout."

39

GILDED
LUNA

Luna took one step, waiting for Spark to continue. She glanced over her shoulder. Shadow and Aurora were further behind.

The corridor was broad, with plenty of areas to hide. Few locked doors were present. They weren't in range to scan what lay ahead.

She closed her eyes as she hid behind another wall, signaling for everyone to halt. Mutations were nearby. Twenty of them, half-Harpy Risen. Coordinates moved in a pattern... The way they moved seemed as if they were ascending and descending.

An image of a staircase manifested in her mind, and Luna drew the power of metal from her hands, creating the shape in her left palm, waving it for the party to see. Her thumb pointed in the direction of the shape.

A mental map of the locations of the Mutations followed suit and appeared as the same element.

Glacieus stared at it and nodded. He shot two silent ice bullets out of his tonfa guns, and they multiplied. With a snap of his fingers, they ricocheted off each other, traveling toward the areas Luna marked and updated.

All clear.

Spark gave them a giddy thumbs up, and Luna beckoned for her to continue. Speeding through the halls, they practically flew up the stairs. Two robotic Mutations were at the top, facing the group.

Even up close, she barely sensed them. Spark threw out both hands, sending shockwaves, powering them off. Nothing else was sensed on this floor… which was a double-edged sword.

It surprised Luna that they even made it this far without casualties or anything else amiss. If they made it out tonight without witnessing a scenario that she'd eventually see in nightmares, she'd question it. She always knew a day like this would come—it'd be idiotic of her to not prepare herself in advance. Fighting alongside the Marauders didn't dispel her notions. At least everyone heeded her warnings.

Anyone could leave this Base almost dead, or dead. If they even had the luxury of bringing back anyone's corpse. Her friends were the hardest to imagine getting killed, but it wasn't impossible. After seeing those relatives on tape, innocent people, colleagues, and her own instructors disappear before her eyes… Who was next? Aside from Sebastian, Star Strike was the closest thing she had to an immediate family. Losing Stream would've broken every fiber of Luna's being. Perhaps Luna would end up in one of those situations where her body was "missing in action" or disintegrated. Regardless, she figured her cause of death would be from a mission. If she worshipped the Gods, like some here and there in this world, she'd pray. But could one blame her?

Worship took a nosedive with each era, and even more so nowadays. She prayed for any glimmer of hope in the past. The Gods, even Celeste, were still beyond reach in their world.

A stretch of intersecting hallways came into view, granting them the wonderful opportunity of having loads of angles to be attacked from.

A faint, cracking sound caught her attention before her aura sensory picked it up.

Ice.

She turned, seeing a glass-like arrow forming in Glacieus' hands.

Another emerged, and each had differing shapes on the lower ends —a circle and three miniature stars. Stars on the left, circle on the right: Astro and Nova Strike.

Glacieus and Luna scurried toward their respective halves of corridors. He paused, sizing up walls and what they could see through the windows—an enormous room with generators.

Where ARE the Mutations?

He frowned and conjured another arrow with stars. Luna closed her eyes, attempting to visualize Astro Strike's locations, and created another map.

Glacieus waved his hand, sending it flying in their direction— faster than it'd take to type a message and wait for someone to think of checking for silent notifications. Anything with sound was a distress call in missions like these—each type had a differing beep.

With those kinds of shapes he could create, it was a pity he didn't stick with training in healing arts when they were kids. His control surpassed hers, and non-elemental aura usage would've exhausted at a slower rate thanks to his lineage's affinity for healing magic. Instead, his training time outside of Recon was allocated to sharpshooting.

Back then, he struggled with it, but wouldn't have faced those same issues nowadays. It was too late, even if he wanted to learn. He shaped his aura over the years to almost solely be used for shooting or enhancing his tonfa fighting style. Luna remembered the excessive time he spent only using his power in that way, making it impossible for his aura to be used for healing ever again.

Astro Strike arrived.

Glacieus motioned for them to enter the room with the generators. He created a thin sheet of ice, allowing it to slide beneath the door.

It opened, and they entered, following Glacieus toward another door that stood at the back of the room. Up close, Luna identified the lock as a lockable thumbturn.

"All others were single and double cylinder deadbolts," said Glacieus.

"What's the difference?" asked Spark.

"Single cylinders are the most common. If the cylinder on the outside is locked, anyone who gets on the other side can unlock the thumbturn and get in. Double cylinders are on either ends and can only get unlocked from a key on the inside," replied Glacieus. "That's a hazard where this place is attacked, and you're locked inside without a key."

Luna nodded. "Lockable thumbturns like this are a hybrid. Thumbturn is on the inside and can only be locked using a key so it's possible to not lock or unlock the door."

"Weird how they have old-fashioned stuff like this!" said Shadow.

"Seeing as how this is the only door with a lock like that, there's gotta be something important behind here," said Glacieus. "These are designed best for when people are gone for extended periods of time... which makes sense, given how they haven't been here in two weeks, judging by the state of the cleanest-looking rooms."

"Do we gotta break down the door?" asked Shadow.

"Unnecessary." Metal aura appeared in Glacieus's hands and slid beneath the door.

Luna sensed it take shape of a key designed for thumbturns. With a swift twist and click, the door opened.

"That's some aura control," said Aurora, impressed.

Spark raised a fist into the air. "Wooh! Convenient!"

"You'd think it'd be harder to get so far into this place," said Aurora.

"Almost as if they don't care as much about it," said Glacieus.

Holographic screens surrounded the room. They projected a map of a maze with black dots spread out. Parts of the diagram remained blank, as if undiscovered.

The Labyrinth.

Glacieus stared at the map. "Blossom must've activated this from the control panel."

A blank section on the map flickered, and more dots filled in.

Luna frowned at the dots. "Live updates, huh? Wondering where they sent this information from. And how powerful their communication devices are."

Spark scratched her head. "When do ya think this place was last entered, Glacy?"

"Still two weeks at the earliest. Gotta be some reason they don't come too often to what is probably the first Base the Typhons ever had."

"I wonder where else they would go," said Aurora. "Do you think they just stick around the Labyrinth most of the time?"

Luna sighed. "No freaking clue. Whatever power they have, it might keep them immune to at least most of the effects of the Labyrinth. There's no other way a mortal could last that long without the aid of Celeste or some other supreme being."

"What are the black dots, though?" asked Shadow.

"Doesn't say anywhere," replied Glacieus. "Wonder how many more of these live holograms they got."

It was faint, but a mass of Mutations were around, somewhat scattered. Luna's hand reached for her forehead, rubbing it and wincing as the familiar jolt of throbbing pain hit. Everything felt fuzzy as the migraine worsened.

Before Luna could peruse for a second longer, she sensed the monsters' locations shifting. She felt sick to her stomach. The pulsing sensation remained on one side of her head, and she had a sudden urge to stab her head with her knife.

Walls shook and Mutations burst through the door.

Different makeups of artificial and aura-based surrounded them.

No alarms?

A barrage of beams made of darkness shot at them and Glacieus came up front, shaking it off him like it was nothing.

Another, resembling a drone but with a mini-cannon attached to it, unleashed its explosives.

Fortunately, Shadow stepped up in time, shrouded in his passive shield.

Spark's currents kept everything away from her and Aurora,

buying the mage enough time to create a bright orange magic circle, creating a heatwave, melting all artificial Risen.

It was as if Luna had taken a painkiller. It would've been wise to let her mind rest for a bit. Who knew what other situations would call for her sensory? There was a reason it passively activated all the time, unless specifically turned off.

Shadow threw Diablos' head, cutting through the remaining enemy.

Luna scanned the room with the same type of cube Stream possessed, saving the information as she waited for Glacieus to finish his observations.

"We're good."

40

BLASTED

ZEPHYR

MORE MUTATIONS GUARDED THE PITCH-BLACK HALLWAYS. STREAM and Leif disabled them with ease again. At the end of a hall, a lone door stood, this time with a different lock from the rest. Stream's gloves deactivated them. Inside was a laboratory, with machines, empty pods of different shapes and sizes, display screens to the left of the pods, shelves with notebooks, and boxes of supplies. Some looked large enough to fit earlier Mutations.

Skye hastily searched every centimeter of the room, like a hunter, relentlessly stopping at nothing for her prey. She almost looked… angry. Zephyr could count on one hand the number of times she expressed anything further than agitation. Every other time, it was comical.

Focus.

Blaze's eyes wandered. "I smell tools and the same metals for Mutations. None used recently."

Stream walked toward the displays. Retrieving a pyramid-shaped remote, it spun upon a button press and the screens illuminated. Her cube also suspended into the air, spinning and scanning. She pulled up a page on the display with her remote. "This one's the most recently updated."

The heading was titled: *Effect of Spiritual Darkness on Eta Geminorum.*

Zephyr had never heard of such a term before.

Spiritual Darkness has far less of an effect on Eta Geminorum, because of its highly concentrated and revitalized core, thanks to the Era of Astra. It appears as if all catalysts within the Labyrinth that enhance Spiritual Darkness have the same knock-on effects for this world.

Dark Spheres increased the spread by drawing and enhancing Risen, but it'd take years for Eta Geminorum to reach the same fate as its sister world. Erebus's power has its limits in its dormant state. Once awakened, Eta Geminorum's resistances would decrease tenfold, but perhaps we can expedite this with other beings of the Labyrinth.

"Who's Erebus?" asked Stream.

The others looked at Zephyr. "I don't know."

Skye held a notebook with her gloved hands. "All these reports are listed as 'Risen most affected by Erebus's enhancements.'"

"Erebus must be who the Typhons got their power from," said Zephyr.

Stream glanced at her screen. "It says here that Spiritual Darkness should never lie in the hands of a mortal. What are they trying to do with it?"

"Maybe they're trying to prove something to the Gods," said Zephyr. "Think of the times in history, when people attained devastating power to send a message, like the Solarian Wars. Everyone thought the instigators wanted power. Instead, they wanted the Gods' attention and to see what they'd do."

Blaze rubbed his hands on the crystal around his neck. "We're in a dying realm where people have given up on hope. Things keep getting worse and worse, even though they should've gotten better by now. Gods still aren't doing anything. Celeste can only do so much, but even she's restricted by her peers."

Zephyr tapped his chin. "Think about it; the Mutations, Dark Spheres, all of it. They're trying to prove a point to the Gods how messed up the Realm is. We were already shot in the foot decades and decades ago, when Nothingness and past eras wreaked havoc on the state of the Realm. If mortals have their hands on Spiritual Darkness and everything that comes with it AND manage to mess up the Realm enough… maybe that'll convince the Gods to play their part and realize how dire this is. And fix our Realm."

"They're not much different from Thanatos and anyone else who's given up," said Skye, setting down the notebook in its proper place.

"Except more evil," said Leif, frowning. "Completely evil."

Zephyr sighed. "We're all trying to accomplish the same thing. No such thing as completely good or evil here. We all have blood on our hands in the pursuit of doing what we think is right."

The cube halted and Stream did a double take when she glanced at her Communicator, almost dropping it. "Communication symbols are gone." She tilted it upward so everyone could see. Sure enough, the normally white icon was clear with an "X" in front of it. The others became that way as well.

"Teleportation icon, too," said Leif. "It wasn't like that earlier. . ."

Stream shook her head. "That's weird… Downloads didn't even finish."

"Maybe we're in an area with bad signal," suggested Leif.

Blaze glanced at the ceiling and groaned. "Of course."

Zephyr turned to him. "What'd you hear?"

The door lit up, and Leif touched it. It didn't budge.

Stream looked visibly shaken as she pressed a few buttons on the keypad beside the door, but to no avail. The displays vanished and sirens blared from the distance. "They know we're here."

"Shit," muttered Skye.

Zephyr's palms went clammy, and his throat tightened. If he started overthinking, all preparations were for naught. He took a deep breath and exhaled. "Stay in position."

Being subtle as possible was out of the question if Typhons were wary of their intrusion.

Skye busted open the locked door with her fists. Zephyr heard blasts in the distance, and Blaze shifted on all fours. They sprinted back to the room, revealing the hidden staircase.

Swarms of Mutations piled up within the halls, appearing stronger than what they encountered earlier. The walls sure would not look blindingly new anymore.

Vibrations traveled, rippling through solid material. *Elena.* At full power, those sound waves could cut through the strongest metals.

They followed the General's alert, backtracking through rooms and sections. Explosions occurred, either caused by Elena or her brother. Swift clanging of metals came, with a hyperresonance succeeding.

Dawn Brigade scattered, and Mutations didn't take notice of Star Strike's arrival.

Ambrose's knives looked as if they telepathically followed him, cutting through steel as if it were butter. His movements were so quick, that Zephyr could barely keep track of where he was, like he was teleporting.

Oscar's photon blasts blinded the surrounding enemy, and he hooked them with his scythe, ruthlessly pressing the switch on its handle, slicing straight through. He slammed the curved blade down onto another, using its weight to spin himself and gather momentum, generating a chariot of light.

"Nice!" said Calypso, behind Oscar.

She released her spells out of her crystal rod with less than a second in between. Calypso was the fastest spell-caster Specialist anyone had ever seen. Mutations released heat waves in Calypso's direction. If it were any other element, it would've dealt a lot of damage to her, who was essentially a glass cannon. Fire aura did nothing to Water Master Calypso.

Calypso spun, splattering purple liquid. She disintegrated remaining Mutations as soon as a single, acidic droplet touched their surfaces.

"Wow..." said Stream once the enemy routed.

Elena turned, facing them. "There you are."

"Glad you're safe!" Calypso nodded at Stream, then the others. "We were afraid you disappeared."

"Why's that?" asked Leif.

"Trinity Trio's missing," said Iyar.

41

QUEEN OF THE FISTS

SKYE

STREAM TOOK A STEP BACK WITH HER HAND OVER HER MOUTH.

"How?" asked Leif.

"Neither Aqua nor Luna sensed them when they were in range," replied Lucia.

Skye's eyes lingered on Lucia, catching hers. She envied Lucia's power, but there was no use dwelling on what she could've had. It was within the Farien name to honor their duty, whatever it took. No matter the stakes.

"We've covered as much ground as possible and have seen no signs," said Calypso.

Blaze shook his head in dismay. Fang was potentially in grave danger, and this was probably the first time the four had ever seen Dawn Brigade look anything less than nonchalant and laid-back. He would've heard everyone's physiological reactions even if he didn't want to, but it wasn't like him to pry.

At least he can't read minds.

"And I'm sure you know by now that Typhons are here somewhere," said Iyar.

Zephyr released a breath. "Right. We need to stick together.

We've covered most of our side, but not everything. Our extraction devices stopped working."

"Figures," said Ambrose. "They disabled all connecting devices within this building."

"We have what we can get," said Elena, nodding. "Focus on the Typhons."

"What's left to cover?" asked Leif.

"Top level," replied the General. "We can also double-check the western wing of this floor."

Star Strike followed Dawn Brigade.

Skye hoped Shadow and the others' paths would cross with theirs. She was prepared to protect till the very end and use all her power at maximum strength—it would take a lot more than complete exhaustion of reserves and energy to kill her.

If anyone so much as looked at Shadow or Zephyr the wrong way, Skye would tear the Typhons apart.

Star Strike devoted their lives to being in danger. Families had to mentally prepare for loved ones to die at any moment. How did her parents do it? Her parents were excellent at protecting Shadow and Cynthia until they were ready...

Was Skye ready to see them deal with what was even more perilous? Perilous enough to where the Marauders had trouble? It also relieved her to have Luna call her out on how she ironically detrimentally affected her teammate's growth. Now, she dedicated herself to preparing them for the worst. She had to prepare herself equally, however.

"Watch out!" cried Blaze.

Lasers shot out of an armada of Mutations.

Skye and Blaze shielded the party. She stepped forward a second after him to activate her durability shield, wincing as her golden boost also covered her.

Blaze was unfazed, even with his passive shield, which impressed Skye.

Skye pointed a beam of light out of Excalibur, and Lucia released her Farien Light out of her staff.

"Guys!"

Luna's group stood before them.

A wave of relief washed through Skye. *They're okay. They're in my sight now.*

"Just in time," said Oscar.

"We have all the information we could get from this side," stated Luna.

"I'm picking up fragments of Trinity Trio," said Blaze. His body might've resembled a wolf-tiger hybrid, but his facial expressions looked human. He looked overwhelmed and distressed over his mentor's status with tightened eyes. "They're unconscious, trapped in some liquid."

"Their aura is being severely drained by darkness," said Luna gravely. "It's not looking good."

Aurora, Leif, Spark, Shadow, and Stream didn't bother to hide their shocked reactions. A Marauder getting a single scrape was one thing, but an entire team being in danger because of anything that wasn't a Level 5 Risen was another.

"Oh, Gods!" exclaimed Spark.

Zephyr exhaled. "Stay calm. We don't have time to process it all."

"Agreed," said Elena.

Glacieus, Blaze, and Skye led their teammates forward, up the flight of stairs to the last level. Skye patted her brother's and Aurora's backs. Signs of distress on Shadow's face reminded her of Lastalia to a lesser extent. It hurt to see him slowly getting desensitized... But it was necessary.

The highest floor appeared maze-like, with halls leading to dead ends, Mutations blocking nearly every centimeter of the area, and blast cannons attached to the ceilings, designed to shoot any intruders in its path.

"How'd they unfold the walls and rotate the rooms like that?" asked Leif.

"Some form of security measurement, I'd imagine," said Glacieus. "Designed to corner intruders and make things easy for Mutations. The sweeper round must've deactivated them."

"Follow my trail," said Blaze. "We'll avoid the dead ends that way."

"Wings of Order are here, too," said Luna. "Either we'll find them, or they'll find us first."

"Can't we just blast our way through?" asked Spark.

Calypso shook her head. "That could collapse the entire building. These new walls aren't very sturdy."

The group tailed Blaze and Luna, while Glacieus, Iyar, Ambrose, and Leif shot at each Mutation hindering their route. Elena, Shadow, and Skye protected the more vulnerable units from the blasts.

As they made it further, rumbling occurred below ground.

Double-doors stood at an edge of the maze. Calypso snapped her fingers, melting all Mutations protecting it as Skye slammed her fists into the entrance.

Inside was an enormous lab with similar pods they had seen earlier. Holographic screens stood, displaying data Skye couldn't decipher. Carts with tools, workbenches, vacuum chambers, and shelves of vials and gemstones, along with other materials, made it seem like any ordinary facility.

Four hooded figures stood by the pods, donning the same robes as the earlier images.

"We guessed it would be you Agents or Cerberus paying us a visit," said a male voice. He sounded the same as in his interviews twenty years ago.

Luna glared at them. "We meet again, Mercury."

He removed his hood, mirroring the visuals caught on camera.

Skye protectively remained in front of Aurora, Stream, and Shadow, with her gaze fixated on him. Her heart thundered, trying to find any ounce of familiarity in his or the others' presence.

"Yes, we've met before, back at Maxia Forest." Unlike Thanatos, none of them seemed bothered about being invaded. He almost looked unimpressed. "We spotted both you and Cerberus there at one point. Except, the latter focused on gathering Celestial Perennials."

"That flower will not achieve their goals," said another man. "Though I admire them for the effort; they've progressed quickly."

"Only Gods can bring back power that has been lost," said Mercury. "They'll only run into adverse side effects."

"I suppose you've tried with Spiritual Darkness?" asked Zephyr, concealing his emotions at the sight of the man he once looked up to. "But even that had its limits, I'd imagine."

Mercury nodded. "Very astute, Zephyr. You seem more intelligent than your father."

Were they there... that night?

Skye needed answers.

Anger swept through her, cumulated from her years of purgatory, at the mere sight of the possible assailants standing before her.

Skye reached for her knives.

Zephyr grabbed her wrist, giving her a look.

She exhaled silently, remembering the exercises taught to her during therapy to maintain control.

"We'd rather not fight you," said a feminine voice. Locks of red curls poked out of her hood as she faced Skye. If Ariadne was here, the other two had to be Electro and Ursula.

"I thought you of all people would fight till the very end to protect the Realm, Ariadne," said Lucia, hands clenched on her weapon. "What happened to Lumière's Sweetheart?"

Ariadne's face fell. "I'm sorry, but this was the only way."

"You're 'sorry?'" asked Iyar, exasperated. "It's a little too late for that. You always have and always will be Electro's sheepdog." Ariadne winced in a way that made Skye *almost* feel slight sympathy for her.

Spark rested her gaze on Electro's fist cuffs. He didn't use his iconic, blue electric currents back in Taonia. Otherwise, they could've pieced it together earlier.

"Your lives have been spent fighting for a cause that cannot be won," said Ursula, sighing and shaking her head. "Blame the Gods. Blame our ancestors. It's all of us versus them."

"Let me guess, you think they'll bring back the old bloodlines you cherish so much, too?" asked Luna. "You'd be pissed if they didn't grant your wish."

Ursula's eyes narrowed into slits, about to object before Electro silenced her with a shake of his head. He surveyed everyone's faces. "Only way to achieve true Balance is to prove how the Gods' understanding of it is a sham and break the cycle."

Zephyr was right.

Gods were never too late with their judgement calls, to where a world had ever been destroyed before. Celeste's absence was a sign they believed the mortals could stop it on their own. Mom always said light could be just as horrible as darkness, and even worse if there was too much. Risen primarily brought darkness, just as mortals primarily brought light. Mortals with aura abilities could summon the power of either, to help maintain Balance, though some in older times feared those with unique darkness abilities.

They were the strongest elements, but most bloodlines couldn't overuse either or else it could corrupt one's mind. If there was too much tipped to either side, creatures from the Underworld or Spirit World would start appearing, which were far too much for any mortal to handle. Though... nobody ever heard of anything like the Undead coming from the Underworld.

A new Realm might mean completely redistributing bloodline power that was lost. Instead of allowing laws of nature to run its course.

Redistribution opened many possibilities. Maybe they could have Alchemists again, more balanced weaknesses and strengths with bloodlines... More balance to non-aura users.

"Surely there's a more peaceful option," said Zephyr. "But you weighed all your choices, right? Mercury? You thought it wasn't worth the risk to die like any other Agent in history and that a less brutal alternative would've taken far too long."

"You sure love analyzing," said Mercury. "You could go on all day, but we don't have the time for that." He stepped to the side, revealing rows of pods filled with electricity behind them. Three hosted the Trinity Trio.

"What'd you do to them?" shouted Shadow.

"You can have them back," said Electro.

"Typhon Strike!" shouted Aqua from the doorway, her team in tow.

Ursula shook her head, disappointed. "Keep bringing your best like that and you'll exhaust your resources."

Electro produced a gadget resembling a Communicator. He pressed a button, releasing the cells. Trinity Trio's Morphic forms glowed an ominous shade. The glow consumed them, reverting the Marauder team back to the human state, still unconscious. Darkness remained, covering their bodies.

What did they do to them? Some experiment? Almost like... the night of the exams.

Skye could've sworn Mercury eyed her.

Her ears rang as her head throbbed. Her mind jolted back to the night of the exams where her innocent, naïve, self laid there. Back with Skye was full of life, full of light, an endless ball of spunk and energy who just wanted to be a hero.

The night Skye Hikari, the human… died.

A flashing image emerged. Mercury stood before her, stabbing Skye's limp body with a blade of darkness, releasing a crystal of darkness inside her body. Pools of darkness surfaced from her.

Skye Hikari, the Host… was born.

He was there... He... put the stone inside me.

Echoes in the depths of her conscious self screeched. She fought hard to silence its agony. Time came to a standstill as darkness rose. Her gloved fingers felt bonier and sweat beaded down her forehead.

One word rested in her mind: kill.

Tear him apart, said the darkness.

Tremors erupted through her being as she reached for her knives, hurling them with all her might as she boosted herself.

Mercury held up a hand. Spiritual Darkness emerged, and it stopped all blades in their tracks. With a snap of his fingers, they shattered into nothingness.

The Typhons disappeared into a dark void.

Darkness overcame everyone in an instance.

Blinded, Skye reached for her brother, but couldn't feel anyone. A sharp twisting throbbed in her chest as she continued to move her hands, but to no avail.

Shadow, where are you?

Explosions were all that was heard along with ringing and collisions of rubble. The Mortal Realm could've been on the brink of collapse, and what was most significant to Skye was that Shadow was alive.

I can't lose both you and Astrid.

∴ ⟨ ∵

SKYE AWOKE, panting and unscathed. She sprang up, brushing dust off herself and recollected her thoughts. Her head spun.

Rubble and debris piled and scattered everywhere, making her location unrecognizable. Portions of walls were aflame and Level 3, 4, and even 5 Risen sprawled alongside Mutations.

Nothing had been found about the Hosts and not a single Undead was seen. No data, no images, nothing. There had to be something in their other Bases.

Witnessing Level 5s made Skye anxious; she hoped Star Strike members grouped with at least one Marauder… and they weren't in critical condition after so many explosions.

Shadow, please be okay.

Ahead, strands of long, brown hair were underneath a crushed pillar.

Skye hurried over, shoving it off her mentor.

Aqua's eyes were closed, and her body looked damaged.

"Aqua! Aqua, wake up!" She grabbed the Lieutenant General by the shoulders, shaking her.

"Skye?" She handed her an Elixir, hoping it would replenish her at least a little. "Thanks." Aqua untwisted the cap and consumed it.

"Thank Celeste you're okay."

"I remember seeing a chain of explosions, but that's about it. Where are the others?"

Skye surveyed the scene. "I don't know. I just woke up here, too."

"I see." Aqua stood up and studied Skye's face. "Why'd you attack them back there?"

Skye winced, as if someone slapped her in the face. Aqua never yelled at her, unlike Storm, but she might as well have done so. "Mercury triggered some of my memories—he's the one who put the stone inside me. If they stayed a second longer, I would've killed them all."

Her mentor shook her head. "Eliminating them right off the bat will jeopardize the Mortal Realm even more. Especially if we don't know how they're causing this. Promise me, you won't be so rash, next time we encounter them."

Skye knew Aqua was right. With the Typhons eliminated, they wouldn't have been able to get answers as easily.

What happened with Dr. Lycaste?

Where did those stones come from?

How did they create the Hosts?

Who is Erebus?

"I promise."

"Good. There's not much we can do now except keep fighting through and finding the others."

They took out every Risen in their path—Aqua with her lance, Skye with her bare fists.

Once Aqua finished wiping her lance, Skye spoke up. "I've been thinking... how would these discoveries affect Star Strike's missions from here on out?"

"First thing's getting them prepared for A-ranked missions. I'll have to assess how well you and Luna have been mentoring them."

"They'll be doing a lot more than eliminating Dark Spheres, that's for sure."

"Anything I need to do besides mentoring and keeping them safe?"

Aqua blinked a few times. "You need to live your life whenever you can with Star Strike. You're young and alive."

"I don't deserve that."

All spare time was allocated to her search. Aqua reminded her of times where Marauders covered for her and her presence wasn't necessary, but she stubbornly insisted on joining them, anyway. Sometimes, she spent extra time on days where it was unneeded to keep herself occupied. Most of the time, she was there to protect the Marauders from dying—if she couldn't die from the Undead; it was more reason to stick around as insurance.

"Have a taste of what life is like outside of an Agent, or you'll regret it forever. I know it's hard, but those memories are something you can hold onto."

Skye thought back to the hugs she shared with her brother and the girls, the mini-shopping trip with Aurora, moments with Zephyr, times where Aurora vented to her, mealtimes, getting supplies together...

"You know a lot about being an Agent. Now, you gotta learn to be a human."

How can I learn how to be something I'm not?

Her fate was changed the night of the exams when all she ever wanted was to be a hero. If none of that happened, maybe she would've ended up being like Shadow or Spark—all filled with light and energy. Maybe she could be with Zephyr.

Skye might've unintentionally contributed to the spread of darkness, but she could also use her god-like power to use it for good as much as possible, before it was her turn to end up like the others. She hoped she'd be able to see Star Strike be the best they could ever be before that time came. For the longest time, Skye kept away to keep her loved ones safe... But was this necessary anymore? Was Aqua right? About cherishing the memories she could hold onto? Before she regretted it forever?

Skye heard a crashing sound in the distance.

The next room filled itself with Level 4 and 5 Risen, a cross between a fallen maze and the halls they traversed earlier. Part of the ceiling was missing, revealing the shining sun.

Aqua's Mark of Lumière appeared in her irises and in a blue

glyph with a water symbol below her boots. She disappeared and reappeared, almost at light-speed, knocking down Level 5s.

Her rays and glyphs surrounded them, and her lance-work had bonus surges of tremendous power. Thanks to the Marking, she chained her aura attacks, releasing them back-to-back with no problems.

Skye boosted herself. She slammed her fist into the ground, creating crevasses and eliminating 4s in one hit. A Mutation the size of a building, resembling an enlarged mech suit, struck her with its arms. Her shield nullified any damage, and she uppercut it with her left fist, sending it high into the skies.

She and Aqua stood with their backs facing each other.

Combined with an aerial flip and back handspring, Skye dodged an explosion and knife-handed another. Risen launched tungsten pillars at her and with one spin kick, she redirected them toward the attackers, and everything shattered upon collision.

The Mutation she sent flying returned, reaching terminal velocity. Skye raised her fist, allowing it to split into pieces that exploded into lingering Risen, one-shotting them.

All Risen disintegrated in minutes. "I'm not holding back."

"I know."

Skye drew the power from her stone, feeling it glow inside. They built her body for battle. A body that could perform rare feats, but at the cost of everything. She might've been a monster her entire life, but for this moment, she was Skye Hikari, a hero.

42

BATTLE OF 1000
ZEPHYR

"Zeph! Wake up!" Shadow yelled.

"Hey… What happened?" asked Zephyr, opening his eyes. They were underground… somewhere. Half-filled with wreckage and holes.

Shadow dusted himself off. "I woke up upstairs and nobody was around."

His back ached. Scrapes were all over his arms and legs, along with a fair amount of depleted aura.

Zephyr triggered his shield on time, but imagined some would've taken more damage than others, depending on how close they stood to the blasts. Prior to the explosions, he sensed several of the Marauders activate protective barriers, especially around the unconscious Trinity Trio.

Further north, discarded bullets from Glacieus' tonfa guns spread out on the floors.

Zephyr kept his eyes peeled for anyone: Skye, Aqua, Luna, the rest of his teammates.

His mind traced back to Skye's quivering self when she faced Mercury. He sensed darkness from her hands. Regular darkness, shaping them. She reached for her blades with no hesitation, as if to kill.

I've never seen her like that before.

A high-pitched scream rang in Zephyr's ears, interrupting his thoughts.

Shadow and Zephyr exchanged glances. *Aurora.*

They spotted scarlet hair buried under a pile of rubble in the next room. "Aurora! Don't worry, we've got you!" yelled Shadow.

Zephyr moved it with his glyphs, and Shadow pulled her out.

"Thanks. I fought off a Risen, and this pile fell on me."

"You all right? You don't have many scrapes," said Shadow, looking her over.

She smiled. "Yeah, thanks for worrying."

A blush crept onto him, and Shadow scratched his head shyly.

"Guys, I'd hate to ruin the moment, but. . ." began Zephyr. "Did you find anyone else?"

"No, I woke up here."

"The others shouldn't be too far ahead. We saw Glacy's bullets, and I sensed Iyar's flames."

"This place looks even more unrecognizable now," said Aurora. "I think they shifted it again when they released the explosions."

"They had little to lose by blowing the place up, if they hardly use this Base and keep copies of their information elsewhere," said Zephyr. "Signals in this place are still busted. I wonder how far we'd have to travel to use the Communicators."

They passed rotated rooms. Zephyr peered inside the first window when he had the chance—everything in it had blown to bits. He imagined others would've looked similar.

Risen and Mutations stood in their path toward the upper regions of the transformed Base. Zephyr could make out a wide-open space behind the enemies where slabs of broken concrete and steel spread out. It was absolute chaos with aura released everywhere to where Zephyr found it difficult to distinguish what was coming from who from the five aura signatures he traced there.

Zephyr focused, closing his eyes and opening them, watching the Mark of Lumière manifest below his feet. He thrust Galeforce at a couple of Risen, sending waves of wind to knock them out faster than he'd ever done it before. Slashing the air in an "X" formation, Zephyr created intersecting glyphs that summoned more blasts, and a wolf made of wind aura emerged, swiping its claws, creating explosions upon contact. More glyphs surrounded the battlefield, and he used it to ricochet back and forth, making himself invulnerable to getting struck while he one-shotted Level 3 Risen with clean slashes straight through them, even the metal ones.

A Mutation spun, glowing silver, turning into a ball of metal spikes, moving faster than anyone could do anything. Zephyr side-stepped, trying to block the attack, summoning aura from his katana. One glyph with a distinct pattern appeared in front of the Mutation, and a green glow shrouded it. The spikes disappeared, moving straight past him without landing a hit.

What in the world?

Aurora's light spell finished casting, creating a photon blast, exploding it into smithereens. Right before it did, a few of its spikes reappeared with the same silver glow from earlier.

"That's... new."

"Cool!" said Shadow.

Feeling lightheaded, Zephyr powered off his Marking. "So, it lasted for a few seconds, huh?"

"Did you disable its aura points?" asked Shadow.

Zephyr shook his head. "I don't think so. I could still feel its aura being drawn out, like it was being stopped. With aura point cancelation, it shouldn't even appear and lasts much longer."

It was surely something to discuss with his clan later. Obviously, it was very limited as of now, but there were hundreds of possibilities for the extent of what it did. It didn't strengthen him, but it gave him more leeway with strategic planning. How fitting.

"Stream, now!" Sully yelled from further ahead. "I'll cover you!"

Their path cleared and Luna, Stream, and Triple Strike were in a hallway toward the east side, filled with another army of opponents. Sully had an unconscious Ava resting on her back as she readied her magic.

"O-okay!" said Stream. She slashed her claws through a Risen, disabling its aura and spun, slashing the air, and creating a spiral of water, evaporating several others.

Ends of Luna's spiked whip extended, snaking through, spinning, and shooting vacuum waves. Mark of Lumière glowed, and she put her hands together, signaling for metal pillars to shoot up and stab through Mutations.

Seeing Luna's Mark of Lumière used in battle always amazed him. According to the data, his brand was supposed to surpass her in terms of raw power, hence the ebony color.

Luna didn't want to be in Unity Squad initially, but she always had Star Strike's best interest at heart, even if her methods weren't as agreeable. Shadow and Leif hadn't revealed what she did that created tension between them, but he didn't want to pry too hard. If Zephyr could become a better leader, then Luna could fix whatever needed fixing.

Stream nodded at the trio. "You guys are all right!"

"Course we are!" said Zephyr.

"Save your aura," ordered Sunny. "We'll take the rest from here!"

Sunny cast her spell within a second, and a meteor storm crashed down upon the Level 4 Risen. A meteor hit the ceiling, creating a hole, allowing sunlight into the room. As a result, Sunny glowed a red-orange, creating a mild heatwave and allowing all Mutations to melt from the increasing temperature in the room, living up to her nickname.

Sully waved her hands, allowing groups of Risen within range to appear suffocated and breathless, asphyxiating them.

Dozens of reinforcement Level 3 Mutations emerged, only for Swifty to clasp her fingers and allow all to collapse by removing their signals. She manipulated the signals of one robotic Mutation, absorbing electricity from it to boost her.

"That's how it's done," said Luna, once the room was devoid of the enemy.

"Were you here the whole time?" asked Shadow.

"Yeah," replied Luna. "After the explosion, Triple Strike found us. Next thing we knew, we were ambushed."

Zephyr studied everyone's physical states. "And you guys, Sunny?"

"I found my sisters attacked when they were unconscious. Miraculously, none of the explosions hit me—we were close to one exit when they occurred."

"What about Ava?" asked Shadow.

"We found her slammed against a wall not too long ago," said Sully. "Before the blasts hit, I covered Trinity Trio with my barriers, but still no guarantee of their fates. Whatever darkness is around them needs to be extracted. Least we know is that they wouldn't have been killed by the explosions."

Aurora looked at Swifty. "Are you coming with us?"

"It's wise to stick together for the time being. We shouldn't risk losing each other again."

"Agreed," said Sunny. "Especially since it's much more difficult to determine everyone's whereabouts all at once."

Swifty beamed at Aurora. "I wanna see what you can do now, Little Candor."

Aurora had a small smile. "And I wanna see what else you can do at full power." Witnessing this interaction made Zephyr want to find Aqua soon.

The following section out east had its walls torn up, revealing the outside, confirming they weren't transported beyond the outskirts of Cordelia and Kadelatha. Dawn Brigade was outside, where Phantom and Reaper Risen surrounded them.

"This isn't your fight," said Sully to Star Strike as she handed Ava to Shadow. "Don't interfere."

Luna looked at Zephyr as if to say the same thing.

"Understood." Zephyr turned to his teammates. "We'll keep guard for anything that comes up from behind. Luna, we can use your boosting as a precaution."

Luna cast white magic circles around her team, temporarily buffing their defences.

Dawn Brigade had weakened already and who knew what they faced earlier alongside potential damage inflicted from the blasts.

A-ranked Agents struggled against Reapers and Phantoms, along with their weaker Level 4 variants. Had Star Strike broken the rules and interfered, they would've given the Marauders more harm than help.

"Formation E!" called Elena.

She and Oscar were in perfect sync, striking diagonally at a Reaper subsequently. Their movements were quicker than Zephyr could keep up with, but the Reaper blocked each strike.

Reapers wore black cloaks, never revealing their faces. All that was visible were their skeleton-like hands holding onto scythes shrouded in darkness. Nobody looked into a Reaper's face and lived to tell the tale.

Most of the time, they spawned alone, like Phantoms.

All Risen they encountered after the Base got blown up had many enhancements cast on them. Zephyr detected nothing other than stronger darkness, but their behaviors made it seem like there was more to it at first glance. Its potency appeared stronger than a Dark Sphere, which Zephyr assumed was Spiritual Darkness; his Communicator spotted nothing abnormal besides power levels.

Before it could reveal its face, Lucia spun her staff, releasing the most powerful beam of light Zephyr had ever seen at a Phantom. A tunnel of light also shot out, transporting Elena from one end to another as the Reaper almost hit Elena.

"Nice!" said Oscar.

Calypso stood behind Elena and Oscar. One hit, and it could've ended in her demise.

Zephyr observed the positions everyone was in to calculate and analyzed the chances they had of winning the fight with no casualties. With the additional factors not in their favor, he predicted at least a team getting critically injured.

Lucia conjured an enormous barrier, blocking everyone from a Phantom's blood-curdling, petrifying scream. The Phantom created a silhouette that teleported behind Lucia, exploding itself onto her, sending her plummeting to the ground.

"Lucia!" yelled Shadow.

Zephyr grabbed Shadow firmly before he jumped into danger.

A Reaper shot Calypso with a dark pulse from its scythe, sending her crashing into a wall as the darkness remained around her, draining life out of her.

Stream gasped. "Calypso!"

Luna clutched her hand.

One darkness symbol conjured by a Reaper struck Ambrose, surrounding his head. He threw his explosives at Iyar, giving him little time to react.

Sully sent healing aqua spheres toward Lucia and Calypso's directions before creating more devastating tidal waves and a bubble that trapped Iyar, only for him to grab the explosives and blow himself up.

Smoke cleared, and both Ambrose and Iyar collapsed. Elena sped toward them along with Oscar, but remaining Phantoms stood in their way.

Another blast threw the collapsing Marauders against the same wall as Calypso, who had darkness disappear into her body. Zephyr heard ugly cracking noises as Ambrose and Iyar both bent at unnatural angles. The most important thing Zephyr had to remember was that they weren't dead... yet.

Sunny and Swifty charged up and massive phoenixes and thunderbirds formed an army. Oscar slammed his scythe onto the ground, creating a tremor that knocked over all trees in the distance, causing stalagmites to shoot up, giving him and Elena an opening to land their strongest strikes.

The impact was so strong that Star Strike got blown back inside and haze covered the outside. It blew away, and Elena slumped over.

Right before one Reaper disintegrated, it launched the same dark pulse as before as its last stand, more potent than before, encasing Oscar, causing him to crumble as Elena caught him. Darkness disappeared into Oscar's body.

They annihilated the enemy, but at what cost?

Aurora ran toward Dawn Brigade and everyone else followed. Green aura emerged from Aurora's tome and Shadow set Ava down to assist.

"I'll take it from here," said Sully.

"Signals still aren't available," said Elena, who had only cuts on her arms. "I'm going to find the nearest spot within range and call for reinforcements." She glanced at Oscar, who was knocked out.

Oscar's face paled and Zephyr sensed darkness growing through his body. He had to hope that he and Calypso were going to get through it.

I need to stop thinking about it. It'll make things worse.

Elena set him down next to the rest of her team. "I'll try to get a signal further from here and call for reinforcements."

"I'll stay here," said Sully, putting her water healing to use. Her amount of aura now could sustain them until more help arrived. "And watch over them and Ava for the time being." She looked at her leader for approval.

Sunny nodded. "Swifty and I'll accompany Star Strike to round up the others."

"They're going to be okay, right...?" asked Shadow gravely. "No permanent internal damage, I hope."

"It's too hard to tell without proper scanning machines," said Sully. "Don't worry about them for now. Focus on finding everyone."

"C'mon," said Luna, still squeezing Stream's hand. "Let's hope we don't run into more armies of those. It sucks to not be able to do anything to help."

"Agreed," said Shadow.

"I've never seen more than at a time before," said Sunny, walking back inside.

"Powering up the Risen with something other than Dark Spheres is something else," said Zephyr.

"If they had the power to do that from the get-go, why bother making the spheres?" asked Luna. "Does it cost more? What else can they do?"

"I'm worried for the rest," said Stream. "What if someone's alone and trapped by Level 5s like we saw back there?"

"We're not gonna keep morale if you keep saying stuff like that!" said Shadow.

"Shadow's right," said Zephyr. "Have enough faith to keep moving forward, but not too much to where you're blinded by it. We don't want self-fulfilling prophecies."

Zero optimism means we've already given up. We need some to have hope.

Swifty looked at Zephyr, impressed. "You sound kinda like the Lieutenant General and President Ziel. I can't describe it, but you have your own unique spin on it, too."

Despite Luna's darker demeanor, part of her lips crinkled into a proud smile.

Zephyr translated her words as, "Keep proving yourself, and I'll respect you as future President."

43

AFTERMATH

SHADOW

EITHER SHADOW WAS IMPATIENT, OR TIME WAS SLOWING DOWN. Whatever the case, exploring the changed layout of the Base felt like an eternity as they ventured southeast.

Aurora had to supply Luna and Zephyr with aura to keep up their senses.

"Two at once. I'm impressed," said Swifty.

"When'd you learn how to do that?" asked Stream.

"Back at the Aquarius Islands," replied Aurora.

"And you've never done it again until now," said Luna. "Well done."

Aurora's eyes widened at Luna's praise. "Thanks."

This was the first time Shadow had heard her say anything positive to Aurora since joining the party. It was a start, but it'd take a lot more than that to undo the extra damage to Aurora's confidence. Since Luna joined, it was far more difficult to uplift her spirits.

Shadow was glad Aurora got the praise she deserved. She earned it.

Next time they faced the Typhons, they'd stop them once and for all. The confrontation might not have gone as planned, but the organization took several steps in the right direction. They made progress.

Level 3 Risen never stopped coming.

Star Strike came close to one-shotting most within that ranking by this point, but that didn't stop their aura from depleting.

Luna brushed herself off after a few battles. "I'm picking up more aura signatures toward the southwest and west side on this floor."

"Nothing upstairs?" asked Sunny.

Luna shook her head.

"I suppose most of the action's on the ground floor."

"That'll make it easier for the reinforcements once they arrive," said Zephyr. "Which should be any minute now, assuming Elena made it in range as quickly as possible."

"Phase Three won't be a picnic with how confusing the layout of this Base is currently," stated Swifty.

Southwest was narrower with more dead ends. Rooms slid and spun, while others pivoted in alternate directions.

Ravagers stood on guard. The Level 4 Risen resembled Beowulves, but were more humanoid in stature, covered in bone-like spines with long, skeleton forearms and claws sharp enough to cut through steel with little effort. Bone plates, masking their faces, with slits for their eyes.

Swifty and Sunny released meteor blasts of their specialized elements, while Star Strike focused on the two closest to them.

Stream came up close to the Ravagers, jabbing into different spots around their arms and body with her fingers, disabling aura points. She slashed them with her claws, releasing explosions of water aura. Aura emitted from their bodies appeared weaker than they should've been.

Both enemies unleashed dozens of beams toward Stream.

"Stream!" exclaimed Luna. A few hit Stream before Luna's whip grabbed onto her, pulling her away.

Spherical forms of light appeared from Aurora's direction. They connected, forming into one large sphere resembling a full moon. It traveled toward the Ravagers, exploding into them. They howled and vanished.

Stream looked like she was about to pass out.

Both Aurora and Luna heaved as they took their steps.

More Ravagers appeared, surrounding the party. Right as they were about to leap and strike, the temperature in the room fell.

"Ari," said Aurora in a whisper.

Time stopped.

Every muscle and bone in Shadow's body went static. A few seconds passed and standing in front of him was a young woman with the same physical features as Aurora and her A-ranked team of six. They annihilated the enemy.

Ari spun her wand. Healing sparkles surfaced, spreading throughout Star Strike.

Shadow readjusted himself as Sunny and Swifty came up to everyone.

Swifty smiled at the elder Candor sister. "Good timing, Arianna. That was an excellent usage of the time freezing technique." Freezing time had a long cooldown and limited uses, exclusive only to Ice Masters. Its success rate wasn't high, so using it was risky.

"Don't mention it," replied Ari. "We came as soon as we heard the distress call."

"Thanks for the help. Anyone else come with you?" asked Aurora.

"Three other teams were right behind us—Willow Strike, Element Tetra, and Eagle Ring. Should be more on their way." Much like her elemental specialty, Ari appeared cold, dignified, and distant, almost robotic, especially with her monotonic voice.

Sunny nodded. "All right, Phoenix Force, you'll stick around the east side with Willow Strike. Direct Element Tetra and Eagle Ring to handle the north. If those areas are clear for a while, help the other sides. We'll continue to accompany Star Strike as we look for Trinity Trio and Wings of Order."

"Understood."

Zephyr turned to Shadow. "Three-quarters of your aura is gone. Be careful, okay?"

Shadow gave him a thumbs up. "Will do!"

Luna pointed south. "The others are this way."

They followed her out of the narrow tunnel for ten minutes.

Once again, they were led toward a wide-open space. One side of the wall was missing, revealing the exterior. Airships were visible in the skies, soaring toward the Base, kilometers away.

Spark, Blaze, Glacieus, Leif, Zetta, Clay, and Blossom were there. In Clay and Zetta's arms were Tiamat and Fang, respectively. A set of dark barriers separated Shadow's party from the rest.

"It'll take a few to disable them," said Swifty.

"We'll go as fast as we can," said Sunny.

Leif looked up after creating earthquakes. "Hey! Zeph and the others are here!"

"Focus on the battle!" yelled Blaze and Luna simultaneously.

Glacieus shot a few with his tonfa guns. "Haha! Leify got yelled at!"

Zetta had a dark circle beneath him, floating above ground with magical orbs in both hands, allowing darkness to overtake Risen and trapping them, allowing lightning bolts to strike them dead.

Clay shot light rays from his staff and then stabbed the ground with it, summoning an army of Golems to do his bidding. Blossom shot exploding arrows that created more to rain down upon the enemy, destroying the remaining Risen.

"Phew, ya did good, Leif!" said Spark.

"Of course, the Great Leif Meister did!"

"You did well, too, Glacieus," said Clay.

Glacieus stiffened. "Thanks."

The barriers disappeared, allowing Shadow's faction to join them.

"Where did you guys come from?" asked Zephyr.

"Leif found me in the northern wing," replied Glacieus.

Leif shrugged. "I don't know where I ended up. Some pitch-black place." He was never the best at figuring out directions. Even with video games, he had the map-awareness of a goldfish.

"Woke up here," said Spark. "Found Zetta, Fang, and Tiamat. And Blaze."

Clay wiped his staff. "Blossom and I landed close to here."

"Then we've seen everyone except Skye and the Lieutenant General," said Sunny. "Crazy how we all dispersed randomly."

"Well, we haven't searched everywhere yet," said Zephyr.

"Anyone been west yet?" asked Blossom. Everyone shook their heads. "I suggest we check there."

Twilight Treader and Raven Mist were two out of the five teams who emerged from the landed airships outside, making their way over to Star Strike and Wings of Order.

"General Elena called us," said Tristan. "The Medics are outside."

Clay nodded. "Good. I need you to take Tiamat and Fang over to them while we focus on finding Hikari and the Lieutenant General. The rest of you can keep the southern side covered."

Shadow knew Aqua and Skye were going to be okay. They could also tank more damage and were harder to hit. Aqua also never took more than minor injuries. He didn't understand why his twin attacked Mercury like that. It was impulsive. But what was more shocking was how easily the man stopped Skye's blades. And destroyed them. At least it wasn't Excalibur.

Luna closed her eyes for a second, focusing. "I'm picking up two aura signatures. Monstrous amounts are being released. No doubt about it; Aqua and Skye are there."

"That's a relief," said Aurora.

Shadow gauged the others. Glacieus and Blaze remained on either side of Luna, eyes dull.

Leif's steps shuffled as they scuffed the floor.

For the first time in Shadow's life, even Spark looked worn out. Her ponytail had several stray strands, lying limp on her back.

A single corridor separated from where they were to the next area.

Armies of Risen were in the space the size of Garnet's Base's ballroom. Flashes of blue and white outsped them.

"Skye!" cried out Shadow, relieved.

"They'll be okay," said Blossom with confidence. "Let them handle it so we can conserve aura for anything unexpected."

The Farien symbol on Excalibur's upper hilt glowed, drawing out the color of the matching gold pattern on its lower spiked blade. Lights burst outward as Skye did a few front handsprings, jumping off the wall, glowing blue.

Aqua's lance enlarged in size and quadrupled, floating in the air, and thrusting into Level 4 Risen, dissolving them with aquatic strikes. She spun her lance, creating hundreds of twisters around the battlefield.

The Lieutenant General was one of the most powerful Agents of their generation, perhaps of all time. It was natural for most of their clan members to have power like hers, but Aqua was an extraordinary case. Luna and Zephyr were the unique ones who didn't have their levels of power, but other skills to make up for it.

"That's our Aqua," said Blossom.

"Yeah…" said Spark in awe. "So cool!"

Skye looked fierce and emotionless in battle. She might've been smaller than Shadow, but her empowering fighting stance made her look towering. Her indomitable spirit radiated from her presence, reminding Shadow of the Daughters of Light.

Dark voids took shape and reinforcements came out. They were about the same size as Aqua and Skye, holding blades. Judging by their size and demonic-like appearances resembling something straight from the Underworld, they had to be Level 5s.

Blaze surveyed the scene. "Oh, no…"

"Don't worry," replied Clay, arms crossed.

Millions of laser beams shot out from them, leading Zetta to shield everyone with his barriers as they stepped further out.

Aqua and Skye deflected and evaded every one, exhausting the enemies.

"Stay back, Aqua," said Skye. "This'll end them quickly."

She stood back. "Don't overdo it."

Something glowed white within Skye's body, and a blue bolt appeared from Excalibur as she raised it above, enlarging and enveloping her. Her eyes glimmered golden. Red and white sparks shot out, filling the room. Winds blew and her hair flew all over the place.

The building rumbled, and parts of the ceiling cracked.

Thick bolts were everywhere, and white rays surrounded a black, spinning circle beneath the sparks. Two waves made of fire and water circled, growing. Crevasses took form, followed by icicles and metal spikes. Skye floated in the air in the center of the circle. A sword made of black aura came forth, hitting the ground, causing everything to burst.

The room illuminated, like it did at Wellsprings Cave.

When it vanished, all enemies disappeared.

Skye opened her eyes, doubling over and clutching Excalibur.

"What was that?" asked Shadow.

The Marauders glanced at each other knowingly.

Shadow ran over to her.

Aurora followed, and so did Zephyr.

"Shadow! You're... okay!"

"Me? What about YOU?"

She stumbled over to them and almost crashed to the ground before Zephyr caught her unconscious self in his arms.

Shadow and Aurora fished out their weapons, and Clay came to do the same. The rest of Star Strike arrived as healing sparkles appeared from Diablos and Helios.

"Hang on, Skye!" cried Aurora.

"Poor girl must've been exhausted from all that," whispered Stream.

Luna shook her head. "Seen nothing like it."

"Super cool to watch," said Spark.

"It's a technique that can only be used wisely," said Aqua. "I've seen her do it once and it, but she's never fainted."

She did that same technique on our first mission. It's stronger here!

"Reinforcements have arrived," said Clay to Aqua.

"Excellent. We cleared the rest of the west," said the Lieutenant General. "Only other voids that appeared recently are on the southern side. Numbers are far smaller than what we had here."

"Might be the last of the waves," said Luna.

"I will stick around here with Sunny and Swifty and ensure the area remains clear," said Aqua. "The rest of you can help those in the south."

"My aura's almost gone, so I'll stay here, too," said Zephyr, eying Skye. "That way, we won't be in your way." Shadow could've sworn he saw Leif and Spark smirk at Zephyr holding Skye.

"Very well," said Aqua. "Luna, if there's no sign of further reinforcements that you can detect throughout the Base, send a signal with your aura. We can retreat from there on out."

"Got it."

With one last look at their leader and Skye, Star Strike trailed Clay south, passing through spotting no further Risen. Wings of Order were the least weary, but even they moved slower, despite trying to go as fast as possible.

"All other teams are there," said Luna, rubbing her temples.

As they backtracked through the familiar path, screams and shouting echoed. The noises grew louder, reverberating through the walls once they passed through the cracked stairwell. Reddish stains surrounding the floors greeted them in the open room where they had last seen Twilight Treader and Raven Mist.

All nine elements zipped back and forth. Twilight Treader, Raven Mist, Willow Strike, Eagle Ring, and other teams took part in the chaos. Risen—Level 3 and 4 stood their ground. Dispersed amongst the scene were lifeless bodies, torn apart with remnants of claw marks.

Shadow's heart careened against his chest. *Did a Ravager do this?*

Laken and the mage from Raven Mist laid stiff, close to where the rest of their team fought. Both had their limbs dismembered, leaking blood onto the tile. Remains of brains accompanied their shredded hearts, once beating with life. Shadow didn't have to get up close to see the sorrow on their teammates' faces.

Several Risen, in the shape of an eye, screeched. Shadow had never seen such a species before, but assumed they were Level 4s. They were the only ones left.

Darkness surrounded them. Within seconds, they exploded themselves, releasing chain reactions throughout the room. Cracks almost completely covered the ceiling along with the walls as tremors erupted. Plumes of smoke rose.

"Retreat!" ordered Clay. He glowed white, spreading it toward every Specialist, boosting their speed.

Zetta's wind spell created a blast, attempting to keep the Base in place before it collapsed. Star Strike sped out first alongside Phoenix Force toward the opening on the opposite end of the room, leading to the outside. Fleets of Lumicarriers rose above, releasing their saucer platforms from their decks toward the Agents. Adrenaline soared throughout Shadow's soul, and he gasped for air. He heard crashing behind them, followed by more rumbling. Shadow looked back, almost tripping as he kept moving, reaching the exterior as he leaped onto a platform right behind Phoenix Force. The only teams missing from the platforms were Eagle Ring and Twilight Treader.

Zetta's wind enchantments disappeared. He looked extra pale as he fell to his knees. Blossom held him steady. The remaining teams were the furthest behind, as the upper levels collapsed onto Eagle Ring, alongside Evelyn, trapping them. More explosions of darkness struck them, disintegrating their bodies.

Shadow's heart sank.

"EVELYN!" screamed Adriel, having landed on a saucer alongside the rest of Twilight Treader.

Right as more chunks of the building were about to crash onto the Specialists, blasts of blue from the Lumicarriers' cannons destroyed them into bits.

Senna and Malcolm pulled a sobbing Adriel into their arms.

Evelyn... you'll be reunited with your brother. . .

The Typhon Base turned into an enormous pile of wreckage and shredded corpses. Shadow tried not to think too hard about everything as fatigue crashed through him.

Out in the distance, Shadow spotted Triple Strike, Aqua, Zephyr, and Skye on another platform. He exhaled in relief.

Star Strike stayed silent while the hovering saucers returned to the docks.

Celia, Eila, and other Medics rushed over with wheeled cots, having the teams sit or lie down. Shadow had never been inside of a Lumicarrier before, but expanded on the inside, resembling a mini, portable Lumière Base. His eyelids drooped, and the room looked fuzzy, making it hard for him to observe the rest.

Next thing Shadow knew, Star Strike was in a medical room with more cots and carts of medical supplies. Celia, Eila, and Clay tended to everyone's wounds.

Skye was the only one unconscious. Zephyr sat at her bedside.

"That should do it," said Celia, dabbing ointment on Glacieus' hands.

"Thanks," said Glacieus, stiffly.

"Take a good, long rest, everyone. Same goes for you, Clay." Celia nodded at her older brother, who wrapped bandages around Blaze's arms. "Honestly, I don't know how you can still function after all those battles."

"Me neither," said Blaze.

"I've never seen the Marauders like this before," said Eila. "You guys were dealing with something else. These Typhons. . ."

Blaze sighed. "I don't want to know what else they have up their sleeve. This is a taste of what they're capable of. How much longer before we can finally end all this?"

"Those explosions dealt more damage than some could take, the Risen were nuts, we don't know what's going to happen with Dawn Brigade and Trinity Trio, and the idea they could challenge our strongest teams is an indicator of what we're up against," said Luna, staring off into space. "We lost so many…"

"Including Evelyn," said Spark, looking down.

Leif shook his head. "Poor Adriel…"

"And all those other teams…" said Stream. "And Calypso. . ."

"Don't dwell on it too much for the time being," said Aqua, coming into the room. "We'll be landing in Garnet soon. Go home and rest up."

"You better follow that, too, Aqua," said Eila.

"Of course," replied the Lieutenant General. "We'll hold a meeting to debrief everything once we're recovered and back on our A-game."

· · **(** · · ·

DAYS PASSED, and Shadow left the Hikari Residence as soon as he could.

During bed rest, he had time to process it all. The Typhons… their Risen… Shadow lost two friends thanks to the Risen over the past five months. Both siblings. The Devaux household would've been a lot quieter from here on out.

Shadow couldn't help but imagine the look on their parents' faces when Adriel and Senna broke the news to them. Last he heard, Adriel spent the past couple of days crying, locked up in his room.

Shadow prayed to Celeste, hoping he'd never had to bear with the same thing happening to his own teammates. Skye was still knocked out. Dawn Brigade and Trinity Trio weren't looking great either. He had to have hope. While others didn't.

"Hey, Shadow!" exclaimed some passerby. "How's it going?"

Shadow walked past them. "All right."

"Ohmygods, it's SHADOW HIKARI!" squealed a fangirl as Shadow cut through Garnet Hills. "Can I have your autograph?"

"Sorry. I'm in a hurry."

"What's HIS problem?" asked the girl, crinkling her nose.

Aurora waited for Shadow outside the Base's entrance. "You're early."

They went inside, making a beeline toward the Medical Wing.

Everyone in the Dawn Brigade except for Elena was in a cot.

Defibrillators hooked to Ambrose, Iyar, and Lucia, as Doctor Trent and Ellen Thorn monitored them. Elena watched Sully and Clay examine Oscar and Calypso, who were across the room, covered in wires connected to an aura extractor. Their skin sagged, appearing paler than a sheet and waxy. Bones protruded within Calypso, making her knees knobby. Oscar's hair thinned and seemed lackluster.

A holographic screen floated beside the Marauders.

"What are you doing here?" asked Elena, turning toward the two.

"They have permission to be off bedrest," said Ellen.

"We want to help," replied Shadow. "What's goin' on with them?"

"Trinity Trio will get through it," replied Elena. "Though... I don't know what's becoming of their powers. That darkness destroyed a lot of their reserves and I assume the Typhons expected it to kill them."

Shadow nodded solemnly. "At least... they're alive."

"What about... these guys?" asked Aurora.

"Oscar and Calypso are the ones we're most concerned about," said Clay. "The others lost reserves and I can imagine they won't be able to fight like they did before, but they'll be all right."

Sully hesitated. "Whatever hit them back at the Base... that darkness technique... it won't stop spreading throughout their bodies. Actually, we'll show you." She motioned for them to come over.

Shadow and Aurora peered at the screen. Diagrams of Oscar's and Calypso's bodies appeared. Areas where the darkness corrupted marked in black, almost covering them. Aura levels appeared as a blue gauge, at their lowest points.

"The more the darkness spreads, the more it drains the life out of you," said Sully. "It's not like extracting electricity or any other element, unfortunately. Or like regular darkness. No matter what, we can't seem to get any of it out."

"What can we do to help?" asked Shadow.

"You can try extracting the darkness with your Gwymond power," said Doctor Trent, looking up from the defibrillator.

"I'll try my best," said Shadow. "I haven't done anything like this before, though."

Aurora's face dropped. "That'll take so much out of you! You haven't recovered fully."

Shadow glanced at Aurora. "I want to do what I can."

"I'll make sure your aura doesn't run out," said Aurora.

"We'll guide you," said Clay. "First, put your hands out. Focus your mind on the darkness inside them."

A white link appeared and attached itself between Shadow and Aurora. Warmth spread throughout him from head to toe. Shadow put his hands out, closing his eyes, concentrating on the darkness within Calypso and Oscar. Thanks to Aurora's technique, Shadow felt himself draw more darkness than he ever had in the past. Darkness emerged, only for some of it to return to their bodies.

"Try again," said Clay gently. "Slower. As the darkness comes out, wave your hands toward you."

Shadow attempted once more. The dark aura resurfaced, and Shadow did as told, moving his fingers inwards first, inhaling and exhaling.

Clay quickly did a hand wave, moving the darkness further into the air.

Sully finished the job, disintegrating the darkness with light. Sweat dripped down Shadow's forehead. He wiped it, seeing a touch of darkness disappearing from the holographic diagram.

Aura levels remained static.

"How do you feel?" asked Sully.

"I'm all right!" Shadow replied, hiding any signs of tiredness.

They repeated the steps.

Shadow stumbled backwards. A twinge of lightheadedness struck him.

"Keep going," said Shadow, avoiding Aurora's raised eyebrow.

Shadow wanted to continue until every ounce of aura bled out. His mind traced back to what he witnessed back at the Base—blood, possibly fatal injuries inflicted upon the Marauders, corpses of Specialists, and people he knew getting killed. Old friends and acquaintances. Gone. Just like that. He was blessed with healing arts for a reason. Shadow Hikari was meant to save lives in more ways than one. Not for the glory and fame. But for the greater good. Like Celeste and Starla de Cordelia. Shadow could recount the stories told by Mom about all the times the Daughters of Light saved the ones they cared about.

Sully frowned at the hologram. "What in the name of Tartarus…?"

Shadow followed her gaze. The spots that were blank a second ago refilled with darkness. "Maybe we gotta be faster about it!"

By the time half the darkness disappeared from Calypso and Oscar's bodies, Shadow fell to the floor.

Aurora and Clay caught him.

The black spots continued to regrow on the screens. "Why does it keep spreading?" yelled Shadow, slamming his fist onto the cold tile. Dozens of needles danced in his head. A sensation of heaviness stabbed him while the edges of his vision flickered.

"Shadow, you need to rest. You're out of aura," said Aurora, biting her lip. "I can't boost you any longer."

Dark circles rested beneath her eyes and the link between them faded.

"We'll take it from here," said Doctor Trent, coming toward them. "We'll try other methods and see what we can do."

Shadow was too drained to open his mouth to argue.

"Go on," said Sully, resting a hand on Aurora and Shadow's shoulders. She and Clay barely showed any signs of exhaustion.

Clay gripped Shadow from behind, easing him toward the nearest cot. "We will keep you posted, okay?"

Once the back of Shadow's head hit the pillow, his eyelids drooped shut.

⁙

"Calypso…"

Sounds of sobbing led Shadow to jolt up. His eyes readjusted, revealing Stream and Luna standing across from him. Everyone who was previously in the room when Shadow fell asleep was present. The crescent moon glowed through the windows. Stream sniffled and spasmed. Her breath shortened, attempting to gasp for air.

Luna wrapped her arms around Stream, stroking her back with tenderness.

"I'm sorry," said Luna, wiping Stream's tears with her thumb. She pressed her forehead against hers.

Not a single ounce of makeup was to be seen on Stream—something unheard of since the girl was a preteen. Parts of her hair swept up into a twisted mess.

Shadow struggled to swallow as he stood, walking over. "What happened?"

Elena released a breath. "Calypso and Oscar are dead."

No. There's no way. These are the MARAUDERS we're talking about! thought Shadow. *How would she know? She's no Medic.*

Shadow glanced at the screens. The General had to be wrong.

Calypso and Oscar's images flashed red—indicating that neither had a heartbeat nor a pulse. Darkness covered their entire bodies. All aura points had been annihilated along with their reserves.

Both were paler than the sheets. Their faces looked at peace... finally given the chance to rest. Elena's words seared Shadow's mind, jabbing into him like ice picks. Every part of Shadow was scorched with grief. It overwhelmed him. Consumed him. It clawed away at his chest, tearing its way through. Tears erupted, flowing out of Shadow. As soon as Aurora saw, she did the same, no longer able to contain it. He felt her trembling arms encase him as she buried her head into his chest.

The Medics and Elena cast Star Strike sympathetic glances.

How's Elena holding on like this?

"We tried..." choked out Aurora. "We really did..."

Luna nodded, reaching her hand toward her for a hug. "You did what you could."

"The last thing she said to me... was that she was glad I was safe," said Stream. "We... We even lost the Marauders... What do we... do?"

Shadow glimpsed the girls' grim faces. Star Strike was the "Beacon of Hope." The most ambitious Dream Team seen in forever. If they weren't motivated themselves, how could they do their jobs?

Keep moving forward. That's what Saylor always said.

"We need to have hope," said Shadow.

44

RECOVERY
ZEPHYR

GLACIEUS' FATHER GRANTED ZEPHYR PERMISSION TO REMAIN BY Skye's bedside in the Medical Wing. He visited her every day, and it wouldn't take long before she'd wake up.

"Keep a close eye on Glacieus, will you?" asked Ellen, before leaving the private room.

"Of course."

Skye looked relaxed, as if in a state of bliss.

Zephyr sat on the stool, reflecting on the past couple of days, digesting everything. It was a lot, but they made it. The organization made loads of progress in months, and Star Strike had a part to play.

Their team's contributions would determine their size of roles in future missions for stopping the Typhons. And Zephyr's trials. The best Zephyr could do for his own wellbeing was to take things one day at a time.

Skye's eyes flew open and sprang up, darting her head. "Zephyr? Where's everyone?"

He attempted to mask everything as much as possible. "Resting or helping the injured." Zephyr omitted the details of all the casualties. Worrying Skye only made him more anxious.

He exhaled, trying to live in the moment with Skye. Zephyr

needed to bask in the light, revel in the happiness and warmth Skye brought him to boost his morale and faith.

"We're at. . . Garnet, right? How did I get here?"

"I caught you when you collapsed and brought you back to the ship."

Skye's hands flew to her face. "Not again..."

Zephyr chuckled. "You know... it's cute when you're flustered like that."

Her eyes widened. "W-who said I was... flustered...?" A light breeze entered the room, pushing stray pieces of hair into Skye's face.

Zephyr reached over, brushing them to the side. It reminded him of the times he tugged on her pigtails when they were little.

Pink stained the apples of Skye's cheeks. If their faces got any closer to each other, they'd be kissing.

"I did," replied Zephyr, smirking.

Beams of sunlight shined through, making Skye look radiant, turning her hair a light brown and brightening the hues of gold in her eyes. Out of impulse, his hand covered hers.

She froze and attempted to withdraw her hand, but Zephyr held it tighter.

Skye's hands were much smaller than his, heavily scarred all over, with thick and jagged edges—a mix of claw marks and slices from sharp blades. He wondered how similar the others on the rest of her looked. His heart felt heavier at the thought of her taking in so much pain.

Her face fell, avoiding his gaze. "It hurts... to look at them. Makes me feel hideous."

His other hand lifted her chin up. "You could be permanently disfigured, maimed, with your face unrecognizable, but you'll always be the same vision of beauty in my eyes."

Zephyr's thumbs brushed her knuckles. His hands and arms were made to hold on to her, no matter how old they were.

About five months ago, Skye and Zephyr were in this room.

Both times, after Skye unleashed a technique with god-like power. That's where most of the similarities ended, however.

"I appreciate everything you've done for me."

Her face grew tender, clutching his hand. "I can say the same for you."

45

RISE OF STAR STRIKE
SHADOW

"SKYE?" SHADOW POKED HIS HEAD INTO THE GUEST BEDROOM.

Skye gazed out the open window at the flower field on the horizon.

"There ya are!"

A cool wind brushed parts of brown hair behind Skye's neck, the breeze touching Shadow's face.

Relatives used the room. It was structured like the Hikari siblings' rooms, except with white furniture and baby blue walls. Bookcases lined the corners. A bureau with a mirror rested against the leftmost wall. A rocking chair stood between the almost empty closet and shelves.

If they had another brother or sister, this room would've been perfect.

"What were ya doin' in the guest room?" asked Shadow as they left the room. Whenever they didn't have guests, Mochi was the only visitor. He enjoyed napping on the bed.

"Oh… I, uh… wanted to see the view of the flowers from here. They looked pretty. A pleasant distraction. From the chaos."

They descended the wooden staircase, holding onto the dark mahogany banister.

Dread filled Shadow over the past week. Word had gotten out about emergency surgeries and conditions worsening within Trinity Trio. Nobody knew what would become of the legendary team if their members couldn't fight like they once could.

Seeing Oscar and Calypso's lifeless bodies was hard enough to accept.

Somehow, reporters got ahold of the scoop before official notices sent out from the organization and rumors buzzed. Luna had crude words to say on their group chat, cursing them out about how they paid zero respect to the team and their families. Star Strike collectively agreed.

Seeing Lumicarriers fly back and forth from Garnet caught enough attention as is. With so many teams leaving the Base at once, it brought more people talking and asking questions. Shadow couldn't leave the house without getting interrogated.

Skye's boots hit the bottom of the front steps, crunching on a leaf that fell from the lone maple tree in their front yard. In some regions, there would be fluffy snow everywhere by now.

Shadow remained by his sister's side while they hurried toward the Base.

After his bout of almost collapsing from exhaustion, the others urged Shadow to return to bedrest. He had more time to process the additional grief that piled into him. He needed to practice what he preached. About having hope. And maintaining morale. Someone had to do it. And it was his job to take.

Shadow had his losses and grievances during his first half year as a Specialist. He'd seen his fair share of destruction, bloodshed, and crises. Was this what descendants of Celeste were doomed to see?

He had to do this for Saylor, Evelyn, Calypso, and Oscar. Their deaths couldn't be in vain.

The number of casualties within the other teams was also nearly impossible to bear. Shadow couldn't imagine people losing their childhood friends, siblings, lovers, and so much more.

Lucia and Ambrose waited outside their usual meeting room when the twins arrived.

Blaze leaned against the wall with his arms crossed, beside Luna and Zephyr.

Spark and Leif stood across from the trio.

"Hey," greeted Lucia. She sounded like she was in pain, swathed in a body brace.

Ambrose limped as he shifted to stand more on his opposite foot. Both of them seemed to force their smiles.

"Holding up, okay?" asked Ambrose, patting Shadow on the shoulder.

Shadow nodded. "I just wanna have this meeting start already."

"Same here. I'd rather go back to training," said Iyar, making his way over to them with Elena on his tail. Prosthetics replaced his hands and forearms that Shadow hadn't seen before. They had blue plating with a black base. The fingers had matching black joints. Chambers were inside the wrist areas, probably holding magazines and shells. "Medics wouldn't let me get outta bed."

Lucia wagged her finger at him. "It's for your own good!"

Iyar pointed his thumb at Lucia. "She's like my mother."

"We know what that's like!" said Leif, smirking at Stream as she entered the area alongside the rest of Star Strike.

"Heh. Well, either way, I gotta get used to these things Blossom made. Have to make up for our loss of teammates, after all."

Everyone except for Elena's faces fell.

Shadow was afraid someone was going to cry again.

Iyar studied everyone's reactions. "It happens, ya know. Can't change what happened. We were all supposed to make it... but mistakes were made. We gotta move on."

"And honor our fallen teammates," said Elena.

Triple Strike showed up with Aqua and Eila.

Swifty and Sunny had bandages wrapped around their arms and legs.

The Lieutenant General opened the room with her Communicator pressed against it.

Shadow scrambled in, struggling to remember where Star Strike sat last, only for Zephyr and Leif to drag him over to the seat between them.

"Sorry we're late." Ava appeared in the room, accompanied by Tiamat and Fang.

Like Iyar, Ava's entire right leg was a mechanical prosthetic. The fundamental difference was that hers had green paint and barrels were present at the heel. The other two had metal pieces scattered throughout their bodies.

Tiamat had his left hand replaced, and Fang's right torso was metallic.

President Ziel walked in with a stoic demeanor.

"I'm happy to see you all here." Ziel seated himself on the head chair after courtesy greetings.

"Yessir." Aqua retrieved her Communicator, pressing a few buttons. "There's a fair amount to discuss at hand."

Images as holograms floated against the blank wall for all to see. Many discovered Mutations, lab rooms, storage rooms, generators, offices, destruction, and a list of casualties with names and profiles were on display. The pictures in the center of the collection were the Labyrinth and the article about Spiritual Darkness.

Ziel listened to Aqua's report, only asking a question now and then.

"They blew everything up, entrapping you between their experiments." The President's chin rested on clenched fingers. "Clearly had very minimal regard for the Base itself. A Base hardly of use. My guess is the same as yours about the Labyrinth being one other area of operations, granted immunity from its effects thanks to this Spiritual Darkness. If they can teleport with ease, they could most likely transport to and from the Labyrinth."

"Has anyone heard of Erebus?" asked Sunny.

"Since the Labyrinth is known to be connected to the Underworld, I'm assuming it's an immortal being of darkness. If it has power like that which can be granted to mortals... it could very much be a disciple of the God of Darkness," said Zetta. "There's a lot we don't know about the Underworld, aside from the areas Celeste traversed back in the day. But that was ages ago. Who knows what could've changed with the shift."

"There's gotta be some drawback to such power," said Iyar.

"It has its limits," said Zephyr. "It can't bring back lost powers... Or turn people into Risen. They used Trinity Trio as extra test subjects for the latter."

"They've got to have more up their sleeves inside the Labyrinth or in other worlds," said Zetta.

Everyone glanced at Wings of Order's greatest mind.

"You think they got the power to transport to other worlds?" asked Shadow.

"Our tracking can't be wrong. We've searched every area thrice and hardly found anything," said Zetta. "Spiritual Darkness opens up possibilities none of us could imagine."

"Either we establish communication between the worlds first, or we find the teleported entrance to the Labyrinth and get answers," said Clay. "We've already tried to do the former for decades, but to no avail."

The first time the organization found the Labyrinth's entrance was by chance. After the Typhons' Expedition, the organization blocked it off. Since the entrance hadn't been entered for so long, it teleported and assumed a new form within Eta Geminorum.

"This time is different. We're stronger than we were twenty years ago and far better prepared in terms of resources. We have a better idea of what to expect in the Labyrinth based on what we found in the Typhons' archives," said Zetta. "We will have to do everything we can to ensure it isn't a repeat of the first Labyrinth Expedition."

Blaze, Stream, and Luna looked uncertain and possibly defeated.

"Ramping up training and prep work needs to start now. That goes for all departments," said Aqua. "Even if we find the Labyrinth, the most we can do is open the entrance and spend more time preparing."

"We won't make the same mistakes as last time and rush in," said Ziel. "And we'll adapt and allocate more funding toward the Portal

Initiative thanks to generous donations from Vertbarrow and Orwyn."

"We'll have to strategize once again new formations within the Marauders," said Aqua, cueing Elena.

"Our reserves aren't as plentiful as before," announced Elena. "Ambrose can't move as fast as before thanks to nerve damage, Iyar can't draw aura from his prosthetic arm, and some of Lucia's light aura points got shut down."

"We've lost a good chunk of our reserves, too," said Ava. "We can still transform, but we're missing half our power. These enhancements may help, but only so much."

"Different fighting styles and training will help," said Elena. "No need to replace any of us with candidates until we retire ten years from now, as planned."

"The second Labyrinth Expedition will be more ambitious," said Ziel. "We'd require more time for preparations." He faced Star Strike. "Star Strike will be invaluable for the Labyrinth mission once they hit A-rank or higher. They will continue to have roles regarding dealing with the Typhons, but on a smaller scale."

"Figured as much," said Ava.

"It took us months to achieve our first aim: finding out the root cause of this spread of darkness. I'm afraid our next objective will be split. Typhons aren't the only ones we'll have to stop." All eyes were on the President. "There's been word of Heracles having adverse side effects—consumers have reached insanity and their powers have gone haywire. So far, only two towns have been attacked during a rampage, but we should not let this persist."

"Of course…" said Iyar.

Others sighed.

"The world is in strife," said Aqua. "Star Strike brought hope and there've been tremendous surges in morale and excitement recently. They're rising as that 'Beacon of Hope' Lumière Inc. envisioned."

"That's what they always called us back then," said Zephyr. "Star Strike, 'Beacon of Hope,' bringing light to the everlasting darkness."

"We've still got a way before we hit that title," Luna pointed out. "Still early to tell, with all due respect."

"I'll stand by Star Strike's side and do what I can to make it happen," said Skye. Her eyes brightened, like Excalibur's when drawn.

For a split second, Shadow remembered the twin-tailed little girl who always spouted off about becoming like the heroes in stories. The same girl who had a light inside her that never truly faded.

She and Zephyr, along with Shadow, wanted a world where people could be happy again. They all wanted to be heroes—that's why they remained with Star Strike. Star Strike was going to be the heroes they dreamed of. After all, they were the Dream Team.

To be continued in
Queen of Blades
Book Two of the Realm of Hope Trilogy
Celestial Legacies Universe

ACKNOWLEDGMENTS

Realm of Hope started as a series of comics when I was a preteen. It evolved into a script for a JRPG-style game that I wrote at age fifteen. Five additional scripts were written throughout the years with every story taking place in the Celestial Legacies Universe, but at different time periods. Eventually, I decided to rewrite each script in the form of a book series. I always loved the idea of creating a universe where several storylines reference each other. Countless revisions were necessary to make my stories come to life, no matter the medium.

I am eternally grateful to have positive reinforcement and encouragement from my peers. I very much appreciate Kathleen Kelley, my Creative Writing teacher, for being the first professional to validate my writing abilities and encouraging me to stick with my passion.

I owe a very special thank you to my editor, Kereah Keller, who pushed me to dive deeper into my characters, plot, and world. This book and trilogy cannot be what it is now without your help.

Thank you to my amazing partner and number one supporter, whose ideas and insight into what works and doesn't work with my story have contributed massively to the polishing of my drafts.

To my childhood friends and beta readers, Spencer and Casey, I am incredibly thankful for your support. You guys have been around since the first conception of the Celestial Legacies Universe and without you, I wouldn't have pursued screenwriting and writing novels.

To my additional beta readers—Tyler, Brenna, Jameel, Sowmya, and Sarah—who are not only excellent at providing their insight, but are also great friends, supporters, and the ones to count on to hype me up.

To my cover artists at MiblArt, thank you for making my vision come to life and creating such amazing eye candy.

To my map artist, Chaimholtjer, thank you for making such a beautiful, hand-drawn map that I can frame on my wall.

To my character artists—Marinacyzgir and Erdjie—thank you for turning my original sketches into a work of art.

To my weapon artist, Mogliarts, thank you for being so easy to work with and creating what I envisioned.

To my header designer, Catherine Downen, thank you for providing designs better than I could ever imagine.

I would also like to thank everyone else who has supported me from day one. I am E.L. Li, and I will continue to write what I want to read.

Made in United States
North Haven, CT
30 November 2023

44791713R00297